To: Donna,

Thank you for being a part of my life.

Best Wishes,

Douglas Roberts

THE INSURANCE MAN

DOUGLAS ROBERTS

LifeRich PUBLISHING

LifeRich Publishing books may be ordered through booksellers or by contacting:

LifeRich Publishing
1663 Liberty Drive
Bloomington, IN 47403
www.liferichpublishing.com
1 (888) 238-8637

ISBN: 978-1-4897-0886-1 (sc)
ISBN: 978-1-4897-0887-8 (hc)
ISBN: 978-1-4897-0885-4 (e)

Library of Congress Control Number: 2016914141

Print information available on the last page.

LifeRich Publishing rev. date: 09/13/2016

This book is dedicated to the 58,479 brothers and sisters who never returned from the Vietnam war.

CONTENTS

PROLOGUE

Rich Coburn could hear the two sets of footfalls walking towards his hospital room in the "pink palace on the hill," Trippler Army Hospital. Two men in summer khakis with long white coats walked through the open doorway.

The first, with silver oak leaves on his collar, picked up the chart from the foot of the bed, and silently started to read.

The other, a Captain, put out his hand, and said, "Rich, I'm Captain Furrilo, and this is Lt. Colonel Aronson. We're from gastroenterology, and we have the lovely job of finding out if there are any little friends from North Vietnam living in your body."

Coburn shook his hand, and blankly stared back. "Captain, I don't understand. I'm a SEAL, why aren't I in a Navy Hospital?"

Lt. Col. Aronson looked over, and kidding said, "we not only treat Army men and women, we sometimes allow Navy heroes in here, as well. I'm told that you are up for the Navy Cross, Coburn, so I guess we'll let you in here."

"Navy Cross, for what" Coburn replied. "I didn't do a damn thing except find my way home. I don't even know why I'm here"

"You found your way home, Rich, all the way from just south of Hanoi. It took you three weeks, and you took nine Charlies down while you were strolling back to our lines. The reason you are here is to find out whether any of the food that you ate on the way, rats, snakes, bugs, and God knows what is still living in that body of yours. While you are here, you'll be talking with Dr. Tramutal of the psych department, as well. Losing the rest of your unit, and coming back alone, after an enemy bombardment, would have severe mental consequences on most men, but you seem to be O.K." Aronson told him, "But the Navy wants us to take a look at you." With a smirk, Aronson continued," I think all of you SEALS, Rangers, and Marine Recon guys, are all crazy anyway."

chapter 1

BOSTON

Seven years had passed since Rich left the Navy, the Bronze Star had been awarded instead of the Navy Cross, college was over, and his MBA in Finance was new in its frame.

Some of the great things in Boston were the myriad of great restaurants within three blocks of Rich's new insurance office at One Washington Plaza.

Usually he bought a sandwich and walked over to the Government Center, to sit on the stairs in the sunshine, and watch the secretaries and other good looking women walk by.

Today, however, it was going to be different. He had received a phone call from a man who identified himself as a Mr. Liberty, who said that he had been referred to Rich, and wanted to meet him at Durgin Park, for lunch, at noon.

As a referral, Rich knew that this was the best kind of prospect, and the prospect's insistence that he would pick up the tab at one of the best restaurants in the city, right around the corner, made it even better.

The line to get inside was long, but Rich had called for a reservation, and when he checked in, the maître'd took him to a table where a man with a bald head, rimless glasses, and an athletic build was seated. Looking more closely Rich saw that the athletic build had softened more than a little bit.

"Mr. Liberty, I'm Rich Coburn, It's good to meet you", he said as he held out his hand.

Mr. Liberty looked at him, and lifted his left hand, turned backward in order to shake Rich's right hand.

"You'll forgive me, Mr. Coburn, my right arm doesn't work very well. It's a pleasure to meet you."

Just then a waitress that Rich would rate an eight out of ten, walked up, and asked if she could bring them something to drink.

Liberty ordered a dry martini, and Rich ordered an O'Doul's. He always drank non-alcoholic beverages when doing business. He'd seen too many guys screw up a meeting when they drank.

"Mr. Liberty, you never told me who recommended that we meet, or told me how I could be of service to you." Rich leaned forward, while looking Liberty directly in the eye. He reached into his jacket, and pulled out a brochure, outlining his services.

"Mr. Coburn, the individual who recommended you has a name you would not remember. He doesn't know you personally, just your record. When I tell you what I need, you will know what services you can provide. I am sure that your brochure does not cover the services I need."

Before Rich could reply, the drinks arrived, and they both ordered roast beef, the specialty of the house. Rich watched the waitress walk away, promising himself that he'd be back in the future.

"Mr. Liberty," Rich said.

"Call me Ben, and I'll call you, Rich" Liberty interrupted.

"O.K., Ben, just what is going on?"

"This is a preliminary interview, Rich, I want to see if I'm comfortable with you, and I want you to see if you are comfortable with me. My position is that of the recruiter. For a number of years I was a recruiter for an agency of the government. Your recommendation came from that agency." The good looking waitress, with a ten for a derriere, came back with their meals, and they started to eat.

"Let me ask you a question," Ben said between mouthfuls of Yorkshire pudding. "I know that you recently received your Master's degree in Finance from Babson, and your undergraduate degree came from Northeastern. How would you feel about traveling outside of the Boston area?"

The timing for an answer was horrible, as Rich had just filled his mouth with some beef, followed by a gulp of O'Doul's. He held up a finger while he chewed and swallowed, and then said, "As you probably know, I've traveled all over the world with the Navy, and gone diving recreationally all over as well. I also go skiing wherever I can. However, I just started my business, and if I'm going to be traveling, it's going to have to fit in with that as well".

"Rich, I'm going to the men's room for a moment. What do you say to our going for a little walk over to the aquarium when I get back?"

Ben took about ten minutes, and was putting his wallet away when he came back. "I took care of the young lady. I hope you didn't want dessert."

They came down the stairs, turned left to walk through the throngs at Faneuil Hall, and headed for Commercial Street, where they turned right.

Ben looked around, and pointed to State Street. "What say we go down to the waterfront on State, and turn to the aquarium, O.K.?"

The stillness between them was eerie, and Rich waited for Ben to start the conversation.

"Rich, there are a number of people who have come together because we believe that this country is going in the wrong direction. We are of the opinion that the present administration is made up of apologists, socialists, and bleeding heart liberals who could care less about the man in the street. As long as they get re-elected, or are able to receive graft or favors under the table, they are happy. We believe that they have given up on our constitution, and are allowing enemy sleeper cells to grow just below the surface, in order to bring this country down."

"Ben, I don't know if you are a patriot, or a nut, but what has this got to do with me, and my insurance business?" Rich asked.

"Rich, the people who recommended you said that you were a no bullshit kind of guy, and that you would probably make that comment. They also said that you were a pragmatist, and would at least listen. Will you do that?"

"Hey, you picked up lunch. Let me ask you one thing first, is Liberty your real name?"

"My real name doesn't matter. What does matter is you. We know that even before we get down to brass tacks, if you are going to be a part of us, you've got to believe the same way we do. We know that you were the smallest guy in your BUD/s class in the SEALS, but you were a leader, and boat captain. We know that when you say you are going to do something, you do it. We also know that you feel there is only one way of doing things, to win. We know that you like to live well, and that you haven't gotten married because you haven't found a girl who loves you as much as you love yourself. We need someone who can think on his feet, follow orders, improvise when necessary, and work under the radar."

"Other than walk on water, what would I have to do?"

"In order to save our country, it will be necessary for you, and others, to eliminate those who want to destroy our way of life, from the cell member to the top of the administration. We have the financial resources to give you whatever is necessary in order for you to accomplish your mission. You'll be able to live the lifestyle you love in the country you put your ass on the line for, not some liberal hellhole. As I told you, Rich, this is an initial interview. Although we know everything that we need to know about you, we need to know whether or not this is something you want to do for your country, your future, and yourself.

I'll call your office tomorrow to see how you feel about it, and if you are positive about the opportunity, we'll meet again to answer any questions either of us may have. If you decide that this is not for you; then we've never met, you'll never see me again; and we never spoke."

Ben turned around, shook Rich's hand, and said, "Thanks for your time; if you've never been to the aquarium, you ought to go. I'll call you tomorrow."

He disappeared into the crowd.

Rich just stood there. He looked towards the harbor, and spoke out loud, "What the hell was that all about?"

The sun was shining down on him, as he walked back to his office, thinking about the last few hours. He thought about what was said, and then his mind wandered back to Vietnam. He thought how much he loved being a SEAL, how much he was elated when the missions were successful, and how he felt as the adrenalin rushed through his body in the middle of a firefight.

He didn't think about the final mission. The rest of his squad was killed while they were in the river, and he was on the shore, when the artillery shells hit the water.

He didn't think about the three weeks it took to get back to his lines. Since all the radios were destroyed, he couldn't call for extraction.

Rich walked into the office, looked at the receptionist, and asked, "Any messages?"

"Nothing for you," said the dark haired Jerrilyn sitting there with a tight jersey, covered by a sweater jacket.

Rich undressed her in his mind, as he walked to his office. He walked into his office, and saw his office mate Tommy Majestic just hanging up his phone.

God, I'd like to poke that Jerrilyn, what a set of knockers," Rich said, smirking.

Tommy laughed, "You and every guy in here."

Tommy and Rich were both just out of grad school, Tommy coming from Boston College. When they both applied to the company around the same time, Bill Finneran, the Branch Manager, introduced them, and recommended that they study together in order to pass their state insurance exams.

The studying led to a close friendship and they chose to share their joint office after they passed their exams. There was a friendly competition between the two, as the agent with the highest production would be rewarded with a larger office of his own, and the loser would get a new office mate, probably a newbie.

The friendship led to Rich joining Tommy and his fiancée, Jennifer on many of their dates, with Jennifer supplying Rich with her friends. Jenny thought that Rich was a good catch for her friends, and Rich liked the selection of women that Jenny brought to him, and the sex was great.

Rich looked over at Tommy, threw a rolled up piece of paper

at him, and asked, "What have you got planned for the next hour or so?"

"I've got some prospecting to do, and then I have a seven o'clock appointment in Brighton. Why?"

"Something just happened to me, and I need your input. How about hitting the prospecting later and listening to me instead?"

"O.K., start talking."

Rich looked at the man whom he trusted like a brother. He never trusted anyone as much, except for the men he left behind at the intersection of the Red and Black rivers, and he trusted them with his life.

"Tommy, I told you I had a luncheon set with a referral at Durgin Park. Let me tell you what happened.

Rich recounted to Tommy every word and nuance he could remember from the meeting, including the waitress with the dynamite ass.

"Tommy, what the hell should I do? What do I tell the guy when he calls me tomorrow?"

Tommy looked at Rich with incredulity. "You're telling me that someone you never met, and who knew people from when you were a SEAL, comes out of the blue, offers you a job as a hired killer, and you don't know what to do when he calls you. Are you out of your fucking mind? He gave you an out. He said if you didn't want to do it, it would be like you never met. What's your problem?"

"The problem, my dear Tommy, is that I think that this country is being led by a bunch of cowardly bastards, who think that the future of the United States should include outrageous entitlement programs, giveaways, and screwing the hard working people like you and me. The problem is that I'm not ready to kill myself starting a new business so that some leftist will tax me to pay for a bunch of lazy animals who think they are the downtrodden and that the fat cats should pay for their drugs. The problem is that I've killed before, and I never regretted it. The problem is that I know that if I do this, I'm not killing for my country, I'm killing because I'm a murderer. The problem is that I don't know what the hell to do, and you're not helping me."

Tommy took a swig of his Mountain Dew, walked over to Rich, and put his arm around his shoulder. "My friend, this is not the kind of problem I can solve for you. I know that you are a decent guy, who knows the law. I know you work very hard, but I don't think this is the way for you to change things.

Run for congress, work on a campaign, make so much money that the taxes don't bother you . One last comment, how do you know that this is for real? You never saw this guy before; maybe somebody is playing a sick joke on you."

Rich got up from his desk, walked over to Tommy's, and picked up the Mountain Dew. He took a swig, and looked straight into Tommy's eyes. "I guess I'll just have to wait for the call. Tommy, please don't say anything to Jennifer. As a matter of fact I'd really appreciate it if you forget this conversation ever happened." Rich stuck out his hand towards Tommy.

Tommy shook his hand, and asked," What conversation."

Rich walked out of the office; walked down the hall past Jerrilyn, waved to her, and went out the double doors to the elevator.

The sun hit him in the eyes as he walked to the garage to get his car, and head north on Rte. 93 towards Chelmsford and home.

Rich turned the steering wheel of his Datsun 280ZX as he took the ramp from Rte. 93 to Rte. 495 south. After a few minutes, he turned to the right on the ramp to Rte 3, and then up the ramp to the Chelmsford rotary. He took North Road by the police station towards his apartment complex. As he drove by the station house, he thought to himself as to how he would feel driving by after killing someone. Maybe he'd change his route.

After parking his car, Rich went up the stairs to his apartment, grabbed a beer, turned on the amplifier, and broke out a package of Chicken Cordon Bleu from Omaha Steaks, from the freezer. He put one of the chickens on a cookie sheet, set the temperature for 400 degrees, set the timer for forty-five minutes, took out another beer, and headed for the shower.

After showering, he ate his dinner while watching his recorded video of the past weekend's football game. Rich went to bed, worn out emotionally from his long day.

He awoke at 5:00 a.m., the same time every day ever since boot camp. No alarm clock was necessary. He walked into the kitchen, drank a cup of coffee which had been brewing since 4:50, put on his underwear and warm-up suit, grabbed his keys, and drove over to McCarthy Junior High, where he ran five miles around the track.

Reversing his tracks, he went home, showered again, grabbed a couple of frozen waffles and another cup of coffee, dressed, and headed to the office.

Jerrilyn looked just as good today, as she did yesterday, but Rich went by the old adage, "You don't shit where you eat, and you don't screw where you work."

One thing Ben didn't say yesterday was what time he would call. Rich hoped that he wouldn't wait too long.

The office door was locked, so Tommy must have had an appointment this morning.

Rich went into the office, turned on the computer, and looked at the list of e-mails.

One pulled his eyes right to it - the standings for the month to date. He'd better be beating Tommy. How would his production be affected if he started working with Ben?

The standings showed two different figures. Production to Date and Monthly Production. Rich was easily beating Tommy in Month to Date by over $2400. Tommy, however, was ahead for year to date by $3100. Rich had better get his ass in gear. There weren't any big cases coming down the road, except for one that Rich wasn't counting on, for $ 8600. It had been around for a while, and qualified as a china egg (made out of china, and therefore never hatches).

The rest of the e-mails were nothing much, changes in product, company policies, and IT changes.

Rich looked at the phone repeatedly, and then at his watch. Time was moving slowly. Rich drank coffee after coffee, walked around the office, and read product news over and over.

Finally his phone rang. It was Jerrilyn. "Rich, I just got a call from a Mr. Liberty. He said that he didn't want to bother you, so not to put the call through. He said that if you would like to meet him, he'll be at Legal Seafood's at 255 State Street at 12:30. Just ask for him at the desk."

Rich wondered why Ben didn't call him personally, and then realized that if he had wanted to tell the police about Ben, they probably would have had his phone bugged. Obviously, Ben knew what he was doing.

Rich looked at his watch once more, and saw that he had about an hour and a half before meeting Ben, if he went.

He pulled a pad from the drawer in his desk, and drew a line down the center. One of the things he learned a number of years ago was to list all of the pros and cons to any big decision that he had to make. Some people called it a Ben Franklin close, but he didn't know why.

At the top of the page he wrote "pro" on one side of the line, and "con" on the other.

Under "pro" he wrote: helping my country, making a difference, being involved, getting rid of scum, having tactical discipline, taking a team approach, doing what I do well, improving lifestyle, acting on instinct, being me.

Next to it, under "Con" he wrote, Is it real, patriotism or murder, following not leading, stress, what's the organization, how big, resources, planning by whom, cash flow for operations, locations, cover, working with a team, compensation.

When he looked at the paper he immediately saw that the "con" column was longer than the "pro" column, which meant that he should make a negative decision regarding the opportunity.

Looking again at his watch once more, he found that it had taken close to an hour to write down his thoughts. If he was going to be on time, he'd better leave immediately, considering he was always five to ten minutes early.

Should he go?

Rich made his decision about his future when he grabbed the pad, shut the light in his office, and went out the door.

He didn't know what questions Ben was going to ask, but if Ben answered Rich's questions to Rich's satisfaction, Rich was on board, no matter what Ben Franklin decided.

When he walked out of the building, Rich was engulfed by a squall with rain blowing sideways into his face. Although the restaurant was close, he grabbed a cab, and gave a large tip to make up for the short fare.

Rich asked for Ben at the maitre'd's desk, and was shown into an alcove with a relatively small table where two men were sitting. Ben Liberty turned halfway in his seat, and held out his left hand, reversed, and said, "Rich, you are a little early; I'm glad; it's good to see you. This other gentleman is Spencer Kohl. Spencer knows everything I know about you, has received my report of our first meeting, and, if you hadn't shown up for lunch, would have been my companion in destroying two delicious lobsters. Please sit down."

Rich looked at the antithesis of Ben. Kohl was about six three, 200 pounds, had a barrel chest, wide shoulders, and looked like a Special Forces poster boy, with close-cropped hair, in a hand made three thousand dollar suit.

Spencer Kohl rose from his seat, looked at Rich, put out his hand, and in a strong, deep voice said, "Rich it's really a pleasure. I've met a number of people from the teams before, and aside from the fact that you are all crazy, you are also all very impressive. From what I read last night in Ben's report, and your file this morning, you are truly outstanding.

Rich looked at Kohl, who was smiling broadly, shook his hand and pulled out the third chair at the table. "Well, Mr. Kohl, I must say that I appreciate the compliment. But I have no idea who you are; I don't know why you are here; and, candidly, I'm not sure why I'm here."

Kohl pulled his shirtsleeves out of his cuffs by another half inch, lowered his head, looked Rich in the eye, and said, "I understand where you are coming from, Rich, and I know that you are wondering about a number of things. First of all, our organization is real; no one is trying to set you up for any reason; and second of all, I am not from the Justice Department. The reason that I am here is that Ben already told you that we wanted to answer all of your questions. Also although we have checked you out all the way back to your first grade teacher, and the little girl you played doctor with under your back porch, we may have some further questions for you. If both Ben and I feel that you would be an asset to our team, and you feel that being a member of our team is how you want to improve both our country and your life, I will be your direct report. You will receive your orders, support, logistics, and an excellent lunch or dinner every once in a while from me. Now what questions do you have from us? By the way, call me Spence."

"Before we get started," interjected Ben, "how about if we get some drinks? " He waved to the waiter, who reacted immediately. "Young man, please give me a dry martini, my friend over here a Glenlivet on the rocks, and if I'm correct, this young man will have an O'Doul's." Rich confirmed the order, and Ben continued, "We have a lot to talk about, so once you bring the drinks, just leave us alone, until we signal you, O. K.?"

Rich sat back, and looked from Ben to Spence, and back. "Gentlemen, since you know so much about me, you are aware that I make major decisions relatively quickly, but I put a lot of thought into it. You will find that I am always candid. Before I decided to come here today, I put together a pro and con list. The pro side brought me here. Your answers to the con side will decide whether we order two or three lobsters before we leave. How about if I go down the list?"

Both Ben and Spence indicated acquiescence.

"Why is this patriotism, and not murder?" Rich said, with his voice low.

Spence pulled his chair closer to Rich. "Rich, when you took out Charlie in Vietnam you did it for the benefit of your country. You did it to keep the capitalistic society of the United States in the forefront of the world; you did it to keep socialism from destroying the American way. You aren't a draftee who did it because he had to or go to jail. You enlisted; you volunteered for and qualified for the teams; you went through BUD/s; you did your job. Now we're in a different world, and you'll have to resort to difficult avenues to get our country back."

"Would I be following someone else, or leading a team?"

"You will be receiving your orders from me," responded Spence, "as well as any support needed. The strategic and tactical planning of the mission will be totally up to you. You'll do the operation in any way you see proper, in order to maximize the outcome. As we find it necessary, you will become part of a team of operatives. As long as the mission will be one on one, you will work alone. If the operation would be more efficient or efficacious with two of you working together, there would be two of you."

"I know this will be stressful. How often will an operation be necessary?"

Ben pulled his chair closer just as the drinks were delivered. As soon as the waiter left, he looked at Rich and said, "There are eight operatives on board now; you will be number nine. We do not want media attention. . If we push too hard, we'll fail. For our country, we can't afford to fail."

"Tell me what you can about the organization. How big is it, what are its resources?"

This answer came from Spencer Kohl. "Rich, obviously we can't tell you too much, as you haven't proved yourself yet. Let's just say that if you took the bottom fifteen companies in the Standard and Poor's 500, that would give you the size of our available resources. I can tell you that the organization spreads over the largest nineteen countries in the United Nations, other than those which are Socialists and Communists, and the division which you will be in is just getting started. We anticipate fifty men, and women, with the kinds of specialized attributes that you have, within two years."

"Who will do the planning?"

Spence answered again." As I said, you will do the strategic and tactical planning in the field, after receiving the orders from me as to the objective.

"How will I receive cash flow for operations in the field?"

Ben chuckled, "looks like we're getting down to the short strokes; money is in the picture. You will receive a budget for field expenses. I won't say it is unlimited, and you will have to account for expenses. But if you need more, ask Spence, and he'll say yes, no, or maybe depending on how much, and why."

"I had a few other minor questions, but there are two that will help me make my decision. First, how do I combine this position with my insurance business, and secondly upon what will my compensation be based ?

This might give you an indication of the resources of our organization, laughed Spence. "If we get together you will be moving to Hartford, Connecticut, which is two hours away. You will become the Director of Sales for the Eastern Division of the company where I am the Vice President of Sales in the Life Insurance Division. You will receive a compensation of $100,000 dollars a year, plus expenses, plus a bonus based on the production of your division. Dependent upon the operations you are called upon to perform outside of the company, your outside compensation will be between $30,000 and $50,000 plus expenses, per operation. Considering the lack of experience you have for the position, I am bringing you in as an asset for a new program, which I know will do well. We'll work out all of the particulars to your advantage. Rich, we knew when we came here how we felt about you; the ball is now in your court. We will call you tomorrow for your answer. We'll even buy that third lobster now, without a decision, O. K.?"

The next two hours were very cordial amongst the three men. Absolutely nothing was mentioned about the earlier conversation, and the Red Sox, Celtics, Bruins, and Patriots took up most of their time together.

Ben promised that he would call at ten in the morning, and Spence would be on the call.

Rich shook hands at the end of the meal, walked out the front door, and found that the old adage about New England weather was true. "If you don't like the weather, just wait a minute." The sun was shining, and it was warmer. He decided to walk back to the office, and think about his options on the way.

By the time Rich reached his building he had made his decision. He was moving to Hartford; he was moving to a new life.

Walking through the outer door of the office, Rich looked at Jerrilyn, and thought how he'd like to celebrate his decision. After all, he wouldn't be working here anymore. He walked up to the desk, looked down at her, and asked her to go to dinner.

Smiling, Jerrilyn said, “I’d love to, Rich, but I don’t think my husband would be very agreeable.” Talk about researching an objective. He had never even looked at her hands to see if she wore a ring; his eyes always looking somewhere else. He apologized, said something about not realizing she was married, and quickly walked to his office.

The door to his office was unlocked, and when he went in, Tommy was sitting there, talking on the phone. “Mr. Goodman, I agree totally, the analysis showed a need for $ 500,000 of capital to cover your obligations. Now all we have to do is to see if your budget allows for the temporary term insurance, or the permanent coverage. Would Tuesday at 4:00 pm, or Thursday at 7:00, when Linda would be there, be better? O.K., I’ll see you on Thursday. I’ll send an e-mail to confirm”.

“Hey, Tommy, it looks like you’re going to win the contest,” Rich winked at him. “I guess we both will.”

Tommy looked at him quizzically, “What are you talking about? How can we both win the production contest?”

“Well, obviously you’ve got a nice sale, and I’ve got some news.”

Tommy stood up, walked over to the door, and locked it. “Does it have to do with the phone call you were expecting?”

“Yes it does. Remember how you said that maybe it wasn’t real? That maybe someone was setting me up?”

Tommy looked at him, a frown crossing his face. “Yuh, it didn’t make sense then, and it doesn’t now.”

Rich sat down on the corner of his desk, and looked at Tommy. He knew he could trust him, but he cut the cards when he played poker with him. “Tommy, it was a setup. It wasn’t real. They wanted to see how I would react. It was a new form of interview by some recruiting company based in Iowa. The whole thing was for a job interview from a headhunter. My name came from a professor at Babson, who told them about me. I met with them again today, and the V.P. of sales was there. The interview took a different tack, and it was all about insurance. They are going to call me again tomorrow, and if I accept, I have to move to Hartford for a job as Director of Life Sales. I can’t believe it.”

"Tommy looked at him wide-eyed. "Director of Life Sales? Are you crazy?

Of course you are going to take it. Why wouldn't you? It's only two hours away. Would you be traveling?"

Rich was glad that Tommy believed him; it would make his cover more believable when he left.

"I imagine that there would be a fair amount of travel. I'll be responsible for the Eastern Division, but I'm not sure what that covers. I know that I know how to sell insurance, and how to manage men, but I don't know what my exact duties will be in total."

Tommy put out his hand and said, "Just don't forget your old friends when you become president of some big bureaucratic insurance company. You seem to be on the fast track, and you can clear that track for your friends. Best of luck, buddy; I'm proud of you."

"Well, I guess that even though they're going to call me tomorrow for confirmation, I ought to go to Mr. Finneran, and give him my notice today."

After Rich met with Bill Finneran for about thirty minutes, he came out of Bill's office with congratulations, and a promise that if he ever wanted to come back, the door was always open.

The ride home to Chelmsford was different tonight. How many more times would he be making it? He'd miss the runs in the morning, but he'd just run somewhere else. He'd moved around enough so that there would be very little nostalgia. Just new adventures.

He got into the office even before Jerrilyn, and started to clean out his desk in anticipation of the phone call. He walked down to the coffee machine, and saw that Jerrilyn had already come in. He was going to miss that body, but he was sure that there would be others to look at.

At 9: 55 he sat at his desk, and looked at the phone. Tommy hadn't come in yet, so he didn't have to worry about security on the call.

At exactly 10:00 am, the phone rang.

"Rich Coburn, may I help you?"

"Rich, this is Ben, good morning, Spence is here, as well."

"Good morning, Ben, Spence, how are you this morning?"

Spence answered, "We are fine, Rich. This is an open line. Have you made any decision on our offer?"

Rich took a deep breath; what he said now would affect the rest of his life. "Yes, Gentlemen, I've decided to join your organization. Now what?"

Spence spoke again, "Rich, obviously we are very pleased. We know that you'll have to give notice to your present employer, and put your things together for the move. I'll have my secretary, Vivian Forkowski, forward the contracts for the Director of Sales position, as well as the benefit forms to your home. She'll also write down the names of real estate agents, and background information on different parts of the city you might care to live in, and the motor vehicle, and utility company numbers. We'll have the moving company contact you directly. They will pack and unpack you, as well as meet your schedule for the move. We know you're coming from an apartment, so that shouldn't be a big problem. We're only a couple of hours away, so we'll expect you to drive your vehicle. You'll be reimbursed for mileage, of course. I'll expect you to be in my office, on Asylum Street, at 7:00 a.m., two weeks from tomorrow for a staff meeting, and other things that we may wish to discuss afterwards. As soon as we receive the signed contracts back, we will notify the local media of your joining us . Any questions?"

Rich put down his pen and answered, "Not that I can think of; it looks like you have done this before, and have taken care of everything. If any questions do come up, whom do I contact?"

Spence answered, "Call Vivian; I'll ask her to put her card in with the contracts. They will be there, overnight."

Rich became a salesman again. "Thank you gentlemen; I look forward to making our relationship advantageous to both of us. If I can be of further service before we meet again, please call me."

"Ben then said, "Don't worry Rich, we will."

The phone went dead.

It was obvious to Rich that the information that was imparted pertained only to the Director of Sales position, and that they'd be speaking about the operational aspect of the job when he met with Spence in Hartford.

Since Rich had already given notice, and in his sales there was really nothing to finish up, he'd have to sit down with Tommy, and go over transferring his client list to him. That way his clients would continue to get good service. He didn't want the office to transfer his clients indiscriminately when he left. He felt a loyalty to them. After all, they trusted their financial future to him.

Rich finished clearing out his office, walked around, said goodbye, and stopped by Jerrilyn's desk on the way out.

"I want to apologize again for making inappropriate remarks yesterday; I never knew you were married. Maybe our paths will cross in the future, and we can have a cup of coffee."

Jerrilyn gave him a 200 watt smile, looked at him, and said, "It wasn't inappropriate, it was very flattering. I hope the girls in Connecticut have the chance I did. Good luck."

Rich went out the door, walked to the garage, put the box of items and pictures in through the hatch, got behind the wheel, and headed north.

chapter 2

HARTFORD

The previous two weeks were taken up with giving up his apartment, taking three trips to Hartford to meet with the real estate lady, finding a rental house in West Hartford that was available immediately, going to the registry, going to all of the utility offices, and meeting twice with Vivian Forkowski, who turned out to be a very efficient, very well put together executive secretary, who knew everything about anything.

At 6:45 a.m. on the designated day, Rich showed up at the front desk of his new employer, and showed the photo I.D. card that Vivian had given to him to the guard.

"Welcome aboard, Mr. Coburn," the guard said, smiling. "We received the news about you yesterday. Your office is on the executive floor. When you get on the elevator, slide your card into the slot above the floor numbers. Otherwise, the elevator won't work for that floor. Here's a copy of the Wall Street Journal. From now on, it'll be at your desk when you get in. My name is Charlie, if you need anything at all. Did you find your parking space O.K.?"

"Yes, Charlie, no problem. I'm a navy man, so the welcome aboard was appreciated. I assume that conference room A is on the executive floor, correct?"

"Just take a left when you get off the elevator, Mr. Coburn. You can't miss it."

Rich found the door to conference room A, and saw Vivian putting down the pads and pens, and adjusting the coffee cups. Doughnuts and bagels were on the sidebar.

Rich walked in the door to a big smile from Vivian. "Obviously you made it, Rich. You sit on the right side of Spence, over here. This young man is Gerry Butterfield. He's your counterpart for the central division. Dave Baxter runs the western division, and his plane was delayed coming in from L.A. last night. So I'm not sure when he'll show up."

Just then a tall muscular black man walked into the room, a suitcase on wheels in tow. He stuck out his hand, and said, "Hi, I'm Dave Baxter, you must be Rich Coburn. We've heard a lot about you."

Rich shook Dave's hand, and then turned to Gerry Butterfield, and shook his hand. Within seconds, Spencer Kohl walked into the room, and Vivian left, shutting the door behind her.

Spence walked to the round table and sat with Rich on his right, Gerry on his left, and Dave across from him. Gerry poured coffee from the pitcher on the table for himself and Dave, and offered it to Spence and Rich.

Spence opened his portfolio, and immediately started to talk. "O.K. guys, the introductions are over, let's get down to business. With the addition of Rich we are going to have a couple of changes in reporting responsibilities, and a realignment of the offices. Rich, you will pick up the Cleveland and Detroit offices in your division. These will come from the central division. Gerry, you'll pick up Dallas and Houston, and Dave, we're opening up offices in Reno, Brea California, and Salt Lake City. This will equalize the divisions more. With Rich not having the experience of you superstars, I'll be working closely with him. I know you'll miss my daily calls, but now Rich can have this pain in the ass in his back pocket. We'll announce the changes in an e-mail this morning. Dave, I want you to meet with the real estate people this afternoon for location alternatives. Gerry, you schedule yourself into Texas, and Rich, you're going on the road to meet with all of your offices. Schedule Cleveland and Detroit first. Gentlemen, I'll be speaking with each of you individually. Next meeting, same time, same place, one week from today. Dave, you'll be on conference call. Dismissed. Rich, let's go to my office, now. Gerry, Dave, I'll get to you as soon as I can."

Spence's office was the size of Rich's old apartment. Upon

entering, Spence took off his jacket, loosened his tie, and asked Vivian to bring the two of them more coffee. "Well, Rich, you've had a busy two weeks. Are you at all acclimated?"

"Spence, of all people, you know exactly how acclimated I am. When I got home the day of the phone call, your shadow was waiting for me, across the street. By the way, he's good, but not that good. I saw him too many times on the way to and from Hartford. I don't know if it was a rental, but a white car is too noticeable when following on side streets. He probably panicked when I lost him, but I went parallel so he could pick me up again."

Spence laughed so hard he almost fell out of his chair. "Ben told me it would be a waste of time, but I figured that it had been a long time since you had been followed. Jungle or West Hartford, it doesn't matter - you are good. Neither Dave nor Gerry is aware of the additional responsibilities you have. As a matter of fact they are more middle of the road politically, so that's the way I would expect you to lean when talking politics with them.

It was purely a coincidence that we aligned the new divisions the way we did, since it came up that your first operation will take place in Detroit, one of the first offices that you will visit. The operation should take place on the day before you visit Cleveland, in order that you will reach Detroit two days later.

I'll have your target file for you at 7:00 tomorrow morning, along with the files for the Cleveland and Detroit offices. If I were you, I'd contact the office managers in order to set up times to meet in their respective cities. As I told you before, the strategic and tactical planning will be done by you. However, I want to see an outline of the plans by tomorrow night. This is a quiet operation. There should be no media coverage other than the fact that the individual has passed out of this world.

Now, go find your office, and ask Vivian to give you all the production and personnel records for your offices, including Cleveland and Detroit. Any questions? I'll see you tomorrow morning at 7:00 a.m."

Rich went to Vivian, right outside Spence's office, and smiled. "Can you tell me where my office is, Vivian?"

"Your first assignment is to find it, Rich. O.K., I'm only kidding. You see that pretty brunette, with the pony tail? Her name is Linda. Go introduce yourself, and ask her where your office is.

Rich walked about fifteen feet towards the elevator, and walked up to the pretty brunette. He looked down, saw the ring, and said, "Hi, I'm Rich Coburn, can you tell me where my office is?"

She looked up at him with beautiful green eyes, and laughed, "I better be able to; I'm Linda Caruso, and I'm your secretary. Welcome, Mr. Coburn; your office is right behind me. Let me show you how to use your electronics console."

After Linda showed him how to use the console, he asked her to get the production and personnel files from Vivian, and asked where the important things like the men's room, lunch room and other offices for the Sales Directors were.

When the paperwork was given to him, Rich found that he had seventeen offices in the eastern division spreading from Maine to Florida, and as far west as Detroit. In those offices were seventeen managers, twenty-one clericals, and eighty agents. A number of the leading agents, by production, were in his division. He didn't have anything that told him about the other divisions, but he had the feeling that he had been given the top division. Considering that he would be spending time on operations, he assumed that he received a division that would really run by itself, without his tutelage. He looked at his watch, saw that 10:00 p.m. had sneaked up on him, and figured he'd ask questions in the morning. Now his only problem was to find his house in West Hartford.

Rich pulled into his space at 6:40 a.m., and saw that a Jaguar was in Spence's space, so he was evidently already there. Walking by, he ran his hand over the hood, and found it cool. Spence had been there a while.

Charlie smiled as Rich walked in. "Guess the first day wasn't that bad, Mr. Coburn; you came back."

"I think you're going to see me around for a while, Charlie. I like my parking space," quipped Rich.

Rich walked into Spence's office exactly at 7:00, and closed the door behind him. Spence said, "Good morning," and handed him a file. He then walked to the door, opened it, and said, "I'll be back in an hour. Please memorize what is necessary for you to accomplish your goal, and take out the target. At 4:00 p.m. I expect a plan, whatever supplies you will need, whether you will need additional logistics at the target location, and how you will integrate that plan with a visit to our Cleveland and Detroit offices.

chapter 3

DETROIT

Rich turned off Route 275 at the Michigan Avenue exit, and headed towards Dearborn. The ride from Cleveland had taken almost three hours on route 80 and 75 which led into 275. He had been unaware, until Spence had told him, that the largest Arab population in the United States was in Dearborn, a suburb of Detroit, as was the home of the headquarters of the Ford Motor Company. Rich knew that there were thousands of good, kind, non-extremist Arabs living in Dearborn. There was also a person whose name was Elijah Anouri who supposedly owned a party store on Michigan Avenue. In actuality, it was a front for a money laundering operation. The dollars were funneled to a political action committee for the benefit of an ultra-liberal senator who always voted for the benefit of the enemies of the United States. The senator was revered in the leftist community in Michigan, and it seemed he had an unending source of cash. Anouri was the mastermind who put the dollars in the senator's pocket.

Rich used the new GPS to find the location of the party store. He parked across the street from the parking lot to the store, and saw the camera locations at each corner of the building. There was no way he was going into the store. He called the store on his throw-away cell phone and asked when they closed. There were two hours to go.

He looked again at the picture that Spence had given him to identify Anouri and placed it in the ash tray.

Two hours later, the lights over the counter went out, and Anouri walked out the door, locked it, and entered a white Cadillac.

He drove slowly down Michigan Avenue, took a right and went to Ford road. He took a left and started to speed up. He drove until he came to Telegraph Road and took a right. He drove directly to a motel on the right hand side of the street, parked around back, and entered room #8. Unless he was delivering the bottle of scotch to someone else, he wasn't being a very religious Muslim.

Rich had been following him the whole way, sometimes three cars back, sometimes right behind him. The intel said that this was his normal Tuesday night procedure . Thirty minutes later, a young boy knocked on the door, and entered. For two hours Rich watched Anouri and the boy perform every sex act that two males could think about. Anouri ran out of steam shortly after the bottle ran out of scotch. He gave the boy a wad of bills, and lay back on the bed. The boy left, and Rich came out of the shadows outside of the window. Anouri didn't move when Rich jimmied the lock and entered.

Rich knew that this was an operation where there would not be any findings in an autopsy, no marks on the body, no witnesses.

Anouri was totally passed out. Rich removed the syringe from the case he carried. The syringe was pre-loaded with 100 mg of succinylcholine, an anesthetic. Not wanting to leave a needle mark that a good coroner would find, Rich opened Anouri's mouth, lifted his tongue, and injected the solution sub-lingually into the body.

Anouri started to have facial twitches. He then started a phase of paralysis, which could last for five minutes or so. After somewhere between three and four minutes his body stopped breathing, and he went to Allah.

Rich was banking on the fact that Anouri never went home on Tuesday night, and never came into the store before six on Wednesday night. His brother took care of the store during the day.

The half life of Succinylcholine was short. There should be no trace of the solution if a toxicity screen was run twenty-four hours later. Rich thought that it would be surprising if the body was found then. Sometimes Anouri didn't leave the room on Wednesdays, so he wouldn't be missed until he didn't show up for work.

Rich locked the door, and climbed out the bathroom window,

closing it as he left. He walked across the street to the restaurant where he had parked his rental car, and headed back to Cleveland.

As he drove down route 275, he set the picture in his ashtray on fire, and emptied the ashtray into the wind. As he drove alongside an eighteen wheeler, he threw the cell phone under the rear wheels. Later, on route 75, he threw the syringe into the bushes, and the GPS found its way into oblivion under another eighteen wheeler on route 80.

Rich thought to himself, as he pulled into his hotel opposite the Cleveland Clinic, "Well, it went just as I planned it. The world is better off, and I have to meet the Cleveland office tomorrow."

chapter 4

CLEVELAND

The meeting with Dwight Porter was set for 9 a.m., and with the office members at 9:30. It was supposed to be a meet and greet, but their production was down, and Rich had a reputation to make.

Dwight Porter was a man who had been in his position for over thirty years. In the military he would be called a lifer, and a short timer. He was just waiting for his time to be up, so he could retire. As time went on production was only decreasing.

An older woman came out to the waiting room, smiled, and said, "Mr. Porter can see you now."

Rich followed her into a sterile office: no pictures, no placques, no charts, and a clean, clear desk. Behind the desk sat the man his personnel file said had opened the Cleveland office. During his years he had built up the office to a point, and it had been declining since.

Rich introduced himself, shook Dwight's hand, put down his brief case next to the straight backed chair opposite the desk, and said to Mr. Porter, "Dwight, I have a problem, and I need your help."

"How can I help you, Rich?"

"Well, here's my problem. I've got an office whose production is decreasing at an increasing rate. It hasn't met its recruiting quota in six years, and it has nine agents who are below minimum requirements. Its manager doesn't submit his expense accounts on time, and when they do come in, they are wrong. What do you think I should do?"

"Now wait a minute, Rich!!"

"No, you wait a minute, Dwight. I know that I'm the new kid on the block, and that you've been here since the Erie Canal was dug. I also know that Gerry Butterfield used to be your boss, and that you originally hired him as an agent. I know he's been covering for you. Numbers don't lie, Dwight. Your office is a losing proposition. There are three options left to me: I can replace you, which would be detrimental to your retirement; I can approve an early retirement; or I can close this office, and make it a sub-office of Columbus. There is one more alternative, but this alternative is not up to me, it's up to you. You have three months to turn this office around, or I'll use one of my three options. Understood?"

Dwight Porter sat stunned.

"I understand. I just didn't expect this. I thought it was just a meet and greet.

No one has ever talked this way to me."

"Dwight, perhaps someone should have talked to you five years ago. Then this would have been a meet and greet. You say that you understand. What do you say we go talk to your team, and I'll be out of here before you have coffee . One more thing, either you can talk to them while I'm in the room, or I'll talk to them while you're in the room. Which would you like?"

"Thank you, Rich, I'll talk to them."

The two of them walked into the room side by side, and the talking stopped.

Porter seemed to grow three inches, as he stood at the podium. "Ladies and gentlemen, allow me to introduce our new Director of Sales for the Eastern Division, Richard Coburn. Let's give him a warm Cleveland welcome."

The applause was loud, and Rich enjoyed it.

Porter continued, "Rich and I have had a heart to heart talk this morning, about individual and team production. There are a number of people in this office who are not hacking it. In all honesty, this office is not making it. Rich has given me, no, he's given all of us, three months to turn it all around. The choice as to what to do is in our hands. In three months, the choice is in Rich's hands. Rich has a very tight schedule today, and is on his way to

Detroit. He didn't want to go without meeting you, and having you put a name with a face."

Rich then took the podium. "Team Cleveland, it's up to you. I've seen one person turn an office around to the positive, and I've seen one person tear an office down. It's up to you as to what you do in the next quarter. My secretary, Linda Caruso, will forward your calls directly to me wherever I am. He turned and wrote a phone number on the board. "This is her number." He then wrote an e-mail address on the board. "This is my e-mail." If there is a reason to contact me. Do it!! If you do what I know you can do, turn this office around, we'll have one hell of a party, on my budget. Thank you for coming in."

The two of them left the room together, shook hands in the hallway, and Rich said to Dwight," I look forward to holding that party."

When Rich had called Spence the night before to say that his assignment had been completed successfully, he told him what he was going to do with Porter. Spence responded, "You're going to build yourself a reputation quickly, as a prick, but he deserves it. He's been coasting, and needs to be either gone, or back on track. When you come back from Detroit we'll talk about your trip. Good luck in motor city."

The flight to Detroit took less time to fly than to go through security, but Rich didn't want to drive through the same toll booths two days in a row. Can't be too careful.

A cab to the Westin in Southfield from Detroit Metro airport took about thirty minutes, This gave him plenty of time to change into casual clothes and meet Kerry Forsyth, the Detroit manager, for a mid-afternoon drink, downstairs.

The Detroit office was in the building next to the hotel, which would make it easy for Rich to walk over there for the next meeting at 10:00 a.m. the next day.

Since Rich was the only customer in the bar at that hour, it wasn't hard for the six foot seven Forsyth to find him. He walked up to the bar, stood next to Rich, and said, "Hi, I'm Kerry Forsyth, I hope you're Rich Coburn."

Rich looked up. "No, I'm a scout for the Pistons, and I'm here to offer you a job." He chuckled, "Guilty as charged. How are you, Kerry?"

"Great, Rich, I'm glad to meet you. I hope that you aren't bringing me the kind of message you brought to Cleveland."

"Boy, the news moves fast," Rich replied. But this isn't Cleveland. You've got good numbers. You're relatively new in the position, and all of your people are on track. How did you find out so fast?"

"We're three hours away by car, but only five seconds by phone. We heard about what happened while you were probably on the way to the airport. The office is buzzing that the guy coming to the meeting tomorrow is an axeman, and heads are going to roll."

"Kerry, let's nip this in the bud. I'd like to go up to your office, dressed like this, right now, and press some flesh. Do you think we could put an impromptu meeting together right away?"

"You're the boss, Rich. You want a meeting, you've got a meeting."

"I understand, Kerry, but that's your office. You're in charge!!"

"Thanks, Rich, let's go!"

They walked over to the next building through the connecting hallway, and rode the elevator to the ninth floor.

As they walked into the office, Rich saw the awards on the wall, the Agent of the month board, and a contest board. They stopped at the desk, and Kerry picked up a microphone. "There will be a meeting in the conference room, immediately. Please attend now, with an emphasis on now!!"

It sounded like a herd of cattle coming down the hall as men and women headed for an unseen conference room. It was like a high school fire drill. The manager had said, jump, and they asked how high.

Kerry indicated that the conference was down the hall, and they walked into a very large room with long tables facing the front of the room. There was paper at each seat, and everyone was looking forward.

Kerry opened it up. "Good afternoon. While I was having some libation with our new Director of Sales, I mentioned that some of you had thought that he came here to be an axeman, and that heads would be rolling. He immediately said, "Let's go talk to them." So, here he is, Rich Coburn."

Rich walked to the front of the first table, and looked each of them in the eye.

"I am not here to threaten or terminate anyone. When I came into Cleveland yesterday, I found an office which was the exact opposite of this one. Their goals were in disarray; yours are written down. There was an attitude of defeatism, where you have a can do attitude. I went to Cleveland to do a job; I came here for a meet and greet. You keep doing what you are doing, and you could win the trophy for best office. If they don't turn it around, they will not be an office. Ladies and gentlemen, we have a formal meeting at 10 a.m., tomorrow. Since most of the agents are not here, we will have that meeting. When you see or talk to your office mates please tell them that I come to praise, not to bury. Thank you."

"Kerry, if you don't mind, I'm going back over to the hotel, and hit the sack. I think that I may have grabbed a little bacteria in the past couple of days. I'll see you in your office, now that I know where it is, at 9:30. Thanks for your hospitality." Rich went back to his hotel, and hit the sack.

At a little after 8:00 p.m. Rich awoke, looked out the window at the traffic speeding past on route 10, and realized he was hungry. He ordered some chicken soup from room service, turned on the T.V., and broke out the files on the rest of his offices.

Shortly after the news programs ended, he laid out his clothes for the morning, including his gym clothes, packed his suitcase with the files, and went to sleep.

At 5:00 a.m., Rich went down to the workout room, ran on the treadmill for an hour, came back, shaved and showered, ordered breakfast and the Journal, and turned on the news. There was no mention of Elijah Anouri.

He called Linda Caruso at a little after 8:00. "Linda, Rich, what's going on?"

Her voice, even at this early hour was cheery, yet all business. "Well, I'm getting all sorts of calls from the clerical corps around the division asking what you are like, and how did you have the cojones to threaten to fire a guy, after being on the job for less than a week? I just tell them that I come to attention every morning, and give you my report, and that there is a whip on your desk. All kidding aside, it's just a typical what's this new guy like. By the way, Vivian was asking when you would be back. I guess that Spence wants to see you when you get back. Nothing else going on."

"Super, do me a favor. I'm going to be able to get out a little earlier, so change my flight to as close to 1:00 p.m. as possible, which should get me to Bradley Airport by 3:00, and into the office by 4:00. Let Vivian know, and fax the flight and times, to this office. I'll see you then."

The morning meeting with Kerry, and the meeting with his team went well. Basically, it was: you are doing a great job, keep it up, and I look forward to spending more time with you the next time I'm in Detroit. Kerry drove him to the airport; Rich caught a flight at 1:15pm, was in Hartford just before 3:00, and walked into his office at 3:30.

Linda looked up at him, got up and walked into his office right behind him, and said. "You have a 4:00 with Spence. Do you want me to wait around? He usually spends about an hour with the other directors when they come back from a trip."

Rich looked at Linda, through tired eyes. Whatever bacteria he caught in Detroit were still with him, and he wasn't in top shape. "No, why don't you go ahead home at your regular time." He reached into his brief case, and handed her all of the personnel files. Just separate the files of Dwight and Kerry and leave them on my desk so I can update them. You can file the rest."

Linda got up, and closed the door. "Rich, can I ask you a question?"

Rich was curious; what was coming next? "Of course."

"I know what your background was, because I helped Vivian,

when she helped Ben, on your background. Of course I was pledged to secrecy, and I'd never say a word. My loyalty is to you. I'm just amazed at the way you have taken over this position, and how you know what to do. How <u>do</u> you know what to do?"

Rich thought for a minute. "Linda, thank you for your interest, but I'm not doing anything special. I have an MBA in insurance and finance, I've led men in the past, and I know what I expect from my people. I then inspect what I expect, and manage for results. When I receive a task, I plan how to accomplish that task, and I work my plan. That's it."

Linda looked embarrassed that she had asked the question, and just said,

"Thank you Rich, I'm pleased that I work for you, I like to be with a winner."

"Linda, let's get something straight. You don't work for me. You work with me; we work together. If I don't get into Spence's office, I won't be working here at all!

Rich walked down the hall to Spence's office. Vivian waved him in, and he walked to Spence's desk and shook his hand. Spence indicated that he should shut the door.

"Rich, to say I'm pleased about this trip would be an understatement. You behaved in an exemplary manner. The impression you made throughout your division, and the company was very positive. Dwight Porter called me the day you were in his office. He didn't call to complain, he called to tell me that he was going to turn his office around. Gerry Butterfield called me to apologize that he hadn't done what you had done. You may have to mend a fence there. Let's go over your report on the two offices. "Under his breath he said, "we'll go over your other report after Vivian leaves."

After about an hour, Vivian knocked on the door, stuck her head in, and said,"Do you need anything before I leave, Spence?" Spence wished her a good evening, denied any need for her services, and told her he would see her in the morning.

Rich asked if he could take a break, walked to the men's room, and said goodbye to Vivian as she walked into the elevator. He watched through the window as she entered her car, and drove out of the parking lot.

Rich walked back into the office, closed the door, and told Spence that Vivian had left.

"That's one of the things that impresses us about you, Rich. You don't leave things to chance." expounded Spence.

"Rich, this operation was as much a test, as anything else. We gave you excellent intel, and you used it. We knew about your background, but we didn't know how you would act in a civilian situation. This guy was a minor irritation to us, and was financing an asshole. But we should have gotten rid of the asshole. When you asked for the syringe and the succinylcholine, we had an idea that you were going to inject him, but we worried about the coroner finding the needle mark, and about finding the drug in the tox screen. I know you used the fake driver's license to rent the car, and paid cash, but what happened to all of the other clues? Where is the cell phone, where is the picture I gave you, of the target, and where is the syringe?"

Rich told Spence where he had disposed of all of the items. He told him where he had injected the anesthesia, in order to avoid the coroner finding the needle mark, and told him why he flew to Detroit instead of driving. Then he asked, "Have they discovered the body? Has anyone stated whether there would be an autopsy? What's going on?"

Our intelligence contact tells us that Anouri's brother called the police about eight o'clock the next night, when he didn't show up for work at six. The brother had a pretty good idea what went on each week, and told the police. After checking several motels in the area they found the body. They found the booze bottle, and the fact that the room was locked from the inside. His family was contacted, and they had the political wherewithal to dispense with an autopsy. There was no toxicity screen, as it seemed that he died of natural causes. So, basically, we got rid of scum, but no one knows that they had better look out. This was not a warning. By the way, here's something for you. He gave Rich a briefcase. I recommend that you lease a safe deposit box and slowly disperse this, over time, to different accounts, or other safe deposit boxes. Any questions?"

Rich had no questions and left Spence's office. He went back to his office, closed the door, sat down, and opened the brief case. There were thirty packets of $ 100 dollar bills with a $1000 wrapper around each. Not a bad bonus, for a few hours work. Rich was a little pissed that it was a test, but guessed that from their point of view, it was necessary. He was pleased that it went so well.

His newly rented house was very easy to find. The office was in Hartford, on Asylum Avenue, and his new home was also on Asylum Avenue, but in West Hartford, a separate city. All he had to do was drive down the street in the right direction.

His real estate agent had mentioned to him that there was a great restaurant in a hotel in Farmington, a nearby town, and there was a nightclub there as well.

Since Rich had not had time to go shopping, there was no food in the house. So he planned on going out, once he unpacked, and took care to place his new briefcase in a safe place.

He called the hotel in order to make a reservation, and was told that it wasn't necessary, but they would make sure he had a table by the fountain. Rich confirmed driving directions from his home, what the dress code was, and walked out the door.

It took only fifteen minutes to get to the hotel, which was very impressive, with a large fountain, and lights that kept changing colors. Rich turned over his Z to the valet, and as he walked into the hotel started to think about possibly buying a Jag, or waiting until the next version of the Z came out. He wouldn't have to worry about his budget as a Director of Sales.

The pretty young lady at the desk indicated where the restaurant was, and a prettier young lady, the hostess, sat him at a window table, where he could look at the fountain, and the changing lights. As she left, she said, "Enjoy your meal, Mr. Coburn, I hope we see you here on a regular basis."

Rich looked at the menu, and chose a surf and turf, and a bottle of California wine. The sommelier was the prettiest of the three that he had met tonight. If this was any indication of the women who came to the nightclub, Rich was looking forward to one heck of a night.

The meal was absolutely delicious. The steak was done just right, the lobster was luscious, even the vegetables were crisp, and tasty. The wine was too good for what he paid, and he knew he would be back here again. He left a big tip when he paid the bill, found out that the server's name was Melissa, and that she was off on the weekend.

Walking out of the restaurant, Rich heard music coming down the hall, and walked over to the nightclub. He looked in, and saw about fifty people, most of whom were about his age. He walked over to the bar, and sat down, enjoying the beat of the music. He ordered his usual drink, an O'Doul's, and looked in the mirror, to see what was going on behind him.

Almost directly behind him was a table with two women, and a man. After a few minutes, the man, and one of the women, a good looking blonde, got up to dance. The other woman, a brunette with a short haircut and dark eyes, sat looking at the other couple. She was wearing a low-cut dark cocktail dress, showing some of her assets. He had been looking at her for about fifteen seconds when she looked over at him, and smiled. Rich asked the bartender to take care of his drink, and he walked over to the brunette's table.

"Hi, I'm Rich, would you care to dance?" She laughed, looked up and said, "Hi, I'm poor but I'll dance with you anyway." Rich laughed, looked into her eyes, and said, "No, I mean my name is Rich." She continued to giggle, "I know, I'm just being a wiseass. I'm Gabrielle, but you can call me Gabby."

She stood up, and they started to dance.

"Gabby, are you here with friends, or has your date gone to the men's room? Am I poaching?"

"Rich, I'm here with my sister and her boyfriend. They decided to go out, and wouldn't take no for an answer, when it came to me. I don't go out very often, because I'm always working. I'm an emergency department nurse, and I love what I do, so I sign up for any open shifts. I work at St. Francis hospital, over on Woodland Avenue."

"I think I've passed your hospital. I'm new in Hartford, and I work on Asylum. I also live on Asylum, in West Hartford and have driven by your hospital on the way home."

"What do you do, Rich?"

"I'm a Director of Life Sales, for an insurance company. Are you originally from Hartford?"

"No, I'm originally from Greenwich, but I went to school in Storrs, at the University of Connecticut. Here come my sister, and her boyfriend. I guess we better stop dancing since the music stopped."

The couple came up to them, and Gabby said, "Rich this is my sister Millie, and her boyfriend, Chad. Millie, Chad, this is Rich."

Rich was invited to bring his beer, and join the three of them at their table.

The evening flew by, and before they knew it, it was after eleven. There was lots of dancing, joking, and drinking. Gabby and Rich became very close for spending such a short time together.

As Gabby and Rich got up to dance he accidentally brushed his hand over her breast. Her nipple came to attention, and the sexual tension carried out onto the dance floor.

Rich held her very close, and she laid her head on his shoulder. After a minute or so, she whispered in his ear, "I believe I feel something trying to impress me." Rich whispered back, and held her closer, "Considering that we are doing vertically that which we should be doing horizontally, and the only thing keeping us from having carnal knowledge of each other is four layers of clothing, I think I could impress you better if we got out of here."

"I can't just walk out on my sister," Gabby said.

"Tell them you forgot that you have a midnight shift, and I'll offer to take you there."

Gabby walked over to her sister and Chad, and started to talk. Rich stood by the side, hiding his excitement, and the lift in his trousers.

Gabby came right to him, smiling, and saying, "Let's go. They know what's going down, but they made like they believed me."

They picked up the car, and headed back to West Hartford.

They were the only car at the light when she reached over, and massaged his thigh, as high as she could go. He reciprocated by reaching down the front of her dress, and massaging her breast.

It seemed like it took an hour to get to his house, but it actually took ten minutes.

They erupted out of the car, and ran into his house. He grabbed her, unzipped her dress, and kissed her, as she ripped off his shirt. He picked her up, and carried her into the bedroom. They tore each other's clothes totally off, and threw them all over the room. She grabbed his penis and placed her mouth over it, while he pushed his face between her legs. After a short time, they reversed their positions, and he entered her. They tested the worth of Rich's mattress, and after five minutes exploded together with mutual release.

As they lay there, Rich looked at Gabby. "You, lady are one hell of a piece of ass." She laughed, "And you, sir, know what the hell you are doing. I feel like I was turned inside out."

After about twenty minutes of cuddling, Gabby kissed Rich's shoulder, sat up, and looked him in the eyes. "Well, Captain Midnight, I'm on shift tomorrow morning at seven. I've got to get my uniform. What are my options?"

Rich looked at her naked body, and had a stirring in his nether regions. "Well, we can both call in sick, or you can wear your dress, or we can get it in the morning."

Gabby saw him rising to the occasion, and got out of bed. "I'm serious, Rich, what am I going to do?"

"O.K.! O.K, ! We can either go to your place, get your uniform, and have breakfast here . Then I'll take you to work in the morning. Or you can stay here until morning, and I'll take you to your place. I think the latter is best, as you'll probably have to get your car in order to get home after your shift. I never asked you where you live."

"I live in Hartford. I guess you're right. We can go there in the morning. But it will have to be early."

Rich looked at her again, caressed her breast, and said, "No problem, I wake up at five. Seems like I'm getting up again, now."

She laughed, saying, "Well, I guess we better get back to bed."

Rich woke Gabby on time, they dressed, and headed to her apartment. She changed into her uniform, and made a quick breakfast. Rich followed her back to his office, since he didn't know the way, and it was on the way to her hospital.

Although it was before seven, Charlie was there to greet Rich, and wish him a great day. Neither Linda nor Vivian were at their desks, although Spence's office door was closed, and the light was on.

When he walked into his office, Rich found a sealed, large envelope on his desk. Upon opening it, he found a file. A note from Spence, asked Rich to review and memorize, and to be in Spence's office at 10:00 a.m. with the file.

The individual named in the file was a Jorge Rodriguez. He was a member of the House of Representatives representing a Hispanic area in Florida. He was Thirty-five years old, a Cuban immigrant, single, and a proponent of allowing every immigrant, legal or illegal, who wishes to do so, to enter the United States. He also wants to offer free hospital care, and welfare immediately. All housing should be given free, and if the individual does not have a job, the government will pay the average wage earned in the zip code in which the immigrant lives. Anyone in the United States for less than five years will not pay income taxes, or have to serve in the armed forces. Any immigrant wishing to go to college will have the tuition and all fees paid by the government.

This is absolutely ridiculous, thought Rich. There would be no people left in the rest of the world. Everyone would come to the United States, and there would have to be ninety percent taxes. The amazing thing about these ideas were that there were liberal representatives, and senators who were considering these wacko ideas.

Linda stuck her head in the door, and said, "Good morning, you're in early. Anything I can do for you, with whatever you are working on?"

Rich looked up. "Good morning. Yes, I did start early. I expect to fall asleep about noon. Actually you can help me with something.

Would you please remind me which offices I have in Florida, and bring me the files on them."

"Sure, our Florida offices are in Jacksonville, and Fort Lauderdale. Terry Evans is the manager in Jacksonville, and Phil Cohen is in Fort Lauderdale."

"Thanks, I'm going to see Spence at 10:00. Do you know if Gerry Butterfield is in? I owe him some talk after the Dwight Porter fiasco, in Cleveland."

Linda leaned back out the door, and looked down the hall. "His office door is closed, and the light is out. I'll ask Tammy, his secretary, about his status. Do you want some coffee?"

"I'd love some."

Linda brought the coffee, and told Rich that Gerry was traveling in his division. She also told him that she left a message for Gerry to contact Rich when he came back to the office.

After Rich memorized some more about Jorge Rodriguez, he finished his Coffee, grabbed the file, and went to Spence's office.

"Good morning, Vivian. Is the boss in? I'm supposed to meet him at 10."

"He's on the phone with Dave Baxter. Do you want me to call you when he's available? Oh, wait a minute, he just hung up. I'll tell him that you are here."

"Good morning, Rich, how are you?"

"Just great, Spence. I just can't believe what was in the file you left for me."

"I just sent Vivian to get the intel file . When she brings it back, I want you to memorize it, and come back to me at 5:00 with what you need for logistics. This operation is not black ops. We want people to know that we don't want far left assholes in this country. That they won't remain alive in this country."

"Rich, the cops are going to be all over this one. So will the feds. Any problems?"

Rich looked out the window, looked back at Spence, and said, "None that I can't handle."

Vivian knocked on the door, and came in with a sealed envelope.

"Here's the information you asked for, Spence. It was at the front desk, as you expected."

"Thank you, Vivian."

Spence picked up the envelope, and turned to Rich. "Here's the intel on Jorge. I'll expect it back when you give me the supply request at 5:00. Remember, you won't need anything like you needed the last time. The operation won't be black. Remember, he could be protected by the Capitol Police no matter where he is. See you at 5:00."

The supply request took some thought to put together. Rich went through a dry run, in his mind, after studying the intelligence information. He'd work the operation in Florida, rather than D.C. Basically there would be fewer agencies around during the operation. In Florida, he'd have the locals, and perhaps a small contingency from the Capitol Police, to worry about. Rich knew that he would get a reaction when he gave his supply list to Spence. "Rich what the hell is this? What kind of collateral damage do you expect?"

"Spence, to answer your question, I don't expect any collateral damage. One of the things you promised me was that I had total planning control, both strategically and tactically. It may seem that I'm going to kill a mouse with an elephant gun, but you told me that you wanted this out of the shadows; you wanted people to know that this target was taken out. Spence, this will do it. By the way, giving me Rodriguez's schedule in the intel packet was perfect. I guess that I'll plan my trip with Phil Cohen so that it coincides with Rodriguez's schedule at home."

Rich went directly home after his meeting with Spence. He called Gabby on her cell phone, and she answered from the hospital. She was on duty from six tonight until six in the morning. It was going to be a quiet evening. It was probably for the better, as he wanted to call Phil Cohen in Fort Lauderdale, to set up a meet and greet.

Rich had taken the Fort Lauderdale file with him in order to review the office, as well as to get Phil Cohen's home phone number. He knew that the Fort Lauderdale office would be the closest to the target, as the only other Florida office was in Jacksonville.

chapter 4

FLORIDA

He dialed Cohen's home number, and Phil answered the phone. Rich had spoken to him when he first took over the division, and the reception was very cordial. They coordinated a date for Rich's visit. Rich put a note in his 'things to do' book reminding Linda to set up a visit for him to Jacksonville on the way home.

According to the intel file on Jorge Rodriguez, he lived alone, in a house in Little Havana, and he had never missed a house vote. So it was pretty consistent as to when he would be home. His overall tendency sexually was towards females. There was no indication that he had any other desires. As a matter of fact he was very close to a researcher who worked outside D. C.

There was no information that he was in any relationships in Florida. No one else inhabited the house, and the alarm system was standard, and relatively easy to bypass, if necessary.

The plan was in place, and the supplies should be waiting for him in Fort Lauderdale. Rich was one of the best. Jorge Rodriguez was going to the liberal congress in the sky.

According to Spence it was going to take about a week for all of the supplies to be delivered to Fort Lauderdale, as some of the materials were not immediately available. Knowing there was about a week left in the congressional session, before a recess, Rich had scheduled the timing to meet with Phil Cohen for the following week. The coincidence had worked out perfectly.

Rich asked Linda to set up the visit to Jacksonville before the trip to Fort Lauderdale, and to work in a trip to New Orleans prior to the Jacksonville trip. He called John Pangburn in New Orleans, and told him that it would just be a meet and greet. He'd be there for a day or so, and then move over to Jacksonville for a couple of days, before heading for Fort Lauderdale.

The week went by quickly in the three offices. As he sat in Jacksonville with Terry Evans, in a restaurant on the banks of the St. John River, he gained the knowledge that the St. John flowed from the south to the north. The only major river he knew of that did that was the Nile. It was just another piece of useless information that he filed away in case he needed it in the future.

When he finished up in the Fort Lauderdale office, he loaded his luggage including the backpack that had been delivered earlier in the day, into the trunk of Phil Cohen's car, and drove with Phil to the airport. He then went into the airport, and the nearest men's room, and took the file out of the backpack in a middle stall. The file contained a Wyoming driver's license, and a credit card with the same name. It also included blueprints of Rodriguez's house, the alarm code, and a map of the streets surrounding it. Surrounding the file were a disposable cell phone, a fully loaded Glock 19, and a sealed in colored plastic package measuring 9x4 inches. There was also a small sealed box, along with a TomTom GPS.

Rich slipped the Glock under his jacket, the driver's license and credit card into his wallet, the GPS and phone into his suit pocket, and left the rest in the back pack.

He left the rest room, and walked over to the car rental company desk. He rented a vehicle for three days, refused the insurance, took the paperwork, and walked outside to the shuttle bus. He was pleased to see that the car was a non-descript grey Chevrolet with 5830 miles on it. He set up the GPS for the address in Little Havana, checked out at the gate, and headed for Miami.

Traffic on Rte 95 and 395 was normal, and he moved along with traffic. The total time was less than he expected, and he enjoyed the music on the radio. He followed the GPS directions, and left the major highway at the exit that was recommended. He drove until the voice in the box told him that he had reached his destination, and verified it by checking the numbers on the front of the house.

He was surprised at the look of the house. Although Jorge was a member of the ruling class he lived as a member of the proletariat. The house was relatively small, although it was on a larger lot, away from the neighbors. There were bushes surrounding the house, and the gardening seemed up to date. There were no indications that anyone was living there, no vehicles, and no cars parked along the block. There were children's toys in the front yards to the left, right, and across the street, indicating that there was no observation by any agency. History had shown that they weren't smart enough to set up toys to disguise a house from what Rich had read.

Rodriguez was not scheduled in until tomorrow, which gave Rich tonight to set up his welcome. He had seen a motel along the way on route 395, and he headed there in order to change, take a shower, have dinner, and rest before midnight.

Rich checked in using the Wyoming driver's license and credit card, and found the room to be adequate. The woman behind the counter told him where he could get some dinner, and asked him some questions about why he was in Florida, and did he drive from Wyoming. Rich told her that he was working for an oil company in Louisiana, and thought he'd like to visit Miami. He rented the car in New Orleans, and it must have been a one way drop off, as the plates were from Florida.

Once Rich was in his room, he secured the curtains, turned on the TV, and slowly removed the large and smaller package from his backpack. He removed the plastic packaging from the larger package, and inspected it. It measured 8.5 inches long, 1.5 inches wide, 3.5 inches high and weighed about 3.5 lbs. The body casing was polystyrene and fiberglass; it was slightly curved and there was printing on one side: "This side towards enemy." What Rich had, and Spence didn't believe he had asked for, was a model M18A1 Anti-personnel Claymore mine. It was shaped like a curved rectangle. This shape caused an effective sixty degree pattern in the killing area. Embedded in C4, seven hundred steel balls of 1/8 inch diameter are included in the charge when the mine is set off.

In the smaller package was a tripwire, a small timer, and an electrical blasting cap, along with a cell phone. Rich had his choice as to how he would set the charge off.

At 11:30, after eating, taking a nap, and changing into dark clothes, Rich and his backpack entered the grey Chevy. He energized the GPS, and headed to Rodriguez's house. He drove down the target street, and noticed that most of the houses were dark. The toys were gone, except for a big wheel in the driveway next door to Jorge's house. Jorge's house was dark, and there were no cars parked in the driveway. Rich drove around the block, reconnoitered the area behind the house, using street lights to help him see what he had to do. He parked in front of a house that was for sale, and had no window curtains, or shades. He then, sticking to the shadows, proceeded to the rear property line of Jorge's house, hoping that there were no dogs in the area. He then proceeded to the rear door, where he put on latex gloves, took out a key case, and after about ten seconds, unlocked the door. When he went in, the alarm system started to beep, until Rich put in the code, and then stopped. It was amazing how many people used their birthday as their code. Rich saw it when he was going through the intel file .

He walked through the kitchen, which was lit by a nightlight, and into the hallway where there was a small table up against the wall. Rich opened the backpack, took out the Claymore, and placed it on the table. He placed the cell phone and the electrical blasting cap next to it, and put the knapsack back over his shoulders. He turned on the phone, and dialed the number after turning on the phone in his pocket. The phone rang, and unless something went wrong, the next time it rang, there would be one less congressman. He connected the phone to the blasting cap, and inserted the blasting cap into the hole on the side of the mine. He shut off his phone.

He then walked back down the hall, set the alarm, and walked out the back door. A car was driving down the street, and Rich stayed close to the house. After it passed, he walked through the back yards, and entered his car.

As he drove back to the motel he saw a surprisingly busy burger joint for this time of the morning, So he went through the drive-through, ordered a burger, fries, and a shake. Adrenalin made him hungry. He had taken off the gloves before he went into the burger joint, and now put them in the bag after he finished the food. He threw the bag into the dumpster across from his room, at the motel.

Taking his laptop from his case, he checked to see when the first flight left D.C. into Fort Lauderdale, or Miami.

Rich didn't have the intel as to which city Rodriguez flew to D.C. from, but he didn't think the congressman would drive to Fort Lauderdale, or rent a car to get back. That left Miami, and the earliest flight would get him in at 10:00. That would get him to his house about 10:45. There was a 6:00 a.m. flight on American, but he didn't think congressmen got up that early.

Just in case, Rich was parked down the block, facing away from the house,

At 10:55 a taxi pulled up in front of Jorge Rodriguez's house. A dark complexioned man of about thirty-five, got out, raincoat and briefcase in hand, paid the driver, and walked towards the house. He was too far away for Rich to match his face to the picture he had. He pulled the keys out of his pocket, while the cab drove away, and entered. Rich could picture him turning off the alarm, walking a few steps, and wondering what the contraption was on the table. That's when Rich called the number.

Nothing happened. Then the whole house lifted off of its foundation, flames shot out of the windows, the walls buckled, and the houses surrounding the target house lost their windows. Rich felt a slight concussion where he was, an eighth to a quarter of a mile away. He knew Rodriguez was dead. As a matter of fact, if they found any part of him, it could have been mistaken for hamburger.

Rich pulled slowly away, and as he turned the next two corners, he heard the sirens coming from many directions.

On the way back to the motel, Rich destroyed the picture, and the cell phone, in the usual way. When he got back to the motel, he took apart the Glock 19, and burned the file in the bathroom sink. He figured he'd get rid of the GPS once he got on 95N.

He turned on the TV, and all of the local stations were talking about how Congressman Jorge Rodriguez's house had blown up. There was no indication that he had been at home, as no body was found. Then there was a breaking news report that a taxi driver had dropped Congressman Rodriguez off just moments before the house blew up. There was conjecture that there may have been a gas leak that set off the blast when he had switched on a light switch.

Investigators from the Miami Police bomb squad, the Florida State Police, The Capitol Police, and Homeland Security were investigating.

Rich, dressed in casual clothes, decided to go to visit Miami. There was a stand at the manager's office with about fifty different brochures outlining everything from flea markets to entertainment parks. He grabbed just about one of everything, and set out for Miami, happy he kept the GPS. He planned on losing parts of the Glock at some of the places he visited, or throwing them away on bridges. There was no way he could get it back to Hartford.

He had a great day visiting all of the places, disposing of pieces of the Glock, smashing the GPS, meeting people of different cultures, and meeting some really nice looking honeys. The trouble was that most of them were with their kids.

When he got back to the motel, he stopped in to see the manager. He told her that he would be leaving very early in the morning to head for New Orleans, and that he'd like to settle his bill, in order that he wouldn't have to disturb her in the morning. She was very appreciative, and took his Wyoming credit card, and settled up.

Rich watched the news for a while, and when he found that the story of the explosion had not changed, went down the street a little ways, found a local restaurant and had dinner.

He bought a paperback at the drug store on the corner, and went back to his room. He read for about two hours, put the news back on, saw that there was nothing new, packed, and went to bed.

At five a.m., Rich awoke, showered and shaved, and put on casual clothes.

He put on the TV and found that there was more news. The people from Homeland Security had found the remains of the Claymore mine. They surmised that Congressman Rodriguez was standing in front of the mine when it was set off remotely. There were no remnants of his body. The explosion had been categorized as a terrorist operation. Rich thought to himself, maybe they should have read the standard on the front of the mine:

"This side towards enemy."

Rich decided not to stop for breakfast until he got to the airport in Fort Lauderdale. He stopped for gas before he got to the airport, and returned the car. He took the shuttle to the terminal, walked to the ticket counter, and bought a ticket to Hartford on the next flight. He had an hour after going through security, so he went down the corridor, and had breakfast. Then he went to the men's room, went into a stall, and bent the credit card and driver's license back and forth, until they cracked into little pieces, and he flushed them down the toilet.

He was looking forward to getting home. He was still running on adrenalin.

Since it was Saturday night he hoped that Gabby would be available. He hadn't told her when he would be coming home, but he hoped she would be available. He really liked her. He sat down, buckled up, and immediately fell asleep.

The next thing he felt was the bump of the wheels hitting the tarmac in Connecticut. He followed the crowd to baggage claim, picked up his suitcases, and went out to his car.

On the way home, he called Gabby. His heart skipped a beat when she answered.

"Gabby, it's Rich, how are you?"

"Rich who? I haven't heard from a Rich for almost two weeks. Where have you been?"

"Well, since we saw each other last, I've been in New Orleans, Jacksonville, and Fort Lauderdale. I just landed, and I wanted to speak to you."

"Gee, Rich, I'm sorry that you were in those non-civilized areas, where there aren't any telephones, or cell towers. I'm waiting for a date to pick me up, so if you have any time, you can call me tomorrow. Bye."

The line went dead.

Rich slammed his hand against the steering wheel. "She was right, but I was on a mission. Then again, she had no idea where I was, or what I was doing, and she is a dynamite piece of ass. Maybe I will call her tomorrow.

Rich's phone rang. "This is Rich."

"Rich, Spence. Where are you?"

"I'm on Route 91 coming from the airport to Hartford. I just landed from Florida."

"Great timing. Come directly to the office. I need to see you. Ben will be there, too."

"Give me fifteen minutes."

Rich depressed the gas pedal a little more, and pulled into his parking space in ten.

Rich went in the front door, and pulled out his I. D. card for the guard.

The red band around the card should have had the guard wave him on. The guard, however, took the card, and compared the picture to Rich's face. He wasn't going to let some unknown, dressed casually, up to the executive floor.

"Nice to meet you, Mr. Coburn. I read that you were aboard, but where I didn't know you, there was no way you were going upstairs. I'm Peter. If there is anything I can do, just ask. Have a great day."

"Peter, it's a pleasure to meet you. You have pride in your job, and I'm glad you're here. I'll have my secretary send a note to the head of security on Monday, telling her that I'm impressed with your demeanor, and the way you do your job. You have a great day, as well."

When the elevator door opened at the executive floor the silence, and semi-darkness was brand new to Rich. The door to Spence's office was closed, but there was light under the door.

Rich knocked on the door, and Ben opened it. "Rich, how are you? I hear that you are doing a hell of a job."

"Good to see you, Ben. What's going down? Hi, Spence."

Spence closed the file he and Ben were reviewing. "Rich, you have done an excellent job on this recent mission. I want to debrief you as soon as possible, but something has come up. The debriefing may have to be a joint debriefing. I hate to do that, but a situation has arisen where time is of the essence."

"O.K. Spence, what have we got?"

"What we have is a situation where you will have no cover story. There are no offices in the location. Therefore, there is no way to get supplies and weapons to you, unless you hump it in. We're under a time constraint. The targets will only be there for eighteen hours, twelve of which are in daylight. They have two Capitol Police guards with them. We have no conflict with the Capitol Police. If at all possible, we'd like to keep them alive. You'll make that decision at target point.

The targets are in upper New York state, in the woods. They are in a cabin that sleeps six, but there are only three people staying there. The road into the cabin will be guarded by New York State Police. The three people are the heads of the liberal wing of the party. They are there to decide who will represent the party in the mid-term elections, as well as to approve the ultra-liberal platform that they will promote during the election.

This is a very important mission. The people in Florida are now looking at the operation as a terrorist mission. When you accomplish this mission, the world will know whom we are after, and who the real terrorists are.

Here is the file. Study it. The advance teams are already at the cabin. The targets are due in at 8:00 p.m., and are scheduled to leave at 2:00 p.m. the day after tomorrow.

Whatever you need, you'll get. Just don't ask for a battleship. Once your plan is ready, give me your list of supplies, and tell me where and when you want them."

Rich went back to his office, and shut the door. He needed to be alone to study the territory surrounding the cabin. He had to plan his insert, although he had an idea that would blow Spence's mind, as well as his egress. As well, he had to plan how to destroy the target. He thought, "When I succeed it's going to be the beginning of getting our country back."

Shortly before 4:00 p.m., Rich walked into Spence's office.

"I want to know one thing before I give you my list. These people are supposed to be top of the line. Why the minimal security? One of the targets is a senator."

Ben turned towards him. "These people don't want a lot of security. The cabin is in a very small town. They don't want people to think they make the decisions. They want people to think this is a democracy. You wouldn't know the cabin was there if you drove by. There is only one road in or out. The Great Chazy River is the only geographically listed water in the area. They're going to be there a total of eighteen hours. Is that enough answer for you?"

"Here's my list. I'm sure that you can get it for me within two hours, considering your contacts. You'll notice that there is no battleship, but I do need some different types of equipment. I'll see you in a couple of days. I think I might need a couple of days off, after this kind of schedule."

chapter 5

NEW YORK

Rich drove home and listened to his blinking answering machine. He heard four messages from Gabby, left over the last two weeks. No wonder she was pissed off.

He changed into his jeans and a sweatshirt, and headed for the airport.

When he got to the private aviation area, he saw a man in a flight jacket waiting at the counter. Rich walked up to him, and the man said, "Are you Phil Doucet? I'm Norm Wern."

"Yes I am, "Rich said, answering to the code name he had given to Spence. "Do you have a jump bag that was left for me?"

"Yes I do. And I've got some weird directions that maybe you can clear up for me."

"Sure, let me get into my jump suit and boots, and we can talk about it on the way. Have you filed the flight plan to Plattsburg?"

"All set, do you want the bag in the aircraft?"

"Yes, please. Why don't you do your pre-flight, and I'll meet you at the aircraft. Which one is it?"

"It's the twin Commanche, starboard of the door."

"Thanks, I'll see you out there."

Rich changed into his gear, got into the aircraft, and sat back as the aircraft took off. He heard the landing gear disappear into the wings and nose.

Once they rose to about 10,000 feet, and leveled off, Rich pulled out a map, and turned to Norm. "Norm, this is what we are going to do. I asked you to file to Plattsburg, as that is where the airport is. Obviously, from the way I'm dressed, I'm not going with you, and you are going to fly back alone. I can't tell you where I'm going, but you'll probably know in a day or two. You've been paid an enormous amount for the flight, and if you ever open your mouth about this trip, you won't see the light of the next day. We have nothing against you, or your family, but this flight never existed.

When we get up north you are going to head to Altona, New York. I am going to jump in that area. Any questions?"

Rich hadn't jumped in about eight years, and it had been out of C-130's where he just walked out the back. Here, he's going to basically open the door, roll out, and fall.

After about an hour and a half, Norm started the Comanche into a steady descent.

Rich had put on his parachute, and tied his pack on a rope, to his left leg.

When they reached 3,000 feet, Rich checked the coordinates of where they were, opened the door on his side, and waited for Norm to power back the starboard engine. When it was ready, Rich shook hands with Norm, said "It's not personal," took the bag with him, went out on the wing, and stepped into the slipstream.

Rich's chute was very similar to the one he had used in the SEALs, and was extremely maneuverable. There were not a lot of lights below him, but he was able to see the reflection from the Great Chazy River. His drop zone was the intersection of the river and Devils Den Road, which would bring him to the southeast of the cabin, and about two miles from the cabin road where the State Police would be located.

There were no headlights on the road, and the intersection was coming up fast. Rich pulled down on the toggles, spilling air, and making for a stand-up landing. Rich took off the chute, rolled it into itself, and put it under the bridge by the side of the road. From his jump bag he then took out a knapsack, which contained a small collapsed rubber boat. He removed his jump suit to reveal a black wet suit, put on a vest which had a k-bar knife

attached, and a bandolier with a rifle attached. He attached two holsters with Glock 19's to his belt, and then headed northwest into the woods. He watched his compass on his wrist as well as the GPS which had the coordinates of the cabin.

It had been eight years since Rich had been in the jungle, but his trip through the woods was as quiet as it would have been in Vietnam.

Before long, the cabin rose in front of him, along with the two Capitol Police. The police were actually walking around the outside of the cabin, one in each direction. They were carrying M-16's and from the looks of it, were wearing 9mm's on their hips. They were looking around, not smoking, and doing a good job.

Rich took position at one side of the cabin, about twenty feet from where the officers were walking. About fifteen seconds from when one passed, the other came around the corner. He took the rifle and the bandolier off, and opened the breech of the rifle. It moved easily, and was well oiled, as he requested.

He loaded a dart with medication into the breech, and closed it. The rifle had a noise suppressor on it, but Rich knew that it was not soundproof.

The first guard to come around was looking right in Rich's direction when

Rich shot him in the throat. He crumpled almost immediately. Rich quickly pulled open the bolt, and exchanged the used dart holder for a new one. Then he quickly closed the bolt and brought the rifle up to his shoulder.

The second guard came around the opposite corner, and saw his partner on the ground. Before he could raise the alarm, the second dart was hanging from his neck, and he was falling.

Rich waited a good fifteen seconds to see if there was any noise or movement. There was none.

He slowly walked up to the cabin, and looked into the window. Seated on the couch, facing the television, three men were watching a football game. Two of them were smoking cigars, and all of them had drinks of some sort in front of them. There were papers on a table off to the side. Rich looked at the men, and knew that these were the people who decided what their party was going to do in the future, as far as a platform. The last election had brought in a leftist platform, supposedly for the sake of change. What it had done was vilify capitalism, build up the number of entitlements, and increase taxes. Rich was really working himself up. He remembered all of the men and women who had died for the beliefs they had in this country and their deaths meant nothing. We were becoming a socialist entity.

Rich took out one of the Glocks, attached a noise suppressor, as the State Police were just down the road, and walked to the door.

He opened the door, walked in, and shot each man twice in the head.

Rich then picked up his brass, walked out, and headed to the river. After a relatively short time, he heard the water, and found the bank of the river. He pulled the personal flotation device out of the knapsack, attached a d-bottle and filled it up with air. He then placed it into the water, got in, attached the hand oars to his hands, and headed south.

In twenty-five minutes Rich reached the intersection he had left earlier, at Devils Den Road. He got out of the little boat, took out his k-bar, and punctured it. He then loaded it with rocks, and threw it into the water, where it sank.

He walked down the road about two miles, and took off his wet suit. He was wearing a shirt and a pair of pants under it, and had been wearing sneakers all night. He quickly buried the wet suit and rifle in the woods at the side of the road.

He took his k-bar and attached it to his left ankle, and placed one of his Glocks in a holster on his right ankle. He threw the vest even further into the woods, with his compass and GPS inside the pockets.

Two more miles down the road, parked just off the road, was an old Jeep.

Spence's logistics people had left it just where Rich had asked them to do so.

Rich got into it, and found the key in the ash tray in the opposite door. He put his remaining Glock into the glove compartment. He didn't like leaving all of the items in the direction of his travel, but he didn't think that the police would find them all unless they had hundreds of people looking for the items.

Rich followed the directions he memorized until he came to route 11. He then followed it east to route 87, and headed south to Albany, the Mass. Turnpike, and route 91 to Connecticut.

Sargent Lou Thera of the New York State Police swallowed the last of his third cup of coffee, and continued to read the novel he started at the beginning of his shift. His partner, trooper Larry Benwick, shifted his body, and said, "When does the next shift of Capitol Police come on?" Thera looked at his watch, and replied, "Actually, they should be here in about five minutes. They usually come on about fifteen minutes before their shift, in order to swap reports from the guys on duty."

Ten minutes later, a black Chevy SUV, with government plates, turned onto the dirt road, and stopped beside the troopers. The two officers inside identified themselves, swapped platitudes, and proceeded up the road.

Five minutes later, all hell broke loose.

The radio, which had been turned down to a minimum level, came to life. "State Police, State Police, this is Capitol Police unit 356. We have two men down, and the cabin has been breached. The senator, and the congressmen are dead. Request immediate assistance."

Thera sat up quickly, spilling cup number four. "Holy shit!! Larry, call for a Captain, and get EMS up here now. Tell them we have multiple casualties; call the locals; call the marines. Let's go!!! Thera turned the car around, and sped up the dirt road.

The first place he ran to was the side of the house where one of the new Capitol Police officers was trying to help the two who were prone, to sit up.

He was having a difficult time, as they were not reviving quickly. The medication in the darts was apportioned to keep them unconscious for four hours. Seeing there was nothing to do, he told the officer that help was on the way, and headed for the cabin. He could hear sirens out on the highway.

When he opened the door to the cabin, he could smell the

copper smell of blood, and the smell of gunpowder. Lying in front of the sofa was the senator, and sitting on the sofa was one of the representatives. Sitting in the other chair was the other representative. All three had been shot in the head, at least twice. There were no other wounds visible. The room had no indications of a struggle. There was no brass visible, so the perpetrator either cleaned up after him or herself, or used a revolver.

Thera looked at the officer, and Larry. "Gentlemen, be prepared for a very, very long day. When we woke up this morning, we fucked up!"

That's when the door opened, and what seemed like a platoon of police came in, led by the local sheriff. Within fifteen minutes, there were a score of police cars from the local and state police, the local volunteer ambulance team, who were working on the darted officers, and the local funeral director, who was the coroner. There was no scene discipline, and if there were any clues about, they were either stepped upon, rubbed off, or sat upon.

For some reason, the local volunteer fire department showed up with an engine and a ladder company, and the chief thought he was the scene commander. They were sent home.

Thera had heard from his captain, and was told to take over the scene until the captain arrived in about a half hour. The FBI, the Capitol Police, Homeland Security, the Governor and State Attorney General, the Justice Department, including the Attorney General, and all of the media outlets had been notified. The scene had all of the elements of a typical cluster fuck.

Spence received a call from his intelligence people. "The sale has been made on the father, and the two children. The lab work has been done, and the applications are on the way."

Spence called Ben. When he picked up the phone, all he heard was, "you recruited the best we've ever had. He's not afraid to make the sale, and his belief in insurance is paramount. I think a bonus is in order."

chapter 6

HARTFORD

Rich drove down Asylum Avenue. As he passed St. Francis hospital he thought about Gabby. He hadn't called her again, but he was absolutely beat. He figured he'll call her tomorrow.

When he walked through the door to his house, the fatigue caught up with him. He put away all of the items he brought with him from the Jeep, grabbed a beer out of the fridge, sat down in a living room chair, and turned on the answering machine. There were no messages, but it didn't matter. Rich was asleep in one minute.

At five in the morning, Rich woke up. His neck hurt from the way he was sleeping. He had spent the night in the chair.

Rich put on a change of underwear, a running suit, and a pair of running shoes, he wrapped a towel around his neck, grabbed his keys, and headed for the track at Hall High School. It had been too long since he had been running in the morning.

He ran for five miles, but the fifth mile was well below the time he usually ran. He was soaked from sweat, and he knew he had to get back on the program. He got home, shaved and showered, spending twice as long as he usually did in the shower, got into a pair of jeans and a sweatshirt, and had breakfast. Then he called Gabby.

There was no answer on her home or cell phone, which indicated that she was probably working. He called her home phone again, and left a message: "Gabby, I apologize. After I spoke with you the last time, I had an emergency situation, and had to leave town. I just got back, and the first thing I wanted to do was call you. Please forgive me. Please give me a call. I'd love to see you again. By the way, It's Rich."

He thought about the brief case that he had hidden above the closet. The alarm was set when he came home, but he checked it anyway. He wondered whether he'd get paid for one in upstate New York, or for three? They still owed him for Florida, but he knew they wouldn't forget. He'd have to find out how to open an offshore account.

He realized that he still had his k-bar and one of the Glocks bound to his legs, and there was still a Glock in the glove compartment of the Jeep. He must have really been tired. He went out to the garage, got the Glock, and placed it in a bag with the other items for disposal.

He drove over to Route 4, went up the hill to the reservoir, walked over to the overlook, and dropped the k-bar into the water. He then drove half way around, and disposed of one of the guns. He drove about another mile, and disposed of the second one. Then he went home.

Rich never felt worn out. He was a young guy, in pretty good shape, and usually exercised. Today, however, he felt worn out. Maybe it was the combination of mental and physical stress from the operation, the driving, the lack of comfortable sleep, and the run this morning, all put together. Rich decided to take the day for mental rehabilitation and watch the football game. "Let's hope the Pats are playing," he thought.

Monday started at 5:00a.m.and Rich went through his routine at the high school, and his morning ablutions. When he turned on the TV while eating breakfast, the only thing on, on all channels, was the execution of three of "our nation's leaders." They built up the three politicians as if they were deities. The day before, there had been a news conference held by the FBI and the justice department. The President also had held a news conference, saying that the terrorists who had caused the world to lose these progressive politicians would be caught quickly, and he would not rest until their capture was accomplished. Rich thought to himself about the fact that he'll have plenty of time to rest, because he doesn't do anything anyway. Rich left for the office, realizing that Gabby had never called him, and figured he'd call her later in the day.

At the same time Rich was driving down Asylum Avenue, Special Agent Donald Minnock, of the F.B.I., Assistant Director Leslie Hyman, of Homeland Security, Lieutenant Bill Guess, of the Capitol Police, and Captain Harris Berlin of the New York State Police were meeting in Albany.

Bill Guess addressed the others. "Well, we know that the perp, or perps, are well trained. We know that he, she, or they didn't want to harm the officers, and we know that their prime targets were politicians. If we combine these killings with the one in Florida, we know that they are well armed. We know that a claymore was used in Florida, and that the shells used here were 9 mms."

Leslie Hyman, although a political appointee, knew her job well, coming from the National Security Administration prior to her appointment. She picked up where Bill Guess left off. "We also have no idea who these people are, how they got here, and how they got away. We know that there was no road other than the one guarded by Harris's people, and that Bill's people evidently were unaware that anyone had come through the woods, until they were hit. There were no footprints, no matted grass, no brass left behind. It's as if they appeared, did their job, and disappeared. The use of the claymore in the Jorge Rodriguez killing makes me lean towards the perps being military. The use of a .45 makes me think military as well, or at least law enforcement, as the most used pistol for cops is the Glock-19 which is a 9mm weapon."

Captain Berlin looked at his colleagues. "Are you saying that police officers killed the politicians, because they used 9mms, and didn't kill the guards?"

Don Minnock, who even looked like an F.B.I. agent would be expected to look like, held up his hand. "Harris, not at all. We have a situation where the suspect, or suspects, are so good that we don't know who did it. The only thing we know for sure is that we have four dead politicians, and no leads. The only commonality that I can see is that the four politicians were all ultra-liberals. Maybe we should start to look at right wing conservatives. With one killing in Florida, and three in New York, we have to look at larger, well-financed organizations."

The four decided to coordinate all of the information their individual agencies developed, and meet again, in four days, in Albany.

Rich pulled into the parking lot, and into his space. He saw that Spence was already in.

He realized that the mornings were getting a little cooler, and figured he'd start carrying his raincoat.

He waved at Charlie, and took the elevator to the executive floor.

Vivian was taking off her coat, and waved to him. He walked over to her, said, "Good morning, Vivian. How are chances for me to see the boss this morning? " She smiled, as she looked at the computerized appointment book that she and Spence shared, and said, "Well, since Spence has blocked out two hours, and your name is typed in, I guess that chances are pretty good. Your time begins at 8:45."

By the time Rich got back to his desk, Linda was already putting coffee on his desk, and bringing his e-mails up on the electronic console. When he walked in, she smiled, put his journal in the center of his desk, and asked, "Am I going to see much of you today? The way you run from office to office, I'm not sure where you are, unless you plan it in advance."

"I'll be here at least this morning. I'll be with Spence for a couple of hours, and then I'll let you know what's going on. Please get me the division production records to date, and the Cleveland numbers on a daily basis for last week."

"Are you going to need a flak jacket for your meeting with Spence, or is everything o.k.?"

"Everything is o.k., as far as I know. We'll see."

At 8:45, Rich walked into Spence's office. Spence indicated for him to close the door. He then stood up, stuck out his hand, smiled, and said "Welcome back, Rich. I can't possibly show the amount of my pride in you, for the job you are doing. You are exceeding all of our expectations. How do you feel you are doing regarding your expectations?"

"Spence, when we first started out I wasn't sure what I expected. It was still a conundrum regarding whether I was moving my beliefs forward, or whether it was murder of people who disagreed with my beliefs. I had lost all religious values in Vietnam, so the actual killing of people never bothered me.

After reading the intelligence reports on each of the people I have terminated, I realized that all of them were diametrically opposed to my values, and my way of life. They all wanted to change the country I believe in. They are my enemy. They deserve to lose the liberty and rights so many people died for, and are still dying for today. I feel that the more enemies of this nation that I eliminate, the more we get closer to my expectations. I'll have accomplished all of my expectations when there are none of these enemies left."

"Wow! That was more of an answer than I expected, but I loved it. Rich, let's sit down and debrief the Florida and New York operations. I've got to admit that you come up with some wild ideas as to how to accomplish your mission."

Two hours later, Spence called Vivian, and asked her to cancel the rest of his morning appointments, since he was continuing his conference with Rich. An hour later he ordered sandwiches and coffee, cancelled his afternoon appointments, and continued his conference with Rich.

At 4:00 p.m. the door opened, and Rich walked out with a brief case. He walked directly to his office, and closed the door. As soon as he sat down, his intercom buzzed, and Linda asked, "Rich, is everything o.k.?"

"Thanks for your concern, Linda, everything is great. As a matter of fact, I'm going to Aruba for a conference for four days. If you can, before you leave for the day, would you please make reservations for me at a hotel on Palm Beach, in Aruba, and let me know the flight times from Hartford to Aruba, and return, leaving Wednesday, and coming back Sunday? Thanks."

Rich then walked over to the door of his office, and silently pushed the lock in the closed door.

He then opened the new briefcase, and counted $200,000.00. Spence had told him how pleased they were with his accomplishments, and that he was being paid for four operations, at the rate of $ 50,000 each. Spence also told him that the board of directors of the organization felt that he could use a break, and he was due a bonus of four days in Aruba, with all expenses paid.

Spence told him that Rich would be given a new assignment on Monday of next week, so he shouldn't get too sunburned.

Linda, in her usually efficient way, buzzed Rich on the intercom. "I have a suite in the tower, with an ocean view, at the Radisson Aruba for you. It has the biggest beach on Palm Beach. There are no non-stops from Hartford to Aruba, or return. You can get a one stop through Philadelphia at 5:30 am, landing in Aruba, or a change of planes in Miami, leaving at 6:30 a.m. and arriving in Aruba at 11:30 a.m. Coming back on that one gets you in at 11:35 p. m .

"O.K., great. Book me on the 6:30 a.m., returning at 11:35 p.m."

"Done!"

Rich spent Tuesday speaking with all of his managers, projecting a budget long before it was asked for, and using the computer to find out as much about Aruba as he could.

The flight left Hartford on time, and headed to Miami. Rich, sitting next to an accountant from Glastonbury, received a history of Aruba. The accountant had gone to Aruba, an island nineteen miles long, and sixteen miles from Venezuela for the last seven years, and loved it. He proceeded to tell Rich that he was staying at the best hotel on the best beach, gave him names of restaurants, and the fact that although the unit of money on the island was the Florin, the American dollar was used everywhere.

When the accountant found out that Rich was a diver, he brightened, and told Rich where the best wrecks were, as well as the best bars and clubs. It was as though diving meant partying, which was not the code that Rich went by. The conversation shortened the time on the flight, or at least it felt like it did.

The accountant was on the next flight, but not next to Rich. Instead, the seat was filled with a six year old boy who never stopped talking to his brother, across the aisle. He also was constantly squirming and kicking the seat in front of him, and was very close to becoming Rich's next target!

Once he got off the plane, Rich had to go through immigration, and customs, and pick up his luggage. When he walked through the airport door, the eighty-six degree weather, which was close to what it was all the time, immediately relaxed him.

He took a cab to the hotel, and couldn't believe the gorgeous flora and fauna, and the friendliness of the staff. He walked through the lobby, and was greeted by a beautiful azure sea on the other side of two fantastic pools. A magnificent white beach dotted with man-made large shaded umbrellas drew him down to the beach, where the vocation of the day seemed to be watching the miniscule bikinis painted on the beautiful bodies of nubile women.

Rich thought to himself about the rewards of what he did. Obviously, the first reward was how someday soon his country would revert back to a strong, vital nation. Secondly, this was one hell of a close second, whether the organization gave him more bonuses, or he had to use his own resources, this was the way he was going to live.

His days became filled with diving in the morning, lying on the beach in the afternoon in the company of a beautiful woman, dining in a top restaurant, gambling in one of the casinos in the early evening, and gamboling with the conquest of the day at night.

On Friday, as Rich followed his regular schedule, the agencies of the F.B.I.,

Homeland Security, Capitol Police and the State Police met in Albany.

There was a major development in the New York case.

Two fishermen had found a parachute, collapsed and rolled up, under a bridge on Devils Den Road. It was new, a military type, with no markings whatsoever. There were no prints anywhere on the canopy, toggles, or the risers.

Now they believed they knew how the perpetrator entered the

area of the killings. They assumed since they only found one chute, that there was one killer. If they found more chutes, they would change their mind.

A memo went out immediately for major manpower to search the area of the cabin, all the way up and down Devils Den Road, and the surrounding woods.

Of course, as soon as the memo went out, the intelligence arm of the organization picked up the information, and forwarded it to Spence.

Within six hours the major media networks were giving out the information, over and over, ad nauseum.

By Sunday Rich had had so much relaxation, that he was exhausted. He requested a late checkout, slept as long as he could, and headed to Princess Beatrix airport as late as possible. They told him that he would need three hours to go through the security process, customs, both Aruban and United States, and make it to the flight. It would be easy in Miami, as the U.S. customs went through their process in Aruba, and there would be no need to do it in the U.S.

Rich slept on both flights home, and was fairly reconstituted as a human being, when he landed in Windsor Locks, outside of Hartford.

On the way home, Rich drove by St. Francis hospital, and realized that he had never called Gabby. He liked her, and he doubted that she would have anything to do with him now, but he'd try to make it up to her. He'll have Linda send her flowers, and candy, and then he'll call. Wait a minute, Spence said he was getting a new assignment tomorrow. May be he ought to wait until he gets back from wherever.

When Rich woke up, he went through his typical morning ritual, but didn't turn on the television, reading his mail instead. When he left, he reversed his direction back down Asylum Avenue, and ended up walking into Spence's office at 7:45.

Spence motioned for him to shut the door, stood up, shook his hand, and said, "Welcome back, how was it? Did you hear the news?"

"It was beyond belief. What news? I haven't been in civilization for four days."

"They found your 'chute, and have about two hundred people searching the grounds around the cabin."

"Don't worry, Spence; there is no way that they can connect any of what I left behind to anyone. The items are all clean, and the actual weapons used are not in New York. I made sure of that. As long as the logistics people covered their asses as to diversifying where they got the items, we've got no sweat."

"Good, I know that they are real pros in getting equipment from different sources, and there is no paper trail. It's good to have you back. Did you relax at your conference"?

"Hell, no, but it was fantastic, as I said."

"Our intelligence people are noticing that the Capitol Police are increasing the protection details for the members of Congress and the Senate. They finally think that they see a pattern in the killings. Liberal politicians are looking over their shoulders as well, although we haven't seen too much change in the voting patterns. We're going to kick it up a notch in this next operation."

"Outline the operation, and I'll tell you what I need to do the job."

"The biggest problem that could arise on this next operation, Rich, is collateral damage. If there is too much, the public will turn against us, and we need the true Americans on our side. We also have to follow our mission, which is to destroy the ultra-liberal government."

"What has to be done? Who has to be taken out? Where is it? I'll put it together with no collateral damage, if possible."

Spence opened his top drawer, and pulled out four files. "These are the files of four senators, as well as the intel file. They are all members of the Senate Budget Committee. They have been cutting budgets for armed services, etc. and increasing appropriations for entitlement programs. These are some of the people who will cause taxes to rise on the average American, and take those dollars to the unwashed masses, and illegals. They must be taken out. The four of them are going to be heading a rally in Independence Hall in

Philadelphia. You can be assured that your recent accomplishments have caused their protection details to be ramped up. There will be maximum coverage from the liberal press, and the place will be full of "give me more" people. This is a tough one. Give me your plan and list by tomorrow morning. The rally takes place on Thursday. Have Linda schedule you in to the Philly office, and then get the flu in the hotel. Good luck."

Rich walked back to his office. As he passed Linda, he looked down, and said, "Good morning. Would you please schedule me into a hotel in Philly, near the office, for Wednesday and Thursday nights, and notify the manager that I'm coming to visit him, Thursday morning. Would you please also book me on flights in on Wednesday morning, and out on Friday morning. Thank you."

Linda, who had been taking notes, looked up at him. "Rich, welcome back. Are you o.k.; can I help?"

"Thanks, I'm sorry if I was brusque, I've just got things on my mind pertaining to this trip, and I apologize for being less than friendly."

"No problem, I just wanted to make sure you were o.k."

"I'm finc. Thanks."

Rich walked into his office, closed the door behind him, and thought to himself, "Yuh, I'm fine. All I have to do is figure out a way to break through a circle of cops, take out four people, get back out through the cops, and not be identified by hundreds of people." He then sat down, and started to figure out how to solve his problems.

He left his office after 5:00, and found his tickets, and hotel reservation in a folder marked Rich, on Linda's desk. He'd have a full day in Philly on Wednesday, and leave about 10:00 a.m. for Hartford, on Friday. He knew that the logistics people would have a box at the hotel waiting for him. Now all he had to do was make a list for Spence, of what he wanted in the box.

Rich drove directly home, had two cans of soup for dinner, and got to work on his plan, and logistics, right away. About 1:00 a.m. he went to bed.

He woke at 5:00, as usual, went over to Hall High, and ran,

came home, shaved, showered and changed, had breakfast, and watched television while he ate. There was no new news. He was in Spence's office at 8:00, reviewed his plan, and list, and then told Spence that he was getting the flu, winked, and said that he would be leaving in about an hour.

He went back to his office, and called the hotel where he had a reservation. He told the desk clerk that he was checking in on Wednesday morning, and was expecting a box, and some clothes in a suit bag. He wanted them placed in his suite as soon as they arrived. The clerk assured him that it would be done, and also confirmed that he could have early entrance to his suite.

Rich pored over the map of Philadelphia, Market Street, where his hotel was located, and Chestnut Street where Independence Hall is.

Satisfied that he knew how to leave one location, get to the other, and get back, he picked up the file on the Philadelphia office, and called the Manager, Thomas Martin. After a brief conversation, assuring Tom that he was doing good job, and that he just wanted to meet him and his staff, he hung up. He punctuated the conversation with a few coughs, and the fact that he had a headache.

He then picked up the file, put it in his briefcase, and walked out of the office.

"Linda, I think my meeting in Aruba has taken some of my energy away. Either that, or I caught something on the plane. Since I'm leaving tomorrow, I think I'm going to go home, and sleep until tomorrow morning. I really feel punk."

"Gee, Rich, I'm sorry. If there is anything you need, please call me. Do you have a doctor to go to?"

"I don't think it's that bad, I think I can catch it by getting some rest. See you Friday."

"O.K., feel better."

Rich drove towards home, passed St. Francis Hospital once again, put a thought in the back of his head to call Gabby soon. Stopped for gas, went to the market, and grabbed a steak, rice, asparagus, and a bottle of domestic wine for dinner, and pulled into his garage.

He packed, memorized what he had to, had dinner, watched a game show, and went to bed.

In the morning Rich went through his usual schedule, saw that there was no new news about New York, and headed for the Airport.

chapter 7

PHILADELPHIA

The flight was uneventful, and took less than an hour and a half. The cab ride added another twenty-five minutes, and he pulled into the front of the hotel.

When he checked in, the desk clerk recognized his name, and made sure to tell him, "Mr. Coburn, your box, as well as the suit bag was taken up to your suite, about twenty-five minutes ago. Please do not hesitate to call upon us if we can do anything at all."

Rich took the keycard, and went on the elevator to his floor.

He found the suite to be at the end of the hall, and through a set of double doors. When he entered, he found the suit bag hanging in the closet, and the box sitting below it. He stowed his own luggage in the closet, walked to the window, and pulled the sheer curtains apart. There was no building across from his room, and he could see the skyline. Philadelphia really was a great city.

He then went to the bathroom, checked the counter space, and the towels.

Everything was going to work out fine.

He walked over to the front door, put out the privacy tag, and came back to open the suit bag. He pulled out a white shirt, with epaulets and gold captain's bars on the collar. Next, he pulled out a hat with gold colored markings on the visor, and a badge on the riser. He then pulled out a Philadelphia Police Department jacket, with captain's bars on the shoulder, and identifying letters on the collar. A gold badge was on the left side of the chest, and a name tag with W. Haggerty was on the right. Above the badge were service ribbons, and on the right chest was a card with a picture and the name of Captain William Haggerty. A belt and black shoes, well shined, were at the bottom of the bag.

He then opened the box. He found a holster with a Glock-19, fully loaded, and an ankle holster with another fully loaded Glock-19. The ankle weapon was a little large, but it was Rich's favorite pistol, so he put up with the inconvenience. He also found a fairly good-sized syringe, filled with what was supposed to be thallium sulfate, and topped with an 18-gauge needle. Another fairly large box was left in the outer box. Rich took the smaller box and took it into the bathroom. He opened it, and found a hairpiece, tooth caps, a mustache, and fillers for his mouth and cheeks to make him look heavier. He also found makeup to darken his skin and hands, and to add grey to his eyebrows and sideburns.

Rich took another shave, showered, and made himself up with all of the items in the small box, using just a portion of the makeup. He then put on the shirt, tie, uniform, and weapons.

When he looked in the mirror, looking back at him was a Philadelphia Police Captain, about fifty years old. He was impressed. Now for the test.

He took the elevator which opened the furthest away from the check-in desk and went out the side door when he reached the ground floor. He walked the two blocks to Chestnut Street, twice returning salutes from patrolmen.

When he got to Independence Hall, there were many different uniforms. The Park Service, the Philadelphia Police, The Capitol Police, Pennsylvania State Police, and, Rich was sure, a number of plain clothes police were amongst all of the workmen and people walking in all directions.

He walked right by the patrolman at the door, who didn't salute, and neither did Rich. Inside was a catastrophe. Rich couldn't see how they would have it all put together by tomorrow.

He walked to the stage, right up to the men at the podiums. "Hi guys, how is your day going so far? Who's in charge?"

"I am, captain, Gerry Golt. How are you doing?"

"Great Gerry, I'm here to check out whoever will be bringing out the water bottles for the senators. Do you know who that will be?"

"Captain, as far as I know, the water is being handled by the Park Police, but I don't know who. Their captain is over there," he said, and pointed to an officer in khakis.

Rich walked over to the officer, a captain, and touched his cap, as a show of respect. "Good morning, captain, I'm Bill Haggerty, Philadelphia Police."

The Park Police Captain touched his cap as well, and said, "Hi, Bill, Hank Terrill. What can I do for you?"

"Hank, I have received directions from the top that I am to check on the delivery of the water bottles to the four podiums tomorrow. Is that under your aegis?"

"You're kidding. They send a captain to check on water bottles? It must have come down from the senate. Those guys think that they are royalty, and everybody else is a peon. I'm sorry for spouting off, Bill. I know that you are following orders. I'm just fed up with this government, and this administration."

"No sweat, Hank, I feel the same way you do. Now where does the water come from?"

"We've got it over here, and he pointed to an area behind the curtain. We've got twelve bottles. I hope they drink it all, and have to piss right away."

"What are you supposed to do?"

"Who will bring them to each podium?"

"We could do it now if you want. All we're supposed to do is leave three at each podium, on the shelf."

"Look, Hank, I know you are busy with everything else you are doing. I'm just supposed to check that they're in the right place, and that the tops are secured. How about if I just check them out, and put them on the podiums where they belong. I'll do it in five minutes; I've got to take a piss."

"Hey, thanks Bill, I do have a lot to do. It was nice meeting you. The men's room is down that hall, on the left."

"Rich walked down the hall, went into the men's room, and waited for a couple of minutes. He didn't have to go to the bathroom, and he couldn't wash his hands or face because of the makeup."

When he got back to the podiums, Hank wasn't there, which

was just what Rich had hoped would happen. He walked behind the curtain, and proceeded to inject the thallium sulfate through the top of each water bottle. He was pleased that the syringe was large enough to carry the amount needed for twelve bottles. He then placed his handkerchief over the top of each bottle, put his thumb over it, and shook each bottle in order to mix the poison throughout the water. He then placed three bottles on the shelf of each podium.

When Rich had just finished, Hank was coming toward the podiums, so they waved to each other.

Rich walked away from the stage, toward the front of the hall. He realized that the hall that he was in was the place where the Declaration of Independence was signed. Tomorrow, hopefully, the American people, through his act, would declare their independence again, this time from a socialist government.

There were no problems for Captain William Haggerty on his way back to Market Street. A patrol car beeped to him, and he waved. They probably never saw a captain walking down the street. He reached the side door of the hotel, again took the furthest elevator from the front desk, and went up to his suite.

He took off the uniform jacket, the shirt, pants, belt, holster, pistol, and the ankle holster and pistol, as well as the hairpiece. He took out the fillers from his cheeks and mouth, took off the moustache, and washed the grey out of his eyebrows. He then showered, and washed the makeup off his body.

When he was finished he called Tom Martin, and told him that he really wasn't feeling well. He said he hated to do so, but he had to cancel tomorrow's meeting, because he would be in no shape to meet with him. He promised to come back soon, and take Tom and his wife to dinner.

Rich then went downstairs, through the main door, and decided to walk down Market Street. He found a restaurant and had lunch. He was famished. Rich walked around to as many historic places he could. Since he was able to accomplish what he was going to do tomorrow morning, today, he decided to go out to Valley Forge tomorrow, and then drive to Lancaster, and visit Amish country.

The last place he went was to the car rental kiosk in the lobby of the hotel. He wanted to leave early in the morning. He leased a car with a GPS system, knowing that he'd definitely get lost in a new area without help. He didn't even have a compass.

Once Rich found out where the car was parked in the hotel parking lot, he went to the hotel restaurant and had an early dinner. He then made two trips, bringing the suit bag on the first trip, and the box on the second. In both cases he took the elevator directly to the parking area, and didn't get off at the lobby floor.

Before he put the uniform into the suit bag, Rich removed the badges from the hat, and jacket, and removed all of the captain's bars and identifying letters from the shirt. He also took off the identifying picture of William Haggerty.

The box contained everything else.

He drove out of the garage, and headed for the reservoir on North 33rd street. When he got there, he scattered both Glock-19s, the clips, and smashed the syringe and needle in many different locations.

He then drove through an area that looked like it had an indigent population. It was here that he put the suit bag on a corner. He knew someone could use the jacket, pants, shirt, belt and shoes. He tore apart the hat, and threw the pieces on different streets. He threw the ribbons, badges, brass letters, and I.D. badge in different empty lots, and the makeup kit in a dumpster in the next town.

He was back in his room by 11:00 p.m., and went to bed. 0500 comes at the same time every day, no matter where you are. Rich woke up, stretched, and put on his work out gear. He put his room keycard in his pocket, took the elevator to the lobby, walked out the front door, did his stretches, and started running. Being in a new city, Rich ran south three blocks, east three blocks, north three blocks, and west three blocks. Then he did it again.

When he got back, he showered, shaved, changed, and went down to breakfast. While he ate he watched the television. The rally at Constitution Hall was all over the news. They were expecting a turn away crowd, and it was due to start at 10:00 a.m.

Rich went back to his room, picked up a light jacket, and headed out.

It turned out to be a beautiful day to be a tourist. The temperature was warm enough for Rich to leave his jacket off, keep his sunglasses on, and just walk around Valley Forge.

He then drove to Lancaster, had lunch, and joined a tour of some Amish homes and shops in the area. They were a wonderful, peaceful people who worked hard, and kept tradition. Rich was impressed.

He spent the rest of the day driving around eastern Pennsylvania, just enjoying himself.

He knew that by now, if everything went as expected, all four of the targets had ingested the 400 mg of thallium sulfate, and each would be dead within a few days.

Rich thought back about his plan.

He had to get by the phalanx of police that would be all over Constitution Hall. He had to get to the targets, and get back out, without being caught or identified. He could get to the targets by poisoning the water, but the poison could not be instantaneous, as only one senator drinking his water and dying, would stop the others from drinking. Therefore, Rich had put enough slow acting poison in each bottle to start the body functions deteriorating. That way they would all drink the poison, and all die. He had been able to walk out of the police protection circle, a day in advance.

The ride back to Philadelphia was uneventful. The GPS had worked perfectly, and he arrived just in time for dinner.

He turned the car in, walked into the restaurant, ordered Chilean sea bass with a sauce, potatoes, a vegetable, and an O'Douls. While waiting for his meal, Rich watched the television, and saw the rally. They covered enough of the presentation by the senators so that Rich was able to see each of the targets drink at least once from the bottles. Since they all looked the same on television, he thought that they drank even more as time went on. The commentator said that the presentation, including questions took four hours.

Rich knew that people talking for four hours could drink a lot of water, and he hoped they did.

After dinner, Rich went upstairs, packed, watched a drama, and went to bed.

Friday morning Rich woke up, did his run, went to breakfast, put on a suit and checked out. He grabbed a cab to the airport, went through security, bought a copy of the paper, waited to board, and entered the plane.

He sat down, opened the paper, and read all about the rally. He read about how the government wanted the American people to be forced to pay for those who could not pay their own way. How everyone should come to the United States, and share what the capitalists have stolen from them. That all of the appropriations for the military should be reversed, and the money given to the poor. He was sure that the senators wouldn't give their money. He got so angry that he just threw the paper on the empty seat next to him. He hoped that the poison was painful, and lasted at least a week to kill them.

The flight landed on time, and Rich went out to the garage, got his car, and headed for the office.

He turned on the news. Although he didn't expect anything to happen this soon, you never knew if luck was on your side. There was no report of any of the senators dying, becoming seriously ill, or being hospitalized.

Rich pulled into his space, and noticed that Spence's space was empty.

There was a pall over the whole office. There was no undercurrent, no talking, just an abnormal silence.

Linda was not at her desk when Rich walked by, but she came into the office right behind him.

"Linda, what's going on? I didn't see Spence's car, the office seems like a morgue. What's happening?"

"You've been in Philadelphia, so Spence said he'd handle the problem. On Thursday, a special agent from the F.B.I., and a detective from the New York State Police came to visit Spence. It seems that one of our agents in the New York office has supposedly promoted himself to vice president of investments, and has been working with a representative of the German government in an arbitrage scheme. The amount of the arbitrage is in the millions."

"How did you find this out?"

"Spence told Vivian, and she told me, asking me to tell you."

"Where is Spence now?"

"He said that he was going to the New York office. You're supposed to call him when you get in."

"Has the law department been notified?"

"Yes, Tommy Mayer, one of the counsels, went with Spence."

"O.k., please get Spence on the phone for me. Thanks."

Shortly after, Linda leaned into the office, and said, "I've got Spence on the line."

chapter 8

HARTFORD

Rich picked up the phone, and sat down. The sweat was running down his sides, and his heart was beating quickly. If the story Spence left was true, and involving Tommy Mayer made it seem so, there was no need to worry.

The fact that the F.B.I. and New York State Police were involved scared the hell out of him.

"Spence, Rich, what's going on?"

"Hi Rich, how was your trip to Philly? I heard that you got sick, and never met with Tom Martin."

"That's right, I spent my trip in the hotel."

"Well, we'll talk about it when I get back. Meanwhile we've got a mess here in the New York office. We have an agent named Abu Ashiri. He's been with us for two years. I think you should have been made aware by now of what he's accused of doing. Not only is he in trouble, but Ralph Woron is in trouble, as well for poor supervision. Tom Mayer thinks he's clean, and we may get the charges dropped on him."

"When will you be back?"

"Since I'm already down here, my wife is going to join me tonight, and I'll see you Monday morning early. O.K.?"

"Good enough, Spence. Have a good weekend."

Rich sat in his chair, looked at the wall, and thought about his reaction in hearing about the police.

When he was in his early teens, Rich lived in South Boston. He was a member of the sabres, a group of teens that today would be called a gang. They didn't do things that are done by most gangs today, and definitely weren't violent.

One of his friends, Sid Schwingo, had a father who owned a market. Five of the sabres, including Sid, decided that they were going to burglarize the market after it closed, and get the money left in the office overnight.

They climbed from the dumpster in the back of the building, onto the roof, and through the skylight, totally ignoring the wire running around the edge, which set off the silent alarm.

Rich was the first one into the back office, and the first to hear the sirens of the Boston Police, who arrived in two and a half minutes. As soon as he heard the first siren, he broke out in a sweat, and his heartbeat started to increase dramatically. In Vietnam, it must have happened fifty times. It was almost as if his body knew in advance when he was going to be in a tenuous situation. What had saved him over the years, was his attention to details, like the wire on the skylight.

Luckily, Sid's father refused to prosecute, and aside from Sid going to military school, there were no repercussions.

On Sunday morning, after Rich returned from his Hall High School run, he showered, and he turned on the television as he sat down to have breakfast.

The lead story was about one of the senators from Minnesota, the oldest of the four who had led the rally on Thursday, being found non-responsive at home, and dying on the way to the hospital. There was no known reason for his death, prior to an autopsy. Of course the government had released a statement deifying him, and the twenty years of service he had used to pilfer from the American people.

Rich had tried to call Gabby the previous day, and she told him not to call her again. She had met someone, and since she obviously didn't even deserve a phone call from Rich, he wasn't even a memory, as far as she was concerned. She then hung up on him.

Rich had lost relationships before, and his attitude was, "Pretty girl, great body, great sex; there were more out there." Aruba had proved it. Rich had no remorse for what he had done in Philadelphia. He truly believed that he was being a patriot, killing enemies who were out to destroy the country he loved, and bring a lifestyle so very different from the one that had existed before.

Rich decided that he was going to spend the day shopping for a new car. The car would have to be one that he could be afford on a $ 100,000 salary, in order to make sure that there was no suspicion that he was making the bonuses which were presently in his closet. Next week, he would ask Spence how one goes about setting up an offshore bank account.

On Monday, the news announced the untimely death of one of the senators from Massachusetts. In this case, it was the youngest of the four senators. The autopsy of the first senator showed little, except that the toxicity report uncovered a residue of thallium sulfate. There had not yet been a toxicity report on the second senator, but the commonality of the two senators having been together at the rally, immediately started treatments on the senators from California and New York.

There was a cry of terrorism from the news pundits. They put the three deaths in New York, the death in Florida, and the attempt on the four in Philadelphia together. All of the dead were liberals. There were no suspects. There was no modus operandi. One by Claymore, that the news called a bomb, three by gunshots, four by attempted poisoning.

The government was stymied, this had never happened before. Considering these were government employees, the typical politicians wanted someone to blame other than themselves, or wanted to take the lead in telling people how to solve the problem. They went in the usual direction; they formed a committee, and held a hearing. As usual, the hearing resolved nothing. They just blamed all of the alphabet agencies, but did nothing positive.

By nightfall, the remaining two senators were being treated for thallium sulfate poisoning. One was on a respirator, and the second was heading downhill. The treatment was started too late. By morning, both had passed.

On Monday, Rich walked into Spence's office at 7:55.

Spence looked rested, and like a cat with a canary in its mouth. "Have you seen the paper? Did you see the news? How are you?"

"No, I haven't seen the paper; I heard that the final two targets were seriously ill, and I'm fine."

"Well, now you can feel better. All four are gone. You've really scored a win for the country. Let me tell Vivian to leave us alone, and then we can debrief your Philadelphia operation."

Two and a half hours later, Rich walked out of Spence's office, with a smile on his face, and a briefcase in his hand.

As he walked by Linda, who was on the phone, she smiled, and mouthed, "welcome back."

In three minutes, she knocked on the door jamb and walked in. "How are you feeling?"

"Much better, thanks. Who was on the phone?"

"Dwight Porter in Cleveland. He knew that you were traveling, and he wanted to know if you had seen his numbers. They're up thirty-seven percent, and I guess he's pretty happy."

"He should be. Please put together a letter from me to him personally telling him that I knew he could do it. I'll sign it when you are finished. Then find a lunch place near the office, buy lunch for the office, and give the restaurant my credit card number. Send them a little note, saying that this is not a reward. But I have to keep you nourished so you can get out there and set a record. Thanks, Linda."

Rich asked Linda to close the door on her way out, and picked up the briefcase. Spence had told him that it contained \$ 200,000 and an extra bonus of \$ 50,000 for doing such a fine job. He had also answered Rich's questions on setting up an account in a tax haven.

In order to set up the offshore account, Rich called the contact that Spence had given him. They agreed to meet at the contact's office at 2:00 p.m. An armored car would come to Rich's house at 8:00 p.m. to pick up the money.

Rich looked at the production records for all of the three divisions, and found that his numbers were the best. This was amazing. He knew that Spence had given him the best division, in order to cover the time he spent away from the insurance job, but his division was increasing production at the best rate.

Meanwhile, the administration in Washington, D.C. was beside itself. There were no clues whatsoever concerning the deaths of the politician from Florida, the three killed in New York, and the four poisoned while in Philadelphia.

All that was known was that in Florida the terrorists used a claymore mine, and that there were none missing from the military. In New York, searchers had found a military type parachute, and the bullets found were 9mm. In Philly, the police knew that the poison was thallium sulfate, but had no idea how it was delivered, considering the protective cover that Rich set up.

The only commonality the victims had was that they were all to the left of center, some very left of center.

The left wing of the party was scared. The votes, and the bills were starting to come to center. The chiefs of the senate and house, both left leaning, were pressuring the socialist leaning President to do something immediately.

The president called the heads of the F.B.I., C.I.A., N.S.A., Homeland Security, and the chiefs of police, in Miami, New York State, and Philadelphia to a meeting at the White House.

The president told all of them that he had no idea if this was domestic or foreign terrorism. There were no clues other than what they already knew, and no one had taken credit for the murders other than the usual Muslim terror organizations who took credit for everything.

He decided that Homeland Security would head a task force of police organizations, using the resources of all of the other agencies, in order to find out who, or what organization, was killing the politicians.

He placed Harold Hastings, the head of homeland security, in charge. He was a political appointee, who used to run the Department of Agriculture. He had no security background, and was a paper pusher who leaned politically in the same direction as the president.

The heads of the other agencies immediately realized that a

non-police policeman like Hastings, had better let them do their jobs, if they ever expected to find the perpetrator, or perpetrators. Putting in non-qualifying people was typical of this administration.

The next day, the death of the four senators was all over the news. The other deaths were added to the total, and the pundits had all the answers as to what should be done, who did it, and what the government should do about it. They were as useless as the politicians.

Spence met with Rich the next afternoon.

"Rich, the government has continued to screw up. They've placed a political appointee in charge of finding out who has been taking out their politicians.

However, they've increased the dollars that they are willing to spend in order to try to find us. Even if we stopped now, they won't let the search die. The question is, do we hit people a few at a time, or do we have a major action taking out numerous politicians, all at one time."

"One of the things we can do, is to come out with misinformation," offered Rich. "We can have information released through a phone call, letter, etc. taking credit by some terrorist organization like Hamas or the Palestinians. They'd love to get credit for killing Americans. Al Qaida would do the same. They're nothing but shit, anyway. The only question that might come up is whether they're smart enough to do it."

"Well, that might work, if we decide to back off our operation. The organization is having a meeting in Boston, tomorrow. When I come back, I'll let you know what the direction will be for us. By the way, I've spoken to some of your offices, and they tell me that you've phoned them, but they'd like to see you in their offices."

"Would you advise that I hold a division meeting, having all of the managers meet in a central city? That way I'd get to meet everyone face to face, and we can put together a production plan. We could actually do it over a two day period, and keep the costs down, while telling them how good they are, at the same time."

"Sounds good, Rich. Why don't you put it together, give me a budget number, and call me once you've got it done. Maybe I'll go with you. I haven't seen some of these guys and gals since the last convention. Vivian and Linda can do the grunt work for you."

While Rich was setting up the divisional meeting, the people in upstate New York, were not sitting around. The number of searchers, in the woods surrounding the cabin had been increased from two hundred to five hundred.

During the first morning that there were more searchers, the vest with the compass, and GPS were found. The vest had no markings, or labels, but the Compass and GPS did have serial numbers that could help in a trace to find out where they were purchased, and possibly by whom.

At approximately the same time, Hank Terrill of the Park Police, was telling the F.B.I. that they should check with Bill Haggerty, a captain with the Philadelphia police, as to why he was the one to place the water bottles on the podiums. Since nothing happened at the rally, the water bottles that were left, as well as the ones that were partially or completely consumed, were discarded. There was no proof that the water bottles were the source of the thallium sulfate.

An hour later, the F.B.I. was looking for an individual approximately fifty years of age, with grayish brown hair, and a grey mustache who had masqueraded as a Philadelphia Police captain.

There were still no clues being found in Florida.

Spence was updated that night by his intelligence people, as to what the police found in New York, and was also told that the F. B.I. was looking for the non-existent captain Haggerty.

While the organization met in Boston to make their decision on the near future of their plans, Rich, Vivian, and Linda were planning for the meet and greet meeting. It was difficult to make any final decisions, as Spence hadn't yet approved the amount of the budget, and they couldn't make a final decision with hotels, airlines etc., without that approval.

The decision was made to hold the meeting in Charlotte, North Carolina, at the Marriott City Centre Hotel, arriving Tuesday morning, and leaving Thursday afternoon. Just about all of the managers could get direct flights from their cities early Tuesday, and would be back in their offices on Friday.

Spence called Rich late in the afternoon, and gave approval for the expenses. He also told Rich that decisions had been made, and he wanted to see him the next morning, in his office. Spence told him that Rich would have to travel alone. Spence couldn't go, as he had to go to the west coast for the week.

The serial numbers on the compass showed that it was purchased on the net, and delivered to a sporting goods store, in France, nine months ago. The GPS was also purchased over the net, and delivered to an address in Malta that no longer existed, a year ago. The names of the individuals that were on the order were false, and the credit cards were stolen. A record was set in getting the information as fast as the F.B.I. did; however, this was the most important case most people could remember. The problem was, though, that the information was a dead end.

Rich wondered what Spence was going to tell him tomorrow. Would he be given another assignment, or would he be sidelined until things quieted down.

When Rich walked in to Spence's office, there were already two cups of coffee sitting on the desk. Spence picked one up, and motioned to Rich that he should pick up the other one.

"It's Columbian; I brought some back from Boston. It left Columbia only two days ago, and it's delicious. There are two packages for you in a bag, on Vivian's desk."

"Thanks for thinking of me, Spence; I appreciate it."

"I've got to take care of my star!"

"What does your intel say about the items found in New York?"

"They tell me that there is no way that the compass and GPS can be traced to our logistics people. I don't think that it would be letting the cat out of the bag if I told you that everything that you had asked for, except for the Claymore, was ordered over a year ago, and had been stored by us. That includes the two poisons that you have used. I must admit that when you asked for the Claymore, I got a little pushback from logistics; however, they had it for you when you needed it. If you ask for a battleship, however, I will have a problem.

Intel also tells me that there was nothing found in Philly, and they really have no idea that a younger man posed as the police captain. They are still looking for a fifty year old grey haired man with, or without a mustache. There is no way that anyone can connect the thallium sulfate to logistics, or in any way to you.

"Well, you've made my morning so far; can you tell me what else was discussed, that I can know about?"

"The first thing I'm going to tell you is that the organization thinks that you can just about walk on water. They have never met anyone who can get into a target, do the job, and get out, like you do.

They have authorized me to increase your bonus from $ 50,000 per target, to

$ 75,000 per target.

The other thing they wanted me to ask you to do is to train another operator to do your job as well as you do it. I told you that the organization had eight other operators. These operators have been terminating lower level targets. They have been hitting fundraisers, local politicians, and possible future candidates across the country. The total number of targets is small compared to the murders throughout the country. No one has tied them together, but our cause has been helped.

We need more than just one senior level operator like you. The best way to get one is to have our best train an associate. How do you feel about it?"

"I honestly don't think I can keep up my schedule of operations, and train a novice, at the same time."

"We don't think so, either. We've decided to take the pressure off you, and us, for a period of three months. During that time, you'll be training your apprentice. Since you won't be doing any operations, unless we have an emergent situation, you'll be receiving a bonus of $ 25,000 a month. There is one more thing. We've chosen the individual we want you to train. She's a former F.B.I. agent, who was a marine before she joined the F.B.I. She is a crack shot, a third degree black belt, and fearless. Before you ask, the reason she left the F.B.I. was a disagreement with her supervisor. He wanted her to tell him why she blew away an informer, and she told him to go to hell. She thinks the way we do, and hates this administration, and where the country is going. She's been a brokerage manager since she left the bureau. She has no idea who you are, or what you've done. All she knows is that we have the best man for the job, in the job, and that if you agree to train her, she is to say how high, when you say Jump! What do you think?"

"Spence, other than when I was with my team, I've always worked alone. My team was trained exactly like I was. I knew I could depend upon them. They were my brothers. I've never trained a female. I never even worked with one when I was in the military. I'm not sure that a woman can do what I do. My other big question is how well was she vetted. How do we know that she's not still F.B.I.? Not that I'm going to, but what if I say no?"

"She's been vetted six ways from Sunday. She's clean. If you say no, then she's gone. But I think it would be a mistake. What's your answer?

"Before I answer, what's her cover?"

She'll come into the same program that you are in. However, since there are only three divisions, and you are doing so well, she will be the assistant director of sales, reporting directly to you. Her administrative assistant will be Linda. We'll give Linda a little fat in her paycheck, since she'll be doing more work. If you say O.K., we'll move Gerry Butterfield into the Chicago office full time, and she'll take his office here. We checked, and there is a nice office space in Chicago. You still haven't given me an answer."

"Spence, one more question. Who decides if she's not panning out . If I want her gone, is she gone?"

"She's gone!"

"When do I meet my new assistant?"

"We're having lunch with her at the Green Parrot, as soon as I call her, and give her a time to meet. Let me call Human Resources, and have them talk to Linda, and give her the news. One o'clock o.k. with you?"

"Fine, but since we have a little time, I'd like to tell Linda myself.

"You can tell her what's going to happen, but she'll still have to go down to H.R. in order find out the compensation. I'll tell them to call her after she goes to lunch."

"O.K., done deal. What's my new assistant director's name?"

"Her name is Julie Lowe. She's about 5' 6", girl next door type of pretty, nice figure, and she can kill you eleven ways before breakfast is served. She's very articulate, very bright, and a total wiseass. You'll like her."

Rich left the office, walked back to his office, asked Linda to come in, and close the door.

"What's up, Rich?"

"Spence just told me that you are getting a raise."

"Why?"

"Why did he tell me, or why are you getting a raise?"

She laughed, "Why am I getting a raise?"

"We are bringing another individual aboard, as the assistant director of sales, who will report directly to me. We'll be connected at the hip, as I'll be training her. The reason you are getting a raise is that you will also be her administrative assistant, or secretary. I don't think that it will be that much more work for you, as the number of our offices aren't changing, and the reports will be the same."

"You said her; what's her background?"

"She was a brokerage manager. I don't know anything else about her. I'm going to meet her at lunch, at the Green Parrot. I assume that she'll come back with us to get the paper work done. Speaking of paperwork, H.R. will call you after you come back from lunch, in order to discuss your raise. I told them to give you $ 500 more a week, but I don't think it'll happen."

Linda laughed, "I don't think it'll happen either. Rich, if working for the two you gets to be too much, can things be changed?"

"Linda, don't worry about it. I won't let it get to be too much."

As Linda opened the door, Spence was coming around her desk.

"Ready to go, Rich?"

"Ready, Spence; let's hit it."

They took Spence's Jag, as there were only two seats in Rich's car. It wasn't long before they were turning into the Green Parrot's driveway. They walked into the front door, and there was a young woman sitting there, in the entrance. She stood up, and put out her hand to shake Spence's. Obviously they had met in Boston.

She was about 5'6" or 5'7" with light brown hair, and if she was girl next door pretty, Spence lived in one hell of a neighborhood. She was a knockout. She was wearing a red sweater, and she really did the sweater justice. The most outstanding feature she had were her large green eyes. Rich was mesmerized by them.

Spence turned, and introduced the two of them. They shook hands, and followed Spence into the restaurant. They were shown to a table in the back, which Spence had asked for earlier. The waiter came over right away, and asked what they would like to drink.

Julie ordered an O'Doul's, and Spence laughed. "That's Rich's drink as well. I guess neither of you want to give anything away by ordering alcohol. Well, I can keep my mouth shut. He turned to the waiter and said, "He'll have one, as well, and I'll have a Glenlivet."

Julie started the conversation. "Rich, is it true that you are the best instructor there is? Do you really walk on water?"

"Yes, Julie, it's true. I do walk on water, but I swim in it much better."

"Don't tell me you were a SEAL! You guys are even crazier than the rangers, and marine recon!"

"Julie, I would have thought you would have been given my background by now. By the way, once you are a SEAL, you are always a SEAL. It's just that I'm not active, right now."

"Don't take offense! Marines feel the same way. Once a Marine, always a Marine. Spence just told me that you were the best. He didn't give me a biography."

"O.K., other than my knowing you are a Marine, and that you worked for the bureau, I don't know much about you, either. I know the type of training you have had, and it's good. What I'm going to train you in is basically how to get in, how to do the job, and how to get out. You'll learn to order just the right number of tools you need to do the job, and most important, you'll learn how to make sure that you take care of the details. Not taking care of the details can get you killed, or caught. You've got to put yourself in the enemy's mind. What is the enemy looking for; what advantage would the enemy have if you didn't take care of a specific detail? If you haven't realized it by now, the enemy is anyone who can change your way of life."

"I look forward to working with you, Rich. Maybe it will help you to know that I have no family. I SCUBA dive, and I skydive. I qualified expert with both the pistol and the M-4 rifle. I, of course, have been trained in hand to hand with the military, but I'm also a third degree black belt in Tae Kwon Do. A major advantage I have, is that I certainly don't look like I do all of that, and, being a female, nobody expects it."

"Well, Julie, let me tell you that you are going to get the same training that a man would get, but if we can use your feminine wiles in the field, we will."

"Rich, I detect a Boston accent, where in the city are you from? I'm from Newton."

"Oh, a rich girl, huh? I was born and brought up in south Boston. Where are you living now?"

"First of all, I wasn't a rich girl. My parents were domestics for a Doctor's family, and we lived with them. They're both dead, and I have no siblings.

I live in Groton, here in Connecticut, but I'm going to be moving to the Hartford area as quickly as I can. Can you recommend any locations?"

"I live on the same street as the office, but in the next town over, called West Hartford. I can recommend a good real estate person."

"Great."

She turned toward Spence, smiled, and said, "O.K., boss, we haven't killed each other; we seem to get along, and I can't wait to get started. What's the next step?"

Spence was right when he said that she was a no bullshit girl. She went right for the bottom line.

Spence looked at her with a partial smile on his face. "First of all, Rich is your boss. I'm his boss. The next step is to have lunch, and then go back to the office, to meet my administrative assistant, Vivian, who will have you fill out all of the paperwork. You'll then meet Linda, who is Rich's admin, and she will also help you with your insurance work. She, as well as Vivian, have no idea what Rich and I do, other than the insurance business. They, as well as anyone else, will never know what the three of us do. Understood ."

"Understood."

"Good! Let's eat," and Spence motioned to the waiter.

Later, Spence and Rich were in Spence's office. Spence said, "I told you she was a pistol. I know you won't take any shit from her, and that's why I jumped at her audacity, to set a tone. If she gets out of hand, terminate her. I don't mean through human resources. She knows too much.

I told Vivian to have her in your office at 7:00 tomorrow morning. It'll probably be about an hour to get to the office from Groton, so she'll be up early. If she's not on time, give her hell."

"Rich walked into his office at 6:45 a.m. Julie was sitting there, drinking a cup of coffee. Another was on his desk.

"I hope you like black," she said. "I figured that's the way a tough guy like you would want it."

"Thanks for the coffee, Julie, but let's cut the bullshit! There is no need to show how tough you are, or to continually be a wiseass. We have a job to do. When I ask you to do something, you do it. Why? Because I want you alive, not because I have something to prove. I respect you and what you have done in the past. I will treat you that way, and that's the way I expect you to treat me. Done?"

"Done."

"Good, by the way, I do drink my coffee black. The way we are going to start our training is in planning. I'm going to give you a target, and a location. You are going to give me a logistics plan. Then you are going to tell me how you are getting in, how you are going to acquire and take out the target, and how you are getting out. I want you to tell me how you are going to do everything, right down to the last detail. Remember if you fail in any way, you are dead.

Linda will be in at eight. She can be very helpful in a number of ways. Just remember anything you use her for, such as transportation, etc. you must do within the aspect of your job as the assistant director of sales. Here is a list of the seventeen offices we are responsible for, and the names of the managers. The New York City manager, is in the custody of the F. B. I. at the present time. I'll tell you about that later. I want you to contact each manager, introduce yourself as my assistant, and set up a time to speak with them every week, verifying their production numbers. Then I want you to back here at 1:00 to pick up a solution problem. I'm going to spend the rest of the morning putting together the solution problem we'll be working on. Any questions?

"Nope, no questions."

"See you at 1:00."

Rich put together a scenario that required a target to be hit in New Orleans. It involved a congresswoman who would be announcing aid to the city. The aid would be administered by a company owned by her cousin. There would be full media coverage and security. The woman wants tax increases on all businesses in the city that are not minority owned. These increases would pay for the $ 5000 in aid being given to each minority member who lost his or her place to live.

When Julie came back at 1:00, Rich handed her the problem. "Did you get to speak with the managers?"

"I spoke with twelve of the seventeen. In the case of the other five, including New York City, I spoke with their assistants, and gave them the times I expected their phone calls with the information I needed."

"Great, now I want you to solve this situation. Don't forget to give me your logistics list. Assume that I can get you anything that you ask for, within reason. No battleships or aircraft carriers, and no bombers. Bring me everything by nine tomorrow morning."

"You've got it, boss. Is there a place a girl can get a drink around here?"

"Julie, its 1:30 in the afternoon. I don't know what your hours were when you worked for the bureau, but I know that we don't work half days around here. What I just gave you is the beginning of a very intense training regimen. If you come back tomorrow, and the solution to the problem is fucked up, you can drink then, to celebrate your new job of being unemployed. I can be civil, I can be your friend, or I can let you die. Think about it. At nine tomorrow morning, you'll give me your decision."

Julie walked back to her office, her head looking down, her ego deflated. She thought, "Who in the hell does that bastard think he is? I could walk up behind him, cut his dick off, and be gone before he knew I was there."

Then her ego calmed down. She thought, "He's your boss, asshole. He's got combat experience with the elite of the elite. He's just trying to make sure that you don't commit suicide on your first mission." He's not just one of the boys, and, so far, he's not trying to get into my pants. I guess I'd better get serious."

Julie walked into Rich's office at 9:00 a.m. with two cups of coffee, both black. She saw that he already had a cup. "Thought you might like a warm up, Rich." she said, and sat down.

Rich thanked her graciously, and put down his pen.

"Do you have the information?" Rich asked.

"Yes, I do, Rich. I also wanted to apologize for being a wiseass, and to tell you that I am one hundred percent committed to doing my job the way you want me to do it."

"Good, that way you'll stay alive."

Rich picked up the pieces of paper that Julie had placed on his desk.

"Normally, you would have received an intelligence report yesterday, giving you a lot more information than you received. Without it, you don't have everything you need. For example, I didn't tell you whether the announcement was going to be inside or outside. You have no idea how many people will be on the dais or stage. Will the cousin be with her? What are your locations, and alternative methods of egress?"

"Why didn't you give it to me?"

"I wanted to see what you came up with on your own. First of all, let's see what you said you needed for supplies."

Rich picked up the sheet, and read off it: brown contact lenses, dark red hair dye, out of state driver's license, fake credit card, k-bar, Glock-19, with two clips, and ammo, sniper rifle with ammo, and scope in a carrying case, New Orleans Saints baseball cap, clear glass eyeglasses, rubber gloves, men's style coveralls (dark blue), men's work boots (size 7 ½) 1 pair knee protectors.

Rich visualized how she would use all of the equipment.

"O.K. you assumed that the announcement would be outdoors, and you were going to set up a sniper location. Considering I didn't give you an indoor or outdoor scenario or intel telling you otherwise, you've got the right idea. Now let's see your plan"

He looked at the plan, and saw that she was setting up a trip, through Linda, to visit the New Orleans office, and meet with John Pangburn, the manager. She would be coming in late in the afternoon the day before the meeting. She would reconnoiter the location for a shooting position. After an early morning meeting with John, she would change into the equipment, again reconnoiter the location, and set up her shooting position. She would take the initiative to take out the cousin, just after the congresswomen, if the scumbag were there. She would then drive to Metairie, a city nearby, rent a room in a motel. She would pay in advance, using the driver's license and credit card she used to rent the car, Then, she would change her eyes, hair, clothes, etc. She would dispose of all of the equipment on her way from Metairie to the New Orleans airport. Her flight home was scheduled for mid-afternoon the same day. An alternate egress was through Biloxi, Mississippi, ninety miles away.

"Nice job. Until I say so, I'd like you to also include in your plan, how you get rid of your equipment. Getting rid of the sniper rifle, and carrying it around until you could, is one of the details you have to worry about. Having Linda make your airline and hotel reservations, except for the Metairie motel, was a good idea. Having the k-bar and Glock-21 were good personal protection items. I use them myself. I probably wouldn't have thought about the knee pads, and would have been hurting when I got home."

"So are you pleased with my first attempt?"

"Let's just say that it seems that you stayed alive, and accomplished your mission."

"O.K., now what?"

"Why don't you go to your office and study the company's products that you will discuss when you go into the different offices. Please be back here at 4:00 pm to get your homework. Have you spoken with the real estate agent?"

"Yes, I have. As a matter of fact, I'm supposed to meet with her this Saturday morning. Did you have anything planned for me over the weekend?"

"No, it's fine; see you at four."

Rich made some phone calls pertaining to production, and answered a number of questions about his new assistant. He then grabbed another cup of coffee, and sat down to put together a scenario.

When Julie walked back into the office, Rich asked her, "Did you destroy any notes regarding the scenario information you gave to me this morning?"

"I may still have some scratchings at my house."

"Destroy them as soon as you get home. On the way home, stop at a Home Depot, or some other place, and get a cross-cut shredder. Any notes, maps, or anything you study or write before a mission should be shredded as soon as you stop working with them. Everything you gave me this morning was shredded as soon as you left the office. That's one of the details you can't forget about. Make sure it's a cross-cut shredder."

"Will do."

"Here is your next scenario, Julie. Remember, I want a list for logistics, and I want you to tell me how you get rid of the equipment you order. I've given you more information, just like you would receive in an intel report. I have a meeting in the morning with the law department regarding the fiasco in the New York office, so let's meet after lunch, say 1:30."

"O.K., I'll be here, ready to go."

Lunch with the lawyers ran longer than expected. Actually it was not the lunch, but the meeting that ran long, so they got to the restaurant late. Rich called Julie, and told her that he'd call her when he got back. He then was transferred to Linda, and told her to clear his calendar for the day.

The scenario that Rich gave Julie was complicated, on purpose. He knew that she had worked on all sorts of cases with the bureau, but she was never the perpetrator. The enemy was never the law enforcement community. When with the bureau, if she made a mistake, it was seldom one that would get her killed, or incarcerated for the rest of her life.

The target was a senator. The location was the home district senate office on the fifteenth floor of a federal building, in the city of Philadelphia, Pennsylvania. The intelligence sheet showed the exact location, a small blueprint map of the building itself, the locations of security, security cameras, access and egress to and from the building, and the hours and days the senator, a female, was in the building. The senator arrived at 7:00 each morning, and left at 5:00 each evening. There was no reason that the target was to be taken out. It didn't matter. This was an exercise, and Rich wanted to make sure that Julie would just follow the scenario, and the order to come up with a plan.

Rich was an hour and a half late for his meeting, when Julie got the phone call to come to his office.

When she walked in he noticed that she had her hair in a French twist, was wearing a pinstriped black suit, a cream colored silk blouse, and black high heels. She was a knockout. "Julie, you look very professional; nice choice of clothes."

She immediately blushed, and her green eyes sparkled. "Why, thank you, Rich, I didn't think you'd notice."

"Remember, Julie, it's all in the details. I notice everything."

"Well, thank you again. Would it be too presumptuous of me to ask how the meeting went? I asked Linda what happened, and since the New York office is one of yours, and therefore, mine, she told me."

"Good initiative in finding out. You should be aware of everything that is going on in our division offices. Abu Ashiri is going down. The case against him is iron-clad. The bureau has everything it needs to put him away. Of course, it'll be up to the courts as to how long he'll go away. Ralph Woron got caught in the middle. He's Ashiri's manager, and has to oversee his business, and business practices. The N.A.S.D. will hold a hearing, and he could lose his license and be fined. The law department doesn't think it will go further than that. The company will go to bat for him, as much as possible. We have to stand by with records, in case the N.A.S.D. subpoena them."

"I don't know Ralph Woron, but if he doesn't serve any time, that will be good."

"Yup, now let's get to your scenario; I'm sorry I was late."

Julie handed him a short stack of paper. "All of my notes have been shredded in my new cross-cut shredder."

"Good, let's see what you've got."

He took the logistics list, and looked at it first. It was relatively short. It looked similar to the last one: brown contact lenses, dark red hair dye, out-of state driver's license with picture and description agreeing with brown eyes, red hair, fake credit card, Glock-19, two clips and ammo, clear eyeglasses, men's style medium-sized coveralls, men's work boots (size 7 ½), cloth knee protectors, two cell phones, 1/8 pound of C-4, dyed brown, detonator disguised as pen, and a black handbag with disguised wires running around edges. Also she wanted a Federal Bureau I.D. and badge, picture to agree, and an empty fudge box.

Rich shifted in his chair, and looked at Julie, "Interesting; I can't wait to read your plan." He looked at her plan.

"Linda will set up a trip for me to visit Tom Martin in Philadelphia. It coincides with dates that the senator is out of town. She'll come in the next day. I'll go down one day early in order to recon the senator's office. I'll go in early, as a citizen, through the metal detectors, carrying nothing that will set off any alarms. I'll walk through the fifteenth floor to see what agencies are on that floor. I'll also check the location of the senator's office, in order to see if it agrees with the blueprints I have. I'll check out if the ladies' room is locked or open to the public. I'll also check to see if the opening to the ventilation system is big enough for me to get into it. Its location is not far from the senator's office. I'll make sure that I'm not seen by anyone in the senator's office.

At five o'clock I'll come back. There will be a different shift manning the metal detectors. I'll flash my badge, and I.D., declare my weapon, and put my handbag as well as my cleaning (coveralls) and work boots through the x-ray machine, Everything (as expected) will pass through. The cell phones, and c-4 (which is in the fudge box) will never be questioned. The I.D. and badge will overrule any thoughts the inspectors might have.

I will take the elevator to the seventeenth floor, and walk down to the fifteenth floor, making sure that I look into the cameras on the elevator. When I reach the fifteenth floor, I'll walk by the senator's office to check to see if there is anyone in the front office. The lights will be on but the door will be locked. Even though there will be no offices open on the floor, all of the lights will be on.

I'll enter the ladies room which is open, and empty. I'll place a sign on the outside of the door that says closed for maintenance. I'll lock the door, and change out of my clothes, and into the coveralls and boots. Then I'll enter the ventilation system, and crawl to the senator's office. The plans show that there is a private bathroom off the senator's inner office. Dropping through the ventilation system into that bathroom, I'll take the fudge out of the box, leaving the box in the handbag, and put my pen into the c-4. The welting at the edges of the handbag become wires which I'll connect to the detonator. The other end of the wires are connected to one of the cell phones. The c-4 and the cell phone will be jammed behind the toilet. I'll climb up on the toilet, get back into the ventilation system, and secure the cover from the inside. Entering the ladies' room from the way I entered, I'll secure the cover, change my clothes, unlock the door, remove the sign from the outside of the door, and go to the stairs which I'll take to the seventeenth floor.

I'll take the elevator to the lobby. My cleaning (coveralls) will be rewrapped in the plastic, and the shoes will be back in the box. I will have been in the building for just under ninety minutes. There won't be any problem in leaving, as I wave to the guard.

The next morning I will be at the building across the street at 6:50. The senator will arrive in her car at 6:55. Her chauffer/security will open the door for her, and then return to the car. I'll give the senator five minutes to get to her office.

If the senator is like most women, she will go to the mirror in the bathroom, in order to make sure that her makeup is on properly. After another thirty seconds, I'll call the number on the cell phone upstairs, and the bathroom becomes a coffin. There are no other casualties, as the staff does not come in until 8:00 a.m.

Rich looked up from the page, into Julie's green eyes. "This is excellent, Julie. However, it is only on paper. If it all worked out this way, it would be fantastic. One of the things we did in the SEALS was plan, plan, plan. There was always one rule. When the first shot is fired, all the plans go to hell. It's true."

"Now let's look at how you discarded your supplies."

Julie sat, and watched, as Rich checked off her logistics list. He crossed off the hair dye, one cell phone, the c-4, and the detonator, all of which had been used. He then read her additional information:

I won't be meeting Tom Martin until 10:00, so I'll have close to two hours to discard the supplies. I'll drive away from the explosion as soon as I can. I know that the place will be full of fire trucks, police, and lots of lookie-loos.

I'll drive over to the Schuykill River, and choose a place where there are no people. I'll field strip the Glock, and throw the pieces, as well as the clips, into varied locations along the river. I'll also throw the glasses, cell phone, and federal badge out into the river, as far as I can. I'll then drive over to a large supermarket, which has a clothes-for-the-poor-box, and discard the coveralls, shoes, and kneepads.

I'll keep the driver's license and credit card with me in case there is a problem in turning in the car. I'll hold on to the Federal I. D. as well.

After the meeting with Tom Martin, and his team, I'll drive back to the airport, and turn in the car. I'll take the I.D. card, driver's license, and credit card, into a stall at the ladies room. Then I'll take my nail grooming kit out of my luggage, and cut the three of them into small pieces. I'll then flush them all down the toilet, and put my kit back into my suitcase.

I'll go through ticketing and security, and come back to Hartford.

"You are good, Julie. You think the way I like. How long do you intend to spend with your real estate agent, on Saturday?"

She looked at him, almost being coy. "Why do you ask?"

"I know that you were trained well by the marines, and the bureau, but if we go on a mission together, I want to make sure that you are good enough with a pistol, and an automatic weapon, to cover my back. I thought that we could go to a range, over in Glastonbury, which allows you to fire assault rifles, as well as pistols. I'd like to see how well you do."

"I had planned on being with her all day, Rich. Are they open on Sunday?"

"I don't know, I'll call."

Rich called, found that they were opened in the afternoon, and reserved two Glocks, and two AK-47's.

Julie said that she would be available, and would meet him at the office.

Rich looked her straight in the eyes, and said, "If you aren't busy tonight, and since we don't have to meet early tomorrow, how would you like to go to dinner? There's a great restaurant and lounge not far from here. I'll understand if you are busy, and it's last minute. But, you have to eat, and I like it there."

Julie looked shocked. "I'd love to, Rich, but when I go to dinner with a man,

I become a wiseass again. Is that permissible?"

Rich laughed, "There are no rules at dinner. You never know, I might be a bigger wiseass than you."

"O.K., let me freshen up before we leave. Should we go in two cars?"

"No, I'll drive. No sense putting two cars in traffic this time of night. If I lose you, you'll never find your way out of this rush hour mess."

Julie came back with her makeup refreshed, and a brightness in her eyes.

Rich got up and joined her, and they went out to the parking spaces. As Rich steered her to his 280ZX, Julie started to laugh. "I knew you would be a Z man: flashy, big engine and a lot of speed."

"Do you know much about Z's?"

"That's my rose and silver one, by the fence."

Rich chuckled, "Flashy, big engine and a lot of speed, Huh!"

The only way Rich knew to get to the hotel was by going from his house, so they drove by it. He pointed it out to Julie, and she made positive remarks.

Fifteen minutes later they were in Farmington, pulling into the hotel.

He gave the car to the valet, and they walked into the front door.

The hostess walked up to them, and said, "Good evening, Mr. Coburn, your regular table?"

Rich was flabbergasted; he looked at her, and said, "How do you do that? I've been here once, and I didn't even call for a reservation tonight."

"That's what I do when one of our clients makes an impression on me. Welcome back." She showed them to the table overlooking the fountain.

Rich looked at Julie. "I have been here only once, when I first came to Connecticut. That's just amazing!"

Julie smiled, "Maybe she remembered you because you kept looking at her while you licked your eyebrows."

"Never happened."

"What's good here?"

"Other than the hostess, the waitress and sommelier aren't bad"

"You shithead; are they better than me?"

"I'm having dinner with you, not them."

The banter went back and forth through the appetizer, the

surf and turf, and the crème brulee, all accompanied by a great California wine.

The conversation stayed light, and they were both smiling as they left the table. A short walk down the hall, and they entered the night club.

There was a table available at the back of the dance floor, and they headed for it. The waitress came over, and they both ordered O'Doul's, and laughed.

They laughed a lot.

Julie was very light on her feet, and Rich was a good dancer as well.

It was starting to get late, and Julie looked at her watch. "Rich, I am having a great time, but by the time I get back to Groton, and get a couple of hours sleep, I'll be coming back to meet my real estate lady."

"I'm having a great time, as well, but I fully understand. We'll do it again."

There was a paucity of conversation on the way back. It was as if neither of them wanted to stop the fun they were having, but they had to do it.

Rich took Julie back to her car, and asked her to call him when she got home. He gave her his cell phone number, hugged her goodnight, waited until her car started, and watched her drive out of the lot.

He thought about the evening with Julie as he drove home. She was a fun person, she was an absolute doll, a good conversationalist, a wiseass, and had a body that was great. However, having a relationship with someone who was your backup could kill you.

Julie called him about an hour later, thanked him for a great evening, and hoped they could do it again.

Rich spent the next day at car dealerships. He really wanted a Mercedes sports car, after he saw it. However, with everything else he spent money on, he didn't want to bring attention to himself considering that he was only supposed to be making $ 100,000 a year.

Rich met Julie at the office, and they left together for the range.

He was in a sweatshirt and slacks, and she was in a sweater, and jeans. He smiled as he thought about using the weapons to keep the guys away, once they saw her.

They went through the orientation at the pistol range, picked up the eye and ear protection, and were issued their pistols. Rich set the silhouette targets at twenty-one feet, the average distance in a gunfight, and they aimed, and fired six rounds. Julie shot a fifty-eight, as did Rich. Both were in the lower right quadrant of the center of the target, with one round in the eight area, further to the right.

They fired six more rounds each, leaving one round in the thirteen round clip. Julie fired a perfect sixty, and Rich hit a fifty-nine. Rich was guaranteed that she would never let him live it down.

They each fired another fifty rounds, with their scores being either perfect, or very close.

They took time out for a quick sandwich lunch, and walked over to the automatic weapons range.

When they got into their shooting booths, each put the thirty round banana clip into the AK-47. The original clip holds fifteen rounds. If the rifle is fully automatic it holds thirty or fifty. Julie lifted and held the rifle, as if she knew what she was doing. After emptying the clip, it was obvious that she did. Rich was equally experienced with the weapon, and they complimented each other.

Rich was impressed. "You can be my backup on any mission," he said.

Julie laughed. "And you can be my backup when it counts."

"How did yesterday go with the real estate lady?" Rich asked.

"We saw about fifteen locations, and I really liked one over on Thomas Drive, not far from you."

"That's great. What now?"

"Well, I want it yesterday, but the people put down that they wouldn't be ready for a month. My agent is going to see if they can get out sooner. They are leasing as well, so maybe they can."

Rich dropped Julie at her car, and said, "I'll see you tomorrow. We've got to solidify the plans for the meet and greet in Charlotte.

"What meet and greet?"

"That's true, you have no idea what I'm talking about. There is a meeting being held in Charlotte, North Carolina, at the Marriott. It was decided upon before you came aboard. I am to meet with all of the managers, and set up a production plan for next year. Now that you're aboard, it will be both of us meeting with them. Tomorrow, please make sure that Linda sets you up with transportation and a room. We'll leave early Tuesday morning, and be back late Thursday. Let's go over the personnel files, as well as the production files, on all of the managers and their offices, tomorrow.

"Will Spence be going?"

"No, he has to go to the west coast for the week. I guess he's probably meeting with Dave Baxter. He's the director of sales for the western division. Before you ask: yes, he has Hawaii and Guam in his division. He always tells the story of how everyone wants to carry his bags when he goes to Hawaii, but no one wants to carry them to Bozeman, Montana, in the winter."

"O.K., but I hope it doesn't screw up my real estate deal."

"If you find that it is going to, cancel the trip. There will be other meetings. However, I'd like to have you with me on this one, as I haven't met all of the managers, and you haven't either. It will be a good time to establish relationships.

The next day, Rich pulled into the office parking lot, looked for Julie's Z, and found it in the first row, behind the reserved spots.

Rich walked into his office to find a cup of coffee on his desk, a cinnamon bun next to it, and a package along with it.

He opened the package to find a listing of all of the offices, the manager for the office alongside each location, the production year-to-date, the increases over the year before, and a red line through Cleveland, as their production number year-to-date was less than the year before. Every other office was a plus. In the final column was a number that coincided with a fifteen per cent increase over where the year end number for this year was anticipated.

Timing was perfect. Rich took a big bite of the cinnamon bun just when Julie walked into the office. He tried to say good morning, and spewed crumbs all over the office.

Julie laughed and spilled the coffee cup that she was carrying. She went to the ladies room to get some wet paper towels, not wanting to leave stains on Rich's carpet.

When Julie came back, Linda was already cleaning up the office, and both Linda and Rich were giggling. Linda said, "Now you know why we don't feed him. Coffee's o.k., but no more buns."

"I promise, I'll never do it again."

After Linda left, and Julie was sitting down, Rich turned to her, drank from his coffee cup, and motioned to the package on his desk. "How did you know what to put together? This is perfect."

"Thanks Rich, but I can't take all the credit for it. I told Linda what I thought we would need for the meeting, and she helped me put it all together. The only thing I wasn't sure of was the increase of fifteen percent for next year."

"You were very close. I received a budget with increases requiring seventeen percent. Some of the offices will exceed that, as they do every year. Others, such as Cleveland, won't make it, unless they have a hell of a year. I'll tell you about them in a minute. All in all, history shows that we should have an average of nineteen to twenty percent.

When I first came aboard, I had a discussion with Dwight Porter, from Cleveland. He's been the manager there forever, and their production was heading the wrong way. I gave him and the agents three months to turn it around. In the last six weeks, he's done exactly that. At the meeting, I may use him as an example to the other managers, as to how you can get more production, no matter what has happened in the past. Just change that final column to seventeen percent, and the figures will be perfect. Also, please confirm with Linda, that meals, breaks, and everything else have been squared away. Make sure that she checks with Beau Parker, the manager in Charlotte, as to whether he wants a room at the hotel. In the past, according to his file, he's requested to go home each night when meetings have been in Charlotte."

"Will I be going down to Charlotte dressed for the meeting?"

"Yes, we'll go directly from the airport to the hotel, drop our suitcases, and start the meeting. Are you going for sure?"

"Oh, I forgot to tell you. I spoke with my broker, and the people will be out by next weekend."

"Fantastic. Again, great report. I've got some things I want to talk about at the meeting, and we can go over it on the plane."

Rich met Julie the next morning at the office parking lot, and headed for the airport. He was pleased to see that she only had one suitcase. He once dated a girl who had to have an outfit for every possible type of weather, including a tornado in a snowstorm, and also for any temperature from thirty to ninety. Besides, the three suitcases that girl would have taken wouldn't have gotten into the Z.

The meeting went perfectly. Julie captivated every manager who was there.

The managers accepted their targets for next year with the usual amount of grumbling as to how it was impossible to keep hitting higher numbers each year. Even Dwight Porter said he was looking forward to exceeding his numbers next year. Rich did use him as an example, and he could see Dwight's ego rise.

On Friday, The Joint Committee on Domestic Terrorism, the new government program set up to find and prosecute the killer or killers of the seven senators, and one representative, met in the committee room in Washington.

The chairman called on all of the members, surrounded by their staffs of at least twenty political lackeys each, to share with the other members, what progress was being made. After calling on everyone, using the "I recognize the gentleman from"...bullshit, they came up with one conclusion: they knew jackshit!! They had nothing from the clues in New York, there wasn't much left of the crime scene in Florida, and they had absolutely nothing in Philadelphia. They couldn't find anyone who looked like Haggerty, although they now knew that he wasn't a police captain.

Friday was also the first day that Julie and Rich were back in the office.

When Rich walked in he found a message that Spence had called on Thursday night. He wanted Rich to call him on Friday morning. He also left a post script that there was a three hour time change, so please don't call him at four in the morning. He also said to call on his cell phone.

Rich waited until ten o'clock Hartford time before he called Spence.

"Hey, Spence, are you awake yet?"

"I've been up since four, it didn't matter what time you called. I heard that your meeting in Charlotte went exceptionally well. The guys loved Julie, but I think that she could have thrown up on their shoes, and they'd love her. Some of those guys think with their dick and not with their brains."

"Spence, she not only looked good, she was good. She had the whole plan put together the day before we left. She handled herself professionally, handled a great deal of the presentation, knew what she was talking about, and took no bullshit. I was pleased to have her there. Not only that, we went to the range on Sunday, and she's an expert with the pistol, and an automatic weapon. She's one in a million. I've been giving her scenarios, and she comes up with a hell of a solution. Give her a bit of experience, and she'll be almost as good as I am. But that's because I'm a damn good teacher!"

"O.K. Mr. wonderful. I'm glad to hear it. Rich there are a few things I'd like to talk about with you, next week. How does your Monday look? Is Julie available, as well?"

"Monday is good for both of us. I was planning on doing a live scenario, but we can do that on Tuesday."

"All right, let's meet in my office at ten."

"Good, have a good weekend."

"You too, Rich."

Rich called Julie, and told her about Monday's meeting with Spence. He told her that he had no idea what the meeting was about, but Spence sounded very serious. From the sound of Spence's voice, Rich said that he wouldn't be surprised if there were other people present.

Rich called Linda on the intercom, and asked her to block out at least two hours for Julie and him to be with Spence.

chapter 9

WASHINGTON, D.C.

Spencer Kohl hung up the phone, and looked out the window of his hotel room at the Willard Intercontinental hotel. He looked down at the White House, a block away, the monuments, and the historic Jefferson Memorial.

The car which would take him on a ride lasting approximately twenty minutes would be coming into Washington on route 66, from Langley, Virginia.

He had been in D.C. all week, meeting with six individuals in the government protective services. He had met with members of the F.B.I., Capitol Police, N.S.A., Homeland Security, and a member of the Joint Chiefs of Staff. Now he was meeting with a senior member of the Central Intelligence Agency.

He finished dressing, grabbed his brief case, went out to the elevator, and went down to the elegant classic lobby. He walked out the Pennsylvania Avenue entrance, and waited. Exactly at eleven o'clock, a limousine pulled up with a driver, and another man in the front seat. The second man left the car, walked up to him, and asked, "Mr. Spencer Kohl?" He nodded and the man spoke again, "Who are you seeing, Mr. Kohl?"

"I am meeting with Mr. Albert Dell, Spence replied."

"Would you be so kind as to follow me to the vehicle, Mr. Kohl."

Spence followed the man to the limousine, entered the rear door being held for him by the driver, and relaxed into the comfortable seat.

The chauffer turned, and said, "Mr. Kohl, there are refreshments in the refrigerator on the right side of the cabinet. The television controls are on top of the shelf on your left. Channel twenty is music, and the telephone is over your right shoulder. The temperature controls are in the armrest, along with a button if you need to contact either of us, up front. We should be there in twenty minutes." The glass partition then rose to the ceiling, and Spence was enveloped in silence.

The car stopped at the booth at the end of the long road through the trees. The two men in the front seat handed identification to the guard, and the car was waved on.

At the second booth, the procedure was repeated, and the car drove on to an entrance to an underground garage. In the garage, the partition was lowered, and the chauffer stopped the vehicle. The man in the front seat, who Spence figured was an agent, opened his front door, and the chauffer came around and opened Spence's door. The agent motioned to Spence, and they walked to a desk where Spence signed in, listed who he was seeing, showed identification, gave his right thumb print, and was given a visitor's badge.

The agent and Spence went up the elevator to the top floor, and went down the hall to the left. They stopped outside an office that had a sign by the door, Albert Dell, Assistant Director.

The agent opened the door, and Spence followed him into an outer office with two desks, behind which were two very efficient looking women.

The closest, a Mrs. Winchester, by the nameplate on her desk, said, "Good to see you again, Mr. Kohl. Mr. Dell is waiting for you." She then looked at the agent, and said, "Thank you, William, we can take it from here. We'll call you when Mr. Kohl is ready to leave."

Mrs. Winchester picked up the phone, pressed a button, and said, "Mr. Kohl is here." She then looked at Spence, and said, "You can go right in, Mr. Kohl."

Spence opened the outer door to the office, and was faced with another door, the space in between making any conversation in the office unintelligible. He opened the second door, and walked in.

Albert Dell was a tall man, about six feet six inches, and weighed about two hundred and twenty pounds. He and Spence had known each other for twenty years, from when they were both field agents for the Central Intelligence Agency. Albert Dell stayed with the C.I.A., and went up the line to be named Assistant Director. Spence decided to go out into the corporate world, and rose to his position as Sales Vice President. Both men were part of the seven members of the organization.

"How the hell are you, you old reprobate?" asked Dell.

"Good, Al. I spoke with all of the other guys over the last week regarding Rich Coburn, and his new assistant, Julie Lowe."

"How is she working out? I know she looked good on paper, and Ben really liked her. He hit the lottery with Rich, but I wondered how a woman would be as a hit person. Notice how I'm being politically correct."

"Fuck you, and your politically correct . You wouldn't happen to have a shot of Glenlivet in your bar would you?"

"I knew you were coming, didn't I? Of course I have Glenlivet. Now tell me about the broad."

"She's not a broad. She's more like a knockout. She's bright, has a good work ethic, and shoots as well as Rich, with both a pistol and an automatic weapon. She's dynamite with her scenarios, and she's great in the insurance business. I just hope Rich can keep it in his pants."

"Do you think that's going to be a problem?"

"So far, Rich has always thought with his head. He has enough military experience to know that when you think with your dick, you die."

"Okay, let's get down to brass tacks. What's so important that you wanted to meet with everybody, especially so soon after our Boston meeting?"

"We decided to back off for three months, in order to give Rich time to train his assistant, and to take some of the heat of him, and the organization. As you know, Rich is so good, that there are no clues which can hurt anyone. I anticipate that Julie, being trained by Rich, on top of her previous training, will be almost as good.

My recommendation is that we let Rich and Julie know that they not only have been working for the organization, comprised of who we are, but have also been under the aegis of the C.I.A. Now they will be working on discovering, and eliminating sleepers who have been in the United States for years. They are going to ask a lot of questions, and I ask that I be allowed to answer those which I feel I can answer with discretion.

The reason that I want to do this is to reinforce their feelings that we are all in this together, fighting a war against the Muslim extremists. That it's not only getting liberals out of our government, but also destroying the enemy that is within our government."

Al had been sitting and listening quietly. He then stood up, and walked to the window. "Spence, we've known each other for what, twenty years? Even a little more. You've always been a straight thinker. What would the purpose be in letting Rich, and Julie, know this additional information? They, or at least Rich, is doing everything you ask, and doing it extremely well, without this additional information. I'm one who believes in need to know. There is no need to know here. What did the other guys say?"

"Al, you know that you are my closest friend in the organization. That's why I came to see you last. I would not do anything unless you agreed to it, but I wanted to feel the temperature of the other guys towards this idea. Each one asked how you felt about it, because we all respect your opinion. After all, you are the top spook, when it comes to field experience. The Director is a political appointee. No matter what they said, if you're against it, it won't happen."

"No, Spence, one of the things I've learned over the years is that I'm not always right. Remember that time in Turkey. If we went into that building like I wanted to, we wouldn't be talking today. You wanted to wait, and you were right. They blew that building exactly at the time we would have been half way up the stairs."

"I remember; the blast scared me so much, I pissed my pants. As a matter of fact, we both had to change our skivvies.

The response to me was unanimous. Everyone agreed with my plan. Everyone, that is, but you. I fully understand your reasoning. We'll put the idea in abeyance."

"No, Spence, don't! Like I said, I'm not always right. There is a lot of brain power, as well as experience, in the organization.

You've got seven people who have different ways of achieving the objectives of the organization, and it will only work using the majority opinion. Please follow through with your idea."

"Al, now I know why you've risen to where you are. You're almost as wise as I am."

"You wiseass! Hey, let me know how it goes. As usual, call and leave your name, and I'll call you on a secured line."

"Al, thank you. I will. You can call your secretary now, and have her call the mute agent who came here with me."

"Spence, it was great seeing you. Let's plan on meeting in New York, with the wives, for a weekend."

Al called his secretary as he watched Spence walk out the doors.

The ride back to the Willard was uneventful. Spence was looking forward to a quick flight back to Hartford.

chapter 10

HARTFORD

Rich entered his office at 7:30 on Monday morning. The light was already on in Julie's office. He picked up two black coffees and walked over to Julie's office. He walked in, put both coffees on the desk, looked at Julie, and asked, "How was your weekend?"

Julie picked up a coffee cup, and looked at Rich. "Thanks for the coffee. Weekend was good if you consider that I was putting my life in boxes, finding things that I thought I threw out, and getting ready to move.

I was up here yesterday, riding around and trying to find where I lived, and went by your house three times. I didn't realize that we were such close neighbors."

"I didn't see you, but I could feel the neighborhood being downgraded," he said with a smirk.

"You know, Rich, you're a shit sometimes."

"Yeah, I know. When are you planning on moving?"

"The end of the week, unless Spence drops some sort of bomb on us at ten."

"I haven't heard a thing about that meeting. His door was closed when I walked by it on the way in."

"Yeah, I looked, too."

"I'll pick you up on the way. I've got to go through some files for a recruit to replace Ralph Woron as manager in New York City. I'll want your input on the finalists. Neither one of the assistant managers has enough experience to run a top office."

At 9:55, Rich put down the files he was working on, and put the three piles of no, maybe, and good, on the corner of the desk for discussion with Julie after the meeting. He walked over to her office, and met her outside of her office door. They then walked over to Spence's office.

Vivian met them outside of Spence's office. "He just called, he's about five minutes out, and asks that you go into his office, sit down, and relax. He'll be here as fast as he can."

Ten minutes later, Spence joined them.

"Hi folks, sorry I'm late. I knew that I had to do an errand this morning, and that's why I set the meeting for ten. About three this morning I heard dripping, and found that my water heater, which is on the second floor, had let go and the water had gone through the first floor ceiling, and ruined my dining room. I've been over to the claims department in the property building getting everything squared away. Glad I work for the company."

What I wanted to talk to you about today, is exactly that, working for the company. I didn't mean to use that as a segue, but it fits perfectly ."

Julie blurted out, "Are we being fired, Spence?"

"Absolutely not!! When I finish you'll know that not only are you not being fired, you are being included in some information that makes you even more valuable than you were when you walked in to the office this morning.

When I spoke with both of you during the recruiting process, I mentioned to you that we were going to go after the people in the sleeper cells that were here in the United States.

In the last four decades, extremist Muslim agencies have been positioning individuals in the United States as sleepers. Some of them are adults, some young men and women, and some children. They have been assimilated into the country and raised as any other American. They have followed the law, and lived amongst us as citizens, and waited. Many have gone onto college, and they have entered all of the professions. Some are lawyers, some are doctors, and some are politicians.

As they came into this country, the Central Intelligence Agency kept track of them, and we know who many of them are. I'm sorry to say that there are many of them whom we haven't discovered.

Obviously, from the way I am talking, the organization has contacts within the C.I.A. The C.I.A. is also known as the company, and that was who I was referring to earlier. The organization has people within all of the alphabet agencies: F.B.I., C.I.A., N.S.A., as well as the Capitol Police, Homeland Security, and the military. We are funded from slush funds in all of the agencies. Basically we are working as an arm of the C.I.A. The relationships that we have are verbal. We have no written orders from anyone. There is a board of governors, if you will, who have to agree on every operation, unanimously. I am one of the board. We are not sanctioned by any agency.

When we told you that we were going after liberals, that was true. All of the individuals that we have eliminated were liberals. There is nothing wrong with being a liberal. It is part of the democratic process. All targets that we have had, or will have in the future, are not only, strong liberals, they are or have been members of cells. They have different religions so as to escape detection as Muslims. They are black, white, and Asian.

About two years ago, our intelligence sources intercepted directives from the extremists' headquarters, activating some of the cells, primarily in the political arena. By having a cross section of their operatives have rallies and speeches and proposing bills, all within the system, the enemy had us leaning more and more to the left when they had the leadership of the country run for the top offices. These people came from the cells. There were questions as to where they went to school, and where they were born.

Even though these questions were never answered, they got elected, and proposed laws that would eventually change our country to socialism. As a socialist society, the Muslims could then take over, establish Shia laws, and the United States, as we know it today, would die.

The reason for this meeting is to let you know the whole story. You are putting your asses on the line, and I felt you should know what and why we are doing what we are doing. You both put your butts on the line before. Rich, you with the SEALS, and Julie, you with the Marines, and the bureau.

You have the right to ask any questions that you have. I must tell you that I will answer anything you ask, as long as it doesn't violate any secrecy acts.

Rich, what questions do you have?"

"Spence, are you telling me that the nine people that I've taken out, including the politicians, were all cell members, and Muslim extremists."

Julie looked at Rich, "nine?"

Rich nodded his head, up and down.

Spence said, "Every single one of them. Your next question will probably be about the three in New York and the four in Philly, together. Yes, together. It was no coincidence that the three in New York were together. Their planning session also included planning for Muslim extremists. The cabin had been set up to record whatever was said. We got them all. I guess, because of you, we could say we got them dead to rights. The four in Philadelphia were to give a speech at a rally. They also got together in one of the hotel rooms. We heard through a directional microphone, their plan to take over, in the future, oil fields in one of our allied countries.

What other questions do you have?"

Julie straightened in her chair, and asked, "What does this mean for us?"

"I'm sure that you have the same question, Rich, but Julie beat you to it."

"What it means to you is that your targets are changing. We decided in our Boston meeting, that not only were we going to lay off our operations while Julie was being trained, but we were going to change up on our targets. We are still going to go after the cell members, but not the politicians. The operations should be easier, as there probably will be less protection for the targets.

Additionally, since there will be less protection, some of the training period could be used for actual operations, and the two of you could work together.

Any other questions from either of you?"

Neither Julie nor Rich opened their mouths. Then Rich looked at Spence and said, "Spence, all of our operations were within the geographical territory of the eastern division. Are Julie and I going to expand our operational territory, or are we going to stay in the eastern division territory?"

"Good question. With your present cover, you've got to remain in the eastern division. However, I'll talk with some of the higher-ups, and see if there is any need for national territory positions within your pay grades. It probably would be much too soon for a promotion from a sales division to a national position."

"I have one more question, Spence," said Rich. "I think with this new approach, as you mentioned before, we don't have to wait the full three months. What would make it possible for us to get to operational status, instead of training status?"

Spence looked straight at Julie. "From what you have reported to me so far, Julie is a great student, and you think that she is just about ready to get her feet wet. All I need is a letter from you telling me she is ready to go. Obviously you are referring to her training in insurance."

"Obviously."

"Any questions, Julie?"

"None. I can't wait to get into the field."

"Good. If neither of you have any more questions, we'll continue as scheduled, and when I receive the letter from Rich, we'll change the operations if necessary."

Julie and Rich walked back to Rich's office, shut the door, and sat down.

Julie was the first to talk. "What the hell was that all about? I came aboard to take out liberals, and he's talking terrorists. I hate terrorists even more than liberals, but terrorists. Who the hell ever thought about terrorists?"

Rich looked at Julie. "You mean that when you were in the bureau you never heard of the Muslim terrorists in the Philippines, or in Indonesia? There's a country called Iraq, where they're killing some of their own people, called Kurds. Lebanon is having a civil war. Julie, they're religious fanatics. That's the worst kind. They'll kill themselves for their cause. The more of them we can take out the better off the United States is going to be in the future."

"All right, what do we do now?"

"I want to do a live practice scenario. If you take out the target, I'll write the letter to Spence. If you don't, we'll keep training."

Julie looked at him for a long time. "Who is the target?"

"I am."

"But you'll know that I'm coming."

"Yes, I will. That makes it tougher for you. I'll know you are coming, but I won't know how. If you use a gun, make sure you use blank ammunition. If you don't, I can't write the letter. If you use another weapon, all you have to do is verbalize that you have killed me. If you use poison, you've got to tell me that I'm dead. Don't use actual poison, but I don't think I have to tell you that. Remember one thing. You've got to suffer any consequences that come from your plan. If you were going to blow up my house, and the cops find you planting explosives, you better be ready with a plausible reason as to why you are planting explosives. If you break into my house, and an alarm goes off, directly to the police, you'd better have a good excuse. By the way, you know me well enough so that you will not get an intel report. As for the supplies, I'm going to tell Spence about this test, and you can get any supplies you need. I'm going to take some time off, and I will be carrying a weapon. If I identify you, you lose. Let me know when you have everything you need, and I'll leave the office."

"I'm going to my office to start to make some plans."

"Good! I'll go tell Spence what's going down. The next time we talk should be when you are ready. Any questions?"

"Only one. Do I get to write your eulogy?"

"Good luck; show me how good you are."

Rich stopped by Spence's office, and told him about the operation. Spence laughed. Then he got serious. "Just make sure that she doesn't kill you. I can't afford to lose you right now."

Rich smiled, "You mean that you can afford to lose me next week instead?"

Spence pulled a file out of his desk drawer and opened it up.

"This is my logistics request file. I'll be interested to see what she requests. It'll give me a good indication as to how she's planning to terminate you."

Rich spent the rest of the day with Linda, telling her that he and Julie were going to visit an actuarial firm in New Jersey, and would be gone for three days. They reviewed all the files he was working on, and sent out any correspondence necessary.

The next morning, at about ten, Julie walked into Rich's office.

"Spence tells me that everything I need will be in my hands by noon. So I guess that you can leave by then." She then slapped him on the back, and said, "See you in the morgue."

Since Julie was getting no intel sheet, and since she had no idea where he was going to be, Rich assumed that one of the items Julie had requested would be a locator bug. She would put it on his car in the parking lot, and follow him on a GPS in her car.

When Julie left Rich's office, it was twenty minutes after she had placed the locator bug on Rich's car. She didn't want him driving away before she could set him up.

Rich left almost immediately. He drove to an Enterprise rent-a-car office not far from his house, and left his car around the back. He transferred the two bags that he had in his car to a new sedan that he had assigned to him. He told the agent that he didn't want to put a lot of miles on his car, and he had some driving to do. Since there was no mileage restriction, this seemed like a smart thing to do. The agent agreed, had him sign a few papers, and show his driver's license. Then the agent gave him the keys, and Rich was on his way.

He thought to himself, "Now let's see what she does when her bug leads her to a parking lot." He drove out route 44 to Simsbury road, took a right on route 185, and headed west into the woods.

Julie picked up the box in Spence's office, and walked by Vivian on the way out. Vivian looked curious as she looked at the box, but Julie ignored her. "See you in a couple of days," floated off behind her, as she walked out to the elevator.

Julie got behind the wheel, and flipped on the GPS receiver to see Rich's location. It showed him stopped not far from his house on Asylum Avenue. She thought, "Is he waiting for me? Is he picking up supplies? What's he doing?" She drove to an area within a quarter of a mile of the indicator. The last thing she wanted to do was drive right up to him, and have him take her out. Game over.

She got out of the car, and walked one block east paralleling Asylum Avenue.

She then walked back to the west, after going about a quarter of a mile to the north. On the corner of Asylum was a rent-a-car office, and Rich's car was parked in the rear.

"That son-of-a-bitch," she said to herself. She went into the office, and looked at the agent. She pushed out her chest, and smiled. "My husband left his car here, and rented another. Could you tell me what he's driving? I'm supposed to meet him, and I won't know what to look for."

"Which is his car?"

"It's the Z, around back."

"Oh, he's in a new white sedan, a Chevy."

Julie thanked him, and as soon as she was out of his sight, she took off, running to her car. That is, if you could call it running, in high heels.

She got into the car, and was about to take off, when she realized she didn't know which way to go. Time to go to backup mode.

When she had left Rich, back at the office, she had slapped him on the back, and had said something about the morgue. This was part of her backup plan. When she had slapped him, she had placed another bug, one of a different type, on his back. It has a range of twenty-five miles.

She changed the channel on the GPS receiver, and there was the magic dot. It was heading west on route 185.

Julie took off, speed-shifted into second, ran up the RPM's and shifted into third, then fourth. She was not going to lose him this soon.

Julie went over the top of mountain road on route 44 so fast that she left the ground. When she got into Avon, at the bottom of the other side, she had to slow down to turn right on route 185.

Then she sped up again in order to get in a position about three miles behind Rich.

They drove about twenty-five miles, three miles apart, until Rich took a left onto a dirt road, that led into the woods. He then went about a mile, and stopped his vehicle.

Julie stopped at the intersection of the dirt road. She didn't want a dust cloud to give her away. She wished that the GPS receiver was portable, just in case he started up again.

She started into the woods, paralleling the road, as quickly as she could go. About a mile in, she came upon a cream colored Chevy four door, parked off the road. No one was in sight.

Julie sat in the same place for thirty minutes. There were no movements, or sounds other than the sounds one would hear in the woods. Dusk would be approaching soon. She had to make her move. Julie went back to her car.

When she got back to the car, she quietly opened the trunk, put on a camouflage jacket and trousers, put on a backpack, also in camouflage, and took out a crossbow and three darts. She headed back into the woods.

Rich sat comfortably in the crook of a limb about thirty feet above the car.

He was waiting for Julie. When he took off his suit jacket, in order to drive to the rent-a-car location, he was lucky enough to see the bug Julie had placed on his back. If he hadn't seen one previously, he would never have noticed it.

He was proud of Julie. She had a back up, just in case the first bug didn't work.

When he changed cars, he made sure that the suit coat was laid out on the back seat, with the bug on top. He didn't want her to lose him.

If he hadn't known about the second bug, he probably wouldn't have been so attuned to the fact that Julie was probably right behind him, and he wouldn't have been looking so intently into the woods.

He spotted Julie about forty yards away from the path. He watched her as she came near his position, and while she sat waiting for about a half hour. He saw her turn around and head back in the direction of her vehicle.

Inside one of the bags he had taken with him were enough MRE's, meals ready to eat, to carry him for five days. He had just finished one when he heard a twig snap off to the other side of the path. She was smart, she didn't see anything from one side of the road, so she's coming up the other.

Rich loved the woods. This was the best place to get into a defensible position. Unless an individual had been trained how to walk in the woods, they usually broke twigs, brushed branches, and made enough noise to warn anyone hiding there that someone was coming.

Rich kept looking for Julie while trying to become a part of the tree. The branches overhead were making the visibility less than what would be expected at this time of day. Suddenly Julie showed up next to the car. She was in camouflage, and carrying a crossbow.

Rich could have let the game go on, but he wanted it to be realistic. The target was going to kill the tracker. He slowly pulled out his Glock, took aim, and pulled the trigger. Even though the rounds were blank, the report of the gunshot caused Rich to jump, and Julie to hit the ground. He aimed, and put two more rounds towards her prone body.

"I believe that you have been discovered and terminated, Miss Lowe," was what Julie heard from above.

"Well, I guess that's why you're the teacher, and I'm the student. I'm awfully glad that you were using blanks."

"Julie, you did a good job. If it weren't for the fact that I knew you had a second bug planted on me, you possibly could have won. A regular target wouldn't have recognized the second bug. I did. The other thing is that you didn't check the high ground. I watched you sitting there for about a half hour, and you didn't look up once. Now let's get the hell out of here before someone calls the state police, and reports some illegal hunting. I'm more worried about your car being out on the main road, than anything else,"

They turned the rental car around, and drove out to pick up Julie's Z.

Rich looked at her in the camouflage outfit, and said with a grin, "If there were guys who looked like that in my outfit, I probably wouldn't have gotten out."

She laughed, and said, "I didn't think there were women in the SEALS, Rich."

"There aren't."

Rich looked into her green eyes. "Since you screwed up so badly, we've got nothing to do for the next two days. Our cover has us in New Jersey. What do you say we get rid of my rental car, go back to our houses, change, get cleaned up, and meet at my house in a couple of hours. Then we can go to dinner."

"Sounds great to me. Should I wear a dress, jeans, what?"

"I don't care what you wear. You can wear nothing as far as I'm concerned.

But if you do, we might not get out to dinner."

I'll meet you at your house at 7:00. p.m. Do you want to go to the place we went last time? The food was good, and the dancing was fun."

"O.K. we'll go there. I'll call for a reservation. See you at my place."

Julie got into her car, and they drove off, following each other until they separated within three blocks of Rich's house.

At 7:00, on the dot, Rich's doorbell rang. He opened the door, and Julie stood there looking absolutely fantastic. Her green dress brought out the color of her eyes, and her hair was up in a pony tail. Her smile brightened the mood.

"Don't you look nice," said Rich.

He was in a sport coat, slacks, and a turtle neck jersey.

"Thank you, sir; you're not so bad, yourself."

They drove to the hotel, talking about the day, and how Julie might have done things differently.

It was like déjà vu, all over again. The valet took Rich's car, the hostess remembered his name, they sat at the same table, had a wonderful meal with a fine California wine, and headed for the nightclub.

Rich realized that he was starting to have feelings for Julie that exceeded his parameters for people who worked with him. He wanted to take her home, and make love to her for the next two days. From the signals that he was receiving from her, he realized that he could probably do that. However, he realized that after he went to heaven for two days, he'd have to come back to earth on the third day, and things would be different from then on. He had to keep to his rules, or when the two of them were in the field, one or both of them could die, due to emotional relationships.

It was almost midnight when Rich asked for the check. They both stood up, and walked to the valet booth. The valet brought the car around, left Rich's door open, and came around and opened the door for Julie. Rich tipped him generously, and they took off.

On the way home, Rich mentioned that if they did this again, he'd pick her up, since now, when they got to his house, she'd have to drive home.

Julie looked over at him, and gave a nervous giggle. "I was thinking that I'd probably drive home in the morning, after I made a great breakfast for us."

"Julie, there is nothing I'd rather do, believe me. I think that you are extremely desirable. You're beautiful, extremely bright, and fun to be with. It's just that we have to maintain the relationship that we have. We can't take it to another level. If you were in a position of danger, in the field, as my partner, I'd react one way, the best way to help you, and the safest for both of us. Add another factor, emotion, because my lover is in trouble, and I get careless, and we both end up in trouble. No one gets out of trouble, because I'm not thinking clearly. It just can't happen."

"Rich, I know that you're right. It's just that you make me so horny, I don't give a shit about the consequences."

"Julie, I have blue balls every time we're together. I've thought of transferring you, or resigning as your instructor, but we're a dynamite team. We just have to live our lives knowing that we can only be the best of friends, or in one way or another break up the team.

"All of this because I have to drive home alone, tonight. All right, boss, I'll drive home by myself. Do you want to do anything together over the next two days?" "Why don't I call you when I get up, I don't want you to call me when you get up, because it'll be too early ."

Rich put his car in the garage, walked out to Julie's car with her, kissed her on the cheek, and waited until she drove away.

At 9:00 a.m., Rich's cell phone rang. Rich was going to answer it, and say "Yes, my horny friend!", but was glad he didn't. It was Spence.

"Rich, Spence, where are you?"

"Actually, I'm not that far from the office. What's going on?"

"Have you had a conclusion to your operational test?"

"Yes, should I assume you are on a secure line."

"Of course, or I wouldn't have mentioned the test."

"Yes. I took out Julie. She had one major flaw. She didn't look to the high ground. We had planned on debriefing this morning. Why, what's up?"

"I would like you and Julie to come to my office as soon as possible. You can debrief at another time. It's important."

"I'll call Julie right away. Are you sure that you want us to come to your office? We had this cover story that would have kept us out of the office for two more days."

"Good thought. You live not that far from the office. Can we meet at your place?"

"Of course. Just look for Julie's car in the driveway, on the right hand side, just before you hit Main Street in West Hartford. Just stay on Asylum Avenue all the way out."

"How long until Julie gets to your place, assuming she's not there already?"

"Very funny, Spence. I can guarantee you she's not. If she's awake, she should be here in less than a half hour."

"Good! I'll see you as soon as I get there."

Rich called Julie. She was awake, and raring to do anything he came up with.

He told her about Spence's phone call. She promised to be there in twenty minutes. He told her to wear something casual.

The door bell rang. When Rich opened the door, Julie was

standing there in a pair of jeans, a blouse, and sneakers. Just then, Spence pulled into the driveway alongside Julie's car. The timing was perfect in proving that Julie hadn't spent the night.

They all sat down at the kitchen table. After the usual small talk, Spence got right down to business.

"We received intel that two individuals from Saudi Arabia flew into Detroit last night. They are here to pick up donations from the Dearborn Arab community to finance terrorism back in the middle east . The money has been donated through organizations that have a front as raising money for the poor.

The organizations are listed as terrorist organizations by the government, but the people who give to the fronts either don't know or don't care. It is imperative that this money does not leave the country."

Spence turned towards Rich. "Not only do I want you to take out the targets, I want you to do it after they get the money, and bring it back. They are due to fly back, the day after tomorrow."

Julie immediately stood up. "You looked at Rich when you said you wanted him to take out the targets. Does that mean that I'm not going?"

"I haven't received a letter saying you are qualified. Rich tells me he took you out yesterday. That's good guys one, bad guys zero."

Spence turned back to Rich, "What do you say, Mr. instructor; is she ready?"

"I'll have the letter for you when we get back. I think she's ready to go. The only question I have is whether or not she'll fit into the Arab community. Women are looked at as second class citizens back in Saudi Arabia. I don't know whether she'll be able to move around near the two targets."

Spence said, "We won't know that until something happens. Here are the two files on the targets. Intel had files already on these scum, and they've brought them up to date. You won't be able to have Linda make your transportation and hotel arrangements, so you'll have to do it yourselves. Of course you'll have no contacts with the Detroit office. Call me with your needs for supplies. Use the usual system. Call my private line and hang up. I'll call you back. Make your hotel reservation first, so I can have the supplies sent to the hotel. Any questions?"

Neither Rich nor Julie had any questions.

"See you when you get back. I'll look forward to getting your list as soon as you can call me."

Spence got up, and let himself out the front door.

Rich looked at Julie. "You're going to get your introduction to what we do while under fire, green eyes. I'll put together a plan, this time. Once you've reviewed it, we'll put together a list for Spence. Meanwhile, why don't you get us a reservation on a flight into Detroit this afternoon? Get it in the name of the company, and tell them the passengers will pay and pick up the tickets at the airport. Also rent a car in Detroit under the name of Andy Darko. When we get there, we'll change it to the name on the fake credit card."

Rich picked up the intel files, and started to read. He stopped in about ten minutes. Julie had been making calls. "Make reservations at the Maxwell-Dearborn hotel for two nights for two adjoining rooms. One for a male, and one for a female. Use Middle Eastern names.

After Rich put together the plan, he went over it with Julie. From the plan they derived a supply list, which they gave to Spence, when he called back.

Julie smiled and looked at Rich. "You know, we could save the company a lot of money if we shared a room."

"We're going to be together day in and day out for the next two days. At least give me six hours a day to be alone."

She grabbed a pillow off the sofa in the living room, and threw it at him.

"Hey, lady, why don't you go home, get some underwear, and whatever you will need as a devout Arab woman, and be back here in an hour? We'll go to the airport in one car."

chapter 11

DEARBORN

Driving to the airport, getting tickets, and flying to Detroit were uneventful. They rented the car, and drove to the Maxwell-Dearborn hotel. The package from Spence was waiting in Rich's room.

They unpacked the two Glock pistols, noise suppressors, and the k-bars. The makeup kit contained oils that would darken their skin, a beard and mustache for Rich, as well as sandals, trousers, a long sleeve shirt, and a kufi, or prayer cap. The disguise for Julie was simple, a burka, a niqab to cover her face, and sandals.

Julie could wear the burka anywhere she wanted to, and no one who looked at her could identify who she was. Although she checked in as a white woman, no one in the hotel could identify her as that person. As long as she was wearing the burka, and the niqab she was a devout Muslim woman.

Rich went into the bathroom with the makeup kit, and looked carefully at the directions of using spirit gum with the beard, and moustache. He would put on the oils first to darken his skin, then put on the spirit gum, mustache and beard. He would put on the kufi before they went out. The bottle label on the oils said that the color would remain for twenty-four to forty-eight hours.

Both Rich and Julie pored over the map of Dearborn, and the alternate ways of egress from the hotel, and routes from the hotel to the airport, approximately twenty miles away.

Also marked on the map were the three locations that the targets would be visiting to pick up the money. Rich had chosen the Maxwell-Dearborn as it was the most centrally located, and it was also was the hotel address written down on the entrance papers to the United States as to the target's location, while in the U.S. Rich was still amazed at the intel information he received. Especially since it was so timely.

Rich told Julie not to change out of her travel clothes, and he stayed in his. He wanted to reconnoiter the area, and also drive by the three locations of the pickups, just in case he could spot the targets. He had pictures of them, taken the day before, at the airport.

Rich and Julie were walking through the lobby when the two targets, and an entourage of three other men, walked right by them. From the size of the three men, it was obvious that they were guards for the targets.

Rich quickly leaned over to Julie, and said, "Keep walking." He then turned and followed the five men to the elevator bank. The five men entered an empty car, and the door closed. Rich watched the floor indicator, and saw it stop, and remain on the fourth floor. About ten seconds later, it went back down to three, stopped, paused, and came back to the lobby where a man and a woman exited. The targets were on the fourth floor.

Rich went out the front door, and saw Julie talking to the door man. She walked over to Rich, and said, "Hi, Honey. This nice guy said that there is a great place to get shwarma right around the corner. " Rich looked at him, and said "Thank you, sir." and they walked away.

Rich looked at Julie, "What the hell is shwarma?"

"Its meat and other stuff, wrapped in pita bread."

"How in the hell would you know that?"

"I have no idea. Somewhere in the resources of my mind. But I had to do something when you left me and told me to keep walking. I asked the doorman where the best place was to get some."

"I left you because our targets walked right by us, with three muscles with them. They looked like the first family of Saudi Arabia. I got their floor, so I'll call Spence, to have intel get their room numbers."

"Do you think they've got the money?"

"No, I think they'll pick it all up tomorrow, and leave the next morning. They have a 10:00 a.m. through New York, and Frankfurt, to Riyadh."

"Do you want to look at the territory?"

"Yuh, let's get the car and ride around."

They drove around Ford Road, Michigan Avenue, and Schaefer.

Rich looked at Julie. "Are we in the United States? With all the signs in Arabic, I'm not sure what country I'm in."

"This is the largest Arabic population in the United States, and therefore the largest Muslim population."

Well, I saw a rib place on the way in from the airport. What do you say we go there, or would you rather get some swarmy, or whatever you call it?"

"Let's go for the ribs."

"Done."

After dinner they drove back to the hotel, and parked. Detroit, and its suburbs had long streets, that were mostly straight, so it was easy to get around. They went into the bar, had a couple of drinks, and went upstairs. To Julie's consternation, they went to their own individual rooms.

Rich was up at his usual time, and since he didn't know the territory, he decided to use the treadmill in the workout room to do his five miles. Fifteen minutes after he went into the room, he heard a keycard in the lock, and Julie walked into the room.

"Hey, sailor, is there room for a poor defenseless female in here?"

"Defenseless, hell. You can be my backup, anytime."

"I think I am."

Julie started her work out on the universal, and then went to the free weights.

Rich finished before Julie, wiped off some of the sweat, and said, "I'll pick up some muffins in the lobby, and meet you upstairs. We can have it with some room coffee, and get into our gear."

She waved at him, and did another rep.

On the way up to his room, Rich picked up four different types of muffins at the shop in the lobby, turned on the coffee when he got there, showered, threw on a robe the hotel provided, and waited for Julie. About twenty minutes later he heard the shower go on in Julie's room, and five minutes later she walked through the adjoining door in her robe. She walked over to the coffee, poured two cups, and brought them over to the table next to Rich's chair. He opened the muffin bag, and they ate like the muffins were going out of style.

"What are we going to do now, boss?"

"As soon as we finish this sumptuous breakfast, we are going to go into the bathroom, and put on the skin dye, in order to darken our skin. Then, I am going to put on the spirit gum, beard, moustache, and the clothes. You, my lovely, are going to put on your burka, niqab, sandals, etc. Under our refinements, we are going to be strapping on the Glock, extra ammunition, k-bar, and anything else we should have. In thirty minutes or so we are going to take the elevator down to the parking garage, and start out for Ford Road.

Then we'll wait for the terrorists, and the rest of the guys to pick up the money."

"I'd better get started, but I only have to go from the mouth up, in case my niqab slips. It won't hurt if I put some dye on my hands, even though I'll be totally covered, just in case."

"I'm going to get started on mine. I'll see you soon."

Thirty minutes later, a man with dark skin, a beard and moustache, a long sleeved shirt worn outside his trousers, sandals, and wearing a kufi walked down the hall, followed by a woman totally covered in a burka and niqab. Just the way she walked showed she was subservient to the man.

As they left the elevator, they met two others, dressed similarly. The man said, "Salam Aleikum", Rich replied," Aleikum Salam." Peace be with you.

They reached the car, and drove to Ford Road. Rich drove, and Julie sat in the back seat, as is done in Saudi Arabia. Women are not allowed to drive, or sit in the front seat.

Initially they drove by the store where the charity maintained its business. They drove about a block and a half, and pulled in. They would watch the front door of the building through the car mirrors. They knew they had time, as the guards and couriers would be at morning prayers. Prayers would be over at 7:30, and they would eat breakfast before they came.

They waited close to an hour before the vehicle finally showed up. The two terrorists and two of the guards went in, while one of the guards remained with the car.

About twenty minutes later, they all came out. One of the terrorists was carrying a gym bag. The two guards flanked the man with the bag. The other terrorist walked behind him. They all entered the vehicle, and drove towards Michigan Avenue.

Rich turned the car around, and followed them. "They'll probably go somewhere to pray, about mid-morning, or pray at the second pick-up point. Are you too warm in that outfit?"

"Not really, I have very little on under it, and you're keeping the cool air on, so that's helpful. Do you think that they'll pick up everything this morning?"

"No, they have to pray after mid-day as well, so there really won't be time for three pickups. We'll stay on top of them until they've made the three pickups, and go back to the hotel. We'll do our hit either tonight, or in the early morning."

The drive to the Michigan Avenue location, inside of an insurance agency, took about fifteen minutes. The vehicle parked around the back, next to a restaurant parking lot. Rich pulled into the parking lot, where the whole back of the insurance agency could be viewed.

The same guard stayed with the car, while the remaining four people went to the back door, knocked, and entered the building. For forty-five minutes, nothing happened. Rich had to shut off the engine of the rent-a-car after a few minutes. A running car drew too much attention. Julie was getting warm.

After another five minutes, the door opened, and the two terrorists followed the guards out of the building. One of the terrorists carried a gym bag, very similar to the first one that they received at the previous pickup point.

The foursome entered the vehicle, and drove by the restaurant's parking lot.

They reversed the direction from which they had arrived, and headed back to Ford Road. Once they turned onto Ford Road they slowed, and stayed in the right lane, as if they were looking for something. After about a mile, they turned into a restaurant with Arabic letters on the sign, and stopped. The two terrorists and one guard went into the restaurant. The other two guards remained in the car with the bags.

After forty minutes, the terrorists and the guard came out of the restaurant, carrying two more meals for the guards who had remained behind. They left the parking lot, and drove further east on Ford Road. Rich followed about a half a mile behind. The target car turned right, drove about three hundred feet, and entered a mosque parking lot. Rich kept driving by the mosque. The terrorists and one of the guards entered the mosque, leaving the two other guards in the car.

Rich and Julie pulled off the street into a gas station, and waited. Numerous cars pulled into the parking lot of the Mosque. Rich walked over to the small building at the center of the gas station, purchased four bottles of cold water, some candy bars, and crackers and walked back to the car. He gave half of them to Julie, and took half into the front seat. They were so thirsty, they just about inhaled the water.

After a period of time, the cars started to exit the mosque parking lot. The terrorist vehicle exited, and turned towards the gas station. Rich waited until it passed, and merged into traffic. They followed the car until it turned onto Schaefer, and headed for the third pickup location.

The third pickup was a copy of the first two, with the same number of people going in, waiting a short time, and coming back with a gym bag.

The next stop was the parking lot of the hotel. The terrorist team pulled into the garage and parked then the five men, and three gym bags went up in the elevator.

Julie and Rich pulled into the parking spot down the row from where the first car had parked.

They exited the car, went up to their room on the fifth floor, and sat down. Sitting on the coffee table was an envelope with a seal over the flap. Someone from intel had dropped it inside the room while they were gone. There was no way that messages could be traced, if none were left on the telephone, or with hotel personnel.

Rich picked up the envelope, opened it, and pulled out the piece of paper inside. He read: 442-1, 444-1,443-3. 1 was always outside, between 442 and 444.

He showed it to Julie. "Well, we know that the guards are in 443 on one side of the hall, and that one is always outside, sitting between the two terrorists' rooms.

In the morning, they'll all be up to pray between first light and sunrise. Let's use the same plan, but hit them before first light."

Julie looked at him with a smirk on her face. "So the Marines are in first, instead of the SEALs, right"

Both Rich and Julie relaxed the rest of the day. They obviously had fit in to the population during the day, but Rich questioned himself on having Julie wear the Burka all day.

Rich called down to room service for dinner for two. Julie took off her Burka, and sandals and washed the dye off of her face. She changed into her travel clothes in order to sign the bill when dinner came.

After dinner they packed, and grabbed some sleep until four in the morning.

At four, Julie redressed into her burka, sandals and niqab. Rich got back into his clothes, including the kufi, adjusted the moustache and beard. They left the room, went to the exit stairs, and walked down to the fourth floor. They opened the metal door, and looked down the hall. About halfway down the hallway there was a chair sitting empty.

Rich and Julie walked towards the empty chair.

The door to room 443 opened, and one of the guards, trying to be quiet, closed it softly behind him, walked to the chair, and sat down. Rich and Julie were almost on top of him when he turned and stood up. He took a stance which would stop them, and Julie shot him twice in the head, from under the burka. The shots sounded like two weak farts, as the bullets moved through the noise suppressor. Rich moved quickly to catch the falling guard, and place him in the chair.

Rich was happy that he was in shape, as the guy weighed about as much as a Buick.

Rich stood to the side, as Julie stood in front of the glass circle in the center of the terrorist's door. She knocked, and waited. One of two things were going to happen. Either the terrorist would be curious as to why a woman in a burka and niqab was standing outside his door, and open it, or he'll be on the phone to his guards, or the terrorist next door, and there will be hell to pay.

Nothing happened.

Julie knocked again, and was answered from inside by a question in Arabic.

She knocked again. He opened the door about two inches, and Julie shot him twice in the face. He fell backwards, into the room, and everything was quiet.

Julie opened the door, and went in. Rich followed, and closed the door behind him.

The connecting door between the rooms of the two terrorists was open. There was no movement from the other room.

Rich crossed the room, and looked through the door. The bathroom light was on, and there was a body in the bed. Rich quickly was at the bedside, and shot the sleeping terrorist twice in the head.

With the doors to the hall closed, they turned on the lights and easily found the three bags. They opened each one, and found it full of money with bands around the bills. They didn't stop to count it.

Rich and Julie quickly carried the three bags of money down the hall to the stairway, and walked up to Rich's room on the fifth floor.

The first thing that Julie did when they closed the room to the hall, was to take off her burka and niqab. She stood there in her bra and panties, with her sandals on.

"Rich, I'm so horny that if you don't do something, I'm going to do something. It happens every time I shoot a weapon.

"Well, my weapon isn't going to be doing any shooting. We've got too many things to do, so put a cover over your libido, or you're fired."

"O.K. boss, O.K. I give up. From now on I'll rub up against the bedpost."

"Good. Put everything that you have, except for your weapon, and ammunition, into a pile. Then go into your room, take a shower, take off any dye that's on your body, and get into your travel clothes. Come back here, with your bag packed, and your room cleaned up.

Rich then went into his own bathroom, took off the beard and moustache, and flushed them down the toilet. He made a pile of all his clothes, and then went into the shower, and rubbed his body with soap, in order to get rid of any trace of dye.

By the time that both he and Julie were out of the showers, the first light had changed the visibility in the streets, and they heard the first of many sirens. Evidently the other two guards had found the body of the third guard, and eventually the other bodies.

Julie came into his room, carrying the clothes that she had worn earlier. "Sorry about before, boss, but you can't blame me for trying."

"Yes I can, Julie. What we do only works if it is kept on a professional level. When we change that level, someone is going to die. If you don't give a shit, that's your problem, not mine. If it happens again, you're through.

"O. K. Rich, I understand."

Rich combined all of the clothes from the both of them, into one pile.

He transferred the clothes from Julie's suitcase into his. He then took the pile of clothes and put all of it into Julie's suitcase. He then took out two collapsible cloth suitcases that he had brought with him, and transferred the money from the three gym bags into the smaller suitcases Finally he collapsed the gym bags, and put them into the other suitcases.

By now the sun had risen, and the red, white, and blue lights were filling the streets. The elevators were stopping on the fourth floor as well, and the bell indicators were ringing almost continuously.

Suddenly, someone knocked on the door.

Rich looked through the peep hole, and saw a police officer. He opened the door, and said, "Can I help you officer?"

"Are you the only one in this room?"

"I'm the only one who slept here. My fiancée, Julie, slept next door, but she's in here now." Rich opened the door wider, and Julie stepped out.

"Did you people hear anything out of the ordinary here in the last couple of hours?"

"What do you mean, out of the ordinary?"

"Well, like shots, bumps in the night, yelling, etc."

"Shots? Did someone get shot?"

"Well, thank you for your help sir!! Have a good day."

"Gee, do you believe that Julie? Someone must have been shot."

Rich then closed the door.

Rich looked at Julie. "Hungry enough for breakfast?"

"I think it would be a good idea. Shall we go to the hotel restaurant? I know it's open by now."

"Great!! Let's go."

Both Rich and Julie went out into the hall, where three uniformed policemen and two plain clothes detectives were knocking on doors, and asking questions. One of the detectives started towards them, and a uniformed officer said, "They're o.k. Tom, I already spoke with them." The detective looked at them, wished them a good day, and went down the hall.

They walked to the elevator, thankful that none of the officers or detectives could see the ankle holsters filled with Glocks, that each of them was wearing.

They both had sumptuous breakfasts, paid their individual bills at the front desk, and had a bellman follow them up to their rooms to get the suitcases. They met the bellman at the front door, put all the suitcases in the trunk, and left for the airport.

As soon as they were two blocks away, they changed direction, and drove towards downtown Detroit. When they got downtown, they found a number of churches with large yellow boxes that had clothing for the poor signs. They opened the suitcase with the clothes used in the operation, and deposited small amounts of the clothing, and sandals in each one of the boxes..

They then drove over to Belle Island where they dropped the makeup kit contents into different dumpsters, and threw the pieces of the Glocks and holsters, off the bridge into the Detroit River.

There was no way that they were going to get the money through the X-ray machines at the airport. They went to the local Federal Express office, had the bags placed in boxes, and sent to Rich's address in West Hartford. Rich was sure that the organization would break even with the cost of shipping, considering the contents.

Rich and Julie then drove out to Romulus to the airport, turned in the rental car, and went to wait for their flight.

As they waited, they watched the news on the television at the bar. The local stations reported the same news every five minutes. Three men had been found dead of gunshots in the Maxwell-Dearborn hotel. Two men who were with them were being questioned. Two of the deceased carried passports from Saudi Arabia. No other information has been given out by the Dearborn police.

Julie looked at Rich, and quietly said, "Not one word about the money. I doubt that the guards will say anything, or they'll be accused of an inside job. I wonder if the guards had weapons, and if they were legal?"

The announcement that the Hartford flight was ready for boarding gave them the impetus to leave the bar, and walk over to the gate. The boarding process was normal, as was the flight to Hartford.

chapter 12

HARTFORD

When they landed in Hartford, Rich called Spence, and told him that both he and Julie were back home, and were planning on coming in to work in the morning. Did he want to see them at any certain time? They agreed on 10:00 a.m.

As they came up the street to Rich's house, they saw that Julie's car hadn't been stolen out of his driveway. They transferred Julie's small bag into her car, and told each other to have a good day, and that they would see each other in the morning. Both were tired, and wanted to go to sleep.

Spence was on the phone when Rich and Julie walked into his office. Vivian was away from her desk, or she would have stopped them.

They started to back out of the room, when Spence waved them in. He continued his conversation while they waited.

"No, Thomas, there is no need to tell them. I'll be happy to tell them. I'm sure that they will appreciate your confidence in them, and will be pleased with the promotions. I can guarantee you that they will be excellent in their new positions. I'll look forward to seeing you and your lovely wife at the club on Saturday. The replacement will be in my office next week for orientation."

Spence sat there, looking at them, like a cat that had swallowed the canary.

Rich spoke first. "Are we the them, that are going to be pleased?"

Julie sat with a look of expectation on her face.

Spence looked back and forth between the two of them. "Yes, that call pertained to you two. However what I want to do first is to debrief you on your trip. I've received the intel report, and you both did a remarkable job. Tell me how you did it."

Rich told him the plan, and Julie told him what happened.

"Excellent plan, excellent execution. Julie, it seems that you have learned very well. There is one question that I have, and you both left out the answer. Where in the hell is the money?"

They both laughed, and said, almost in unison, "What money?"

Before Spence had a case of apoplexy, Rich told him that they should have it by the next day, and told him how they got it out of Detroit.

Spence congratulated him on thinking outside the box, and then asked, "Did you insure it?" and laughed.

Spence looked at the two of them. "Do you know where Vivian has gone?"

They both shook their heads, and Julie said, "Where?"

"She has gone down to the printing department in order to get you both your new business cards. She has already ordered your desk plates, and the signs for your offices. The announcement will come out by e-mail tomorrow. When you walked in I was talking to the president, telling him that he didn't have to come over to tell you. However, I anticipate that you'll be called to his office for a handshake tomorrow."

Rich looked confused. "What are you talking about?"

Do you remember last week when you asked me if you would only be working in your division? I told you that I didn't think there was a national position within your pay grades. However, I brought it up in the staff meeting, and although you are both relatively new, the president thought that you two would be perfect for two new positions: the National Director for General Agents, and the Assistant National Director for General Agents. You'll move over to the other side of the floor, and you will be given a new Administrative Assistant. Linda will have to stay here, in order to break in the new Life Sales Director. Julie, your life position has been eliminated. I was right when I thought that there was not a position in your pay grade. Both of your pay grades have been increased by one level. Congratulations!!

"Oh by the way, Julie, you have a new parking space, next to Rich, on the left side of the lot. You both will continue to report to me.

Rich asked, "Who's taking my place?"

Spence looked directly into Rich's eyes.

"Phil Cohen, the manager from Fort Lauderdale. He's a young tiger who wants to move up the ladder. I'm not sure coming inside is moving up the ladder, but he seems to think so. He'll be here next week. His family will be coming up at the end of the school year."

Rich smiled, "He's a good guy. His numbers are good, and he has a good reputation. I'll be happy to help him any way I can."

"Good. Why don't you two work out of your house tomorrow, Rich. I don't want FedEx to leave those boxes on your front steps, and go away. Why don't the two of you go and say something to Linda. She's aware of the situation, and you'll be on the same floor, but you still can go make nice. Spend the rest of today moving your personal stuff to your new offices, and meet your new admin, Tina."

After Julie and Rich spent some time with Linda, and thanked her for everything she had done for them, they went looking for their new offices. Rich's new office was in the rear corner of the building overlooking a tree covered hill. Julie's office was right next door.

They found Tina, a willowy blond, sitting in front of Rich's office, at a desk covered with pictures of children. After speaking with Tina, they found out that all of the pictures were different shots of her son and daughter, and she had worked for the company for six years as an administrative assistant in property and casualty. Her boss had just retired, which made it possible for her to take the open position supporting their two new positions.

She seemed very willing to do whatever they asked her to do, even though neither one of her new bosses had any idea of what they were supposed to do.

Rich and Julie spent the rest of the afternoon moving their personal items from one office to another, as well as reading the position descriptions that Human Resources delivered to them. They also received their new compensation levels, and both were very pleased. Rich thought about the recent trip, and wondered about the brief case. Maybe he and Julie would get paid their bonuses when the cash was brought in, tomorrow.

Rich asked Julie if she wanted to come over to his house tomorrow, to help wait for the money, as well to put together a plan for their new positions that would agree with their job descriptions. She immediately agreed to do so.

FedEx delivered before ten, as requested originally, and Julie beat them to Rich's house by fifteen minutes.

They opened the boxes in the living room, after checking that the boxes hadn't been opened. They had drawn lines across the tape, and the continuous lines were not interrupted. The suitcases were inside, wrapped in shrink wrap.

They opened the cases, and started to count. By the time they were finished, their eyes were wide open. They had a pile of bills with wrappings around each one thousand dollars. They had a total of two million, three hundred thousand dollars. That could buy a lot of armament for the terrorists.

Rich called Spence: "The package has arrived. I'd rather not drive it over, but unless you have other ideas, that's what I'll do."

"Do you have any equipment with you?" Of course Spence was referring to the Glocks they wore in their ankle holsters.

"Yes, both of us do."

"Then bring it."

Rich called Tina, and asked her to have a two-wheeler at the guard desk, so that he and Julie could bring some things upstairs.

When they got to the office, Rich went over to Charlie at the desk, and picked up the two-wheeler. He then went out to the parking lot, put the two suitcases on the two wheeler, and went upstairs.

Spence was expecting them when they walked into his office. He wasn't expecting the amount of money that they told him they had.

"Nice job. Not only did you take out the targets, your collateral damage was a plus, and you brought back some future pay checks, as well. I have no other questions about the operation, other than what you have already told me.

There are two briefcases here, one for each of you, giving you your bonuses for the killing of the two terrorists. Please just give me your expense reports, and I'll have the cash for you right away. Now, go start your new cover. Any questions?"

Neither Rich nor Julie had any questions.

Walking back to their offices, Rich looked at Julie, and said, "How about going to the Green Parrott for lunch. I've worked up a hunger for one of their peanut coated satays, and an O'Doul's."

She looked at him and replied, "I was going to go downtown. With this new job, we're going to be doing a lot more traveling, and I've got to buy some more clothes."

Rich smirked at her. "That's a woman's big cry: I don't have anything to wear!"

"Well, I don't."

"Have fun, I'll see you when you get back. I'm going to lunch."

When Rich got back, there was a list on his desk of the General Agents, by state, with whom the company had contracts. Tina told him that it had been sent over by the sales department of the property and casualty division.

General agents represented the company, but did not use the company exclusively. They used other companies, as well, for different lines of business. All of the agents on the list used the company for property and casualty, but few, if any, used the company for life and investment business. It was going to be up to Rich and Julie to get the agents to use the company for this line of business. Ultimately, when there were a number of General Agents in a specific territory using the company, the servicing of these agents would be through the individual sales offices such as those who had reported to Rich and Julie, and their jobs were to find new General Agents.

Julie walked in the door at about the same time that Rich had finished the list.

Rich looked at her. "What, no packages?"

She laughed, "I was only gone a little over an hour. How much could I buy? Actually, I left them in the car."

"Did you leave your briefcase there, as well?"

"No, I left that in my office. I figured it was safe, here."

"Good. Here's a list of the General Agents. Decide where you want to go first. Unless Spence gives us another operation, we choose where we travel. At least initially, then it's where we have to put out any fires that may come up."

"How about Hawaii."

"Look at the list. There are six General Agents in Hawaii. California has over two hundred. Where do you think the powers that be would like us to go?"

"Well, I guess I can wear my new bikini in California, as well as Hawaii."

"I'll check with Spence, see if he has anything for us, and then we'll make our decision. Meanwhile, I want you to call this individual. He can help you set up a place for your money. It's one of those details I'm trying to teach you about."

"Thanks, Rich."

Spence did not have an operation ready at the present time, but he asked Rich if Julie was ready to work alone on an assignment.

Rich answered, "She was cool as a cucumber in this last assignment. She did everything that I asked her to do, and she didn't hesitate to pull the trigger. I just wonder whether or not she was leaning on me, in case anything went wrong. When we get another assignment, I'll let her put together the plan, and carry the load, as much as possible."

"O. K.; in the field, you're the boss. Enjoy your trip to wherever. Keep in touch, in case something comes up. Call Tina every day, to tell her your itinerary. If I need you, I'll call."

Rich went back to his office. On the way, he stuck his head in the door of Julie's office and asked her to join him.

"Spence doesn't have anything for us right now, so we're going to California. Do you want to go north or south, San Francisco or Los Angeles? Just about half of the General Agents are in each part of the state."

"I've always liked the northern part of the state better, so why don't we go to San Francisco? If I remember the list correctly, there are a number of agents in Sacramento, as well."

"Then that's what we'll do. Pack tonight; figure we'll be gone for ten days; and be in here by seven tomorrow morning. We'll put together a plan in the morning, get a noon or so flight, and continue with it on the plane. With the time change we should get in around early evening."

"O.K. Do you want me to send in Tina for her to make the arrangements?"

"Please."

When Tina left his office she had the instructions as to the approximate times of the flights, the hotel, rental car, and whatever else was needed. Rich gave her his preferences for airlines, seats, car companies and types of cars, and hotel chains. He wanted her to know what he wanted in the future.

He also asked her for Dave Baxter's telephone number. He thought that he would call Dave to see if he would be in that part of his territory at the same time that he and Julie were there. He thought it would be good for Julie to meet him, and it would be common courtesy to call him, since he would be in Dave's territory.

chapter 13

SAN FRANCISCO

The only flights out of Hartford to San Francisco International Airport had connections. There were no non-stops, so they changed planes in Chicago. It seemed rather stupid to go south to Atlanta, in order to go west to San Francisco. That added another hour to their trip.

When they finally reached San Francisco, the time change gave them plenty of time to take a taxi to Union Square, and check into the St. Francis hotel before dinner.

They got into casual clothes, went out the front door of the hotel, and walked over to Chinatown. The walk turned into a discussion for five to ten minutes as to where they were going to eat. Each of them had their own favorite place in Chinatown, and reveled in the stories of past experiences. Rich finally gave in to Julie, and they went to her favorite place.

Rich had to admit that the meal was excellent, the service was great and the atmosphere was authentic. They both overate, and the walk back was lengthened in order to try and walk off the overly satisfying meal.

After about a half hour, they went back to the hotel, agreed to meet in the workout room at five the next morning, and went to their individual rooms.

The sky was still dark when they rose and met downstairs. They went through their routine, and went back up to shower and change. They set a time to meet for breakfast, and grab a cab to California Street where they were to meet with the San Francisco General Manager of the company's property and casualty division.

An hour and a half later, the cab left them at the front door of the western divisions' property and casualty building, and they walked inside. They read the information board, and took the elevator to the eighth floor to meet with Boyd Carrington, the General Manager.

Carrington had been briefed on the two life people who now sat in his expansive office. He was to help them in any way possible to penetrate the ranks of the General Agents in order to have the agents sell life insurance to their clients.

"Rich", Boyd said, "I'll do what I can to help you and Julie. I've taken the list of all of the General Agents that we deal with, and put a star next to those who are either personal contacts, or people who I know will do business with you, if I put the pressure on them. There is a check mark next to the star, for you to contact them right away. I called them yesterday, and they said they'd meet with you. Good luck, and keep me in the loop."

"Boyd, thank you. I'll make sure that Spence Kohl is fully aware as to your jumping on the life bandwagon. I'll definitely keep you in the loop, and if there is anything we can do, please don't hesitate to call on us. By the way, do you know if Dave Baxter is in town?"

"I don't think so. He was here just last week, and he has such a large territory, I only see him about once a month. Talk about large territories, you two have got a doozie."

"You're right, but I think once we've gotten our feet wet, we'll split up, and each of us will cover a smaller area."

"Well, take care, and get us some production. So long."

Rich and Julie went back to the St. Francis, and picked up a rental car that Tina had reserved. They then spent the next three days calling on General Agents in the San Francisco area. They met some very nice, professional people and they met some real turds. Thankfully, the number of turds were few.

On Saturday they did the tourist thing. They went to Fisherman's wharf, Pier 39, Alcatraz, the Muir woods, and drove across the golden gate again, to go to Sausalito.

They were just pulling in to the garage at the St. Francis, when Rich's cell phone rang. They looked at each other with excitement.

Although the last three days had been fruitful, they hadn't done anything that made their adrenalin levels rise, and they were both adrenalin junkies.

Rich picked up his phone, and hit the button. "Rich Coburn."

"Rich, it's Spence. How's it going?"

"Good, Spence, it's been a good week. We're making good headway with the General Agents, and Boyd Carrington has been putting just the right amount of corporate pressure on people, to do business with us."

"Rich, I didn't anticipate that this would come up this fast. I have another operation for you and Julie for next week. I tried to call you at the hotel, but evidently you aren't there. However, I am on a secured line. How long until you get back to your room?"

"We were pulling into the hotel garage when you called."

"Good, there's a sealed package at the front desk for you, under your name. All the intel is in the package. When you have put together your plan, call my line, and I'll get you your materials delivered right away. Please don't ask for an aircraft carrier. I'll speak to you whenever."

"So long, Spence; speak to you soon."

Julie looked at Rich, "Well what's going down? I can only hear one end of the conversation, turkey. What's happening, and when?"

"Easy, easy; Spence had nothing to do, so he just called to see what was going down."

"Bullshit! From what I did hear, you didn't expound on our calls this week, which means he called for something else."

"You're right, smarty pants. We have an operation for next week. The intel will be waiting when we go upstairs . This is going to be a good one, because you are going to put together the plan, with my supervision, and you are going to order the supplies."

Julie sat back, with a smug look on her face, and looked at Rich. "This is going to be the best plan you have ever seen, and we'll use a minimum of supplies."

"Julie, don't go off half-cocked, you don't know who we have to hit, how many, and when. Once we see the intel, then we'll decide on the plan, and the logistics."

They went to the desk, picked up the package, and went up to Rich's room.

Rich called Tina's answering machine, and gave her the list of General Agents that he and Julie were to see on the first three days of next week. He gave her the telephone numbers, and asked Tina to call them in order to tell them that due to unforeseen circumstances, he would have to postpone the meetings. He then told Tina that something had come up, and they had to make the change.

While he was calling, Julie was reading the Intel report. When Rich finished the call, she looked at him, and said, "Holy shit!!"

Rich looked back at her, and asked, "What's your problem?"

"My problem is that the target is a Deputy Commissioner of Police for the City of San Francisco, and she is a woman."

"Why do they want her terminated?"

"According to the first page of the intel folder, she's not only a fundraiser for Hezbollah, an arab terrorist organization, but is a protector of prisoners who are members of the Muslim Brotherhood. Additionally, she is thought to have initiated and masterminded two bombings of military recruiting centers. I knew that this area was a hotbed of leftist thinking, but a Deputy Police Commissioner?"

"Remember what people say about the left coast. If you got rid of all the fruits and flakes, all you'd have left are the nuts. It's the granola coast."

"Rich that's not fair to all the good people out here."

"My feeling is kill them all, and let God sort them out."

"I've heard that before, and I didn't like it then."

"Yes, miss liberal, keep your own confidence, but put together a plan to take this asshole out of existence."

Julie worked with the intel report, and her plan for terminating the target. In approximately two hours, she pulled out another sheet of paper, and listed the items for the logistics list. She then handed both the plan and the list to Rich. "What do you think, boss?"

Rich went over the plan and the list, with a fine tooth comb. He went over the plan again, and again.

"Julie, I think you have put yourself in too many situations where the only outcome is for you to be captured or killed. I know you want to be aggressive, but it borders on being reckless. You don't have to prove anything to me; I know that you're good. Please refine it and do spend more time taking care of the details. Also I don't like your exit strategy, so refine it."

Two hours later Julie gave him what he wanted, and they called Spence. He called them back to get the list of supplies. He told them that there were supply locations just outside of San Francisco, and they'd have what they needed, delivered to their hotel, within two hours.

The next thing that they did was get out maps of the city, and the intel report. They found police headquarters, the physical location of her home, type of car, home of her driver, route of travel, and most important, her normal routine. They also had a total background on her ex-husband, and her children, all working in other cities.

Julie looked at her watch, and asked Rich, "What do you say we go out to dinner?"

"I think it's a good idea, except I want to wait for the supplies. I've been feeling naked walking around without a k-bar and a full ankle holster."

"I know what you mean."

Julie went off to take a shower while they were waiting, and Rich reread the intel report. He knew Julie had the capability of memorizing something once she had read it, but he didn't know if she missed anything. He sure wanted to make sure that he hadn't missed a thing.

About an hour later, there was a knock on the door. Rich looked through the eye piece in the door, and saw a courier, in uniform. Rich opened the door and collected a mid-size box. It wasn't especially heavy, and was unmarked. Just as a check, Rich asked the courier what was in the box. The man said he had no idea. When the box was delivered to the Courier office, they were told to get it to Rich, as quickly as possible. Rich signed the form, tipped the courier, and put the box on the coffee table.

The first things that Rich saw when he opened the box were the two holstered glocks, four mags of ammunition, two sound suppressors, and two k-bars in their sheaths, with belt clips.

He pulled them all out and put them into two piles. He checked the mags in the weapons, and found them to be full. He pulled back the slides, and put one into each of the chambers.

Julie walked in from the other room, and he gave her one of the piles, telling her that there was one in the chamber.

They both put on the full ankle holsters, without suppressors, and clipped the k-bars to their belts, with only the handles showing.

"Now can we go to dinner, boss?"

"Yes, we can."

They walked up the hill to the Mark Hopkins, and went for a drink at the Top of the Mark. It was a stunning view from the top floor of the hotel on one of the highest hills in San Francisco. The city looked beautiful at dusk. They tried to see Sausalito where the Deputy Chief lived, and could see the Golden Gate Bridge which led there, but didn't know where it was on the green treed land, on the other side of the bay.

After having a drink or two, they decided to go for ribs, over on Geary Boulevard, a place that both of them knew.

They left the Mark Hopkins, walked a short distance down the hill, and took a right, a short cut they both knew.

About five hundred yards down the street they both saw three men coming up the sidewalk. From the way they were swaggering, and the fact that the hairs on the back of Rich's neck were standing up, Rich said, "Let's cross the street." As they crossed the street, so did the men.

Rich bent down, as if to tie his shoelace. When he stood up he placed his glock in his belt, under his jacket, and unsnapped the k-bar. Once he was standing, Julie did the same thing.

The men were no more than one hundred yards away. As they came closer, they spread out, and blocked the sidewalk.

Rich and Julie crossed the street again.

The men jogged over to the side of the street they were now on, and started to talk.

"Hey, Chica, what are you doing with this little guy, when you can have a real man?"

Julie laughed, "He's the only real man here. You punks can go and fuck yourselves."

The one who had spoken reached out and grabbed her breast.

Julie took her left hand, and crossed it to her right shoulder. She then flattened her hand and brought it straight out into the throat of the big mouthed jerk. As he grabbed his throat, she brought the heel of her right hand up under his nose, driving the cartilage into his brain, killing him instantly.

The remaining two pulled out knives, and were about to attack, when Rich shot them both in the groin. Julie finished off the quick altercation by shooting them both in the head.

Neither Rich nor Julie had had any time to put noise suppressors on their weapons, but it didn't matter. Both suppressors were back in the hotel.

Rich looked at Julie, and said, "Let's get out of here, somebody will report those shots."

They walked across the street, and took the next right, and then a left, following the general direction that they had started out to follow.

"Remind me never to grab your breast," Rich whispered.

"I can guarantee that you'll get a different reaction."

They had gone four blocks before they heard the first siren.

Julie turned her head to Rich. "Well, at least there will be three less scum on the welfare rolls. Maybe they would have been better off staying in their own country."

"That doesn't sound like my liberal friend, who's always for the underdog," answered Rich.

"I'm just fed up with these assholes coming to our country, breaking the laws, and having no respect for the people who are paying for them to live. The only people who are worse than them are the politicians who vote to give them everything. I can almost guarantee that they were illegals."

They were just about to take a left down the next block, when a black and white pulled up next to them. The driver lowered his window, looked toward them, and said, "Excuse me folks, may I ask you a few questions?"

They both walked to the patrol car, and bent down to look at the driver, and his partner.

"Of course officer, how can we help you?"

"Do you live in the neighborhood?"

"No, sir, we're from Connecticut. We're in the city for business, and we were going to Victor's, down the block, for the best ribs in the city."

"Where are you staying?"

"The St. Francis."

"This isn't the way that you would walk from the St. Francis."

"You're absolutely right officer, we went to the Top of the Mark for a couple of drinks, first, and to discuss some business. We took a short cut in order to get over here."

"Did you see or hear anything out of the ordinary?"

"Like what?"

"Like any noises, or did you pass three men walking together?"

"I don't remember three men. Julie, did you see anyone like that?"

"No, but I did hear a car backfire. As a matter of fact, I thought that it was odd. It backfired once, then there was a short period of time, and it backfired twice more. I never heard a car do that."

"Thank you, folks. Do you have a business card, in case we need to reach you? How long are you going to be in town?"

Both Julie and Rich reached into their pockets for their business cards. Both of them did so while making sure that the Glocks and the k-bars didn't show when they pulled back their jackets.

"We're not sure how long we're going to be here. We have open tickets to go back to Hartford. We really didn't know how long we needed to be here to accomplish what we need to do. Should we call when we leave?"

The officer took both of their cards, looked at them, and raised the window half way. "No need to call us. If we need to talk to you again, which I doubt, we can get in touch. Sorry to have interrupted your evening. Enjoy your ribs."

"Thank you officer; have a safe evening."

Julie said to Rich, "I wouldn't do his job for anything. When I was with the bureau I didn't have to put up with the scum he does every shift."

Julie and Rich enjoyed their ribs, a couple of O'Doul's, and crème brulee for desert. Each went to their respective restrooms in order to place their weapons in their holsters.

It was amazing. They had just killed three human beings, covered it up with the local police, and felt no remorse. Are they psychopaths, or just people who consider that they are the tools to be used in making this country better? Both of them felt that they were the latter, but thought about the former.

The filling meal, the leisurely walk back to the hotel, and all that had happened to them this evening, gave both of them a level of fatigue that they hadn't had in a long time. They knew that they were going to sleep well tonight. When they got to the hotel, they went upstairs, said they'd meet in the gym at five, and went to bed.

After working out, and having breakfast, they went over the plan one more time. They had destroyed all of the copies of the logistics sheet, and the intel file by burning them in the toilet, and flushing the ashes.

One of the items on the intel sheet was that the Deputy Commissioner loved to shop at the high end women's department stores on Market Street, on her lunch hour. Another item was that she left her home in Sausalito at 7:15 a.m. every day in a car driven by a sergeant, for the approximately twenty-five minute ride to her office.

Rich and Julie were waiting, fifty yards down the street from the Deputy Commissioner's home when a black Lincoln pulled into her driveway. She came out the front door, in uniform, and got into the car. They followed the car over the Golden Gate Bridge to route 101 to Bryant Street. With traffic, it took approximately twenty-five minutes.

In accordance to Julie's plan, they left Bryant street, took a left on 6th Street, and a right on Market Street. They were at the high end stores in three minutes.

"I don't think she'd call for her driver, to go shopping. It would probably take less time to walk," Julie said, as she put in her brown contact lenses to go with her wig of dark red hair. She then left the car, and went into the department store with the circular escalator. There was no place to park, so Rich continued down Market Street to the embarcadero. He then turned around, and drove back down Market Street. Julie still wasn't in front, so he did it again. This time, as he came opposite the department store, Julie flagged him down. He picked her up, and went back to Bryant.

"I think that the department that she'll go to is on the fourth floor. There are dressing rooms in the left rear corner of the department, and the cashier counter is in the right rear corner. There are cameras in the ceiling over the cashier, and also at the entrance to the dressing rooms. There are no cameras in the dressing rooms themselves. There are chairs for waiting husbands, or boyfriends, just outside the dressing rooms, which can be observed by the cameras. The cameras are about fifteen feet high. I think we should put the car in the garage here across from the headquarters building. You can get into your gear in the garage, and we'll be ready to go."

They parked the car in the garage for people visiting the courts, and different departments of police headquarters. Rich put on a sweatshirt with University of San Francisco on it. He then put on a blond wig, and sunglasses. He put on a baseball cap, and pulled it low over his face. He transferred his Glock from his ankle to his waist, and pulled the sweatshirt over it and his k-bar.

Julie transferred the k-bar and Glock to her handbag.

They walked out of the garage. Julie walked across the street to the steps of police headquarters, and sat down on a bench to the right of the stairs.

Rich stayed across the street, and leaned against the wall, in the sunshine.

At approximately 11:35, the Deputy Police Commissioner, in her uniform, walked down the stairs, went to the edge of the sidewalk, and her car pulled up in front of her. They had been screwed.

As soon as the car pulled away, Rich crossed over, picked up Julie, and they walked towards 6th street.

"Well, we didn't expect that, so let's hope she doesn't want to walk in the street in her uniform, but still wants to shop." Rich picked up the pace, and said, "When we turn onto Market Street, let's hope that we see the car parked at the curb. I couldn't park there, but nobody's going to bother a police sergeant in an assigned vehicle."

As they turned right onto Market street, they could see the black Lincoln parked just where they expected it to be. Julie went up to the fourth floor, and Rich followed about fifteen people behind her. Julie went to the area she had been in earlier that morning, and there was the Deputy Commissioner with a salesgirl, carrying a number of outfits for her.

Julie walked through the racks while Rich walked, head down, to the left corner of the store, and sat in what they called the husband's chair.

Julie took two outfits over her arm, and walked into the dressing rooms. She put one outfit over the door in front, and went into the second door, forcing the salesgirl to bring the Deputy Commissioner to the last dressing room, furthest away from the sales floor.

Julie left the dressing room door partially open, in order to see the Deputy Commissioner walk by. As soon as the last room was filled, Julie attached the noise suppressor to the glock, and walked out of her room. She walked over to the last room, and knocked.

"Yes."

"I have another outfit that I believe will go along with the type you picked."

"Thank you, one moment."

She unlocked, and opened the door, and Julie shot her twice in the head. She then went back into her room, placed the weapon and suppressor into her bag picked up the outfits, and slowly walked out of the dressing room.

As she expected, the salesgirl was waiting outside the door. She handed the outfits to her, and said, "They looked better on the racks than they looked on me."

The salesgirl smiled, and said, "sorry, come back soon."

Julie walked to the escalator, with Rich fifteen yards behind her.

They were down to the third floor before they heard the first scream.

Julie walked to the right when she left the front door, and entered the store next door. She bought an inexpensive sweater, and went into the ladies room, and took off her wig, and put it with her contact lenses into the bag. She put the sweater on, after she removed the tags, over her blouse.

Rich, meanwhile bought a light jacket, went into the men's room, and put his wig, cap, sunglasses and sweatshirt into the bag. He took the tags off of the jacket and put it on over his shirt.

When they walked out of the front door, it was pure chaos. There must have been fifteen police cars, all with their flashers on, parked all over Market Street. They turned right, towards the embarcadero, and walked about two blocks before they turned right, walked down to Bryant and turned right again. They walked a few blocks to the garage, and drove out, saying "Have a good day," to the cashier.

They drove out to the Cliff House, on the ocean, for lunch. They walked along the cliff, threw their Glocks and k-bars into the ocean, and drove back to the St. Francis garage.

When they reached their rooms, Julie went to freshen up, and Rich picked up the phone.

Rich called Tina, and asked her to set their appointments for the next day, and fax their itinerary to them. He told her that she should set appointments for the following day if any that they had cancelled were left over. He then asked her to transfer him to Spence.

"Spence, how are you?"

"Fine, Rich, How are things going? I heard from Boyd Carrington. He was impressed by you and Julie. He says that you're calling on a number of General Agents, and you are being well received."

"Glad to hear that. Just wanted to let you know that we are achieving our objectives, in all cases."

"Excellent. Any idea as to when you guys will be back?"

"We figure that we are going to stay at least through the end of next week. We have enough G.A.'s just in the bay area, to keep us busy that long."

"Great. Just keep me informed of anything out of the ordinary, or if there is some way that I can be of help ."

"Thanks, Spence, we'll be in touch."

Julie walked in just as Rich hung up the phone. "What's going on?"

Rich told her about the phone calls, and they sat down with the list of General Agents, and made their appointments for next week.

The time passed quickly as they did their job with the General Agents, and spent their free time as tourists. Before they knew it, their time was up, and they were leaving for Connecticut.

Neither one of them realized how taxing the two weeks had been until they both fell asleep on the way to Chicago, and then again, on the way to Hartford.

chapter 14

HARTFORD

The weekend flew by, doing all the things left to do after a road trip: paying bills, mowing grass, doing laundry, sleeping, and getting your head together before you go back to work.

Rich and Julie arrived at the company cafeteria at about the same time, to pick up their coffee. During the time they were gone, the coffee machine had been removed. From now on, you either brought in your cup of coffee, or bought it at the cafeteria in the basement.

Some kind soul had brought a box of Dunkin' Donuts into the sales department, and two were suddenly missing, after they walked by the table.

Tina was waiting with a package of phone messages for each of them, as they walked by her desk. She also had a message that they were to meet with Spence, in his office, in thirty minutes.

They called some of the people back, and then Julie stopped by Rich's office on the way to see Spence.

They both walked in, saw the briefcases on the floor by Spence's desk, and closed the door behind the two of them.

"Good morning Julie; good morning Rich; welcome back. How are you both feeling?"

Rich said, "Super, how about you?" Julie looked at Rich, "Me too."

Spence leaned forward, and said, "I can't believe what's going on in San Francisco. The F.B.I. has been asked to come in, because the city police have absolutely no clues. Intel tells me that they are exactly where they were a week ago. They are looking for a red haired woman, with brown eyes, about 5' 6" and a man between 5'

8" and six feet with blond hair, who might be associated with San Francisco University. That's all they could get out of the security cameras, and the sales people.

They have film from the place next door that show two people with those descriptions coming into the store, but never leaving. The trail ends there. They reviewed the cameras from every garage in the area with no luck. They are totally stymied. Great plan, and great execution."

Rich literally patted Julie on the back. "Spence, this was Julie's plan, and Julie's execution. I was just the overseer. She deserves all the credit. I dare say that she is ready to go on operations on her own."

Neither Rich nor Julie mentioned the incident with the three men.

Spence reached down by his desk, and picked up the briefcases. He gave one to each of them, and smiling, said, "The organization was extremely pleased with the Dearborn contribution that you brought back. They approved a bonus for each of you, on that operation, and an extra bonus on this operation, as well. Don't spend it all in one place. Now go to work."

They went to their individual offices, and then Julie walked into Rich's office, and closed the door. She walked close to his desk, and lowered her voice. "Do you think that we should have told Spence about the creeps that we had to waste?"

Rich, his voice also lowered, responded, "I think that some things left unsaid should stay that way. First, it wasn't sanctioned; second, how would we have explained to the police why we were carrying weapons? Let's just leave it alone. I don't believe there were any witnesses to the action, so we can't be hurt. Forget it."

"That jerk really paid the price for a quick feel, though, didn't he ?"

"Why do you think I don't want to touch you," laughed Rich.

Rich pulled the list of General Agents from the file in his desk, and looked at Julie. "We should put together some sort of letter for Tina to send out to those people we can't see for a while, letting them know that we are offering our line to all General Agents. The

General Managers in each Property and Casualty office have been notified to get on the line to all of their G.A's, and then to call us when they need the personal visits. Let's work together on putting together a letter. I guess the first thing would be to put together bullet points, and then flesh them out."

"Sounds good; I'll get working on it right away. Any idea where we'll go on our next trip?"

"We only hit about fifty percent of the agents in the San Francisco area, but for obvious reasons, I don't want to go back there right away. California has the most G.A.'s so I guess we'd hit southern California. The regional office there is south of L.A. in Brea. I'll call the G.M. there, and see when it would be convenient for him."

"Fine, I'll get started on the letter."

"O.K.; so will I."

About ninety minutes later, Julie came into Rich's office with her list of bullet points and sat down. Rich put it next to his list, and crossed off the duplicates. They still had eleven points as to why a General Agent would want to use the life insurance line of the company.

Julie picked up both sheets of paper, and stood up. "I'll take these, and see if I can put something together that we can send out."

"Sounds great. I'll look forward to seeing it."

Forty minutes later Julie walked in, and laid a piece of paper on his desk, and sat down. Rich picked it up, read it, and looked at Julie. "This is perfect. I don't want to change a thing. Let's go with it."

Rich called Tina in. "Tina, please take this letter, written as is, with both names on the signature line. Once I review it, please run off enough copies so that each General Agent receives one. Then give it to Julie to sign each copy in blue pen. Finally, bring it to me for my signature in blue. That way it won't look like a copy. Also please bring me the name and telephone number of the G.M. in Brea."

"His name is Jerry Bernard; I'll write his number for you. I've been dealing with him for a long time. Nice guy, been around forever."

"Thanks, Tina."

Julie stood up and walked to the door. "I forgot she worked on the P & C side of the company. She probably has a lot of contacts. She'll be a good asset for us."

"Yes ma'am, she will. By the way, I don't know if you realized it with all this work, but neither one of us has eaten lunch."

"I'm really not that hungry. Will you bring something back for me, like a small salad, or something?"

"Sure, I'll just go downstairs. I'll probably bring something back as well."

They worked for the rest of the week on sending out letters, calling Jerry Bernard, and setting up appointments for the next week. The first appointment was at 7:00 a.m. with Jerry Bernard.

The following weekend was cut short since they had to travel on Sunday in order to be with Jerry Bernard on Monday morning, in Brea.

Tina made the reservations for them to fly through Chicago again, as there were no direct flights to Los Angeles. The rental vehicle would be waiting at the airport, since Brea was thirty-five miles east of L. A. They would be staying in individual suites at the Embassy Suites in Brea, five minutes from the regional office.

They planned on staying one week, in order to test the market in the area. They could always come back to L.A. if things went well.

Rich picked Julie up at her home, and they drove to the airport, late on Sunday morning. They boarded the plane for Chicago, and then connected to Los Angeles. They picked up the rental car, and drove east for about a half hour. Following the directions given to them by the hotel, they arrived with no problems. They checked into their individual suites, and met thirty minutes later. The people at the front desk recommended a smokehouse bar-b-que not far away, and they went there for dinner. They then went to their individual rooms, expecting to meet the next morning at the workout room.

chapter 15

LOS ANGELES

After working out, they had breakfast, and prepared to meet with Jerry Bernard.

The meeting with Jerry was similar to the meeting with Boyd Carrington.

Jerry had called a number of people, and appointments were set in addition to the ones that Rich had set back in Hartford. The G.M. was very supportive, and offered to help in any way possible.

Rich and Julie spent most of the week calling on General Agents. The G.A.'s seemed to be more receptive in southern California, than in the north. Some were ready to sign contracts as soon as they walked in the door.

Spence called them on Thursday night. They were due to leave early the next morning.

"Rich, Spence. This is not going to be a habit. It's just that a window of opportunity has come up, and both of you are close.

"I want you to grab a flight to Las Vegas. There is a state senator there who has just submitted a bill to the Nevada legislature which will invite illegal aliens to come to Nevada. He says that there is plenty of land and resources for them, and he wants to establish an additional tax to pay for them. There is no guarantee that it will pass the state senate, but it is thinking like this that will open the flood gates from Mexico and South America. In addition, this will be an easy way for more terrorist cells to enter the country. It's already projected that twenty years from now, just after the turn of the century, that Nevada will be at least fifty-one per cent Hispanic, mostly illegals.

The reason that we have a window of opportunity is that the Nevada legislature meets in Carson City. Security is much better there, as there are many legislators in town. This guy will be in Las Vegas for the weekend.

He's holding a fundraiser there on Saturday night. I believe it'll be at the Sands, but I know that the Intel sheet will have it.

I know that we have a moratorium on federal politicians, but this guy is state. By the way, I know how good you are. I thought that you might like to know that all of the investigations on your past operations have come to a halt. Officially they are still open, but there are no more clues for them to follow.

I've reserved rooms for you at the Riviera, under your names. Have a great vacation. Since you're so close, you decided to take a long weekend in Vegas. The intel file will be waiting for you. Call me with your needs. Good luck."

Rich knocked on the connecting door to Julie's room. He told her about the call from Spence, and asked her to cancel the flights for tomorrow, while he called to make flight reservations on a different airline, for Las Vegas.

chapter 16

LAS VEGAS

McCarren Field was far different from the airport in Los Angeles. It was much smaller; there were slot machines just about everywhere; and the atmosphere was far different. Instead of the hustle and bustle of a large airport, there was an excitement that ran through the people getting off the airplanes and walking through the hallways.

They grabbed a taxi to the Riviera, and enjoyed watching the people walking by, as they drove down the strip.

They checked in, picked up a package and went to their rooms. After putting away their luggage, they met in Rich's room, and went over the intel file. They jointly made up the list of what they needed, and Julie called to leave a message for Spence. Spence called back within five minutes, and reminded them that there was a three hour time difference, but everything would be there in the morning.

Julie went back to her room and went to sleep, after agreeing to meet Rich in the morning.

After working out, they went to breakfast, and took a short walk in the warm morning sun. They were amazed by the number of people who were walking the strip so early in the morning.

At eight-thirty the front desk called Rich to tell him that there was a box for him at the desk. He went down to get it, and brought it back to his room.

Once they opened the box, they put on their Glocks, but left the k-bars in it.

In both cases they put the guns in the waistbands of their shorts, covered by their shirt and blouse.

They went over the intel once more before destroying the file.

Walking outside, they felt the warmer temperature. Since going out earlier the temperature must have gone up twenty degrees.

They walked over to the Sands and went into the main door of the roundish hotel. They went over to the reader board, and found that the fundraiser was to be held in ballroom A at 8:00 p. m.

They asked at the desk for the location of ballroom A, and were told to go to the second floor. They walked up the stairs, and found the ballroom. They went in, and found that there were people setting up tables, chairs, and a small stage, with a podium. At the back of the ballroom were doors leading to the back of the house, and the kitchen area.

As they walked around the area, a guard came over and said, "Can I help you, folks? This isn't a public area."

Julie smiled, and looked around. "We're thinking of getting married, and we wanted to see what the place looked like, and the facilities to service the ballroom."

"Well, congratulations, ma'am; are you locals?

"No, why?"

"Just asking, ma'am. Most people here work for one hotel or another, and usually the hotels give a discount to their employees. I didn't recognize either of you, and I've been here since it opened. So I figured you must work for another hotel, and didn't know if you knew about the discounts."

"Why, thank you. That's very nice of you. No, we're from Kansas, but we're thinking of moving here. So we thought, why not get married here?"

Ma'am, sir, your best bet would be to go down to the desk, and ask to see the wedding planner, Marlene. She can handle everything you need. You tell her that you know Tom Parker, and I said that you should receive my employee discount. I've been married over forty years, so I'm not going to use it."

Rich walked over, put out his hand, and said, "Tom, I'm Bill

Townsend, and I really appreciate that. If the little lady and I decide to do that, you've got an invitation to the wedding."

After shaking hands, Julie and Rich walked out of the kitchen area.

"Did you see the exit out of the kitchen?" asked Julie.

"Yes, I saw one out to the left, and another one down the hallway to the right. There was also a freight elevator down the hallway as well."

"Good, I didn't see either exit, although it was on the intel sheet."

"There was also a fire door, just to the left of the ovens, that wasn't on the intel sheet. It was probably added after intel looked at the blueprints."

They left the ballroom, and walked downstairs. When they got to the bottom of the stairs, they looked in all directions for possible exits.

Walking back towards the Riviera, they discussed the plan further. There was a gnawing in Rich's mind, and he couldn't place what it was. Something wasn't coming together; there was a detail that wasn't planned for yet.

They walked up and down the strip, stopping in different casinos, and then rented a car at the Riviera, and drove around the area. There was more housing than they had thought, and new areas popping up. The downtown area was still a little seedy, but the area north of the strip, called Summerlin, was very nice.

Late in the afternoon, they got dressed in advance of going to the Sands.

Julie put on a blond wig, blue contact lenses, a pair of black slacks, a white blouse, and a white waiter's jacket. She placed her k-bar and the Glock, with the noise suppressor attached, into her waistband.

Rich put on a brown and grey wig, blue contact lenses, black slacks, white shirt, and a white waiter's jacket. He also placed his Glock and suppressor, as well as his k-bar, in his waistband.

Rich looked at Julie, and said, "Don't forget this," and handed her a nametag that said Kate.

He put on his tag, that had Harvey written on it.

They went down to the garage, got into the car, and took the three minute trip to the Sands. They could have walked, but Rich wanted the car there in case they needed it. They parked in the rear of the lot, near the rear exit.

They walked in the front door of the Sands, walked up the stairs, and into the kitchen area, like they owned it.

Rich immediately looked for the person giving directions. He walked up to him, stuck out his hand, and said, "Hi, I'm Harvey, and this is Kate, where do you want us?"

"Do I know you?"

Rich surreptitiously glanced at his name tag. "Kirk, don't you remember, we worked together over at that wedding at the Riviera. What are you doing, getting old?"

"I've got a million things on my mind. I'm sorry, Of course I remember you.

You're good workers. How are you, Kate?"

"Let's see; here's the board. Kate, you take tables nine, ten and eleven. Harvey, you take twelve, thirteen, and fourteen. When we do the hors' d'oeuvres, just rotate the trays as you go in and out. There will be security in uniform, and they aren't to eat, or drink. There also will be three state cops in plain clothes who will be close to the senator. You basically can tell them by their haircuts. They look like marines. You can grab some food now if you want."

That was the missing detail that was bothering Rich: plain clothes security, and state cops, to beat it all. You can pick out uniformed security when they're near the target. We should have planned on it.

People started coming in at 7:45, and Kirk started his team going out with the hors' d'oeuvres, and sent the bartenders out to give out drinks. At 8:15 the senator came in through the door leading from the kitchen to the outside hall. There were three men, in suits, accompanying him. Just as Kirk had described them, they looked like marines, all in great shape. The senator walked around the kitchen, shaking hands with everyone, and talking to some of them, mostly the Hispanics.

Julie walked right up to the senator, and shook his hand. When she turned away, the senator's eyes followed her. Rich felt a pang of jealousy.

Rich sidled up to Julie, and whispered, "Watch the three who came in with him. They're state cops, We didn't figure on them . Watch yourself.

After three quarters of an hour of hors' d'oeuvres, the wait staff was told to start serving salad. Bread and butter had already been placed on the tables.

The senator, two other city dignitaries, one of the state police officers, and two other people, were sitting at the dais on the stage near the podium.

Every time Julie had to go into the kitchen, she made sure to walk by the senator, and smile at him. Rich watched the senator's reaction as Julie walked away, watched him undress her with his eyes, and got angrier and angrier. He told himself to be more professional, and stopped his anger when he realized the man would be dead in fifteen minutes.

The rubber chicken dinner was served, as well as the dessert, and coffee.

As soon as the coffee was served, Rich went into the kitchen, and walked through the door to the hallway. He then walked down the stairs, and waited for the screams.

The senator wiped his mouth with his napkin, stood up, and walked to the podium.

Julie walked to the door to the kitchen, and stood beside a post on the outside of the door. The senator was about six foot four, and stood tall above the podium. Everyone turned towards him as he started to speak. Julie leaned against the post, as if she was listening to the speech. At the same time, she reached inside the jacket, and grabbed the butt of the Glock, which had the noise suppressor attached.

She looked at the state cop on the dais, and he was looking at the senator. She looked for the other two cops, and couldn't find one of them. The uniformed security people were looking at the senator.

She slowly brought out the Glock, blocked it with her body, and aimed it at the senator. She pulled the trigger twice, the noise suppressor did its job and the senator started to slump. The officer on the dais rushed to grab him, as Julie walked into the kitchen, and through the doorway to the hall.

The second officer rushed up to the senator, as did the uniformed security.

The third officer ran towards the kitchen, and burst through the doors. He had seen Julie, gun in hand, as soon as the senator had been shot. He looked around the kitchen, saw that Julie wasn't there, and ran out the door to the stairs.

He took the stairs two at a time, and could hear Julie below him. As he turned the final corner, he shot once at Julie, before two bullets hit him in the chest.

Rich had heard the commotion from upstairs, and was expecting Julie. When he heard two sets of legs running down the stairs, he made sure to look beyond Julie, to stop whoever was coming after her.

He had shot the officer just after the officer had shot his own gun at Julie.

Julie was hanging on to Rich. There was a spreading red stain on the lower right side of her jacket. She'd been hit.

Rich picked her up in both arms, ran out the front door, and to the rear of the parking lot. He got her into the car, and went out the back of the lot onto a side street.

Sirens seemed to be coming from all directions. Rich drove slowly down the side street parallel to the strip. When he got to the end of the street, he was at Sahara Avenue. He pulled into the front of a closed store, and went around to Julie's side. He opened the door, and looked into her ashen face.

Rich turned Julie so that he could lift the white, now mostly red, jacket and see what the bullet had done. She was a very lucky young lady. The bullet had entered the lower right quadrant in the back, and had gone through to the other side and had exited in the front. It was a true shot clean through. Rich had no idea if it had nicked anything, or had gone through any organs during the time it took to go through her body, but at least the bullet wasn't inside of her.

He put the jacket over the wounds, and tied the sleeves around it as tightly as he could. He then took off his belt, and wrapped that tightly around the jacket as well.

He drove the car about two blocks down to an open gas station, went into a phone booth, and called Spence collect.

When Spence picked up the phone, Rich said, "Call me back; emergency!" and gave Spence the number. It was after midnight in Connecticut.

The phone rang almost immediately after Rich had hung up.

"Rich, Spence, I'm on a secure line. What's going on?"

"Julie's been shot. I don't think its life threatening, but I'm no doctor. Do we have help in Vegas?"

"Hold on."

Rich held on for what seemed like ten minutes.

"Rich, I'm going to give you the number of a doctor. Tell him that you have a company problem, and you need his services immediately. He'll tell you what to do. Keep me in the loop."

Rich called the number. It rang six times before anyone picked it up.

"Yes."

"I have a company problem. I need your services immediately."

"Do you have the problem personally?"

"No, it's a girl I work with."

"Who gave you my number?"

"Spencer Kohl."

"Where are you?"

"At a gas station on Sahara Avenue, near the strip."

"Do you have a car?"

"Yes."

"What are you driving?"

"A rental car. A new Chevy, white."

"Drive north on Sahara as far as you can go. There will be someone in a black Pontiac. Her name is Sylvia. Do what she says. What is your name?

"My name is Rich."

"Goodbye, Rich."

Rich drove the car all the way up Sahara Avenue, as far as he could go. It took about ten minutes. There was no car at the end of the road.

About a minute later, a black Pontiac pulled up, and an older woman lowered the car window.

"I am Sylvia; what is your name?"

"My name is Rich."

"What is your problem, Rich?"

"My partner has been shot in the lower back, I think it's a through and through. But she's bleeding a lot."

"You will follow me, no matter where I go. Do you understand?"

Rich got behind the wheel, and started off after the black Pontiac.

Julie started to moan.

"Julie, are you awake? Can you hear me?"

"What's going on? Where am I?"

"You've been shot. You're going to be all right. The bullet went through. We're going to a doctor. Try not to move."

"I fucked up, boss."

"We both did. We didn't take care of the details."

"Where's the guy who shot me?"

"I killed him. I'll tell you the story later."

"What about the senator?"

"We'll check the news. I have to follow the car in front of me. Don't talk. Just rest."

The car went right on Charleston Boulevard, and pulled into a driveway. The woman put her hand out the window, and waved Rich on into an open garage.

The garage door closed behind the car. A door on the left of the garage opened, and a man walked in. Rich got out of the car, and walked to the man.

"Are you named Rich?"

"Yes, my partner is on the other side."

"Let me see how she is."

The man took a flood light off the wall, and went to the other side of the car. He took the belt and the jacket off Julie, and looked at the wounds. He put on a pair of gloves, and examined the wounds more closely. He went in to the door that he came through originally, and Rich could hear voices.

The woman came back out, and put pressure bandages on the entrance and exit wounds.

She turned to Rich, "Pick her up as gently as possible, and bring her inside.

Watch out that you don't hit her head on the door jamb."

Rich carried her inside, and at the man's direction, he laid Julie on what looked like an operating table.

The man then pointed to a door, and said, "I'll be out as soon as I can. It looks like it didn't hit any internal organs, but I have to be sure. There will be another man joining me. I called him when you called me. I need him to assist. You may turn on the television if you like. If you are hungry, the pantry and refrigerator are open to you. It may take a while, if we find anything. Do not come back in. Thank you."

Rich walked out and went down a short hallway. A bathroom was on the right, and the kitchen a little further down on the same side. A living room was on the left. The door at the end of the hallway, probably a bedroom, was closed.

Within minutes, Rich heard another vehicle, and looked out the living room window. The Pontiac was gone, and another vehicle, a Plymouth, was in the driveway. Rich heard the garage door go up, and then down. Then he heard another door close.

Rich went into the living room, and turned on the television.

He heard the commentator say, "And now the continuing coverage of the murder of Senator Victor Ponder, and state police sergeant Dominick Pallazio. The police have said that there is evidence that Sergeant Pallazio most likely has wounded or killed the attacker of Senator Ponder.

People who were in the lobby said that there was a man dressed as a waiter at the bottom of the stairs when the woman who shot the senator came down the stairs. As the woman reached the bottom of the stairs, the man pulled a weapon, and as soon as there was a shot from up the stairs, the man shot twice up the stairs. The woman then came to the bottom of the stairs, and fell into the arms of the man. He then picked her up, and ran into the parking lot. Police are checking with all hospitals and clinics for these two suspects.

The woman is approximately thirty years of age, about five foot six, blonde hair, in a white blouse and waiter's jacket, dark slacks, and black shoes. The man is between thirty and thirty five, with grayish brown hair, between five foot eight, and six feet tall, dressed similarly to the woman. Sources tell us that they were wearing name tags with the names Kate and Harvey. Stay tuned for further developments, and biographies of senator Ponder, and Sergeant Dominick Pallazio."

Rich watched the biographies of the senator and the sergeant, since he obviously had the time.

The sergeant was a hero in the past, before he was assigned to Senator Ponder. Rich felt sorry for the man, and his family. He was only doing his job, but then again, so was Rich.

The senator was the hero of those who wanted everything, but were not willing to make the sacrifices, or wait their turn. He was an ultra-liberal in a conservative state, and somehow kept getting re-elected. You either loved him, or hated him. Those that hated him, really hated him. Those that loved him loved him more depending on how far left he went. After this latest bill, the left loved him more and more.

A half hour later the door to the medical area opened. The man walked down the hallway towards Rich, very slowly.

"Your partner was hit in the lower right quadrant of her back. The bullet exited, in the lower front quadrant of her body, without hitting any vital organs. I have given her antibiotics, and bandaged the wounds. The biggest problem that can arise is infection. I have called and spoken with Spencer Kohl. He has requested that we keep your partner here for the time she needs to heal, and that we keep track of her in a safe house, and treat her medically. We will do so.

Rich, your partner is a very lucky girl. The track of the bullet was very close to vital organs. She owes you her life. She would have died of exsanguination, or bleeding to death, if you had waited much longer to call us.

We have contacted a clean-up crew, that we work with. They will pick up your vehicle, and clean it of any bloodstains. If the stains are too much to clean, they will replace the front seat, or any other parts, that are needed. The car will be delivered to you the day after tomorrow. The key will be left at the desk.

While your partner is here with us, we will destroy her wig, and contact lenses, as well as all of her clothes. We found weapons on her person. They will be buried in the desert. We will purchase new clothes for her, as well as replace her ticket on the air carrier.

Since I doubt that you want to walk around in your bloody clothes, I will send one of our associates to purchase clothes for you. I will need your sizes. I assume that you have weapons as well. When we take your clothes, we will also take your weapons, and dispose of all of it. I also believe that you are wearing a wig, and possibly contact lenses. Please include them. We will send you back to your hotel by taxi. Do you have money with you?"

"Yes, I do. I can't thank you enough."

"No, Rich, from what I saw on the news before you called me, it is I that should thank you. If you will wait here, an associate will be here in just minutes.

Just tell Spence that he'll receive my bill when the young lady returns to her home. By the way, what should we call her?"

"Her name is Julie."

"Thank you. I'm sorry we had to meet under these circumstances."

Rich couldn't believe how efficient the organization was in everything they did. He was driven, by taxi, back to the Riviera, wearing his new clothes. The rental car showed up on schedule with what looked like a new front seat, and it had been washed. He had a ticket on a flight back to Hartford, and included in the ticket wallet was a telephone number that he could call to speak to Julie.

chapter 17

HARTFORD

Spence had notified the people in the office that Julie and Rich were in an automobile accident, and Rich was fine. Julie, however, had been hurt, and needed a couple of weeks in Las Vegas, to recuperate before she came home.

Rich was, however, a little shaken up, and would be out for a couple of days.

The time at home went by very slowly for Rich. He kept thinking of the one thing, the one detail, that they forgot. It could have killed Julie. Lack of attention to details cost people their lives, caused operations to fail, and causes to be extinguished. Julie had put the plan together, but getting shot wasn't her fault. Rich was the overseer. He almost lost Julie.

He called her three days after he got home. He was going in to see Spence the next day, and resign.

She sounded a little groggy, but was excited to hear from him. She said that the company was really taking care of her, and that nobody could believe that the bullet missed her small intestine. They were still worried about infection, but she wasn't running a fever.

The people were very nice, and they bought her some very nice clothes, even though she wasn't going anywhere.

Rich apologized. He said that if it weren't for him overlooking the obvious detail, she wouldn't be in Las Vegas while he was in Connecticut. She replied that the plan was hers, and as usual, was aggressive. It wasn't his fault at all.

He then told her that he was going to resign.

Julie got really pissed. She felt that he had saved her. If it weren't for him, she'd be lying in the morgue in Vegas, with a toe tag. If he resigned, she would hunt him down, and shoot him in the crotch. She made him promise that he wouldn't resign. Then she made him promise again.

Julie was not a quick healer. Two weeks spread to three, and then four, before the man in Las Vegas would give her the green light to go home.

Rich had acquiesced to Julie's threat of shooting him in the crotch, and had not resigned. He wanted to talk with her before he did the deed.

Rich found that the relationship had gotten closer, when Julie had been shot.

When he thought he was going to lose her, he realized how much she meant to him. He didn't think he was in love with her. He just felt that she was like an appendage to his body. It was as if the appendage was cut off, since she wasn't with him.

The meeting with Spence finally came, five days after Rich came home. It would be almost four weeks before Julie joined them.

The debriefing was thorough. As usual, there was no clue left for the police.

The federal government became involved, and the bickering in congress as to what to do, and how many committees to convene, slowed the investigations even more. Metropolitan police in Las Vegas and the Nevada state police, were, like previous police agencies, completely stymied. They followed every lead, and nothing panned out.

All that was said was that true professionals must have planned the assassination, as the leads were not leading to any solutions. They were looking for a man and a woman. It is believed that the women is seriously wounded, or dead.

There was one question that Spence asked. "Rich, we both know that things can go wrong, no matter how well that things are planned. I think you once told me that the reason that the SEALs worked so well was that every contingency was planned for, but once the first shot is fired, the plans all go to hell. What part of the plans went to hell? What contingency wasn't planned against?"

"Spence the plan was excellent. Julie put the plan together, but I O.K.'d it. The contingency that wasn't planned for was plain clothes security, in force, in addition to uniformed security. It was totally my fault.

Spence, if you believe that my error in judgment warrants it, I am totally prepared to offer you my resignation."

"Rich, I can understand how you feel. I've had partners wounded; I've had partners killed. We live in a world of conflict. We try to eliminate the bad guys, but sometimes, instead, we lose a good guy. Thank God in this case, no one was lost, except for the police officer. You grew up the same way that I did. Although our generations may be different, we hold women in high esteem. When one gets hurt in doing her duty, we blame ourselves. There is plenty of blame to go around. Both of you are culpable. If I hear one more word about resignation, I will take the letter, attach it to a baseball bat, and shove it up your ass! Do you understand?"

"Yes, but…."

"Enough! No buts!!! There is a briefcase next to my desk for you. I'll hold Julie's until I can give it to her personally. I may deduct the bill for her medical costs directly from her part."

"But Spence."

"I'm only kidding, I'm not an asshole. Look, take a few more days. Everyone will understand, especially me. If I need you, I'll call you. Come back when you get bored."

"Thanks, Spence, I'll probably be bored by tomorrow. However, I think I may go home to Boston, and visit my family."

"Good, now get out of here."

Rich got out of there; as a matter of fact, he went all the way to Boston.

He was born in south Boston, one of three boys, to an Irish-American family.

His mother and father never left Southie, as it was called. His two older brothers couldn't wait to get out, and went away to college. Timothy went to Dartmouth, in New Hampshire, and then on to Yale Law school. He was now a partner in a large Chicago law firm. Patrick went to Northeastern in Boston, and lived at the dorm. He went to Jefferson Medical College in Philadelphia, spent his residency at George Washington University hospital, and was now an emergency center physician in Atlanta.

Rich was the baby. When he was seventeen, his father became very ill. In order to make sure that there was enough food on the table, Rich left home, and joined the navy. He was an accomplished swimmer in high school, so when he told his swim coach that he was going in to the navy, his coach called an old buddy, and once Rich finished boot camp, the coach arranged for Rich to have an audition to some outfit called the SEALs.

When Rich showed up, he was the smallest of all the people there. Some of the larger guys started to rib him, and told him that he'd never qualify to pass the swim portion of the test. He won every heat. In another test, he spent the longest time of all of them sitting on the bottom of the pool, holding his breath.

It would be fair to say that the relationship between the coach and his buddy made it possible for Rich to audition, but it was one hundred per cent Rich that made it through the rest of the training and to the day that the Trident, signifying that he was a SEAL, was pinned to his chest. Shortly after graduation, he was sent to Vietnam. It was during his second tour that the rest of his platoon was lost, and he ended up at the pink palace on the hill.

As he drove down the street where his parents lived when he was born, he remembered how it was when he was younger, and was glad that he left when he did.

His mother opened the door, and he enveloped her in his arms. His father was sitting in his favorite chair, and looked much more frail than Rich remembered. The questions from the both of them, as to what was going on in Hartford, did he have a young lady, etc. went on for the two days that he stayed with them . He had nothing new to tell them.

Rich came back to Hartford the day before Julie was coming home. She called him and gave the flight number and time she was due to arrive.

Rich was standing outside the jetway when she walked out, pulling a rolling bag. She looked like dynamite, not like someone who had a foreign body enter and leave her.

She greeted Rich with a tight hug, and he returned it. He grabbed her bag, and they walked towards the garage.

"How do you, feel? How was the flight? Do you have any pain?"

"Hey, I'm fine. The trip was good. Connections were fine. No, I don't hurt.

I just can't believe how well they treated me. There was someone in my room twenty-four hours a day. Did you know that the Doctor was the chief of surgery at one of the biggest hospitals in Vegas? One of the people who stayed with me, told me. What's going on here in Hartford?"

"Well, I took a couple of days, and went to Boston see my mother and father. Everything else has been on hold. I was in touch with the General Agents, and the two G.M.s when I got back, while I was at home. I imagine that you'll have light duty for a while. Spence told everyone that we were in a car accident, so back it up. By the way, I missed the hell out of you."

"Well. The doc said that I should take it easy, and not exercise for a while, so I guess that you don't have any worries about my jumping your bones."

"Gee, that's too bad, because I'd probably enjoy it."

"You mean…?"

"No, the rules haven't changed. Just because I missed you doesn't mean that I've changed the rules."

Rich drove Julie to her house, helped her in with her luggage, and made sure the house was comfortable for her.

They talked about what to do about dinner, and decided that Rich would bring in Chinese. They ate, talked about nothing for about an hour, and Rich left with Julie's promise that she would call immediately if there were any problems.

When he got home, Rich called Spence, and gave him the news that Julie was home. Of course, Spence already knew. He probably could have told Rich what they had for dinner.

chapter 18

NEW YORK

F.B.I. special agent Donald Minnock rolled out of bed when the phone rang, and walked across the room. He never liked having the phone by the bed, as he wanted to be fully awake to take a phone call. He always had a pad of paper by the phone, along with a sharpened pencil.

"Don, its Harris Berlin."

"Hey Harris, how are the state police treating you?"

"Not too bad. Look, we've got a lead on the politician case. I know it's been a while, but something has happened. I called Leslie over at homeland security, and Bill Guess, at the capitol police, and gave them the information.

When we were searching the woods, a boy scout troop helped us look for clues. They decided to take their tenderfoot scouts for a walk through the area, to show the new guys what the old guys had done.

One of the tenderfeet, if that's what you call them, saw a piece of black neoprene sticking out of the ground. He called over the scoutmaster who called the sheriff in Altona. They dug up a shallow hole that contained a wet suit, wrapped around a rifle that shoots darts.

Bill Guess can't make it up here later today, but Leslie can. Can you meet us in Albany, at the federal building at 1:00 p.m.?"

"I'll be there, Harris, but I'll need it to be at 2:00 p.m. I'm testifying on a case this morning. As a matter of fact, you beat my alarm clock to the punch."

"Sorry, old buddy, I tried to let you sleep. I called the others first. Two o'clock is fine. See you at the conference room."

Don went downstairs, kissed his wife and little baby, and grabbed breakfast. He was excited. Maybe something will come of this after all. Absolutely nothing had come from the parachute, which he had sent to the lab in D.C. There were no skin cells, or DNA that could be found, and there were no markings or labels on the chute itself. It was the same type, however, that the military used.

After breakfast, he went upstairs, showered and changed, and put on the typical white shirt, dark suit, striped tie, and highly buffed shoes of an F. B. I. agent. He put on his shoulder holster under his jacket, checked that his safety was on, and put his weapon in his holster. He then went downstairs, kissed his family once more and went off to court, and his meeting afterwards.

Don kissed Leslie on the cheek, and shook hands with Harris. He took off his jacket, as did Harris. Leslie kept hers on.

Leslie spoke first. "O. K., what have we got?"

Harris replied, "It's all right here," and pointed to two evidence bags containing a wet suit in one and a rifle in the other.

"The Sheriff's guys knew what they were doing. They bagged the items as soon as they dug them up. They wore vinyl gloves, and sealed the bags immediately."

Don leaned over the table, and looked at the bags. "I'll have these sent to the lab in D.C. right away." He picked up the phone on the table, and called his office. He asked that they send a courier right away to the conference room .There was evidence that had to be delivered to the lab immediately.

"All right, what else do we do?" said Leslie. "Should we get some more people, and go over the area again? I thought we had searched everything in the area before. Who knows what else we missed?"

Don looked at Harris. "Where was this discovered in relation to the area we searched? Was it near the river?"

Harris answered, "No, as a matter of fact it was found near the road, which means that he or she had to walk away, with the rifle, from the river. I don't think the perp swam down the river, which means that there had to be a raft or a boat that came down the river. I think we ought to check the river again."

Don agreed, as did Leslie.

This time it was Harris who picked up the phone. He called his commanding officer, and explained the situation. He waited silently for about two minutes, then said, "Yes Sir, I understand," and hung up.

Harris turned to the other two, smiled, and said, "There will be a full dive team, as well as the auxiliary to the state police, and a national guard unit at the site tomorrow morning. They will search the Great Chazy River, and the riverbank, from an area by the cabin to the intersection of the river and the road, where they found the chute. Folks, we're back in business."

chapter 19

HARTFORD

Rich went into work the next day. He was greeted by Charlie at the desk. "Hey, Mr. Coburn, how are you doing? I heard that you were in an accident out West. How's Miss Lowe?"

"Thanks for asking, Charlie. I'm fine, just some bruises. Miss Lowe just came back yesterday. She was in the hospital for a period of time, but she's much better. She'll be on light duty for a while."

"If you see or talk to her, please give her my regards. She's a nice lady."

"Thanks, Charlie, I will."

The "how are you feeling," and "how's Julie," continued through most of the morning. It was nice to know that people cared, but it had reached the level of being a pain in the ass.

After giving Vivian the same answers he gave everyone else, he walked into Spence's office.

Spence looked genuinely pleased to see him. "Now you look like your old self. I guess that your ride to Boston, and the fact that Julie is back in town, has brought you to life. I've got something to share with you. Please close the door."

Spence told Rich what was going on in upstate New York. He then asked,

"Can they get anything off the wet suit, or from the rifle?"

"I was fully clothed under the wet suit, so there was nothing they can get off of the suit itself. I didn't wear a hood, so there's no connection there. I wore sneakers with no pattern on the sole, and I wore them home. I wore vinyl gloves, which I stuffed into my pants pocket when I took off the suit. The shirt and pants were disposed of, including the gloves, back here, when I got rid of the jeep.

The rifle had no serial number because your people sent it to me that way, and again, I wore vinyl gloves, so there won't be fingerprints. Even when I brought the rifle up to my face, in order to aim the rifle, I wiped it off afterwards. Can you think of anything else?"

"Rich, I think you thought of everything. I won't worry until they tell me something else, which I don't think will happen."

"When do you think Julie will be back? How is she mentally? Being shot makes you realize how vulnerable you are. Some people have their mind screwed up permanently after it happens."

"I'm no psychiatrist, but I think Julie is too strong to have any permanent damage. She was a marine, and an F.B.I. agent, and she's seen a number of dead people. She seemed pretty normal last night, when I picked her up at the airport, but only time will tell. As far as when she'll be back, I don't know. If she's anything like she was when we left, she'll want to be back yesterday. If she asks, I'm going to recommend that she doesn't come back until next week. She needs her strength."

"Keep in touch with her. Let me know how she is. I'll call her today, in order to welcome her back. We've got to get you two back on the road with the G.A.'s."

Rich walked over to his office, and went through the how are you's with Tina. She gave him his stack of messages, and the get well wishes from everyone who called. Rich spent most of the day on the telephone calling them back.

He also called Julie.

"Hey, malingerer, how are you doing? I didn't want to call earlier, due to the time changes between Vegas and here. How did you sleep?"

"I woke up a couple of times, because there was no one in my room. I'm sure I'll get over that. Spence called a while ago, and was very nice. I told him I wanted to come back tomorrow, but he said to wait until next week. What do you think?"

"When I was in his office, I told him that I was going to

recommend that you wait until next week. I want you to get all of your strength back. I'm going to work you pretty hard, and I don't need any pantywaists."

"I've never been a pantywaist, and I'm not about to start being one. You can throw anything you want at me. I'll get it done!"

"Julie, I'm only kidding. Take it easy!"

"Gotcha, I knew you were kidding."

"What are you going to do for dinner tonight?"

"If you didn't ask, I was going to send out for a pizza. Now that you've asked, what ideas do you have?"

"Well, I'm certainly not going to cook. You've been under a doctor's care long enough, as it is. How about if I go over to Gianni's for ribs and corn?"

"Sounds good. How about seven?"

"Good. I'll be the guy with the flower in his buttonhole."

Rich called until five-thirty, which was only two thirty, on the coast. It was unbelievable how many people knew about the auto accident, and were concerned for Julie and him. The G.M's, both good marketers, called everyone to make sure that the G.A's didn't think that Rich and Julie dropped the ball, and that an auto accident had been the reason that the people from the home office didn't get back to them.

He called in the order to Gianni's, and drove to East Hartford to pick it up.

He then drove over to West Hartford, to Julie's house, and got there fifteen minutes early.

He rang the bell, and no one came to the door. He rang it again, and still there was no reaction. He waited, rang it a third time, and waited. If she didn't come to the door this time, he was going in anyway. She might have passed out. Then the door opened.

"You, sir, are early. Here I am trying to make myself presentable, and you won't give me the time to do it."

She looked more than presentable. The only word that came to his mind was delicious. What a beautiful woman! Her hair, which was in a pony tail the day before, flowed over her shoulders. Her silk blouse set off her eyes, and the slacks were just perfect, outlining her eloquent rear end.

"Julie, whatever look you were going for in your mind, as far as being presentable, you have succeeded. You are absolutely fantastic."

Julie, curtsied, and said, "Thank you, my hero with ribs. Please come in."

They ate the whole order of two racks of ribs. Julie went after the ribs like they were going out of style. The corn was a yellow blur, as it was consumed. Rich was happy that she had a good appetite.

Rich got up to help throw away the paper plates, and she reached around him to throw away the cups. They were face to face, two inches apart. Julie looked into Rich's eyes, leaned forward and kissed him. She had no idea whether he would kiss her back, or pull back, and fire her. She did what she felt she had to do.

Rich dropped the plates into the sink, put his arms around her, and kissed her back. Their tongues sought each other out, and he pulled her close.

Then he remembered her wounds, and released her.

"Julie, remember what the doctor said. I want to hold you, but I don't want to hurt you. Either physically, or mentally."

"I understand, Rich, but I'm not made of glass, I won't break."

"I'm not worried about you breaking, just cracking."

The mood was broken, at least for now.

"Rich, I know your rules. If you want to fire me for that kiss, do it. You were all I thought about for the four weeks I spent in the safe house. I dreamed about you every night, I thought about you every morning. You were the reason I recovered. I've never felt this way about any other man. If we can't work together in the future, I can live with that. I just can't live without you."

"Julie, when I carried you out of the Sands, my heart was broken. I thought I lost you. My life was given back to me when the doctor said that he thought you'd be all right. For four weeks you've been the only important thought that I've had. When I saw you at the airport yesterday, I couldn't believe it. My reason for living had returned to me. I have never felt this way about any other woman. I know that we are meant for each other. If I have to, I'll give up everything for you. I love what I do, but I think I love you more. I say I think, because I don't know what love is. I want to make love with you, but we can't, not until the doctor says so. My rules can go to hell. Maybe the easiest thing to do is work separately.

Rich and Julie spent the night in Julie's bed, in each other's arms, and followed the doctor's orders.

Rich spent the rest of the days of the week contacting General Managers, and General Agents. He spent the rest of the nights with Julie, alternating their houses for dinner, and for sleeping. It was extremely difficult to follow the doctor's orders, but they did.

chapter 20

NEW YORK

Don Minnock called Harris Berlin three days after they had met at the Federal building..

"Harris, Don Minnock, how are you doing?"

"I'll know better after you tell me why you called."

"Well, I've got good news, and I've got some not so good news. The lab has gone over the wet suit inside and outside, and found nothing. That's the not- so-good news. The serial number was removed from the rifle, but an acid wash brought it back. We've started to go after the serial number with the manufacturer, and hope to find where it was sold, and to whom. I haven't called Leslie or Bill yet, but I'm planning on it, when I hang up."

"Thanks for calling me, Don. I'll wait to see what's come up. Maybe we caught a break."

"I'll get back to you as soon as I hear anything."

chapter 21

HARTFORD

Spence called Rich into his office.

"I just heard from one of our intel people at the bureau. They were successful in bringing out the serial number on the rifle. The manufacturer is foreign, so I don't know how successful the bureau will be in getting information, and we may be able to suppress it at the source, anyway. Logistics tells me that the rifle was purchased in Bangladesh, and it'll take years to trace it. I share whatever I can with you on your cases, so I wanted to bring you up to date."

"Thanks, Spence, I appreciate it."

"How's Julie doing? Will she be back on Monday?"

"She is bored, and can't wait to get back to work. There's no reason I know of, that would keep her from being here on Monday."

"Good, you can use her proclivity in writing letters, and charming the General Agents. Where are you going next time?"

"The most lucrative areas are in California, since they have the most G. A.'s.

However, we can go just about anywhere."

"Can you think of any way that we can clone the two of you? There really is no way that the two of you can see every G.A."

"I've been thinking about that a lot. Either Julie and I can go around the country to each of our sales offices, or someone from each office can come to a central location, from each office. Then we can conduct a training session on how to deal with G.A.'s.

Each office would have an individual who specializes in General Agents. That individual is compensated based on how much business comes from the G.A.'s. In the beginning you give them a base salary that decreases over time. This gives them the incentive to go out and get more business.

In that way, the support for the G.A. is local, and the sales office can be there for the G.A."

"I like it, Rich. Why don't you flesh out a budget for the training session, and a salary level that is consistent throughout the country, and an approximate cost of the program. I'll kick it upstairs, and see if we can get the funding."

Rich spent the rest of the day working on the training budget with Tina. She worked on hotel and transportation costs, and he worked on the training materials, and the costs associated with them.

Rich drove home at the end of the day, looking forward to seeing Julie. They had spent last night at his house, so she would be waiting for him when he got home.

Last night Julie had brought up the idea of them moving in together. They could save one of the lease payments each month, and they could play house.

Rich reminded her that they no longer had to worry about lease payments, and that they were playing house now. They had to keep up appearances, and keep their relationship, as it was, professional as far as anyone else was concerned.

He pulled into the driveway, and looked up at the living room window. Julie was waving to him, like a little girl.

He ran up the stairs, and the door opened magically. He went in, kicked the door shut behind him, and Julie jumped into his arms. If he held her any tighter, he'd be on the other side of her. Then he realized that he might be hurting her, so he let go.

She grabbed him tighter, and said, "I called the doctor, told him that I was feeling wonderful, and asked him if I could exercise. He said that my body would tell me when to stop. I can't stop until I start. Let's go to bed!"

"Julie, there is nothing that I would like more than to make love to you. I'm pretty sure that I'm in love with you, and that's the reason why. When you were shot, and I thought you were going to die, I died inside. I can't let that happen. I've got a job to do, and you've got a job to do. We can't do that job properly if we become further involved. Unless either one of us resigns, then it isn't going to happen. The only other alternative is to tell Spence that we can't work together, and I can guarantee he'll want to know why."

"I know you're right. I just wanted my cake, and sex too. Can we put a time limit on it? Like one of us has to resign in six months, or something like that time period?

"Why don't we just go along the way it is? Aside from both of us being horny, it's the only way I can see us continuing."

"Rich, you're the only man that I've ever offered myself to, on a platter, and you turned me down. You know that can give a girl a complex."

"O.K., gorgeous, since we understand each other, let's have dinner, and find out some more about you. It's something I've wanted to do, and since we have nothing to do tonight, I'd like to just sit and talk. Is that O.K.?"

"Fine, but I'm not going to tell you about the first time I got laid, or things like that."

The sexual tension dissipated over dinner, and they talked about their individual day. After cleaning up from their meal, they went in to the living room, and sat down, each with a glass of California wine in their hands.

Julie looked at Rich, and asked, "Well, what do you want to know?"

"Sweetheart, all I know about your background is that you lived in Newton, with your parents, who were domestics for a Doctor's family. I know that you were in the Marine Corps, and that you were with the F.B.I. as an agent. I was told that you left the bureau after a disagreement with your supervisor. That's all I know about your background before I met you."

"Here we go, boss. The autobiography of Julia Marina Lowe, with added features.

My parents came to the United States from Sarajevo, which was Yugoslavia at the time, and is now Bosnia. They came to my uncle's house in the west end of Boston. Shortly thereafter, I was born, and they moved to Dorchester. My father found a job as a chauffeur for a doctor in Newton. He was a renowned cardiac surgeon, and very wealthy. After a couple of months, the doctor asked my father if my mother and I would like to move into the house. She could be a maid and as well, a nanny for their two children, and my father could be a chauffeur, and all around handyman. It worked out to be a perfect situation. I was brought up as a member of the family. The doctor paid my tuition, and I went to Sacred Heart with the other girls in the family, even though I wasn't catholic.

When I was about to graduate high school, Doc asked me where I wanted to go to college. I had a good business head, and told him that I wanted to go to Bentley, in Waltham, and major in accounting. His reaction was that I could go wherever I wanted, and that he would pay for it. He was the most generous man that I had ever met.

During my fourth year at Bentley, my father and mother were killed by a drunk driver on Commonwealth Avenue, in Boston. The doctor, upon hearing the news, had a heart attack, and died on the way to the hospital. It was the worst time in my life.

I graduated magna cum laude from Bentley, and decided to go to New York to work. While I was in the city one night, three men grabbed me, put me in a car, drove me to Harlem, and attacked me, repeatedly. I couldn't fight back; I didn't know what to do.

Three days later, after my hospital recuperation, I joined the marines. No one was ever going to take advantage of me again.

I went through officer's candidate school, and with my degree in accounting, was assigned to lead a section in the payroll department.

So there I was, at the end of my hitch, with a degree in accounting, enough knowledge to not only protect myself, but enough to kill guys a lot bigger than me, and no place to go.

At that time, in order to be an agent, you had to have an accounting degree, or a law degree. Today, it's different. I applied, took the exams, and went to Quantico for training. Having been there with the marines, it was like going home again.

I was assigned to cases that had action in the streets. I wanted to be where the action was, and due to my background, they gave it to me. I established relationships with informers in the gang areas, and there were some real good kids, who got the wrong end of the stick. The liberal laws had the victims suffering instead of the perpetrators. I had a meeting with an informer early one evening. When I got to his apartment, I heard screaming. I, along with my partner, knocked down the door. He was buggering a young kid who couldn't have been more than ten. I pulled the bastard off the kid, and the cocksucker swung at me. I shot him in the head. The kid ran out the door, and my partner chased him. The kid got away.

My partner and I put together a story that the informer swung at me. However, he was unarmed, and I didn't have a cold piece. My supervisor gave me a ration of shit about how the perp had rights. I told him to take his rights and jam them up his ass. The bureau and I agreed to separate.

I was working as an accountant for a major auto company, when Ben found me. Now you know all about me."

"Wow! you're a tough broad. Only kidding, Julie. You've had quite a different life, with a lot of disappointments, and tragedies. Not only am I proud to love you, I'm proud to know you.

It had taken them almost three hours to have dinner, and have Julie tell her story. They talked for about another hour, and went to bed.

In the past, Julie always undressed in the bathroom. Tonight she undressed in the bedroom, in front of Rich's appreciating eyes. If he wouldn't come around one way, she decided to try another. She knew she had an absolutely fantastic body. She went to bed without a night gown. Rich spent the night with pain in his scrotum.

Julie was welcomed by everyone, when she walked into the department on Monday. Everyone was concerned, and it showed.

Spence came out of his office, and walked over to Julie. "Hey, crash, how are you doing?"

"I can't wait to get back to work, Spence. I was going bonkers at home."

Well, Rich and I were talking about some things that the two of you can do. Once you get your sea legs back, pick up Rich, and come on over to my office. Glad to have you back. The team wasn't the same without you."

"Thanks, Spence, I'll be over shortly.

"Julie stopped by Rich's office, said, "we have a royal command performance in Spence's office to talk about what you two have spoken about. Want to give me a hint?"

"Do you mean the training program?"

"I don't know, do I?"

"Wise guy. The only thing that we talked about, that you weren't already a part of, was the training program. It's not complicated. I'll let Spence give you his perception of it."

Julie walked over to Spence's office, followed closely by Rich. They walked in to the office, and closed the door behind them.

Spence picked up the brief case that was remaining from the Las Vegas operation, and gave it to Julie. "I believe this is yours, Julie. I told Rich that I was going to subtract the cost of your medical care from it, but then you would have to pay me. Obviously I'm only kidding, we'll take it out of your next bonus. I'm so glad that everything worked out medically for you."

Spence then went over the training program idea, regarding the General Agents. He also outlined the budget, and how much it would cut out of the budget sending Rich and Julie all over the country.

"I haven't received approval yet, but I want to get going on the program, and start to increase the bottom line, using increasing sales from the G.A.'s. I'd like you two to put together a training program, as soon as possible. Rich, I know you've been working on it, and now with Julie back, we can get more planning done, faster. I'd like to kick off the training module within three weeks. Of course, if we don't get approval, the whole thing is moot."

Rich and Julie went back to their offices, and started to put an outline together for the training program, itself. Meanwhile Tina got on the phone with the travel department to find the most centralized city to bring people into, from all of the offices.

Spence will have to set up a conference call to all of the Sales offices, as well as the General Managers, in order to break out the new national program, once the budget has been approved.

Rich and Julie worked into the early evening on the outline of the training module. When they were both weary, and bleary-eyed, they decided to go to dinner, before going home. Neither one wanted to go through a sit down dinner at a nice restaurant, so they ordered a pizza, and picked it up on the way home.

After finishing the pizza, they each poured a glass of wine, their third of the evening, and sat down to watch the news.

They were absolutely amazed when the news story came on that a suspect had been arrested in the murder of the deputy commissioner of police in San Francisco. It was just a headline, and the story wasn't fleshed out. Both of them couldn't wait to speak with Spence, in the morning.

They continued to watch the news. Rich was about to say that he was going to go to bed, and looked over at Julie. It had been a big day. She was fast asleep. Rich put a blanket over her, and went to bed.

The phone rang at 6:45 a.m. It was Spence.

"Rich, Spence. I know that you get up early, so I hope that I didn't disturb your breakfast.

"Not at all, what's happening, Spence?"

"I'm on a secured line. Did you see the story about San Francisco?"

"Just as a headline. I was going to stop by your office when I got in."

"They've got some poor guy who is claiming innocence, as a suspect.

He's a student at the University of San Francisco, who's had run-ins with the law in the past. I've spoken to our people at intel, and they say that there is no way that this guy will go beyond being a suspect. He doesn't even look like the guy on the video. I just wanted to bring you up to date. I think that the San Francisco police want the people there to believe that they are still working hard to find the killer, when they aren't really doing much at all."

"Thanks for calling, Spence. I appreciate the update."

"No problem. I'll see you when you get in. Say hi to Julie for me. See ya."

Rich called Julie, right away. She had gone home to shower, and change.

"Julie, I just heard from Spence. We were talking about the situation in San Francisco, and we were ending the call. He said, 'I'll see you when you get in' and then said, 'say hi to Julie for me.' I swear to God that he knows when I fart. I really think he knows about us."

"If he knows, he knows. There's nothing we can do about it. Meanwhile, what's going on in San Francisco?"

Rich told her what Spence had said, and assured her that there was nothing to worry about.

She said that she was just about to leave, and she'd see him at the office.

He pulled in next to her in the parking lot, and she was still sitting in her car. He walked over to the car, and asked if she was all right. She told him that she had just pulled in, and saw him turn in to the lot. She figured that they could take the elevator together, and if no one was in the elevator with them, she could give him a good morning kiss.

After saying "good morning" to Charlie, they walked over to the elevator, and Julie put in her card. The door closed, and she hit the stop button. She turned to Rich, put her arms around him, and kissed him. He realized that she didn't have her lipstick on, because she didn't want to smear her face. He pulled out the stop button, and the elevator started to rise.

When they got to their offices Tina came over and told them that Spence wanted to see them right away.

They walked over to Spence, who greeted them with a smile. "The training program has been approved. Now we've got to set up conference calls, travel arrangements, and all the rest. Have you got an outline module set up for the training?"

"We worked on it until O dark thirty last night. I think it's ready to be fleshed out. Do you have any location that you favor, or should we let the travel department tell us where we should go."

"I don't have any favorites, why don't you let them tell you where to go."

Julie, smiled, and said, "People have been telling me where to go for years."

"Well, let's get hopping on this. I've got to call property and casualty, and get their feeling on who they want to talk to their G.M.'s, We also have to call every sales office, tell them the plan, and have them let us know who is going to represent the office at the training session. Use Vivian, and Linda, as well as Tina, to get as much done as possible. Have fun, guys. Keep me in the loop."

The travel department picked Kansas City, Missouri for the training session.

According to them it offered a central location, good airline connections, and excellent prices for hotels and food. The Marriott Downtown was large enough for their meetings. Now it was up to the administrative assistants to book all the airline tickets, as soon as they had the names of the attendees.

The session would allow for everyone to come in the night before, then have two and a half days of training, everyone leaving on the afternoon of the third day.

Spence spoke with all of the G.M.'s, Rich spoke with all of the sales office managers, and the different parts of the training session were put together.

Two weeks later, all of the representatives of the different sales offices, as well as Julie and Rich, met in Kansas City for the training session. The General Managers had audio of the whole meeting, as they couldn't take the time out of the field. All of the exhibits had been sent to them prior to the meeting. The managers of the sales offices would be briefed by their representatives.

The trip for Julie and Rich was different. They made sure that their rooms were not adjoining. They were only together when business required it. They didn't even have meals together. But accidentally one morning they both showed up at the workout room, at the same time. Considering how they felt about each other, they didn't want anyone else to pick up any vibrations, between them.

Rich and Julie came into the office the Monday after the meeting. Spence called them in and congratulated them on having a great training session. The platitudes from the field had reached the company president, and he had called Spence to congratulate him, and asked that the congratulations be passed on to Rich and Julie.

Being the wiseass that she is, Julie quipped "if he feels that good about it, I won't turn down a raise," and laughed.

Spence laughed along with her, and replied, "From what I understand, there will be another source of income coming up soon."

Rich immediately brightened up. "Where, when, and who. Both of us, or just one, and which one?"

Spence got up, walked over and shut his door. "I have no information as of yet. All I can tell you is that under normal circumstances, I get a call from the intelligence people asking if our operations people, that's the two of you, are available. That could be a day in advance, three days in advance, or a week in advance. Intel then puts the info necessary for an operation together, and sends it to me. In turn, I give it to you. You put an operation together from your point of view, the action portion, we get the logistics together, and you put your ass on the line.

I received a call earlier this morning, asking if my operations people were available. I answered in the affirmative. As I said, I have no idea when, or if, I will receive another call."

Rich was excited. "Spence, as you know, I enjoy the insurance business, immensely. However, it doesn't have the risk factors that go along with my other vocation. I need the adrenalin rush. I know that Julie feels the same way. We are ready, whenever the call comes, day or night."

"Take it easy, Captain Marvel; the reason you're here is what you just said. It's the adrenalin rush, but that only lasts as long as you do the job right, and stay alive. You're the one who says that it's all in the details. You are a great team, but you are also excellent as singles. You make me proud. Let's just do our insurance job right now, until I get the call."

As they walked back to their offices, Julie said very quietly, "Should I change my hair color, or just be my natural, beautiful self?"

"Well, when you were a redhead, you really turned me on. The blonde didn't do much for me. In all reality, as long as you wear a tight sweater, I don't give a shit if you're bald."

"You sexist bastard."

"Why am I sexist? Because you've got a nice body, and I appreciate it."

"If you really appreciated it, you'd be getting some. You're the one who is always saying no."

"I think that we've spent enough time on that subject. This is not the place to discuss it further."

Both Rich and Julie spent the next two days calling around the country, talking with those individuals who attended the training session. They also spoke with the managers of the sales offices, and General Managers. They called those General Agents that they had called on previously and told them about how they now had local service, and tried to make the sale.

On Thursday morning they walked into the office five minutes apart. They made sure that one or the other left five minutes earlier in order that they didn't arrive together, even though they spent the previous night together.

Julie was winning her argument. Even though they had not consummated their relationship, their closeness and sleeping together was winning Rich over to Julie's side of the discussion.

As they got to their desks, Tina told both of them that Spence wanted to see them. They gave each other a glance, and walked a little faster to Spence's office.

They walked in, and shut the door behind them.

Spence welcomed them, and motioned them into two chairs, on either side of his desk. "I just received the call. The reason, I am told, that it took so long to come back to me after the first call, is that this operation is different. It involves taking out two targets, in two locations, simultaneously. You will have to split up, and put together your own plans. You will execute individually, but it has to happen at approximately the same time. You can choose which one you want.

The people we are after are running an across the border underground railroad for illegal aliens from the Mideast. The illegals go into Canada with student visas, or visitors' visas. They then go across the border from Abercorn, Quebec, into Richford, Vermont on the property of the Richford Country club. Four members of the brothers of Islam were brought through last month. These people are suspected of having blown up two military recruiting offices, and killing three Marines. Also, they are part of the cell in Montpelier that we are keeping tabs on. We expect to move on them through the F.B.I. in the near future.

This operation will be different as one end of the railroad is in a foreign country.

What we want to do is hit both ends of the trail at as close to a common time as possible. That will give us the opportunity to stop the line at both ends, in order that they don't have one end still going, and just add the other end quickly.

Both of these locations are in the middle of nowhere. Vehicles obviously would be noticed going into the area. For example, the last census showed that there were only 366 people in Abercon, most of whom only spoke French. Unknown vehicles would be spotted right away. There is a border crossing station on the Vermont side. It's a natural for both of you to jump in, since both of you are skydivers, and Rich has also done it in combat. The problem I see, is that it will have to be a low jump. The closest airport is Montreal, but we don't want to file a flight plan over international borders. Whoever is going to Canada has to worry about the radars picking up a cross-border flight.

I assume that you will ask for a chopper pickup, and we can get both of you on the same flight.

Julie, I'm afraid that your Marine Corps experience as an accounting supervisor didn't give you much experience in the forest, or jungle, but I know that you can use weapons, no matter what the terrain.

The other thing that makes this different is that each location not only has our target living there, but they are surrounded by hangers on, who hate us. Don't worry about collateral damage. The more of these creeps we take out now, the better humanity will be later.

I should have the intel report in my hands this afternoon. I'll give it to you as soon as I receive it. Now who wants to go where?"

Rich spoke first. "I'll take Canada. I can glide further with a military chute, and might even be able to jump inside the U.S. border, if the location is close enough. We'll both be able to jump out of the same aircraft, if the locations are that close, so we'll make it a little bigger plane than the last time."

Julie looked at him, and said, "What last time? You've done this before?"

"Yes I have. I'll give you the benefit of my experiences when we go over the intel sheets. Spence, we'll need an extra day for planning, and logistics if we're going to do this together.

Spence shook his head up and down, "No problem. My understanding is that the targets are getting ready for a transfer this Sunday.

Julie looked back and forth from Spence to Rich. "I guess that leaves me in Vermont. Should I pack my skis?"

Spence stood up. "I'll call you as soon as I have the intel reports."

The meeting was over.

Rich was explaining to Tina that he and Julie were going to be out the rest of the week, as they were going to visit another insurance company up in Boston, for a meeting. Julie walked out, and embellished the explanation with how she was going shopping at Nordstrom's.

The call from Spence came three hours later. Intel had delivered earlier than expected. Both Julie and Rich took their individual intel reports, and took off early in order to start their preparation for the mission.

Rich verified that Julie had her jump suit, boots, helmet, goggles, and everything else needed to make the jump. He knew that they would get the logistic bags when they got to the airport, but she would want those items that she had used before, and had broken in.

They went through the intel sheets individually, and then jointly. Then they put together their plans the same way. They reviewed them, and gave suggestions to each other. Rich went over the discarding of their equipment and clothing, repeatedly. As far as he was concerned, these were the details that could get them caught later. The other details were what could get them killed during the mission.

They called Spence and he returned their call on a secured line in order to get their list for logistics.

Rich requested that the flight north be ready to go at 4:00 a.m. He hoped to jump just as the sun came up, and approach from the east, with the sun at his back, especially where it would be a low jump. That way the sun would be in the eyes of anyone looking up in the sky, but Julie and he would have the visibility to jump.

They used the next day to study the demographics of the area, and go over maps surrounding the locations of the targets. Even though there were few ways out, they planned an alternative egress from their respective areas.

Julie left Rich's house late in the afternoon, in order to get her clothes ready for the flight, and to get to bed early. She had a feeling that she wouldn't be getting much sleep over the next couple of days.

Rich said that he'd pick her up at 3:00 a.m. and drive directly to the civilian air terminal at Bradley field. She was to be dressed to fly. The chutes would be waiting.

The names of the targets were Hadma Ibrahim in Canada, and Mohammed Anouyi in Vermont. Rich and Julie had intel on both of them. They were both Saudis who came on student visas to Canada, and then crossed into the U. S. Both crossed back and forth, through the forest, with impunity.

Rich picked up Julie exactly on time. They drove to the airport in almost perfect silence, thinking about what was going to happen during the rest of their day.

As they turned into the terminal, Rich saw an unmarked C-47, the military version of the DC-3. It actually was overkill for two jumpers, but it was going to be easier to get out of, than his last jump was. Julie was used to jumping through a door, so it would be easier for her.

They walked into the terminal, and there were two men, in flight gear, sitting in the lounge. Both were about six feet and very trim. They each had a jump bag with a number one on one of them, and the number two on the other. One of the men walked over to them. "Hi, I'm from the company, are you Rich?"

Rich smiled impishly. "I'm pretty comfortable, but I wouldn't say I was Rich. Yes, my name is Rich, and the pretty young lady is Julie."

"Good, we're here to take you flying. Bag number one contains what Julie asked for, and bag number two is yours. We know that you want to get to the jump zones at sunrise, and approach from the east. Sounds like you've got a military background. Let's get going."

Modern aircraft have nose wheels, whereas, the C-47 has just a tail wheel, as well as the main landing gear. It also has a door about two thirds of the way back along the fuselage. This door is how they all entered the aircraft, and how Rich and Julie would jump out, when the time came.

The pilots entered the cockpit, went through their checklist, and revved the two engines. The plane rolled to the end of the runway, received clearance, and started to taxi. As they picked up speed, the tail rose, and at take off speed, they rotated and were in the air.

The co-pilot came back, and said that the first jumper would be Julie, and that he would come back to open the door for her. They would be jumping from five hundred feet. Julie should wait until she reached the door to hook her jump bag on to her clip. The door would be left open for Rich. However after they dropped Julie, they then would make a large circle in order to approach from the east once again, and drop Rich.

Before they knew it, the co-pilot was back, and indicated that they should follow him.

Julie stood in the doorway, and looked down. She had never jumped from such a low altitude. Her stomach was in her throat. The co-pilot told her that as soon as the green light was on, she should throw her bag out the door, and follow it immediately. The light came on, and Julie was out the door.

Rich stepped into the doorway, as the plane banked to the left, and made a large circle. The circle became an oval, and when it started to go west, with the sun behind the plane, the light turned green, and Rich stepped into the void.

Both Rich and Julie waited just a few seconds before they pulled their D-rings and floated to earth. In both cases their jump bags hit the tree tops a second before they did. Their helmets, face masks, suit and gloves kept them from being seriously cut, as they fell through the branches. Each of them hit the ground, rolled, and stood up.

chapter 22

VERMONT

Julie wrapped her parachute, unclipped the jump bag from her leg, and took stock of where she was. The forest was very quiet, and the umbrella of leaves above made it darker than it was above the forest. She scooped out a hole at the base of a tree, took off her mask, gloves, and helmet, which she added to the chute already in the hole, and covered it up. She then spread the pine needles onto the top of the hole. She opened the bag, took out the compass, and put it next to her watch, on her left arm. She then attached the GPS to a short lanyard on her left hip. Putting on her vest, she attached two grenades, her k-bar, and extra clips of ammunition to it. The holster, and the glock, with the suppressor, went on her belt. She then pulled out the heaviest piece, a knapsack. Inside was a MAC-11 machine pistol and two mags. She left the Mac-11 and the C-4 and detonator in the bag. There was also a small radio transceiver in the bottom of the bag.

Having had the experience in the past, Rich acted more quickly in rolling up his chute, taking the protective items off, and burying them. He opened up his jump bag, and removed all of the items that Julie had removed from her bag. However, he removed the MAC-11, put a sling on it, and put it across his chest and shoulder. He put duct tape on the clips reversing one so that he could load the mags into the weapons quickly. He also left the C-4 and detonators in the knapsack with a small radio transceiver.

Both Julie and Rich turned on their GPS's which already had the coordinates of their individual objectives programmed into them. Julie's target was about eight hundred yards or a little less than a half of a mile from her location. Rich, on the other hand, was, according to his GPS, over twenty-five hundred yards away.

Julie assumed that there would be some outlying security, and took her time going through the forest. Rich, however, knowing what to look for, moved more quickly through the forest.

Both arrived approximately at the same time within two hundred feet of the target locations.

All was very quiet surrounding the two locations. Julie saw a house with a porch, in the middle of nowhere, near a large shed, or barn like structure. A dirt road ran west from the back of the house. She thought to herself, who the hell puts a porch on a house in the woods? There was a dark skinned man, sitting in a chair, on the porch. He was fast asleep.

Rich observed a small cabin, also on a dirt road. According to his GPS, the dirt road led to a paved road which headed south. Next to the cabin was a large barn like structure, with one visible double door on the west side. There was absolutely no one observable at either structure. There was, however, smoke emanating from the chimney, giving a clue that there was someone inside. Both Julie and Rich circled their objectives at about two hundred feet away. Julie saw two more men outside of the barn. Both were sitting at a table, drinking something out of cups. They were talking loud enough for her to hear them, but she had no idea what they were saying.

Obviously there were at least three people that she had to worry about. From the picture she had of Mohammed Anouti, he wasn't one of the men.

As she continued her circle, she came back within sight of the porch. There was a fourth man on the porch. He was without a doubt berating the man she had seen before. There was a lot of loud talk, and hand and arm waving. It was all coming from Mohammed Anouti.

Julie attached the noise suppressor to her Glock. She took aim at Anouti, and pulled the trigger twice. He flew back against the porch wall, and slumped to the floor.

The dark skinned man had no idea as to what had happened. He turned to Anouti, at the same time that the right side of his head disappeared in a spray of blood.

The two men from the barn were just coming around the corner when Julie had taken out the second terrorist. She had risen to her full height, in order to get the shots off.

Both men opened fire at the same time that Julie dove to the ground. She pulled the trigger four times, while aiming in their direction. Neither the men nor Julie hit their target.

The men split up. One going behind the house, and the other into the woods trying to flank Julie.

Julie reached into her knapsack and retrieved the MAC-11 with its metal 32 round magazine. She wanted as much fire power as possible.

The man who went behind the house sneaked a peek to see where Julie was. She let loose with the machine pistol, taking off the wood at the corner of the house. She heard a scream, but didn't see if the target was actually hit, or had the shit scared out of him.

Julie started out to her right, in order to be able to see behind the house. All of a sudden there was noise behind her, and an arm came from behind, and wrapped around her throat. Julie reacted quickly, grabbing the arm, and turning to her left. She lowered her hip, and threw her attacker over her right side. When he hit the ground, Julie didn't hesitate. She aimed the pistol at his head and pulled the trigger, obliterating his face.

Now it was time to check out the guy behind the house. Julie continued to her right, so that she could see around the corner.

When she came around to the back of the house, while still under cover of some trees, she saw a body on the ground. Keeping under cover as well as possible she ran to the other side of the house and watched the body. He did not move. Julie came to within ten feet of him, and pulled the trigger on the MAC-11. One more terrorist had become a martyr for Allah.

She then walked around to the front of the house, and checked the bodies on the porch. Both were dead. She stood next to the window, and looked inside. The room she could see was sparsely furnished, and there were no people.

Rich taught her to always worry about the details. Standing to one side of the door, she turned the knob, opened the door, pulled the pin, and threw in a grenade. She then threw herself off the porch, and hunkered down. The concussion of the explosion caused the front wall of the house to bulge out, and fall. It exposed the back rooms, which were empty.

Julie ran in a broken field run to the door of the barn. The door had a board holding it shut. She went around to the other side, and found another door, similarly held closed by a board. She had no idea if anyone was inside. She was not about to open the door, and get a face full of lead.

She cut the block of C-4 in half, and placed a half on the door at one side of the barn. She pushed the detonator into the smaller block, and flipped on the receiver. She then walked around to the other door. She placed the other half of the block on the second door, inserted the detonator, and started walking towards the house.

When she had reached the other side of the house, she pressed the detonator switch, and the barn was demolished. Boards were falling for a good ten seconds. When she went back to the area where the barn had stood, there were no more bodies, just the carcass of a truck, and some mechanical tools.

chapter 23

CANADA

At the same time Julie was causing destruction in northern Vermont, Rich was reconnoitering his target in Canada. After he watched for fifteen minutes, the only thing moving was the smoke coming from the chimney.

The mission reminded him of the one in upper New York State. The major difference here was the security. There didn't seem to be any security whatsoever at this location. That meant one of two things: the targets were satisfied with their security, because Rich hadn't seen any, or they were so stupid, that they didn't think that they needed it. Rich believed that it was the former.

As he very slowly crawled on his belly towards the cabin, he saw the video line up in the tree. He had no idea how many video feeds that the enemy had, but he was sure that it was more than one. He didn't move, but the video camera did. It swept the area in a thirty degree arc. That meant that there were many more, in order to cover a complete circle. It also meant that these people were ahead of the game in security.

Since the camera was high in the tree, it covered an area above his on the ground, or much further out from where he was. He hoped that when he came close to the cabin, whoever was watching the video had missed him, due to the early hour. He doubted that there were many visitors, and the terrorists may be overconfident with their security. Intel somehow had missed the problem.

He inched towards the video feed. It took him fifteen minutes to go five feet.

While he was lying in wait, he remembered a time in Vietnam

that a poisonous snake had crawled over his legs. He was amazed that it didn't detect his body heat. Now he was moving a miniscule amount of distance while keeping alert for any movement from someone else.

He came upon the video line, at the base of the tree, and slowly removed the k-bar from its sheath on his left shoulder. He cut the line, and turned his body towards the cabin, to see if there was any reaction.

Within three minutes, the door to the cabin opened, and a man came out. He was carrying an AK-47. It was not Hadma Ibrahim. Rich waited until he entered the tree line, and came into the forest. He aimed the suppressed Glock at the man, and pulled the trigger twice. The man fell forward silently. Rich didn't move. He waited for at least three minutes. Another man came out the door. He also carried an AK-47. He was much more alert than the first man, and looked from left to right. He called out in what sounded like Arabic. He also entered the tree line, and started towards the area where rich was lying on the ground. He evidently saw either Rich or the first man as he raised his rifle. Before he could get off a shot Rich dropped him with two shots to the head.

Rich started to move backwards, on his belly. He went deeper into the forest. He came upon a fallen tree, and took shelter behind it, as he looked into the open door of the cabin. Nothing moved. There was no movement whatsoever at the outer building. Everything was quiet.

All of a sudden four men ran out of the double doors in the barn, all were firing wildly into the woods. Rich didn't move.

He took the two grenades off his vest, and placed them behind the tree.

The enemy was not disciplined, and yelled back and forth. They entered the woods, and separated, but they were very noisy. One walked right by Rich, and stopped five feet away. He started to turn, and would have tripped over Rich. Rich jumped up, reached around the man, grabbed his chin, pulled back, and cut his throat from ear to ear with his K-bar. The cut was deep enough to sever the man's vocal cords, and he didn't make a sound. Rich lowered him to the ground, and looked for the other three. The three remaining Arabs came together, at the body of the second terrorist who had entered the woods. Rich pulled the pin, let go of the spoon, counted to three, and threw the grenade into their midst. Three fewer Arabs.

Rich thought about the score. Six Arabs dead, none of whom were Hadma Ibrahim.

The terrorist obviously knew that he was under attack. The men had not returned, and the grenade was far from silent. Rich just didn't know where Ibrahim was hiding. He started off to his left, in order to circle the cabin, and see if there was a rear door. As he got to the far side of the house he heard a vehicle engine start. He ran through the woods to the side of the dirt road. A panel truck shot out of the barn, through the double doors, and onto the dirt road. He moved the MAC-11 into his hand, and aimed through the windshield. The truck was picking up speed as it came upon his position.

He led it perfectly, and pressed the trigger, holding it down. The thirty-two rounds entered through the windshield, and the driver's window and into the driver. The truck went on for another hundred yards, and came to a stop. Rich moved along the side of the road, in the woods, until he reached a point that made it possible for him to see into the cab. The driver was obviously not going to be a threat. Hadma Ibrahim was dead.

Rich went over to the truck, opened the door to the back, and found that the only person in the vehicle was the now dead Hadma Ibrahim.

Rich went back into the woods, and walked in a straight line to a point where he could observe the cabin door. Everything was quiet. He ran to the cabin, jinking back and forth, until he reached the front door. It continued to be quiet. He crouched down, and looked inside the doorway. The room was full of video screens; otherwise, it was empty. He went into the room, and through a doorway. The remaining two rooms were bedrooms, with two cots in each room, and clothes all over them.

Rich walked back out the front door, after surveying the area in front of the cabin. He pulled the pin, released the spoon, and threw his remaining grenade into the room full of electronics. He then ran to the barn.

Looking through the double doors Rich saw an empty barn. Off to the right side was an office, and a two room apartment. To the left was another room with four bunks.

Rich went into the office, and found a filing cabinet. The top drawer was full of paperwork. He removed the C-4 and the transceiver from the knapsack, and put the papers inside. There could be plenty of intel, or absolutely nothing in what he took, but he figured he'd let the intel people make that decision.

He placed the C-4 in the office, inserted the detonator, and walked out of the barn. He walked into the woods, passing the still smoldering remains of the cabin, and pressed the detonator button. The barn disintegrated.

As the barn was disintegrating, Julie pressed the button on her transceiver, signaling the helicopter that she was ready to be picked up.

Rich pressed his button a short time later.

Once both signals had been received, the chopper pilots lifted off, and the channel was opened so that there could be two-way communication between the pilots and the people on the ground, as well as directly between Julie and Rich.

It wouldn't have been good to have Julie call Rich while he was in a precarious position, or vice versa.

Rich called Julie, and they told each other what they had accomplished, and how things had gone. They then said that they would see each other shortly, and speak then.

Rich sat in the woods, and cleaned up around the fallen tree, in case he had left any clues as to who was there. He looked skyward, and waited for the chopper.

He could hear the whup - whup of the helicopter blades before he saw anything. Then his transceiver woke up. "Alpha, this is big daddy, Alpha, this is big daddy. How do you read?" Rich picked up the radio, and pressed the button: "Big Daddy, Big Daddy, this is Alpha. Reading you five by five; standing by at the coordinates; the landing zone is cold, repeat cold."

Then Rich saw the chopper. It came in low, flared out, and landed next to the remains of the cabin. He was aboard, and they were out of there in fifteen seconds, heading to Julie.

When he got aboard, he was given earphones, and could hear the call to Julie.

"Bravo, this is Big Daddy; Bravo this is Big Daddy, how do you read?"

"Big Daddy, Big Daddy, this is Bravo. Reading you five by five. LZ is cold, LZ is cold; standing by at coordinates. Bravo out." She sure sounded like a Marine.

The chopper was in, picked up Julie, and was on its way south, before they realized the pickup was over.

There wasn't much talking on the way back, due to the noise of the chopper, and the fact that all four people on the chopper could hear each other.

When the helicopter landed at Bradley, one of the pilots came back and asked both Rich and Julie for anything that they wanted to dispose of, in addition to all of their weapons.

They both turned everything over, and Rich laughed. "I can't believe that I covered discarding the items so vehemently with you, Julie, and all we had to do was give it to the company's pilot."

chapter 24

HARTFORD

The couple picked up Rich's car at VIP parking at the civilian air terminal, and headed into Hartford.

Rich picked up his phone, and put in a call to Spence. "Hi Spence, Rich, how are you?"

"Fine, Rich, how was the meeting?"

"Everything went well; we accomplished everything that we intended to accomplish, and both of us had a blast."

Spence chuckled. "Well, I'm sure that you guys must be worn out, with all of the meetings. Why don't you rest up, and tell me all about it on Monday."

"Sounds great; have a good weekend! Bye, Spence."

He turned towards Julie, "We don't have to go in until Monday. What do you say we go down to New York City tomorrow? We can drive down to New Haven and take the train in to the city."

"That sounds great. I'd say let's do something tonight, but since you're so old, you probably need to go to bed early."

"Actually, young lady, I am beat. It's been a long day for each of us. What time is good for you to leave?"

"How about 10:00 o'clock? That way we can get into the city for a late lunch."

Rich pulled into Julie's driveway. She leaned over and gave him a kiss goodnight, and he drove over to his house.

He picked up the mail, walked in the door, and sat down to read it. All of a sudden everything that happened since early this morning caught up to him.

He felt exhausted. He took off his jumpsuit and walked to the shower. He swore that he fell asleep in the shower, before he went to bed.

No matter how tired Rich was, or when he went to bed, he woke up at the same time every morning. This morning it was an effort to open his eyes. Once his eyes were open, there seemed to be a problem with his brain making his muscles work. Everything hurt.

He forced himself to move his body out of the bed, and into his running outfit. It was a major movement to put on his running shoes, and walk to the door. He forced himself through his morning run, came back to shower and got ready to pick up Julie.

By the time he was to pick up Julie, he was recovered enough to act normal, and not wince when he walked.

Julie was her usual ebullient self, and acted like yesterday was a regular day at the office.

They drove to the train station in New Haven, and took Amtrak to the city.

Lunch was great at the Carnegie Deli, and they spent the day walking everywhere in the city, including museums, tourist traps, and the stock exchange. They went to Times Square, and were able to get tickets for a play that night.

They weren't dressed for a formal dinner, but they walked into a fine dining establishment like they owned the place. No one stopped them, and they had a wonderful meal.

The play was more humorous than they expected, the seats were great, and it was a joyous time.

After the play, they took a cab over to the east side, and went to Julie's favorite bar, on First Avenue. When she was with the bureau she was there at least three times a week. They spent a couple of hours there, and took a cab to the train station.

It was there that they found that they had missed the last train back to New Haven.

It had been an absolutely fantastic day. They spent the day walking and holding hands, hugging, and just being a couple. They walked out of the station, and Rich turned to her. "I have an idea. Since we're going to have to stay in the city, why don't we go to the Ritz Carleton.

We're having a classy day, and that's a classy hotel. It'll probably cost us the same as a cab back to New Haven, but I can afford it, and you're worth it."

They grabbed a cab over to the Ritz, and were fortunate enough to be able to get a room. No one asked why they didn't have any luggage.

The room, and the accoutrements were amazing. Neither of them had ever stayed in a hotel like this before.

They looked out the window at the city, and the lights were beautiful.

Rich walked over to Julie, put his arms around her, and kissed her deeply. Their tongues fought each other, and their bodies were as tight together as possible.

Rich caressed her breasts, and started to unbutton her blouse. They kissed each other's necks, and as soon as Rich unbuttoned a button, he replaced it with his lips.

He took off her blouse, and buried his face between her breasts. She was gasping for breath. He discarded her bra. She was fighting to get to his belt, to undo it, and unzip his pants. He unbuttoned her slacks, unbelted her, and forced her pants down. As he kneeled in front of her, he leaned forward, and forced his face between her legs. He reached up, pulled her underpants down, and forced his mouth into her moistness. She was gasping for air.

He stood up, removed his pants, socks, and shoes, and stood there. His erection was strong, and standing up. She stepped to him and removed his shorts. As she kneeled, she wrapped her hand around him, and placed him in her mouth.

He rocked back and forth, and then reached down, picked her up, kissed her again deeply, and led her to the bed. He ripped off the covers, and laid her down. He started to kiss her on her shoulders, worked his way down to her breasts, kissed across her stomach, and ended between her thighs. She was moaning continuously. He took her legs, separated them, and put them over his shoulders. He forced her legs back gently, and entered her. They started rocking slowly, and then he penetrated her deeply and more deeply. Their movements increased, faster and faster, until they both released, and collapsed.

There was no sound except heavy breathing. Then she looked up at him, and said, "That was fantastic. The only problem is that I can never trust you. You broke your rules."

"I guess you're right. I can't be trusted, and as soon as I can, I'm going to break the rules again."

There was no more rule breaking that night, as both of them fell asleep within ten minutes.

At five a.m. Rich opened his eyes. The first thing he saw was Julie's nipple.

Then Julie woke up and stretched, that was all Rich needed to break the rules again.

They hadn't planned to stay over, so they didn't have any gym clothes. Rich convinced Julie that they didn't need any clothes in order to get their exercise this morning.

After exercising they went downstairs, and spent the gross national product of a third world country, for breakfast. Funny how hungry you get after exercising.

After breakfast, they checked out, walked some more around the city, and caught the train to New Haven. Rich knew that they called it the mile high club when a couple had sex in an airplane, but he didn't know what they called it when a couple had sex in a restroom on a train. Whatever they called it, he and Julie were charter members.

They drove back from New Haven to Rich's house, and spent the rest of the weekend breaking the rules.

chapter 25

HARTFORD`

On Monday morning they left Rich's house early in order to get to Julie's, so that she could change into her work clothes. They then left for the office.

As they entered the parking lot, Rich noticed that Spencer's car wasn't in his space.

They said good morning to Charlie, got on the elevator, closed the door, and started to kiss. They stopped when the elevator did, and before the door opened.

When they got to their desks they expected to find a note telling them to go to Spence's office. Instead they found Tina, asking if they saw Spence.

Rich asked, "Where is he supposed to be?"

Tina responded, "He's supposed to be here. He missed a seven and a seven thirty appointment. He's never missed one appointment, never mind two."

Julie asked, "Did they call his house?"

"Yes, Vivian called twice, and called his cell phone. No one answered. Vivian cancelled his appointments until we hear from him. You two were scheduled for 9:30 a.m.

The floor seemed empty. Spence had been gone many times, but there was an undercurrent of concern that something had happened.

At 10:00 a.m. Mrs. Kohl called. Spence had experienced a heart attack at six-thirty this morning, on his way to work. His car had crashed into an electrical pole. She was called by the Hartford police. He was in I.C.U. at St. Francis Hospital, and only close family was allowed to see him. He was considered to be critical.

A pall fell over the whole floor. No one knew what to do. Julie and Rich sat in his office, drinking coffee.

Suddenly, Rich realized that he knew somebody at St. Francis, Gabby. He looked at Julie. "I dated a girl before I met you. She's an emergency room nurse at St. Francis. Maybe I can find out something about Spence."

He picked up the phone and called the emergency room number listed for St. Francis Hospital.

Rich explained to the secretary that he wanted to speak to an emergency room nurse named Gabby, about a patient.

"This is Gabby."

"Gabby, this is Rich, please don't hang up. I need some information about a patient."

"Rich, unless you're the patient, I can't tell you anything."

"I understand, but my boss, Spencer Kohl was brought in by ambulance this morning. Preliminary diagnosis was a heart attack. I just want to know what his prognosis is."

"Rich, like I said, I can't tell you anything. I don't know the patient; I was not his nurse, and I don't know anything about your boss. All I can say is that if what you say is actually true, he's probably in I.C.U. and his status is critical."

"Thanks, Gabby, maybe we can have a cup of coffee."

"Bye, Rich."

He looked at Julie. "She didn't tell me anything we didn't know."

"What was this coffee bullshit ?"

"I was just being nice. It didn't mean anything."

"You want any more exercise, it better not mean anything."

Rich called Vivian and told her what had happened. She was crying, and wasn't the only one who had tears in her eyes. A number of the people had worked with Spence since he joined the company, years ago.

At one o'clock, Loren Kohl called the office. She told Vivian that Spencer Kohl had died from a heart attack, at 12:30. They cried together.

By five o'clock, the calls from the field exceeded one hundred.

The time of the wake, and the days until the funeral went by quickly. The field, as well as the company, acted as if a statesman had passed. Spence had been a professional in different careers, over the years.

The largest church in Hartford was full, and overflowing for the funeral. People came to town from all over the country. One man who had known Spence for twenty years came all the way from Israel. He was a well loved man.

Julie and Rich had known Spence for a relatively short time. However, they were very much affected by his death. They went right to Rich's house from the funeral.

They were both thinking of the same question. "What now?"

Rich, who always looked at things from a logical point of view, outlined the situation. "First, although we have contracts with the insurance company, we really worked for Spence. Second, we made more money working for the organization. Third, whoever replaces Spence will not work for the organization. Fourth, since we don't know what the organization is going to do, we just have to wait to hear from them and the company.

They sat for a while, each in his or her own world, before going to bed.

The next day they walked into their offices. Both had messages from human resources, and Ben Liberty.

Rich called human resources while Julie sat next to his desk. The human resources people said that they were calling to allay fears that there was going to be a rapid replacement of Spence. Rich was told that he and Julie should continue to do what they were doing. There were no changes in objectives.

An hour later there was a memo to all personnel stating that Dave Baxter, the Director of Life sales for the western division was named to take over Spence's position, on an interim basis.

Rich looked at Julie, and said," Looks to me like Human Resources doesn't know what the hell they're doing. When did they start calling personnel, human resources? I've never heard of inhuman resources.

The next call, the one to Ben Liberty, required that the doors to the offices be closed.

Rich called Ben, while Julie listened in on the same extension on her phone, in her office.

"Ben Liberty."

"Hi Ben, its Rich and Julie, on an unsecured line."

"Good morning. I saw the two of you at the church yesterday. I looked for you after the service, but couldn't find you."

"We're sorry, Ben, that we didn't meet."

"It was a miserable day. You two only knew Spence for a short time. I've known him for many years, and I'm going to miss him."

"I know we'll miss him as well, Ben."

"Look, I want to see the both of you tomorrow, if that fits into your schedules."

Rich looked at Julie, who shook her head yes. "We can do that, Ben. Tell me the particulars."

"How about if we meet at the Marriott, in Farmington, at 11:30. That way we can either meet first, or eat first. Up to you."

"Sounds good. We'll be there at 11:30. Anything we can help with, in order to set it up?"

"Nope, I'll see you then. Be casual."

"Bye, Ben."

Both Rich and Julie sat silently for about fifteen seconds. Julie was the first to speak. "What do you think? Are we fired? Do we work for Ben? What do you think will happen?"

Rich shrugged. "I'm not going to try and second guess anything. I don't think we're fired. We're too good, and we've succeeded at everything they've given us. I don't think we'll work for Ben, because he's a recruiter. He probably does something else, but I don't think he's an operations man. I think that we ought to wait until Ben talks to us, and not jump to any conclusions."

"Since we don't have to meet with Spence, and we have nothing scheduled, how about we go to your place, put on our exercise clothes, and exercise until tomorrow."

"Young lady, you are insatiable, and I love it."

The next morning Rich picked up Julie, and they headed out to the Marriott. It was the same hotel and restaurant that they had gone to before. Julie never realized that it was a Marriott.

The valet recognized the car, and the couple. "Welcome back to the Marriott; enjoy your lunch."

Rich acknowledged the valet, and both of them walked to the front desk. They were about to ask for Ben when he walked up to them, and stuck out his hand.

"Hi Ben," they said, in unison.

"Good morning, folks, how are you?"

"Good Ben, do you want to eat, or talk?"

"Let's go up to my room, that way we can relax over drinks and lunch."

They went up to Ben's suite, and sat down in the living room. Ben poured coffee for all of them, and indicated the mini-bar in case they wanted something else.

Ben started the conversation: "Let's take a look at where we are. Due to the tragic death of Spence, you are directly affected. We do not have anyone else in the insurance company who is in the organization. Therefore, you cannot stay with the insurance company, and stay with the organization. Either or both of you can stay with the insurance company in your present positions, as long as they want you. No other insurance companies have an organization person in a senior management position. Since that's where your backgrounds are, there would be no positions for you.

An alternative would be for you to leave the insurance industry, and work solely for the organization. As you know, the organization works under the aegis of the Central Intelligence Agency. The only way that you could work as a member of the agency would be as contract employees. There would be some differences as to compensation, and there would be no benefits such as you get from the insurance company now. As a contract employee, you would be paid $ 100,000 per target named. There would be no salary such as you are receiving from the insurance company. There is one other major difference. The targets can be anywhere in the world. Questions?

Julie spoke first. "I was just injured, as you know, in Las Vegas.

If we were contract employees, and one of us was injured, would we be taken care of medically? Or would it be on us?"

"All of the medical connected to an organization operation would be covered the same way that you were just covered in Las Vegas."

Rich chimed in, "What about expenses and logistics for an organization operation?"

"All expenses and logistics for an organization operation would be covered. If you want to upgrade to first class airfare, you pay the difference. There really will not be any difference from the way you are operating now.

You will report through me, and I will give you your operational orders and logistics. You will receive your compensation the same way that you always have, but you will receive it from me. You will also debrief with me. Any other questions?"

Rich looked at Julie, and said, "I can't speak for Julie, but I have no more questions. When do you need to know?"

"I need your answers by tomorrow; you can call me here. If you know earlier, call me. Julie, do you have any more questions?"

"The only question I have, Ben, is when does this take effect?"

"There are no operations that are scheduled for the near future, basically in the next two weeks. That would coincide with the notice that you would give your employer, if that were your choice. Any other questions?"

Neither of them had any questions.

"O.K., then, let's go to lunch."

They had an excellent lunch, made lots of small talk, found out that Ben was based in Chicago, and originally was from Kansas City.

They promised to call Ben before noon. Then they picked up Rich's car, and headed home.

As they drove home, they were quiet. Then Julie broke the silence.

"The way I see it, these are the alternatives:

Either we stay with the insurance company, receive a hefty salary, have a safe existence, keep all of our benefits, get promoted, make more money, and live the American dream. Or, we become self-employed with no life or disability insurance, no social security in the future, no 401k, or paid vacations, and the possibility of a lot of money. Added to that we could be killed, wounded, disfigured, found in a back alley, or even the front alley. How do you see it?"

"I see it the same way."

"Do you want to write the resignation letters, or should I?"

"I'm the boss; I'll write them."

"Let's call Ben."

They called Ben as soon as they got home.

"Ben Liberty"

"Ben, Rich, Julie is on the extension. We're calling from my house."

"Have you made your decisions?"

"Yes, we have. How long will it take to get contractor's papers set up?"

"That's great Rich! I personally am very pleased to have you aboard, and I know Albert Dell of the Agency will be ecstatic. The papers are in my briefcase. They are the standard contractor's papers, and just have to have a few things filled out. I've got all the information I need to fill in the blanks.

I'll do that tonight, and go back to my office tomorrow. We'll have two copies sent to each of you. Sign one, and send it back. Keep one each for yourselves. Where do you want the courier to deliver them, your Asylum Avenue address?"

"That'll be fine Ben; we're looking forward to working closely with you. We think it will be good for everyone, all around."

They celebrated their new partnership by taking a shower together, and going to bed very early.

The next morning, Rich and Julie called Tina into the office, and told her of their plans. She was shocked, and asked them what they were going to do.

They told her that they had decided to open a consulting company for life companies that wanted to use their General Agents as a new distribution arm.

They asked her not to say anything until they had submitted their resignations to the human relations department.

Rich wrote both resignations, asked Tina to type them up, and gave Julie hers for signature.

Then they both went down to Human Resources, and gave them the two week notices.

The human resources Director accepted the resignations, with regret of course, and told them that their compensation and benefits would continue for two weeks. He also asked them to leave all company property at their offices, and remove themselves, and their personal effects by the end of the day. To say he was pissed, would be an understatement.

Of course, Tina told Linda and Vivian what had happened. They both came to visit Rich and Julie, and express their sorrow that they were leaving, and to wish them good luck in their new venture.

Rich and Julie made a couple of trips down to the car with their personal stuff, and turned in their badges and keys, before they left.

On the way home, Julie decided that she was going to propose an idea to Rich.

"Now that we are partners, we've got to keep down costs. We'll be getting large sums of money, but until we do, we've got to watch our pennies. What we've made so far can start to cover our retirement, or bad economic times.

We're both leasing our homes; we're together as a couple; why don't we get rid of one of the houses?"

"Why you hussy, you want to live with me, without the benefit of a formal arrangement? Actually, I was thinking about it. What would it take for you to get out of your lease? My place is bigger, after all."

The next morning Julie called her real estate agent, and asked what it would take to cancel the lease. The penalty wasn't bad, as there was someone else that the real estate agent felt would like to move in. Julie said that she was able to get out within two weeks.

That was what the two of them did for the next two weeks. They slowly packed boxes with Julie's belongings, and carried them over to Rich's house. They hired a small moving company to move her furniture. They celebrated the placing of her name on the mail box by going to dinner at the Marriott.

At the beginning of the two week period, a courier interrupted their morning with a delivery. The contracts were exactly as Ben had said they would be written. They each signed a copy and sent it back to Ben, by courier.

Now that they were unemployed, and eager to get to work, they called Ben.

"Ben, Rich, how are you?"

"Fine, Rich, how are you and Julie."

"We're great. By the way, Julie is living with me now. We felt it would be better for communications."

"That's the first time I ever heard it called communications, but congratulations."

"Thanks, Ben. When can we get to work?"

"There is a possible operation in Hawaii, but I believe that it's in the beginning stages. It might take another week to ten days to finish the intel on it. I'll check it out and get back to you tomorrow. Now don't go telling Julie that you're going to Hawaii. There may be an operation that comes up earlier In Bozeman, Montana."

"Very funny, Ben. I think we've had our turn in the woods. I'll look forward to hearing from you tomorrow. Take care."

The fact that they weren't going to go to work, when they weren't on operations, finally hit them. They were going to have a lot of time on their hands in between operations.

Since neither of them was the type of person who could just sit around, they had to find something to do.

Rich, not one to let things go, asked Julie, "What are we going to do while we wait for an assignment? Neither one of us is a couch potato."

"Well, I'm not going to join the Junior League, or Time for Tots at the library. Got any ideas?"

"How about if we open that consulting firm that we told the girls at the office that we were going to do?"

"What do we know about being consultants?"

"Considering that we were doing it within a major insurance firm, and that it was starting to work, we know enough to sell it to other companies. We won't travel around the country doing it; we'll tell them how to do it. We can show them how well we did it for our old insurance company. The nice part is that as consultants we don't have to be at the office every day. We'll know our travel schedule, and we can say when we are going to be available."

"Sounds good. How do we do it?"

"The first thing we have to do is put together the actual plan that we are going to sell. Then we have to put together a marketing plan, and market ourselves. There is a listing of every life company that has any kind of distribution system. We can start with the larger ones, and go from there."

"All right; boss, we're back in the insurance business. Let's get to work. What do you want me to do?"

"Never ask me something like that. I might tell you, and it has nothing to do with insurance! O.K., let's get a pad of paper, and start listing things."

For two weeks, they listed, talked about, and wrote down a plan that they should follow in order to have a product to sell. They wrote down everything that they did in the past regarding general agents, and put together a system that the other insurance companies hopefully would buy. Once they had the outline of the product done, they were about to start on a marketing plan.

Then Ben called.

He asked Rich and Julie to meet him at the Marriott since he liked the food there.

Ben was flying in that night, and asked them to meet him for breakfast, and then they'd go to his room for a discussion.

Rich and Julie left the house at 7:30 a.m., and arrived fifteen minutes later.

Ben was waiting for them in the restaurant.

When they came in, Ben stood up, and waited for them to walk over. The table was set for three. He kissed Julie on the cheek, and shook Rich's hand.

"It's so good to see you two. I'm very proud of each of you, and it's great to be working with you. Order some breakfast; there's a buffet if you want."

They sat and ate for about a half hour, and after Ben signed the check, he led the way to the elevator and up to his room.

"We have a target that we want you to take out. You can act as a team, or either one of you can do it."

Rich interjected, "We work well as a team, Ben, and it gives us a way to play off each other."

"O.K., then take it as a team."

"The target is in France. He is a major player in the terrorist network. He is involved in setting up cells all over the world, not just in the United States.

He is a multi-millionaire and lives in the outskirts of Paris on an estate. He is surrounded at all times by a number of guards. When he travels, it's in an armored car, and when he's at home, there are patrols around the estate. I have an intel report on him. There is no time constraint on terminating him. This gives you plenty of time to reconnoiter the situation, and make your plan. It's a hell of a first operation, but I have full confidence in you.

The logistics will not be delivered to you until you have been able to observe the situation, put together your plan, and request your needs. There is a telephone number in the intel report that you should use for logistics, and everything else you need. I request that you memorize it, and destroy it when you destroy the intel report. There is no concern about collateral damage. Just don't take out the civilian population of Paris. He has a private mosque on the grounds of the estate, so that he doesn't have to leave the grounds to pray. There are two first class tickets in the package. They are a present from me. Don't expect First Class from now on, unless you pay for the upgrade. The dates are open . Best of luck."

He handed a large yellow envelope to Julie, kissed her on the cheek, and shook hands with Rich.

"Any questions?"

"Rich spoke: "Just one. Do we call you in Chicago when we come back, after completing the assignment?"

"I'll know when it happens, but let me know that you are home safely."

They left Ben's room, and walked down the hall to the elevator.

Julie, in a low voice said, "It looks like we're really going to have to study this one. Do you speak French?"

"Hell, no. I have enough trouble with English."

"When do you want to go?"

"I think we ought to go as soon as possible. We've really got to reconnoiter the locations that this guy goes to when he leaves the estate, as well as the estate itself."

"Well, we'll have to take enough clothes for a while, and we probably want to check if there is an apartment in the Paris area that belongs to the company. If we're there for a longer time than usual, hotel costs will be ridiculous. I know they cover all costs, but we shouldn't take advantage of them."

The accommodations became moot, once they opened the intel file. An apartment location was given, and a car was rented for their use. The charges on the car would start when they picked it up, and end when they turned it in.

chapter 26

PARIS

They left two days later on a flight to New York, and then directly on to Paris. When they reached the airport in Paris, they took a taxi directly to the address that they had been given in the intel report. The key to the apartment, and a key to lock the mailbox were supposed to be in the mailbox, and they were.

The apartment was spacious enough, as there were two bedrooms, and they were only going to use one. A place to park the car was included, and the refrigerator was stocked. The heat and air conditioning were part of the rent, so they had nothing to worry about.

They took out a map of the area, and looked for the address of the target. It seemed to be about a half an hour away, and there were a number of ways in and out of the street where the estate was located.

They took a cab over to the car rental office, and picked up their car. It was not a sports car; it was a small square car, but it would be sufficient for their needs. At least the driving was on the right side of the road.

They drove around a while in order to find out where they were living, and they found that next to Boston, and Tokyo, the worst drivers they encountered were in Paris.

They then followed the map, and tried to find the estate. Actually it wasn't very hard. They found it in about twenty-five minutes, and it was very large. The only thing visible from the road was the main gate. It was barred by two large gates. There was an electric card reader next to the gate. The gates were in contact with a twelve foot brick wall that spread out on either side of the gate. The wall must have gone for five hundred feet in either direction, before it turned into the rear walls. There were cameras every twenty-five feet or so.

They could not see the house. The road back from the gate had grass on either side, as far as one could see.

It was not going to be easy to get inside, if that was the way they chose to follow.

The road going by the estate did not have a place for anyone to be able to park and watch the gate. If they were going to follow him when he came out of the estate, they would need two cars. They would have to park a car in each direction, away from the gate. If they parked right, and he went left, they would lose him, and have to try again.

The intel report showed the target to be single, and approximately forty five years old. He was Lebanese, and a religious Muslim extremist, who made his money in arms sales. He was also involved in oil futures and land sales. He did not drink, watched his diet, and had a passion for the opera. It was not known what his propensity was for the gender of a companion, as he was always alone, except for his guards.

The intelligence report showed where his box was at the opera house, so they would have to check if there were any available seats near him.

Other than his trips to the opera, there were no other locations listed that he visited on a regular basis.

They drove back to their apartment building, parked in the reserved space, and went up to their apartment.

The jet lag was catching up with them, as well as the fact that this operation looked like an almost impossible challenge. In spite of the fact that there were so many things going through their minds, they were exhausted. So they went to bed early.

There was no exercise equipment in the apartment, and they had no idea where there might be a gym, so they started their day by running around the blocks near their apartment. Not only did that give them exercise, but they were able to find out what was near them, such as a bar, bakery, and restaurant.

The two of them dressed in tourist type clothes, and went to the opera house.

They inquired as to the schedule of performances and were given a pamphlet that listed all of them. They saw that there was a performance in two days, and asked if there were any seats near the box number that the target had purchased. They were disappointed to find out that there were no seats available, except for those in the balcony.

The young lady behind the glass was very cordial, and said that she had studied in the United States. She loved Americans. She asked if she could look further in order to see if there were seats near their friend's box. She found that there was a box available for a special performance being held in the middle of the next week. Would they be interested?

Each box held five seats. Did they have friends that they would like to have accompany them?

They purchased five tickets for the box at the special performance, and also purchased balcony seats, in the first row, for the upcoming performance.

As they walked away, Rich asked Julie, "How did she know we were Americans?"

"Do you think it was because we spoke English with an American accent, the fact that you are wearing a Red Sox cap, or the American flag pin that you are wearing on your lapel?"

Two nights later they were alongside the road about one hundred feet from the gate. In order for the target to get to the opera, their car had to go in this direction.

They watched the gate closely through the mirror, as they did not know what type of vehicle was being used to carry the target.

Suddenly there were headlights turning in their direction, coming out of the driveway. In less than a minute a black Mercedes limousine passed them, picking up speed. Julie wrote down the license number, and they edged onto the road and followed the Mercedes.

It took them about twenty-five minutes to get to the opera house. Rich pulled up behind the Mercedes. When it stopped, one man left the right front seat, and one came from the left of the rear seat. Both walked to the right rear door, and opened it. Another man got out, and looked around. A third man left the rear seat, and the three guards set up a phalanx around the target. They then walked to the front door of the opera house.

As the car left, Rich pulled up, and Julie opened her door, and stood there for a moment in her gown. Rich leaned over, and closed the door. He pulled forward and gave the car to the valet. He walked over in his rented tuxedo to pick up Julie, and they entered the opera house.

Both Rich and Julie checked their coats, and went up the stairs to the balcony, and their first row seats. As they sat down, they swept their eyes around the theater, looking for a box occupied by four men. Both sets of eyes settled on the box closest to the stage, on the left side. Rich took out the picture of the target that he had received in the intel file, and compared it to the faces he saw through his opera glasses. Julie did the same. They both saw the man, sitting in the middle of the box, with a guard on each side, and one behind him. He was about six feet tall, handsome in a rugged way, black hair flecked with gray, and impeccably dressed. There was a small table in front of him, with two bottles of water, a silver pitcher, and four glasses.

At intermission, the target and his guards did not leave the box. The door to the box never opened. At the end of the performance, they also stayed in the box. They waited approximately ten minutes before leaving.

Rich and Julie also waited. They looked under their seats and the seats behind them as if they had dropped something.

When the terrorists left, they walked out the door to the box, and were gone before Rich and Julie had reached the first floor. They picked up their coats, and walked towards the exit. As Rich walked out of the front door, he saw the Mercedes turning the corner.

Once the valet had returned their car, they started towards the apartment.

Rich had a fantastic sense of direction, and although it was now dark, he found his parking space, and they went upstairs.

Rich took the studs out of his tuxedo shirt, and removed his cummerbund. He had removed his bow tie, and lowered his braces. He took off the shirt and trousers, and stood there in his undershorts. Julie took off her gown, and all of the accessories that a woman wears.

"In five days I become a penguin again. It doesn't make sense that I rented the tuxedo, and I have to bring it back tomorrow. Then rent it again next week. It's just not efficient."

"Well, at least I didn't have to rent this gown. I'll just get another tomorrow when you bring back the tux."

"Shall we start to put the plan together, in order to get the logistics list together, or should we do that tomorrow, and just screw our brains out tonight?"

"I vote for losing my brains, what about you?"

"I was brainless to begin with, so I've got nothing to lose."

They went to bed.

The next morning they stopped at the bakery on their way back from their run. They had a cup of coffee, and some breakfast buns that were much too delicious and fattening. If they were going to eat this way in the morning, they were going to have to extend their run.

Their morning was taken up by the return of the tuxedo, and the purchasing of a gown. Rich told the tuxedo rental people that he would pick up the tuxedo rental on Wednesday, and return it on Thursday. Julie had the kind of figure that required a little alteration to make the bust larger. Other than that she could wear it off the rack.

After completing their errands, they decided to drive by the estate one more time, to check out any alternative means to destroying the target. The road was well traveled, and there was no way to get over the wall without the cameras catching you. Also they were sure that there were other cameras surrounding the house, if they came in by parachute. If they came in as delivery people, they were positive that there were procedures set up to make sure that there was security. Another aspect was that they didn't speak French, so they couldn't behave as if they were locals. The estate, therefore, was not a killing ground.

Since the vehicle itself was armored, the only way to attack it would be by a rocket propelled grenade, a bazooka, a roadside bomb, or a radio detonated mine. Attacking the car was a viable alternative, but considering the amount of armor, it might not work.

From what they had seen so far, the most viable time and location would be when he was outside the vehicle, in a location other than the estate.

Their first opportunity would be at the opera, at the special performance in the middle of next week. They would be near enough to him, since they had their own box. They only hoped that it was on the same side of the theater.

Julie called the opera house, and gave them the box number that they had purchased. She asked where the box was located, and found that they were two boxes away from the target box.

The time passed quickly. The only function required of them was calling the special number for logistics, ordering what they needed and receiving the supplies the next day, at the apartment. Before they knew it, it was Wednesday, and the opera was that night.

Rich picked up the tuxedo, and Julie went along for the ride. When they got home, they took a short nap, dressed for the evening, including everything they had ordered from logistics, and left for the opera.

The entrance to the box seating area required them to go up a short flight of stairs, and turn down a hall. All of the doors to the boxes were open, except those whose ticket holders had already arrived. They found the box number that corresponded to the number on their tickets, and entered the box. There were five chairs, and a small table at the front, as well as at the back.

Before they closed the door, a waiter showed up, asking what type of libation they would like. They ordered bottles of water. When he brought them, Rich gave him a nice tip, and he left. The box also contained a curtain to the left, and a curtain to the right, in order to give the box holders more privacy.

Where they were sitting gave them a direct view of the target's box. The seating arrangement was exactly as it had been the previous week.

They looked over, and the target was looking directly at Julie. He nodded his head and smiled. Julie looked back, and smiled as well. He then looked at Rich, and did the same. So did Rich.

The opera started.

At intermission there was a knock at the door, and the waiter was there once again. This time he had a bottle of Christal champagne, and two flute glasses.

"This is from Mr. Khalid in box one, with his complements to the beautiful lady, and the handsome gentleman."

Rich replied, "Please thank Mr. Khalid for his generosity, and his obvious good taste. I hope he will allow me to do the same when we meet again."

The waiter carried the message back, and Mr. Khalid acknowledged it with a wave.

The opera started its second half; when it ended there was a standing ovation.

As the theater started to empty, Rich rose from his seat, stepped behind the curtain, and withdrew a silenced .22 from the waist of his trousers, behind the cummerbund.

The target and his guards remained in their seats, as they had done before.

Julie walked to the back of the box, so that it looked empty to the target and his guards.

After five minutes, Rich moved the curtain away from the wall. He had a direct line to the target. He aimed, and fired twice, hitting the target both times in the head. He then turned the gun immediately to the head of the man behind the target, and shot him twice in the head.

There was utter confusion in box one.

The two remaining guards drew their weapons, and searched the area around their box. There was nothing to be seen. They had a problem getting by the body of their colleague, before they ran out into the hall, before they ran to the management.

Rich and Julie walked out of the box, the gun already back behind the cummerbund, and the bottle of Christal in Rich's fist.

The crowd carried Rich and Julie with them. There was no indication that the killing had been reported.

They made it to the valet and their car was brought to them. They entered the car, and drove away. There were no sirens, no chaos, no screams, no problems . It was just another night at the opera.

They heard the first sirens, as they drove around the roundabout a mile away.

They drove over to the Seine, walked like lovers along the side, and when they got under a bridge, Rich threw the .22 and the noise suppressors into the river. Julie reached under her gown, unhooked the holster and Glock from her leg, and threw them into the river. It was the smallest list they had ever asked for, but it was all they needed.

They went back to the apartment, put on the television, and saw the first notice of a shooting at the opera house.

Two men, a Zachary Khalid, a wealthy French citizen from Lebanon, and a man who worked for him, were shot while attending the opera. The shooter or shooters must have used silencers, as no weapon was heard. Police say that the bullets were of a small caliber. There are no suspects.

"I thought that it was a nice touch for him to send the champagne. I almost feel bad for ending the life of a no good bastard terrorist."

"Looks like we just earned our first pay check as contractors", said Julie.

"The funny part of it is that it probably was the easiest operation we've had.

When do you want to go home?"

"If we go tomorrow, let's go late in the day. I want to pack, buy some souvenirs, and just take it easy. It's a long flight, and then we have to transfer to Hartford."

"The ticket is open, but I don't know whether or not there are seats available tomorrow. I'll find out."

chapter 27

HARTFORD

Rich was able to get a flight in the late afternoon, which connected to a flight to Hartford. They finally got home about 9:00 p.m. They had called Ben as soon as they landed in New York. Ben was aware of the outcome of their trip, and was pleased that they were back in the U.S. He set up a time to meet with them in two days, in order to debrief them, and bring them a briefcase.

Two days later they had caught up with their sleep, and were back on east coast time. They met with Ben at the Marriott, debriefed, and picked up their briefcase.

Rich called his contact, and delivered most of the money to him for transfer to the offshore account. Now that they were no longer on anyone's payroll, they had to keep living expenses, plus a small slush fund.

It didn't take long for them to get back into the swing of things regarding their consultant practice.

Once they decided upon what their product was going to be, they had to decide upon a marketing plan.

Rich thought back to his marketing courses from his M.B.A. classes.

Marketing was defined as bringing a customer and a seller together at a specified price, for a specific product. Rich didn't necessarily agree with that definition, but it gave him an indication of what they had to do.

Julie put together a list of those companies that they had to contact, and the list was lengthy.

Over the next month, the two of them put together a marketing plan, had brochures printed and sent out, and followed up with phone calls.

They were ready to start making appointments, when Rich looked over to Julie and said, "You know what I've been thinking?"

"Of course I know what you've been thinking. You want to know why Ben hasn't called us with an assignment. You're as itchy as I am for some adrenalin running through your bloodstream. I'm surprised that you've waited this long to bring it up."

"Shall we call him?"

The phone rang. "Wouldn't that be a coincidence if that was Ben?" he asked.

"This is Rich."

"Rich, how are you? It's Ben."

He looked at Julie. "Ben, you won't believe this, but Julie and I were about to call you."

"Great minds must think alike. Can you meet me tomorrow at the Marriott? I've got some things to talk over with you. How about dinner? I can't get away early in the day."

"Dinner at the Marriott is fine. How about 7:30?"

"I'll see you then."

Rich smiled, went over to Julie, and kissed her. "I think we're back making the big bucks."

"Sounds good to me. I'm glad he made it dinner. I've got nothing to wear to lunch."

"I don't believe you! You made me empty one of my closets which had my clothes in it, so you could have a third closet for your outfits."

"Yes, but he's seen my outfits."

"He's seen my suit too. I'm not going out and buying another suit."

"You'll never understand."

The misunderstood Julie, and the misunderstanding Rich left their house at 7:00 p.m., and drove over to the Marriott.

It felt good being recognized by the valet, as well as by the charming hostess. She led them to the table by the fountain, and Ben was sitting there, with a drink in his hand.

He stood as they arrived, kissed Julie on the cheek, and said, "What a lovely dress, I don't think I've seen it before."

Julie preened, curtsied, and said, "Thank you Ben, If it were up to my friend here, you wouldn't have seen it at all. I bought it this afternoon."

"Well, it's lovely. I like your suit too, Rich."

"Thanks Ben. I bought it about a year ago, and I like it, too."

Julie quickly got tired of the banter, and sat down. The men did the same.

Ben and Rich ordered the surf and turf, and Julie ordered lobster. They ordered drinks, and a bottle of domestic wine. They toasted to each other's health, and successful operations in the future.

When they finished their dessert, Ben looked back and forth between the two of them. "What do you say we go upstairs, and have a discussion?"

They went to Ben's suite, and sat down in the living room.

Ben looked at them both, again, and asked, "How are things going?"

Rich looked at him. "The business hasn't really started up yet, but we're close to starting up our sales efforts."

"Can you get away at this point?"

"Not only can we get away. We can't wait for our next assignment."

"The assignment that I am about to discuss with you will be the most difficult that you have been given. As a matter of fact, the organization isn't sure that we want to give it to you, at all. It will entail your working together, and working individually, as well as working with another team of two men. Every assignment has been dangerous, but this could be a suicide mission if it doesn't work out the way that you plan it."

Rich looked at Julie, but spoke to Ben. "Who has control, us or the other team?"

"We are giving you the lead, Rich. The other three members of your team will follow your orders. This is one of the reasons that the organization had some misgivings. The other two agents have been around for a lot longer than you two. Additionally you are contractors, and they work directly for the agency.

You two are to fly to Charlotte, North Carolina, tomorrow in order to meet the other team. You will spend the day together checking each other out, seeing whether or not you can work together. Do you want to put your lives in the hands of either one of these guys? Do they want to put their lives in your hands?"

Julie asked, "Can you tell us anything about them?"

Ben answered, "I'm not being flip; find out for yourself."

Rich chimed in, "Can you tell us anything about the mission?"

"First, Let's see if you guys can work together before we break out the intelligence files."

"Can you tell us what country we'll be working in?"

"No! What I can tell you is that the team won't have any problems with the language."

"Do they know who we are?"

"All they know is that you are a male and a female, and that you've been very successful, and are very professional."

Ben looked at Julie. "You won't have to go out and buy a new dress for tomorrow's trip. Any other questions?"

Neither Rich nor Julie said a word.

"Well, since there seems to be no more questions, here are your tickets for tomorrow. The two others will meet you at the airport. They have your pictures. The flight leaves for Charlotte at 8:00 a.m., and returns around 4:00 p.m. If only one of the four of you feels that there would be a problem in working with any of the other three, the mission will be off for the four of you. Understood?"

"Understood," repeated Rich.

Julie shook her head yes.

"Call me when the two of you get back, and let me know your feelings. If the four of you are copasetic, we'll meet again, later in the week."

Ben walked them to the door, and wished them luck.

They walked silently down the hall, took the elevator down, and picked up the car. They started down the driveway before a word was spoken.

Julie spoke first. "I don't know if I like this. We've always worked either singly or as a team. I'm not sure that I want anyone else involved. How do we know who these people are?"

Rich answered her. "That's what tomorrow is all about . I know how you feel though. In Nam we joined up with a ranger outfit, in order to attack a village. I didn't like it, and expected problems. What happened was that we found that they were trained well, knew what they were doing, and we wouldn't have been able to achieve the objective without them. We just didn't have the firepower. I think that this operation is just too big for the two of us, and that's the reason that they increased the attacking force."

"I love it when you use big words like attacking force to describe us."

"You like it when I use big things, whether it's words, or something else."

"Yes, wiseass, I do."

"Let's just see what tomorrow brings."

chapter 28

CHARLOTTE

The flight was normal, and they landed at Douglas International Airport in Charlotte, on time. They didn't know if someone would be holding up a card with their names on it, or what. All that Ben had told them was that they'd be met, and that the two men had their pictures.

They walked down the concourse through security, and looked around. They saw two men, around their age, leaning against the wall, looking at them.

They walked over, and Rich said, "You've been made. I'm Rich, and this is Julie."

The taller one smiled, and said, "What if we weren't the people who were to meet you? What would you do then?"

Rich smiled back, and said, "I'll bet that you've never seen me dance. I looked around, didn't see two men standing together amongst the greeters, and took a chance. You were also eyeballing us, although you could have just been appreciating Julie's body."

"Rich," Julie said, with a bit of scorn in her voice. But, she was loving it.

The shorter one said, "You found us. I guess Ben was right when he said that you were good. I'm Lou Geiss; this is Andy Burton."

Rich and Julie both stuck out their hands, "I'm Rich Coburn, and this is Julie Lowe."

Lou looked back and forth between Rich and Julie. "Our car is in the garage. We booked a room at the airport Marriott so we can talk. Is that O.K.?"

Rich answered for the both of them. "That's great. Let's go."

On the way to the garage, Julie asked, "Are you two based here in Charlotte, or do you come out of D.C.?"

Andy answered, "We're actually from D.C., we flew in an hour before you did . Lou lives in Georgetown, and I live in northern Virginia. Are you both from Hartford?

Julie spoke first. "We are now, but we're originally from Boston. We never met, until we started working together in Hartford. What do you know about us?"

"We really don't know anything about you at all. Ben is our handler with the company, and he said that there is a mission that will require four operatives. He said that there were two contractors who would complement our way of doing things. He also told us that you had done only one operation in Europe, and a partial operation in Canada. All of your experience had been here in the U.S."

"Does that mean that this operation will be overseas?"

"We don't have any idea about the operation. All Ben told us was that we were to meet you in Charlotte, and decide whether or not we could trust you with our lives, and that you were contractors, as I said."

Lou turned the rental car into the driveway at the airport Marriott, and the four of them went up to the room that was reserved.

Rich sort of took over.

"Why don't we get comfortable, and ask and answer any questions that we have about each other. How does that sound?"

Andy and Lou sat on one side of the living room, and Rich and Julie on the other, with the coffee table in between.

Julie got up, held up the coffee pot on the side of the dresser, and said, "Anyone else want coffee?" Everybody said yes, and Julie opened up the mini-bar and pulled out some cookies that she put on the table.

Rich said, "Why don't I start, by giving you my background."

Both Lou and Andy nodded their heads, and sat back.

Rich started with his Boston roots, went through his military background, his education, how he was recruited, his time in the insurance industry, and brought his history up to date, with his new business with Julie.

Andy asked a few questions, mostly pertaining to Rich's time in Vietnam, and the types of missions he had been on individually, and jointly.

The only question that Lou had was whether either Rich or Julie spoke any foreign languages.

Julie went into the other room, and brought back the coffee, and another package of cookies.

Andy leaned forward to take a cup of coffee, and said, "I guess I'll go next."

He sat back, got comfortable, and started to speak. "I'm originally from Ojai, California. I had the normal upbringing. My Mom was an accountant, and my Father was an aerospace engineer. I have two sisters, both younger than I am.

I went through the regular schooling, played three sports in high school, and was the valedictorian for my high school class when we graduated. I went on to Stamford, and graduated in the top two percent of my class, with a degree in international business.

I was recruited directly out of college by the company, was sent to language school to learn German, and went back within the last five years for Arabic.

I was also in Vietnam, but with the company, and although Rich never knew my outfit, we knew his. I have a fantastic regard for the Navy SEALs. You guys are the best trained warriors I've ever met. My hat is off to you.

After Nam, I was transferred to covert operations in Europe. I was involved in a number of operations in numerous countries. On some of those operations my German and my Arabic were very valuable.

I started working on operations with Lou a few years ago, and then we were both transferred to Langley. We started working with Ben a little over two years ago. We both knew Spence Kohl for a number of years, and were sorry to hear that he had passed. What questions do you have for me?"

Julie looked at Rich, then back at Andy. "Have you ever worked with a woman as part of your team?"

"No, I never have. I've never met any women in covert ops. I know that there are some, that they are very professional, and that they do their jobs very well, but I never have worked with one."

"How do you feel about it?"

"I have full faith in Ben and the company. If they believe that you are good enough to go on any mission with me, then I believe you are good enough.

I don't believe that they would put me in any more danger than the danger involved with the mission."

Rich then leaned forward, looked Andy in the eyes, and said, "Would you put yourself in extra danger to protect Julie, because she's a woman?"

"Julie is a very attractive woman, and I'm as chivalrous as any other man. However, when it comes to working together, I'm going to put my ass on the line for her, as much as I would for you, or Lou, or any other operative. No more, no less."

Rich looked at Julie, "Any more questions?"

"Nope."

"Then it's your turn."

Julie did the same as Rich. She gave her childhood background, her education, military background, and F.B.I. experiences. She then went through her recruitment, apprenticeship to Rich, and partnership in both operations, and their new company.

The only question that Lou had was, "How would you feel about taking out another woman, or God forbid, a child?"

"If the target, or collateral damage, were a woman or child, then I would feel the same way that I would feel if it were a male. The operation comes first."

Andy stood up to get a cookie. "Julie, have you ever been shot, or wounded in any way?"

"A few months ago I took a bullet in the lower back. I was luckier than you can believe. It was a through and through. No one could believe it. If it weren't for a company doctor, I wouldn't be here."

"That wouldn't have been in Vegas, was it?"

"How would you know that?"

"There were rumors that a woman had been shot on an operation, but I didn't know whether it was true or not."

Julie stood up to get more coffee. "Any other questions, gentlemen?"

Neither of them said a word.

Lou leaned forward in his chair. "I guess that it's my turn. I'm originally from Denver, actually Englewood. I also went through the normal schooling, and was one of two valedictorians in my class. I went to George Washington in D.C., and majored in drinking beer, and getting laid. Somehow I stayed out of trouble, and my grades were good enough to graduate with a degree in history. I was going to try to go to law school, but I couldn't get in to a good school, plus my father wouldn't pay for any more schooling. The government wouldn't give me any loans, and I was shit out of luck.

I saw an advertisement for a job with the C.I.A., and I somehow passed the test. I went to the farm, and graduated."

Julie interrupted him.

"The farm?"

"It's boot camp for the C.I.A."

Rich interjected, "I hear that it's a lot more difficult than that."

"Well, it's not hell week, but it's not a picnic."

"Anyway, I found that I had better accept some responsibility, and grow up, or I wasn't going to make it; so I grew up. My first assignment was in France, and I didn't speak French. However, I found that I didn't need to speak anything but English, and since my weapon was German, it didn't care if I spoke any language. I was in covert operations my total time in service, until I came to D.C. Andy and I worked together in the field, and we were both transferred to D.C. at the same time. That's me, what you see is what you get."

Rich looked at Julie. "Any questions?"

"Yes. Both of you have told us about your work, but nothing personal. I think we ought to know about that as well. Are either of you married? Do you have children?"

Andy answered first. "I lost my wife to cancer last year. I have a twelve year old daughter. My sister lives with us, and takes care of her when I'm gone."

Lou smiled. There isn't a woman stupid enough to marry me. I'm single, and I intend to stay that way. What about you two?"

Julie answered, "We met when I was recruited. Since that time we've worked together on operations, and just recently, I moved into Rich's house. We're partners in a consulting business when we're not on an operation. I guess you can say that we're partners in everything. One thing I want to assure you of, is that we look out for each other, in the same way we look out for other partners. We work very well together which makes us an asset to anyone who works with us."

Rich looked at everyone in the room. "Anyone for a late lunch?"

The tension in the room disappeared. It was a signal that they probably were a team.

They went downstairs to the restaurant, ordered burgers and beers, and had a long lunch.

Lou finally said, "I think that we know each other enough to give Ben a decision. Do you guys have any questions or comments before we go back to the airport?"

Rich looked at Julie. "Anything?"

"I know everything that I have to know. I'll never recommend that any of my girlfriends date Lou, and I know a young lady who can use some dresses that I have."

Rich said, "I guess that does it for us. How about you guys?"

Andy looked at Lou, "What do you say, partner, any questions?"

Lou looked at Julie. "Do your girlfriends look like you?"

Everybody laughed. They motioned for the waitress, paid their bill, and walked to the rental car.

Ten minutes later they were all shaking hands, and the meeting was over.

chapter 29

HARTFORD

The flight was easy, and they drove back to Rich's house. They had discussed the day on the plane, and both made the decision that they could easily work with Andy and Lou. The phone was ringing as they walked in the door.

Rich reached the phone first. "This is Rich."

"Mr. Coburn, my name is Helen Burke. I'm calling on behalf of the Hartford Courant. We have a new subscription package for people in your neighborhood. I notice that you are not one of our subscribers. Would you like the weekly subscription, or weekly and weekend?"

"Helen, thank you for the opportunity, but there is no one in this house who knows how to read." He hung up.

Julie laughed. "That poor person was only doing her job. Why did you do that?"

"I was expecting it to be Ben, or Andy, or Lou. Not a salesperson. We just spent a day with a couple of really good guys, and I didn't want to buy a damned newspaper."

"O.K., O.K., shall we call Ben, or what?"

"Yuh, let's call him."

The phone rang.

Rich said, "If that's another salesman, I'm going to cut his balls off."

Julie picked up the phone. "Hello, this is Julie."

"Julie, its Ben. I hope I'm not interrupting anything. When did you guys get back?"

"Hi, Ben. We walked in five minutes ago. How are you?"

"Fine, dear, fine. Did you enjoy your day in Charlotte?"

"Yes we did. It was a pleasure meeting with Andy and Lou. They seemed to be professional, and they've been around. We think we can work with them. Have you heard from them?"

"Yes, they called me before they flew back to Dulles airport. They were impressed by both of you, and they also said they'd like to work with you. May I speak to Rich, please?"

Julie gave Rich the phone.

"Hi, Ben, how are you."

"Good, Rich. What do you think?"

"As Julie said, we think we can work together. Did you tell them that I'd be in charge?"

"It was explained. Can you two be in D.C. tomorrow afternoon for a meeting at Langley?"

"Yes, we can. Which airport?"

"Someone will meet you at Dulles. I'll reserve seats for you on the 11:35 a.m. flight. I don't know how long the meeting will be, so I'll leave the other end open."

"O.K., Ben, we'll be there."

Rich gave Julie the plan, and they went out to an early dinner. They had to fly out again tomorrow, and the running around was taking its toll on the both of them. They went to bed early.

chapter 30

LONDON, ENGLAND

Imam Ahmed Cheemar looked at the lieutenants of his personal army of followers. Since he had found Allah in prison, and changed his name, the same group of men had followed him as his personal protectors.

No one but the six lieutenants and the Imam knew that they were all in prison together. None of the other followers in the mosque knew anything about the backgrounds of the holy one and his close brethren.

Most of the members of the mosque would be horrified to find out that the Imam and his circle of friends were in actuality terrorists, working against the West. The members also had no idea that the terrorists were funded by being one of the largest heroin and PCP traffickers in England.

Originally all from Muslim countries, the group came together at Wandsworth prison where they were all prisoners. Cheemar, a natural leader, and a self-trained religious zealot, led the prayers in the prison mosque, and continued once all of them had been released.

Once out of prison, the group had to find a source of income. Drugs were the fastest way to earn money, and one of the group had contacts in Afghanistan in order to get the product. After a short while, they became one of the largest dealers in England.

Every dollar that they earned went towards setting up attacks on the population surrounding the Muslim enclave, and trying to wipe out western influences within the area.

Now they had escalated. They were going to attack the RAF base at Lakenheath. The base, although a Royal Air Force base, housed the 48th fighter wing, a U.S. Air Force unit. Intelligence about the attack had been derived from a number of sources, mostly from intercepted phone calls amongst the members of the group. There was no human intelligence though, and that made the C. I. A. very uncomfortable.

Cheemar was sitting in a back room at the mosque. His closest underling, Abdullah Yinni, a thirty-four year old from Yemen, walked in, and addressed the Imam. "All of the preparations are made; the trucks will be here at 2:00 a.m. next Monday. All of the weapons will be loaded. We will destroy the planes, and be away, before morning prayers."

"Thank you, Abdullah. What of the others?"

"Everyone knows their assignments, and are, as I am, ready to become martyrs for Allah.

"Excellent. I wish to go over the assignments and the timing once more. Give me the assignments."

"Umar and Hussain will be driving the trucks. Waqar and Akram will be stationed on the backs of the trucks firing the RPG's at the planes. Hassan and Farook will be manning the machine guns which will also fire out of the back of the trucks."

"Where will the trucks come from, and what size will they be?"

"You are aware of that, oh holy one."

"I know of what I am aware; tell me!!"

"The trucks will be covered 6 X 6's, and will be stolen from the armory at Cheltenham. We will steal the trucks tomorrow night, and hide them in the lorry park, next to Umar's brother's house, under large tarpaulins."

"Tell me the plan. Everyone must know all phases of it. We cannot afford to have someone do something incorrectly, and ruin the mission."

"The trucks will be here at 2:00 am. You and I will lead them in a car that has government plates, and is painted like an RAF vehicle. If we are stopped, we have the papers for two trucks following an officer. We go to the field and follow Leeds Road to the area of the American fighter wing at Lakenheath. There are no lights along the fence at that point. We cut through the fence, leaving the embedded communications wires until last. We have six minutes from the time of the cut until the security people are at the flight line. We know this from the timing that we checked a few weeks ago, when we cut the wire to test the response time. In six minutes, we can destroy all of the aircraft on the flight line, return to the hole in the fence, and head back down Leeds Road.

One mile down leeds road, we abandon the trucks, and pick up the two cars that Farook's family will leave there for us. We leave all heavy weapons in the trucks, take only hand held weapons with us, and separate. Car one with you, Abdullah, Umar, and Hussain in it will head north. Car two with me, Waqar, Akram, Hassan, and Farook will head east. We will drive until sunrise when we will all go to areas with Mosques, and pray. The listing of mosques will be given to the drivers. They have been visited in the last week, in order that we know exactly where they are. We have timed the distance from the starting point to the location, and we should have no problems in finding them. In two days we are to head back here to the mosque. In the two day period, all of the men are to go to local hotels, and wait. Is that your plan, my leader and friend?"

"That is my plan, my friend. You are to make sure that each and every one of the others knows it as well as you do. Now leave me."

Abdullah bowed, turned, and walked out the door.

chapter 31

LANGLEY, VIRGINIA

Five o'clock came early, but both of them jumped out of bed for their exercise, had breakfast, and called the airport to confirm their reservations to Dulles. They still had a couple of hours to kill, so they went back to bed, but not to sleep.

They figured that they should dress nicely since they were going to the C.I.A. headquarters. At least they assumed that was where they were going. Was there anything else in Langley, Virginia?

They walked into the airport at 10:30 a.m. and went to the United counter . They picked up their tickets, and verified that their return trip was open. There were flights back almost every hour from 4:00 p.m. on.

Julie looked professional in a pin striped business suit, and high heels. Rich looked very businesslike in a dark suit, and a red power tie, shined shoes, and a briefcase. He had to have something to carry his pad of paper.

The flight to Dulles took a little less than an hour and a half, and was non-eventful.

As they walked out of the jetway, they saw the sign for baggage and headed that way. Before they had walked fifty feet, a poster boy for the C.I.A., right down to the crew cut, walked up to them, and asked their names. When the names agreed with the captions on the pictures in his pocket, he looked at Rich, and said, "Please follow me." They walked through a non-descript door and down a flight of stairs to another door. When they walked through it, there was a limousine, with a driver waiting for them. The person who met them opened the nearest rear door, and walked around to the other side to open the other door.

Julie entered the closest door, and Rich walked around. The agent closed both doors, and sat in the right hand front seat.

The locations of refreshments, telephone, television, etc. were explained to them, as well as the air and heat controls, and the divider between the seats was raised.

Julie looked at Rich, and mouthed, "What if we were prisoners?"

Rich looked back at her, and mouthed, "We are."

After about fifteen to twenty minutes, they stopped at the first guard shack, went through to the second guard shack, and went into the basement entrance. The agent and chauffer got out, opened the doors, and Julie and Rich left the vehicle.

They went to the desk, picked up their pre-pictured badges, gave their thumb prints, which were verified immediately, and went in the elevator to the top floor, with the agent.

They left the elevator, turned right, and walked to a double door office closed off by thick wooden doors. The plaque on the wall read, Albert Dell, Assistant Director.

They walked in and faced two women. The nearest one looked at the agent, and said, good day, William. Are these Ms. Lowe, and Mr. Coburn?"

"Yes, Mrs. Winchester. You are correct."

"Thank you, William; we'll call you if they need a ride back."

"Yes, Ma'am."

Mrs. Winchester rose, and walked around her desk. The other woman ignored them as if they weren't there.

Mrs. Winchester put out her hand, and welcomed the both of them to Langley.

"Mr. Dell is presently in a meeting, and will be with you shortly. Mr. Liberty, and two other gentlemen are in the conference room if you would care to join them, or you can sit here with me and have a cup of coffee. Totally up to you."

Julie smiled, and said, "No offense please, Mrs. Winchester, but I believe that all of the gentlemen, as well as the two of us, will be meeting with Mr. Dell, so we'd be pleased to go to the conference room now."

"Excellent, my dear, please follow me."

They walked into the conference room, and Ben, Andy and Lou, all stood up and smiled. The smiles were met by Rich and Julie smiling right back, and everybody gave each other a hug. The hugs given to Julie seemed to last a little longer than those given to Rich.

Everyone sat down, and fifteen seconds later Mrs. Winchester brought in another carafe of coffee.

Ben looked around the table, tented the fingers of his hands, and spoke.

"It's good to see all of you together for the first time. When I spoke to you individually, after you first met, it seemed like a love fest. Everyone thought the other was better than sliced bread. I've never seen an easier melding of a team. The reason that we are here today is to meet with my boss, Albert Dell. Al is an Assistant Director of the company, and is in charge of covert operations. Normally he doesn't get involved with an operation at this level. The problem that we have is that it's in England. The British could have handled it with their M-5 people, but the target in this case is American. They have the jurisdiction, since it will formally involve a Royal Air Force base, but the tenant of that base is an American fighter wing.

Al should be here shortly, and I'll let him go through the drill with you, and answer any questions.

Do you have any questions?"

Knowing that any questions that they had would most likely be covered by Albert Dell, they sat mute.

The door opened, and Albert Dell walked in. He had a box in his hands, and he placed it on the table. On the outside of the box was written "LONDON."

He nodded to Andy, Lou, and Ben. "Andy, Lou, Ben, good to see you. This must be Julie and Rich. Hi, I'm Al Dell."

Julie smiled, said "Hi," and sat forward. Rich nodded and sat forward as well.

"I was extremely pleased when Ben called me and told me about the merger of the two top teams who are sitting here. We have a problem in London, and we need people of your caliber to solve it.

The people in M-5, our counterpart in London, have asked us to take over the running of this operation. We both felt that although we have worked together on operations in the past, only one agency should be involved in this one.

As I said, this is in our bailiwick, and we make the rules. Sometimes in Great Britain they would rather arrest the perpetrator, and put him on trial. I want to underline the following. On the enemy side, NO ONE IS TO BE LEFT ALIVE! I don't care if there is collateral damage; I don't care what we have to do. I'm not giving these scum the chance to walk on a technicality and come back after us again. Are there any questions or comments on that?"

No one said a thing.

"All right, let's get down to the briefing."

He passed out seven pictures.

"The picture labeled A. is that of Ahmed Cheemar. He is the leader of this cell. He is the Imam of a mosque outside London. All of the other members are subservient to him, and belong to the mosque. All of them met in Wandsworth prison. They were there for what we would call felonies, and spent time together.

The second in command, and closest to Cheemar is Abdullah Yinni. His picture is labeled B. The other pictures are as follows: C is Umar Khan, D is Hussain Yemer, E is Waqar Missan, F is Akram Musan, G is Hassan Kamar, and H is Farook Bughami. All of them are from Arab countries, and their backgrounds really don't matter at this time. However, I have in the intelligence files all the individual information.

We have no human intel on this operation. All intel has been picked up from conversations given to us from M-5 and the NSA. If the plan that they have is successful, they will have hit us hard, and cost us millions of dollars and a lot of aircraft.

We could wait, and start an investigation, but that's not our objective.

Their plan is set to go off next week. The timing, as we know of it, is outlined in the intel folder.

Basically what we know is that there will be a car and two trucks used to attack the Royal Air Force Base at Lakenheath. The United States has a fighter wing based there as an addition to our forces in Europe. The objective of the attack is to surreptitiously enter the base by cutting through the fence, and run down the flight line destroying aircraft as they pass. They then will leave the base, destination unknown.

There was a penetration of the base a while ago, using the same method of cutting the fence, but no one entered the base. We believe that it was done to find out how long it would take for the reserve security force to respond to the area of the penetration of the fence.

We have been in contact with the commands of both RAF base Lakenheath and the 48th Fighter Wing. They in turn have tripled security on the flight line, and moved more security into the area. All of it has been undercover. We want to get these guys.

There are maps in the box, showing your backup positions, if you don't succeed in your primary.

Your primary objective is to destroy the cell before they leave for the base.

If, for some reason, this is not accomplished, you are to intercept them on the way to the base, or at the fence. I'll leave it up to you, and your leader Rich, as to the means of accomplishing your objective. Any questions?"

Andy held up his pencil. "Will our weapons be waiting for us there, or do we take them with us?"

"I'm going to let Ben co-ordinate the weapons you require. You'll take them with you when you fly out of Andrews Air Force Base. You'll be using a Gulfstream Jet. You might as well be comfortable on your flight. You'll land at Lakenheath, and pick up a car. There is a safe house awaiting you, in London."

Lou asked the next question. "When do we leave?"

"Be at Andrews at noon tomorrow. Pack for a week."

Al Dell picked up the intel box, walked over to Rich, and put it down in front of him. He then put out his hand, and said, "It's been a pleasure meeting you and Julie. I would wish you the best of luck, but you are too good to need it."

He then shook hands around the table, and left.

Ben stood up, and gave a card with B-221 written on it, to each of the team members. "When you get to Andrews tomorrow, give this to the Air Police at the gate. They'll take you to this building. There is no need to tell them who you are, or give them any information. I know that this is the best team I have ever put together. I know that you have the background, the knowledge and the wherewithal to make this a fantastic operation. I'll see you tomorrow, and then when you get back.

He walked out the door, and they could see him enter Al Dell's office.

Rich took over.

"Okay, we've got our marching orders. Candidly, I wasn't overly impressed by our briefing. We'll have to put it together on the flight over, tomorrow.

I'll call Ben when we get back to Hartford, to give him the weapons list.

If you've got any personal preferences for handguns, just bring them with you, or call Ben as well, so you'll have your favorites. Any questions?"

No one spoke.

"O.K., Well, see you tomorrow. Do you guys have transportation?"

Both Andy and Lou said that they drove over, and would see them in the late morning.

Rich, carrying the box, and being followed by Julie, walked back to Mrs. Winchester, and asked for transportation back to the airport. Before they left he fit the contents of the box into their carry-on luggage.

The limousine dropped them off at Dulles, and they flew back to Hartford.

chapter 32

HARTFORD

Once they reached their house, Rich and Julie sat down, and went over a weapons list. After they agreed, Rich called Ben, and gave him the list.

Ben told him that everything would be waiting for the team tomorrow.

He also told them that their tickets were purchased, and would be waiting for them at the airport, and reminded Rich that they would be flying into National Airport. The flights left every hour, so they could choose what was best for them.

Rich started to read the intel, and Julie joined him. They broke for a quick dinner, and went back to reading. About nine o'clock they broke their concentration, in order to pack, and went to bed.

The next morning, they flew to National, and grabbed a taxi to Andrews Air Force Base.

chapter 33

ANDREWS AIR FORCE BASE, MARYLAND

At the main gate they disembarked from the cab, and walked up to one of the air policeman at the gate. Both of them gave him the card, and watched his expression change. He went from disinterested to oh shit, and picked up the phone. "Please send an escort vehicle to the main gate for transportation to B-221." He then turned, looked at them, and said, "Ma'am, sir, your vehicle will be here quickly. Please allow me to put your luggage here, by the bench."

Before they were able to sit down, a jeep pulled quickly up to the gatehouse.

A sergeant jumped out, picked up their luggage, threw it in the back, and held the door for Julie. Since there were no other doors, Rich assumed that he was to jump in the back, and did so.

The sergeant didn't say a word, and they quickly found themselves next to a large building which had B-221 on a small plaque next to the door.

There was a camera trained on the area outside the door. When they walked up to the front, a voice came out of a speaker saying, "Please state your name, and hold up your card. Thank you." They did, and the door buzzed open.

They found themselves inside a large hanger housing three aircraft. Next to a white Gulfstream were two men who were loading mid size boxes into a hatch. Rich assumed that this was the weapons cache.

Just then a door to an office on the other side of the door they had entered, opened.

Ben, Andy, and Lou walked over to them and shook hands.

One of the men at the aircraft walked over, and took both suitcases, carrying them back to the aircraft.

Ben said, "Everything is ready for you on the aircraft; the apartment has been stocked; your tools are loaded; and a car is waiting for you at Lakenheath. There is a map in the glove compartment indicating the location of the apartment. The intel box tells you the location of the mosque, and where we believe the attack is going to take place."

Rich said, "We studied the intel box last night. We'll open it up to Andy and Lou as soon as we get aboard."

"Well, then, let's get going. Your flight is scheduled to leave in twenty-five minutes."

They all shook hands with Ben, and walked over to the plane. They let Julie walk up the stairs first, and followed her in. They found chairs and sofas, and a table with four comfortable chairs around it. Each of the chairs had seatbelts, and they all sat down in them.

Just then a young lady came out of the rest rooms, walked over to them, and introduced herself. "Hi, I'm Lindsay. I'm your flight attendant, and I'm here for your safety, and to help you in any way. Anyone want something to drink, before we take off? We've got about twenty minutes."

No one took advantage of her offer.

They started to go through the intel box, and were totally consumed with the contents, when the door closed, and the outer door to the hangar opened.

The engines started to spool, and the plane moved towards the outside world.

There was a static sound, and then they heard, "Good morning folks, this is Jeff Todd, your pilot, and I'm up here with Gary Whyte. We're going to take you to London, England today. We expect the total flight time to be seven hours and fourteen minutes, and we'll be flying at 37,000 feet. Lindsay will be back there to help you with anything you need. Shortly after takeoff, she'll be serving lunch. We'll talk with you later."

The flight was long and tedious. The work that they were accomplishing took the full amount of the flight. The new team worked very well together, and the respect for each other showed.

chapter 34

LONDON

The landing was perfect, and as they taxied, they could see many fighter planes, as well as cargo, and one or two Gulfstreams, like theirs.

They pulled into a large hangar, and parked between two more Gulfstreams. The door opened, and an air force captain came aboard.

"May I ask for the individual in charge, please?"

"Rich said, "That's me."

"Sir, I'm Captain Dolan. Would you and your party please follow me to the commanding officer's office."

The team picked up the intel and followed the captain down the stairs. On the way out, they stopped to thank the pilots and Lindsay for their work.

The team walked into the commanding officer's office. On the way in, they saw their luggage, and the weapons bags being placed in the trunk of a car, and a box was put on the roof of the vehicle.

An air force colonel was standing behind the desk. "Ma'am, gentlemen, welcome to England. My name is Colonel Wick. I'm fully aware of why you are here. I won't ask any questions. All I want to do is offer you any help I can. I know that you've been briefed on the changes we have made here at the base. If you need anything, anything at all, just ask, and you'll have it. Is there anything that you need right now?"

Rich answered, "Thank you colonel, we appreciate it. I don't believe that we need anything at this point. I understand that our vehicle is being loaded, as we speak, and we'd just like to get going."

"Let's see where we are." He walked to the door, and saw the vehicle sitting there. "Looks like you're set to go. Good luck, I hope I don't see you again until you're on your way home."

The vehicle was roomier than they thought it would be. The four of them were able to spread out, while Julie directed Rich, who was driving, where to turn. They arrived in about fifteen to twenty minutes.

The apartment was, in actuality, a small house. There were four bedrooms, a living room, a kitchen, and two bathrooms. There was a garage under the house, and the whole building was cleaned and polished.

They pulled into the garage, and unloaded all of the luggage and weapons bags. They took the box off the roof of the car. Rich put Julie's gear in one of the rooms, and his own gear in another. He was about to explain, when Julie just said, "I understand."

Both Andy and Lou picked up their 9mm Glocks from the weapons bags, and Julie and Rich picked up their Glocks. They pulled on their Kevlar vests, as an added protection, since they were now up against a small army.

They reconnoitered the area around their house, and found their way into the Muslim area. After they found the mosque, they looked at the surrounding streets for entrance and egress possibilities.

The parking lot of the mosque was about one third full. There were no people to be seen, just cars.

They drove around the streets in the area, seeing signs in Arabic, advertising Hallal meat and mid-east specialties.

The map showing where the attempted fence cutting had been was in Julie's hands. They headed for Leeds road, after doubling back to the mosque, in order to time the trip.

When they came upon the place where the attempted break took place, they knew why the terrorists had picked the location. There was a straight piece of road for about a quarter of a mile in each direction. Anyone at the fence would see a car coming well in time to hide. The side of the road was level right up to the fence, making it easy to drive a vehicle from the road to a point inside the base. The fighters were parked fifty feet inside the fence, along a taxiway that any vehicle could drive down.

Across the road from the location of the attempted break was a patch of woods where vehicles could be left until they were needed. The tree line was sparse, allowing space between the trees. There was a covering of brush about three feet high.

They stopped, and walked into the woods to see how far back it went, and what the cover was like. Even though the tree line thickened as they went further back the brush thinned out, allowing for less cover.

The team got back into their car, and headed back to the house. On the way, they swung by the mosque. It was time for prayers, and Rich wanted to see if there were more cars. The parking lot was full, and there were cars parked in the street.

Rich commented, "That's what I was afraid of. There are a lot of members of that mosque. When there were no prayers, the parking lot was still one third full. I know that Dell doesn't care about collateral damage, but he's not here, or in charge of the mission. We also know that he said that we should hit these scum at the mosque, before they went out to the base. I disagree.

The mosque is their territory. They know every nook and cranny. They may have tunnels, or safe rooms, or anything else they could use to escape.

I know that as scene commander I can make any operational decisions there are, but I respect your opinions. Andy, what do you think?"

"I have to agree with you. The woods and the fence area are as new to them as it is to us. They may have been there before, but the odds are equal outside of a building, and if I can't have the long side of the odds, I'll take those that are even."

"Lou, how about you?"

"I agree with Andy, and with you. I don't think the odds favor us if we hit them at the mosque. There was nothing telling us when it was going down, though, so it'll be difficult setting up any kind of ambush."

"We didn't need to know when it was going down, if we were

going to hit them at the mosque. If we are going to hit them somewhere else, somehow we have to find out when they are planning for it to go down."

"Julie, what are your thoughts?"

"I have to agree with the rest of you. However, I think that it is imperative that we know when the operation is going to happen. It could happen, and we'd be sitting on our butts, waiting."

"You're absolutely right. Let me think about it, and see what to do."

They came back to the house, and had dinner. Andy turned out to be a great cook, and they all ate well. They spent the evening reviewing the intel once more, and they went to bed relatively early.

The next morning Rich awoke, and turned on the television. The news story of the morning, even though it was early, was how the armory in Cheltenham, less than a hundred miles from London, was broken into during the night. Two large covered trucks were stolen, as well as some armament.

Rich immediately woke everyone up, and they gathered in the living room to watch the news.

Excited, Andy said, "This is it folks; I can feel it. The bastards are going out tonight or tomorrow. They don't want to have to keep those trucks where they can be discovered. It's going down!"

Everyone became animated.

Rich quieted everyone down.

"Look, all we know for sure is that two trucks, and some arms were stolen from an armory. The odds are good, but not great, that the Muslims are behind it. We still have a problem. We can assume that it's going down, but when? Tonight, tomorrow night, how do we know?

We can put a stakeout at the mosque, but then what? If the trucks show up at the mosque, what do the rest of us do? If we decide that we use a stakeout, then we need another vehicle. Or we drop three of us out at the area across from the fence, and one does a stakeout at the mosque. How long do we carry it on?"

Julie, calm, and in a level voice said, "How about what you just said? We know that they're not going to do it during the day. If we leave three people in the area across from the fence, and one across from the mosque, with radio communications, that person can call the three and let them know that it is going down. Then the person takes off, and joins the ambush before the bad guys get there."

Rich looked at Andy and Lou. "Guys?"

Lou answered first. "Sounds good to me."

Andy concurred, "Me, too."

Rich looked at the three of them. "O. K. who is at the mosque?"

Andy spoke next. "I think I'm the natural. If anyone notices me, and comes over, I'm the only one that speaks Arabic. I obviously won't park directly opposite the mosque, but an unknown car being anywhere for six hours, is going to stand out, and be suspicious."

"Makes sense," said Rich. I agree with the six hour time limit as well. When and if it goes down, it'll be between midnight and six. We can start tonight, and keep going until something happens, or you guys qualify for your pension."

They then called Colonel Wick, and were told that he was off the base. Rich was told that if it were an emergency, they would call the colonel, and have him call back. Rich requested it, and three minutes later the phone rang.

Rich picked up the phone, and repeated his phone number. The colonel answered with, "This is Colonel Wick, with whom am I talking?"

"Colonel, this is one of the three men and one woman who flew in to your base from the states. Do you know who I mean?"

"Yes, I do. What do you need?"

"We need another vehicle, in addition to the one we have. We'd like to pick it up at your office, or have it delivered to a public place, where we can pick it up. We need it today."

"You've got it. It's Sunday, so the best place to pick it up would be my office. I'll clear the gate for you. Just tell the guard that you are coming to see me, and use the name Willie Pete. The car will be outside my office in one hour. Anything else I can do for you?"

"Not at this time, Colonel. Thank you for being so responsive, and so quick to return my call."

"Hey, we're on the same side, right. Have a good day."

Rich told the others what was happening, and asked Julie to accompany him. "There's no reason for everyone to drive out to get the car. Why don't you two make sure that the weapons are set to go, and loaded ."

Rich and Julie drove off to pick up the car, and when they used the name Willie Pete they were escorted directly to the commanding officer's office. There was a car parked just outside the office, with a key in the ignition.

The air policeman called the front gate, and cleared their exit with the RAF gate guard.

Rich and Julie drove their respective vehicles back to the house, parking the extra car in the driveway. They would use the car in the garage for the stakeout.

They loaded each car with what was needed for their respective jobs. The stakeout car would have Andy's 9mm on his person, with a MAC-11 and a sawed-off Mossberg shotgun under the seat.

The ambush car was loaded with each person's individual weapon, four MAC-11's, five claymore mines, the electronics, and clackers for each, and three rocket propelled grenades. There were also a half dozen hand grenades, and the necessary clips and magazines for the Glocks and the MAC-11's.

The time until approximately 10:00 p.m. was taken up with relaxation, final preparations, and checking of the radios.

The threesome in the ambush team left for the area across from the fence. Andy waited until 11:45 p.m., and then left for the street where the mosque was.

Andy drove by the mosque, and parked facing away from the mosque, about a quarter of a mile down the street.

He could see the front of the mosque, and the surrounding area, in his rear view mirror, as well as his side mirror. Everything was quiet, and there were no lights on in the parking lot.

Andy learned long ago that smoking on a stakeout was the wrong thing to do. The cigarette called attention to the fact that there was someone sitting there. He had parked under a tree in order to use as much of the shadows as possible. A burning cigarette ash would show up for hundreds of feet. He had no problem, as he had given up smoking years ago.

He tuned in a local radio station on his battery operated radio. Listening on the car radio would either run down the battery, or require him to keep the car running.

The team in the other car drove out Leeds Road to the location of the ambush.

They turned off the road into the woods, and drove as far back as they could.

They turned the car around, so that it was facing towards the road. They unloaded the weapons, and covered the car with as much brush as necessary. They didn't want the truck headlights to reflect off the glass of the car.

They split up into three sectors. Each had a Rocket Propelled Grenade, a few standard grenades, their personal weapons, and the MAC-11's. Lined up next to them were the clips and magazines for their weapons. Every two Mac-11 magazines were reversed and duct-taped together for easy insertion into the weapons. They were there to fight a war.

None of them smoked, as they didn't want the smell of smoke to be in the area, and give them away.

It was midnight on a Sunday night. The base was as quiet as a monastery.

Andy looked at his watch for the thousandth time. They were starting to play the same songs over and over on the radio. Another hour, and he could go home. He started to think that the six hour shift was too long. They couldn't leave the mosque at five, as it would be light in a short time, and the mission would be in conflict with prayers. He was going to recommend that the stakeout be shortened to four hours, from midnight to 4:00 a.m.

Lying in one spot without moving for hours reminded Rich of Vietnam. The big difference here was that there were not poisonous snakes lying in the jungle with him; there was not one hundred percent humidity and ninety degree temperatures. The dry brush and lack of bugs made it almost comfortable, but the six hours were long. Rich was thinking, as it was getting lighter, that they ought to call off the six hour shift tomorrow night, and make it four.

At six o'clock Rich called Andy, and called off the wait. He told him to leave quickly, before the members of the mosque showed up. Andy was gone in the time it took to turn on the ignition.

The ambush team loaded up the car, and drove to the house.

Julie was the only one who stopped for breakfast before turning in to bed.

Everyone else just went directly to their rooms.

Around one o'clock there was stirring in the house. Rich came out of his room first, then Andy, Lou, and Julie walked out of theirs. They each walked over to the refrigerator, and found what they wanted for lunch.

They all sat down at the kitchen table, and ate silently. In about three minutes, Julie asked cheerfully, "How is everybody this morning?"

Andy said that it was afternoon; Lou shrugged, and Rich didn't bother to answer.

Rich looked at Andy, and said, "What do you think about cutting back the time on the stakeout? It seems to me that they wouldn't attack after 4:00 a.m."

"You must have been reading my mind. I think that they have to have time to get through the fence, do the deed, and get the hell out of Dodge with time to go where they are going, before first light. They have to be done by 4:30 a.m."

"O.K. let's change the stakeout from midnight to 4:00 a.m., instead of 6:00 a.m. The ambush team will change their time also. We've got the two vehicles, let's recon again in the two areas this afternoon. We can't be too careful, and miss something.

The team spent the rest of the day, and the early evening going back to where they had been, and noticed a few small additional things that would make the ambush easier. For example, there were trees that they could put claymores in.

At 10:30 p.m. the ambush team left for their assignment, and Andy left an hour later. Both vehicles, and their occupants took up the same positions they had the night before.

As Andy drove by the mosque, he saw four cars in the parking lot. It had been empty at this time last night.

At 1:45 a.m., Andy saw a car coming down the street, towards him, and crouched down further in the seat. Within two minutes, two large trucks drove by him, going in the same direction. They all pulled into the parking lot of the mosque.

Andy turned on the car, and started to move. He picked up the radio as he drove, pressed the button, and said, "Rich, it's Andy, Bingo, Bingo. They just pulled into the parking lot of the mosque. A large car, and two six-by's. I'm on my way. Get ready."

Andy's radio woke up. "Roger, Roger. Understand one large car and two six-by's. Come join the fun." The radio went back to sleep.

Ahmed Cheemar walked to the door of the parking lot, and directed the trucks to back into the area of the entrance to the basement. He then directed the drivers to go into the basement and help the others load the RPG's and machine guns into the trucks. He was dressed in an officer's uniform of the Royal Air Force. Abdullah Yinni was dressed as an enlisted man, since he would be the officer's driver. Everyone else was in regular clothing. Most of them were in shirts and jeans. All of them wore assorted side arms.

In a very short time, the trucks were loaded; the men were either behind the wheel or in the back of the trucks, and Ahmed and Abdullah had entered the car.

Cheemar leaned forward, and gave Yinni the order. "Go, in the name of Allah."

The small convoy took off for Leeds Road.

Rich walked around to the individual points of the ambush. He checked everybody's weapons and cover, and gave assignments to each one. He checked the fields of fire and alternative locations.

The team placed the claymores about five feet off the ground, in the trees, facing towards the road, and in front of their positions. They made sure that the position that Andy would take was behind the firing line.

Andy joined them within fifteen minutes, and assumed his position. The two cars were as far back as they could be placed, and covered with brush.

They waited.

They could hear the trucks coming in the quiet early morning. Soon, a car could be seen, slowing down, and pulling to the side of the road.

Yinni could be seen backing the trucks into the woods.

He then joined Cheemar, who was already across the road, cutting through the fence, and making sure that he didn't cut the alarm wires.

The terrorists remained in the trucks, awaiting the order to race across the road, through the cut fence, and out to the aircraft taxiway.

Rich hit the clacker for the claymores. Three of the five went off, decimating the truck on the right, and killing the three terrorists in the driver's seat, and the back of the truck.

The people in the other truck had no idea what had happened. They were totally undisciplined, and not knowing what to do, they opened up with the machine gun.

It was totally illogical that they would hit anything, but their first bullets stitched across Lou's throat, above his vest, killing him instantly.

The fact that only three of the claymores went off meant that there was an interruption in the wires connecting the five in parallel. Rich, or someone else had to set them off individually, as this was their first line of the ambush.

Cheemar and Yinni opened the trunk of the car, and grabbed weapons. They ran across the road, and took up positions using the trees for cover.

The team held their fire, rather than give away their positions. Silence took over the night.

Andy was about fifty yards from the second truck. He picked up his RPG, and aimed it at the truck. He got up on one knee to aim. The movement was seen by the machine gunner in the second truck, and he sent off a burst at the area Andy was in.

At the same instant, Julie aimed her RPG at the truck and fired. The truck lifted up off the ground, and disintegrated in a ball of fire. There were three more martyrs in the truck.

Ahmed Cheemar saw the departure of the RPG from Julie's position, and fired his AK-47 at the shooter. A bullet punctured her right shoulder, just to the right of her vest, and pushed her back against a tree.

The wildly shot machine gun, fired simultaneously with the RPG, emitted eight rounds. Four of them hit Andy's right leg, severing his femoral artery, and giving him a death sentence.

Rich had been slowly moving towards the connection to the claymores, dragging an RPG and carrying his MAC-11 across his back.

All of the action had taken less than three minutes. He had no idea that his team had been destroyed.

All he knew was that Cheemar and Yinni were still alive, and that the two trucks had been destroyed. No one could have been left alive in either of the trucks.

Cheemar told Yinni to try to get to the car. If Yinni could swing it around, Cheemar could get in, and they could get away.

Rich could see vehicles running up the taxiway towards them. The calvary was on its way.

Yinni ran across the road, and got into the car.

Rich slowly picked up his RPG, aimed, and fired at the car. Yinni would never reach his Imam.

Rich slowly flanked Cheemar, and came up behind him, on the road.

Cheemar knew that all was lost, and decided to run. The military was coming, and he had to get out of there. He turned around, and there was Rich, pointing his MAC-11 machine pistol, with thirty-two rounds in the magazine.

He smiled at Rich, and said, "You win; I surrender."

Rich pulled the trigger and filled the body of Ahmed Cheemar with thirty-two rounds.

"You're right; I win."

"Drop the weapon, and get on the ground. Spread eagle."

Rich immediately dropped to the ground, dropped his weapon, and spread out his arms and legs. He looked at the individual holding an M-16, with an air police arm band, and captain's bars on his collar. "I've got three more people in the woods. Please check them out."

The captain yelled, "Reed, take two guys, and search the woods. There are supposed to be three more. Treat everyone as an enemy."

He then turned to Rich. "Who the hell are you?"

"Your Colonel Wick can identify me. I'm with a government agency. The people in the trucks are terrorists, so is the person in what's left of the car. The son of a bitch soiling the honorable uniform I just punctured is their leader."

There was yelling going on in the woods. The policeman called Reed ran up to the man holding the M-16, "We've got two dead, and one wounded. I already called for an ambulance. They're all Caucasians. One's a woman.

Rich looked up. "Is the woman dead?"

"No, she's wounded. She took a round in the shoulder, but I think she'll be o.k. The two guys are dead. One took a number of rounds in the throat, and the other bled out after his leg was almost shot off. Who are you people?"

Rich ignored the question. His heart was broken. Two of his people were dead, and Julie was shot.

The captain's radio squawked.

"Do you have any I.D.?"

"No."

"How am I going to know if you're a good guy or not?"

"Just ask me. Seriously, Colonel Wick knows who I am. I guess he'll just have to eyeball me. How long until that ambulance gets here?" They heard the siren in the background.

"It's on the way. There's a number of agencies who use women in the field. Which one are you from?"

"I'll let Colonel Wick tell you. By the way, I'm sure he's been notified. When do you expect him?"

"Any time now. If you don't mind wearing cuffs, you can stand up."

Rich rolled over, and placed his hands in front of him. The captain cuffed him, and helped him up.

The ambulance pulled up, and the captain indicated that there were men in the back with the wounded person, and that there were two bodies. One of the medics called in for two more ambulances for Andy and Lou, while the other medic ran back with a gurney in the direction that the captain indicated. The other medic followed right behind him.

A car with USAF on the side pulled up, tires screeching. Colonel Wick erupted out of the back seat, and ran up to Rich, and the captain. "Take off the cuffs; he's one of ours. What's the situation?"

The captain answered first. "There was no penetration of the base. There was a firefight here, and it looks like we lost two, and had one wounded. There are no more terrorists here. This gentleman was holding a MAC-11 when I came upon the location, so I treated him as a hostile."

He looked at Rich, "I hope that there are no hard feelings, sir."

"Absolutely not. You did your job."

The medics were pushing the gurney towards the ambulance, and Rich walked over to intercept. Julie was unconscious. Rich looked at the nearest medic. "How is she?"

"I'm not a doctor, sir, but she looks like she's going to make it. I don't think she'll use that shoulder for a while, but it should be back to normal, with time."

"Thank you, where are you taking her?"

"We have a hospital on the base, sir, and the docs are first class. We'll take her there."

"Thanks. Where will the other two go?"

"They'll go to the base morgue, at the same hospital, sir."

"Thanks."

Colonel Wick walked up to Rich. "Sorry about your people. I know I owe you a lot of gratitude, and so does the United States government."

"Colonel, I'm going to need to go over to the hospital. Can you get me clearance to get on the base?"

"Just tell them you are Willy Pete, and tell them where you are going."

"I'm sure that you are going to have to file a report, as I will. I'll be here as long as the young lady is in your hospital, and you can reach me at the house at any time if I can help with your report. He gave the number to the colonel. Thank you for all that you have done, colonel."

"No, thank YOU!! I'm sorry for your casualties."

"Thank you. I can only drive one of the cars back, Colonel. Would you take care of the other one? Thanks."

Rich took Andy's car, since it had the weapons in it. He knew that the air force would pick up the remaining weapons. As he was leaving, he mentioned the two remaining claymores to the air police captain, and explained the firing problems to him. It had been a horrible day. They had achieved their objective, and there were seven dead terrorists, but what a price they had paid.

Rich drove back to the house, showered, changed, and called Ben.

"Ben Liberty."

"Ben, Rich."

"Rich, how are you?"

"Right now, not too good."

"I don't like the sound of that. What happened?"

"We accomplished our mission. The terrorists are dead. But Andy and Lou were killed, and Julie is in the hospital, with a round in her shoulder."

"Oh, Rich, I'm so sorry. Are you o.k.?"

"Physically, I'm fine. Mentally, I'll have to let you know. I just wanted to bring you up to date. I'm heading over to the hospital now."

"Please give Julie my love, and tell her that I will call tomorrow. Is there anything else I can do for you?"

"I guess you can take care of the notifications. I'm sure that you will notify the local office or whatever you do in a case like this. Julie is at the base hospital. The fighter wing commander, a Colonel Wick, has been great. He doesn't know any of our names, so I guess I'm called the one who wasn't shot, if you need me."

"Thank God for that, Rich. I'll speak to you tomorrow."

"I'll either be here or at the base hospital. Thanks, Ben."

Rich went down to the car, and removed the weapons. He put

them inside the house, along with his vest. Then he took off for the base hospital.

The name Willie Pete got him an extra yes, sir, and an escort to the base hospital. When he tried to describe who he wanted to see, or find out about, he hit a stone wall. They couldn't give him any information without a name.

Finally, he asked for whoever was in charge, and a lieutenant colonel with an attitude, came out. He started to give Rich a ration of shit, until Rich said that Willie Pete told him to come here, and how many women did they bring in tonight who was a civilian, and been shot in the shoulder. To add to it, he asked the name and serial number of the lt. colonel, and after writing it down, said, "Now do you take me where I want to go, or do I go over to Willie Pete, and have you sent to Thule, Greenland?"

"Sir, I don't think that will be necessary."

"What makes you think that I give a shit what you think?"

He was introduced to someone in green scrubs who Rich assumed was a doctor. Rich asked, "How is the young lady who was brought in with a shoulder wound? I'm her partner."

"She's in recovery. I believe that she'll be fine after a little time to heal.

There was some damage to the shoulder, but I don't think she'll have too much trouble in the future, unless she wants to pitch for a major baseball team. She'll be out for a few more hours. You can either come back, or I'll have one of the nurses take you to the room where she'll be, after she leaves recovery."

Rich chose the latter, and sat in the room for about two and a half hours, until they brought Julie into the room. She was awake, but she looked very pale.

Once the nurses had transferred her to the bed, took her vitals, and left the room, Rich bent over and kissed her. "Young lady, you scared the shit out of me. You've got to stop getting shot. This makes twice, and that's two too many."

"I think you shot me to keep me from going shopping. What's the story, how are the other guys? Where are they? Is everyone o.k.?"

"One question at a time. First, you." He then told her everything that the doctor had told her, and embellished the part about not pitching for a major league team.

Then the tough part came.

"I'm sorry to have to tell you this, sweetheart, but Andy and Lou didn't make it. They were both shot."

"Oh my God, are you telling me that they're dead?"

"Yes, baby, they didn't survive."

"How did it happen?"

"I don't know when or how it happened, sweetheart. It was during the firefight."

"But they were wearing vests."

"So were you, honey, but they don't cover everywhere ."

"Oh, my God. Oh my God, we just met them a week ago."

"I know, I know. Look, Julie, you've got to keep up your strength. Why don't you lie back, and get some sleep. I'll talk to the nurse, maybe she can give you something."

"O.K."

Rich went out to the nursing station, and talked to the nurse. She contacted the doctor, and then gave Julie a shot. Julie went to sleep, and Rich went back to the house.

When he got to the house there was a strange car in the driveway, blocking his entrance to the garage. Rich walked into the house and found two men, both in coveralls.

The first greeted him by name. "Hi, are you Rich Coburn?"

"Yes, who are you."

"We've been sent by Ben. I'm sorry about your team. How's your hospitalized agent?"

"Hopefully, she'll be out soon."

"I'm Jake Lemo. My partner Bill and I are here to take all of the effects of Andrew Burton and Louis Geiss for return to the family, after we go through them. Do you know of anything that wouldn't be in their rooms?"

"There are some weapons, and personal effects over here," and Rich gave them to Jake.

After they left, Rich made himself something to eat, and went to bed. He was mentally and physically exhausted.

Rich went to the hospital early the next morning. When he entered Julie's room, he found her to be fast asleep. He sat in the chair, and watched her breathe. He followed the sinus rhythm on the monitor; he checked her oxygen saturation on the other monitor, and looked at her blood pressure readings.

Rich was bored silly.

About twenty minutes later, one of the nurses came into the room. She told Rich that there was a phone call for him from Colonel Wick.

Rich went to the counter, and picked up the phone.

"Yes, Colonel, how are you?"

"I'm fine, Rich. I got a call from a Mr. Ben Liberty, and he gave me your and Julie's names. He also informed me who you were, and told me that I was to treat you like he would, which was like a father to his children. I can guarantee you that you will receive every courtesy of this office. You need anything, you ask; you get it. Understood?"

"Yes, colonel, thank you."

"Rich, I think we ought to get together to go over what you can tell me for my report. I know we both have to turn in reports, and it might be easier if we worked on them together."

"I agree colonel, when would it be convenient?"

"Any time that's convenient for you. Just call my office, and they'll let me know that you are coming over."

"It's a deal. I'll probably be over this afternoon, but I'll give you a call."

"Great. Give my best to Julie, and I'll see you later."

Rich hung up the phone, and walked back to Julie's room. She was awake, and talking to the doctor. Rich waited outside the room, until the doctor left.

Julie had seen Rich start to come in, and then back out. She called for him.

Rich walked in and Julie greeted him with, "Hi, there, what's happening?"

Rich answered by asking a question. "What did the doctor say?"

"Well, he said that I was lucky with the path of the bullet.

However, I'm not going to get over this in a day or two. Once I get back to the states he says that I'll have to go through physical therapy, and it'll be a while until I'm one hundred per cent."

"Did he tell you how long you'll be here?"

"I asked him, and he said that it'll be a few days anyway. It really will depend on how I react to treatment. Can I get some breakfast? I'm starving."

"I'll send in the nurse. I have to go see the colonel, today anyway, so I might as well go down there while you're eating."

"O.K., I'll see you later."

Rich called and went down to the colonel's office, and spent an hour or so, going over the reports that each of them would have to file.

Additionally, the colonel told him that the base information officer had been able to cover up the action, and that nothing reached the media.

Rich spent the next week going back and forth from the house to the hospital. The air force wanted to make sure that Julie was as well as could be expected, before they released her to go back to the states.

After leaving the hospital, Julie spent two days at the house, before they decided to fly back to the states.

Rich and Ben had been speaking daily, and keeping up on Julie's condition.

Ben didn't want her to be discharged too early, and she wasn't.

The plane was waiting for them when they arrived at the base, and the colonel was there with his aide to see them off.

chapter 35

ANDREWS AIR FORCE BASE, MARYLAND

There is nothing like landing in the United States, when coming back from abroad. Both Rich and Julie wanted to kiss the ground of the greatest nation in the world.

When the door was opened inside the hangar, the first persons aboard were a customs and immigration team, who made a perfunctory inspection, and left right away. They didn't even check their luggage.

The next person aboard was Ben Liberty.

"Welcome, home!" He looked at Julie. "We were worried about you, young lady. How are you feeling?"

"I'm good, Ben. I have to go through therapy, and obviously I'm still in a sling, but the doctors said that my shoulder will be as good as new, within a few months."

"You're a brave girl, Julie, and according to Rich's report you had no problem taking out one of the trucks, with three terrorists in it. We're proud of you."

"Thank you, Ben."

"Al Dell sends his best. He was, of course, devastated by Andy and Lou's death, but we all know that it can happen to every field agent. There will be a ceremony honoring the men later in the month. You'll get notification. Two more stars will be up on the wall honoring our heroes."

"Rich, your report was received and reviewed. There will be an inquiry into what went on. We also have received a copy of Colonel Wicks' report, which by the way paints you as superman, and has been turned over to the inquiry people.

I know that this is going to hit you in the pocketbook. You and Julie will receive no more assignments until the inquiry board rules."

"I expected something like this, Ben. After all, I lost two experienced men, and had my remaining agent wounded. I walked away. People are going to wonder about that."

"Well, enough of this kind of talk. Your luggage has been loaded into the trunk of a car at the foot of the stairs. The driver has your tickets back to Hartford, and I promise that I will leave you alone for a week. By the way, Julie, you will get a call tomorrow from an orthopedic team from Hartford Hospital in order to set an appointment to review your treatment. They'll recommend your therapy, and all billing will come to me."

Ben hugged Julie, making sure that he didn't hurt her, shook hands with Rich, then hugged him as well, and walked out the door.

Rich looked at Julie. "Well, are you ready to go, lefty?"

chapter 36

HARTFORD

They took a taxi to National airport, flew comfortably back to Hartford, and drove home.

Julie received the call the next afternoon, and went down to Hartford Hospital. The doctors there found that she had received excellent care, and set her up for therapy, starting in a week. The therapists were based in West Hartford, and Julie wouldn't have to go far to get there. In the beginning, Rich would have to drive her.

A courier came by about a week later with the remuneration due for the assignment, and they set aside a fund to live on while the inquiry was proceeding.

They had a lot of time on their hands, and worked up a number of appointments for Rich to have regarding the General Agency concept. He made sure that the appointments didn't interfere with Julie's therapy, and she made quick progress in getting back to normal.

The time at the ceremony in Langley, honoring Andy and Lou, brought the day of the battle back in their minds, and meeting relatives brought tears to everyone involved. Rich gave a speech; Al Dell gave the eulogy, and Ben acted like a father to both of them.

During the time that they waited for Julie to heal completely, they lived, they loved, and they relaxed. The business started to pick up, not enough to take off, but enough to get started. If they had to live on only the amount of money they made from the business, they wouldn't have been able to visit the Marriott, which they did twice a week.

Rich was sitting in the living room, watching replays of the

Hartford Whalers hockey team games, when Julie walked in, at the end of the day.

She had said that she was going to the hospital to find out the results of her last blood test.

When it came time for dinner, Rich walked into the kitchen, and found that there were three places set for dinner.

He looked quizzically at Julie. "Are we having a guest for dinner?"

Julie smiled, and said, "Yes, in seven and a half months. Rich, I'm pregnant!!!!"

Printed in the United States
By Bookmasters